MAY GOD STRIKE THEM DEAD

Chuck Evanson

ISBN: 979-8-9987123-2-6

FAINT PRAISE — AND MORE!

"It has all the punctuation marks and
paragraph indentations one might expect
to see in a genuine piece of writing."
THE FRESNO DAILY GRIEVANCE

"Bullets and blasphemy, sex and sensationalism.
Not exactly the four pillars of literature, but still …"
THE ALBUQUERQUE FLYSWATTER

"A book sure to glow warmly in your fireplace."
THE OMAHA WINDSOCK

"Is the author the savage beast he appears?
Or is he in fact a trenchant expositor of
metaphysical chicanery? Because if it's the latter,
we're dealing with some really big words here."
THE SHREVEPORT DREDGER

"Downright brainy in spots,
but you could skip over those."
THE CHATTANOOGA BLOODHOUND

"Make no mistake. When the nuns catch you
with a copy, they'll smack your head with it."
THE SCRANTON SCRATCH PAD

"This whole thing has to be some
kind of a joke. Am I wrong? Anybody?"
THE MONTPELIER GRAPEVINE

TO DANA

ONE

When I looked up from my desk, she was leaning on my office doorframe with her hand on her hip and her sensuality flowing over me like a spill from an aphrodisiac tanker. Her full lips and high cheekbones were so perfect you'd think they'd been fashioned at some plastic surgery clinic in Miami Beach or Beverly Hills. As if she needed a boost from a cosmetics counter, her hair cascaded in platinum, her sky-blue gaze was set off by smoky eye shadow and her mouth was done up in a torrid red. Adding to the impact, a white sleeveless blouse and a black skirt were tailored to accentuate the narrows at her belt and the hourglass curves above and below.

For all I knew, the lady flaunted the same dazzle every time she ran an errand, but she seemed awfully spectacular for anyone showing up unannounced in a run-down commercial building at ten in the morning. Especially in a burg like mine. The carefully engineered glamour had me concerned about motives and manipulations, though no cautionary instincts could have mattered much. Not at that moment, because whether her beauty was a natural phenomenon or a work of art, whether she was in a jam or only staging a gambit, her image and presence were enough to snap a guy's head back. And enough to start him off on her side.

She stepped nearer to me and without glancing at the door behind her, reached around and flicked it shut.

"Someone is trying to kill me," was all she said.

Not the standard visitor; not the standard overture.

I put down the book I'd been reading since returning from the Pulptown Strangler sentencing. "Jack Harbinger," I said. After a perfunctory half-pushup from a seated position, I nodded toward a crinkled leather chair on the other side of the desk.

She approached it in a languid rhythm but stopped short. She pulled at the collar of her blouse and said, "It's difficult for me to sit comfortably."

Calmly and casually, she cocked a thumb over her bare left shoulder. "Would you mind?"

As she turned one-eighty, I scanned everything from her risqué heels on up, looking for a problem to correct. She checked out wonderfully until her fingers went to the nape of her neck and parted those blond waves.

High on her back was the dangling handle of a Sears Craftsman ice pick.

"Jesus!" I blurted for lack of anything intelligent.

I stood up, opened a drawer and took out some antiseptic cream, a clean cloth and a premium adhesive bandage — the kind I always used for bullet holes. I hurried to where she waited and got behind her. From close by, I could see that the attack must have been a reckless jab, with the pick landing inches away from any expert's target and not driven in deeply. Channeling a stream of hair to one side, I used the cloth to extract the tool, drawing its filed spike through a crimson stain on the white fabric. I laid it on the desk.

Quicker than I could react, she grabbed the weapon for a close examination.

"Slow down," I said. "If there were any prints, you've smeared them."

"Sorry, I wasn't thinking." She put down the pick and laid her clutch purse beside it. Facing away from me, she undid several buttons and lowered her collar below the damage. There was blood but not a fountain of it.

Dabbing at the droplets, I applied the cream over the puncture. I tore the bandage out of its packaging and gently covered the injury. It was heady work, touching her like that. She was the one who had been stabbed, but I was the one whose legs were wobbling. I put away the detritus of first aid.

"Thank you," she said distantly. She repositioned her collar, fiddled with her buttons and turned to me with some of them left unfastened. It took all I had to lift my line of vision up to the level of eye contact. I made myself speak.

"Did you drive yourself over here with that thing stuck in your back?"

"I like to think of myself as resilient," she said. It was a non-answer, which could have been intentional. "A superficial wound, at worst, and I had a tetanus shot last year." With a lithe motion, she took her place in the client's chair. Although she had to be hurting, she nestled against the backrest as if nothing traumatic had occurred. I sat down behind the big oak desk and settled in to give her a listen.

She was as shy as a showgirl. Crossing her legs and flashing a thigh, she breathed in dramatically. Her breasts were straining against the blouse and peeking out from the unbuttoned breach. They weren't going to make a break for it, but they were definitely considering their chances. Meanwhile, she gave me a subdued smile and tossed her hair like she was waving a magic wand.

Then suddenly the posing was gone and she allowed herself to wince.

From a deep drawer I pulled out a whiskey bottle and two glasses. I poured drinks, hers for the pain and mine for the jitters. I shoved the first tumbler across the woodwork and returned the bottle to its nook. Her liquor was gone in a single swallow. I took a measured sip of mine. With a crisis overcome and both of us ready for conversation, we set our glasses down.

She said, "I see you have some time off today," and pointed at the worn paperback on my desk.

"*1984*," I said, picking up the dystopian novel. "I figured I'd better read it again. We're only six months away, and I'm reminding myself what to expect."

She surrendered another smile. "Given your occupation, you should expect trouble. Same as any other year. But I doubt you're anticipating the kind portrayed in the book."

I shrugged, nodded in agreement and stowed the tattered volume. "And you would be …?"

"Roxanne Delaplaine. I suppose I was too distracted to mention it."

"My hunch, Ms. Delaplaine, is that you haven't been in this area very long."

"Quite perceptive. What tipped you off?"

"It's been five minutes and you haven't brought up the Green Bay Packers."

"Oh, that. No, we didn't practice your religion on the West Coast and I haven't converted to it since arriving. Or maybe I should call it an addiction. I've noticed that most of you around here are compulsively fixated on your little team up the road." She fanned herself in the muggy heat of late June, her red fingernails fluttering. "Even now, in the off-season. And you? Are you in withdrawal?"

"I'm dandy. I've been watching the USFL."

"Not familiar," she said.

"A new pro football league. Games in the spring and summer."

"Then you're doubly addicted."

"Guilty. Now, about that ice pick."

"Please, I wouldn't fret over such a trivial thing. On my way here, I stopped at the Church of Saint Opius to light some votive candles. I'm nondenominational but I thought it couldn't hurt. I must have broken some rule when I was reciting my prayers or folding my hands. A nun attacked me but missed the spinal column."

"So, it couldn't hurt, huh?"

"I had heard stories about overly strict nuns. I wrote them off as tall tales."

"Well, you shouldn't have," I said. "Any description?"

"All I remember was a black habit. In a hasty retreat, as the saying goes. Never mind. It's nothing."

"Maybe. Regarding your earlier point, my schedule is open for the next few days."

Technically, my schedule was open for the next few decades.

"I've never hired a private investigator before," she said. "I'll admit I'm apprehensive about a stranger sleuthing through my private life. There have been some questionable associations in my past, and I haven't always been the model of morality."

I was never so glad to hear anything in my life.

"We all have our dirty little secrets," I told her. "Mine is that I get a hundred dollars a day, plus expenses."

She lifted her chin, straightened herself and tilted her head. It was a small gesture, but nothing less than imperious. "I was prepared to pay twice that."

"I'll stick with my quote," I said. "But you're a great negotiator."

"Don't misinterpret me. I haven't retained an investigator, but in the past, I've done some research on several of them. Including their fees."

"When and where?"

"You're very nosy," she said. "But then you would be. Nothing ever came of it, so you don't need to know when and where. Or why."

There was a protective shield around her, but fortunately the shield was invisible. Damn, she was something to look at.

"Off limits," I conceded. "Back to the numbers. The charges you're talking about may be the norm wherever you're from. They wouldn't fly in Pulptown, Wisconsin."

"It's simply that … Do you get work every day?"

"In this town there are long gaps between murders."

"You're putting me on," she said, eyeing me sideways.

"Okay, there are a lot of minor assignments for every major one. But no, the work isn't steady. Then there are clients who can't pay their bills."

"And this is how you're amassing your wealth?"

"Gosh, Ms. Delaplaine, I generally have to know a woman for a whole week before we start quarrelling about my income."

Her eyes twinkled — involuntarily. She offered up an edgy, "Pardon me."

"Wealth is a relative concept," I said, maybe trying to defend myself. "Depends on what's important to you. I make enough to buy burgers and beers and a few bullets a week. When I get sapped in the back of the head, I can scrounge an aspirin. I sleep indoors almost every night and I have a car that may run another month or two without throwing a piston rod at me."

"How impressive."

"Also, I have a portrait of Madison in my safe."

Her eyebrows perked up. "You mean a five-thousand-dollar bill?"

"I mean an oil painting. It's an homage to the skyline of the state capital."

"I'm sure." Her eyebrows fell back into neutral.

"A client gave it to me in lieu of cash. I'm told it's worth at least a hundred portraits of Washington, if that's how we're counting our money these days."

"We're not," she said. "But you've missed my meaning. If any of this ever comes out, I can't be perceived as hiring some cut-rate, sporadically employed gumshoe."

"I'll try to keep that part quiet."

The joke didn't take. Her eyes were done with twinkling.

"Undoubtedly a fruitless discussion," she said. "It's obvious that yours is not a lucrative operation. I suppose that would account for the décor."

Appraising the seedy office and its battered furniture, she let a touch of disdain cross her features. She had the aura of someone who felt she was too good to find herself in a den like mine, and I wouldn't have argued otherwise. To anyone successful, its finer appointments must have looked dismal.

The desk was bare except for the essentials. Next to the usual blotter, lamp and pens there was a phone with an answering machine and a Rolodex full of contact information. My workload was too light to require an in-box or an out-box. There were no pictures of my wife and kids because there were no such persons.

On the wall to my right, a framed P.I. license and a few other documents were hung, though seldom noticed. Beside those were some fairly unblemished rectangles, spaces where former tenants had once displayed photos or diplomas and then watched the wallpaper surrounding them turn dingier by the year. At my back, there was a credenza that didn't match the desk. Around the rest of the room, I had an olive drab filing cabinet, some swayback bookshelves, a water cooler and a stand supporting a portable typewriter. The heavy old safe protecting the oil painting squatted in a corner. The carpet had footpaths trampled into it and the ceiling fan was paralyzed, its four blades deployed uselessly around a cluster of frosted lightbulbs.

Such was the ambiance in the world headquarters of the Jackson T. Harbinger organization.

She waved her red nails again. "Don't you have air conditioning in here?"

"It's broken," I said. "So is the fan. And those windows behind me are up as far as they'll go."

"Marvelous." She appeared eager to change the subject, but not to bring up the issue that had put her in the client's chair. Her eyes focused past me, aiming at a trophy on the credenza. "I see you're a tennis champion." The award was the lone ornamental doodad in the office, meant mainly to take a genteel guest's attention off a corroded fire escape outside the windows, a murky river below and a grimy factory on its far bank.

"Racquetball," I said. "Only second place. And only a gym tournament. But I have a good backhand kill shot."

"Kill shot ..." I could tell the words were rolling around in her head. "I like an athletic man," she said, now working me.

"How can I help you, Ms. Delaplaine?"

TWO

"What brought me to you was this." She rooted around in her purse and came up with a neatly folded sheet of paper. It was brown and coarse, like the disposable toweling they might use in an auto shop. "I received it about a week ago. There have been two more since then." She unfurled the paper on the desk.

It was the craziest damn thing. Drawn across the top was a crude skull-and-crossbones. The outline of the skull was scrawled unevenly, as if whoever drew it had been struggling to control his hand. The eye sockets were spasmodic swirls. The nasal cavity was sketched in with a few slashes of ink, and the teeth were lined up in a repulsive grin. A pair of crossbones were drawn under the skull just as wildly. Some of the strokes in the image made it look like the goof who produced it was stabbing at the paper. Below the graphic, lettering was thrown down in a similar, erratic rush. The text was loopy, but it had a menacing quality all the same.

Blindly shall you wander the night, and therein shall you find your ultimate destruction. The false and foolish hope of life must now be unmasked as the certainty of death. Ask not why the shroud of extinction lies upon your burdened shoulders. Know only that you are powerless to unravel its grim and horrifying fibers. I am in the same America as you and ever closer do I approach. Anonymous

I was nearly sure she was pranking me, but her eyes didn't give anything away.

"Happily," I said, "he's in the same America as you. That narrows it down a bit."

"Please don't make light of the threat. That reference may have to do with some oblique form of symbolism. The obscurity makes it all the more frightening."

"You're serious?"

"I'm *extremely* serious." Now she was angry.

"My apologies, but the entire thing seems a little flaky. This feels like it's from someone who's only trying to rattle you for a hoot."

Her eyes were as soothing as branding irons. "And if you're wrong?"

"If I'm wrong," I said, trying to recover, "then you're right and there's no percentage in underplaying it. Let's have a look at the other two."

She unfolded a second sheet of paper and laid it on the desk. It had the same demented drawing and lettering. Still, it had a twisted eloquence.

Your steps upon the earth have not yet placed you within my deadly radius. But take no solace, no respite from terror. For the world outside your chamber awaits your final and fatal excursion. And as you emerge, you shall be dispatched in the bleak reaches of helplessness. Anonymous

She laid down the third sheet, still with a straight face, and smoothed out its creases.

You have failed to reveal yourself. It is of no consequence. I speak with cosmic authority, and upon my command, the night's firmament shall obediently cast its inescapable light upon you, guiding me to your side. Then what pathetic wailing shall befoul the night! For yours is the fate of the feeble and fainthearted, while mine is the destiny of the dealer of doom. Anonymous

"Nice touch with the alliteration," I said. "Do you have any idea what this guy is talking about?"

"As I said, the language is obscure. All I know is that I can't go anywhere without looking over my shoulder."

"I can sympathize." I tried to sound compassionate without crossing over into gullible. "If these are genuine, whoever did them might have spent time in a mental institution. Or should have. The squiggles are unhinged. Hard to evaluate the tone of it, though. Sort of off base for a murderous rage."

"How do you mean?" she asked. Her lips tightened with annoyance.

"The lingo is — how to put this? — piss elegant."

"You have a rather plebeian way of expressing yourself," she said dismissively.

"Let's phrase it this way: The text is full of pretentious hyperbole. Comes across like the work of a narcissist with delusions of grandeur. Sound any better?"

She stiffened in her chair, raised her chin again and looked down her exquisite little nose at me. "Somewhat," she said.

Maybe she thought I wasn't qualified to be a death threat critic.

"How are the threats delivered?" I asked.

"All three were mailed to me at work. Local postmarks. There were no return addresses, of course."

"We won't get any leads from fingerprints. The paper is all wrong. Are the envelopes made of the same stuff?"

"Thrown out, but yes. They looked home made."

"You mentioned questionable associations," I said. "Let's start with those."

"That was overstated," she said demurely. "The occasional rebel that one dates in one's youth."

"Your youth wasn't that far back."

"Those men … some of them boys … came and went years ago," she said. "I never felt as if I were in jeopardy, and there was never anything about them that would sink to the level of homicide. I only meant … well, I'm not sure what I meant."

"I'm not either," I said. "For now, let's get more current. That bit about cosmic authority. The folks down at Saint Opie's really love that kind of talk. Are you sure they're not mixed up in this?"

"I don't see how they could be involved."

"To begin with, somebody on their roster just pumped a shiv into your back."

"I told you. That was a nervous response to a minor infraction."

"The word *nervous* doesn't exactly capture it."

She slid off the subject again: "You seem to be acquainted with Saint Opie's. Is that your church?" Her voice was softening and the branding irons were cooling.

"I went to grade school there," I said. "One of those things your parents make you do. Mom and Dad were wrapped up in the faith, and they had some idea the place would give me a moral grounding."

"And did it?"

"Mostly, it gave me bruises."

"You must have been a bad boy," she said provocatively.

"I asked the nuns too many questions."

"And look at your vocation. Questions all day long, I would think."

"That connects. Have you been to the police?"

"I don't trust the police," the lady said.

Time ticked away. Someone had to make noise and it wasn't going to be me.

"For reasons I'd rather not go into right now," she said after a tense pause.

I took off my wristwatch and held it in front of my face long enough to make a point.

"Then how about going into it now?" I said.

She got mad at me again.

"You can't maneuver me, Mr. Harbinger. I'm not your everyday client. Believe me, I'm like no one you've ever met before."

"Yeah, I know the type." I strapped the watch back on.

"Are you under some impression that your attitude is endearing?"

"Truce. I'll behave myself. But when people don't want to go to the authorities over problems like this it's almost always because they have something to hide. And then, when a P.I. starts digging, whatever it is they're hiding tends to come up from under the ground and get him punched in the stomach or plugged in the gizzard. Or worse."

"Malappris," she said Frenchly. Then in an instant she was all sincerity and pleading. "I'm in danger and I don't know why. I'm here to get some professional assistance. Is that too mystifying to comprehend?"

She was being difficult but she was also being gorgeous. Her long, thick lashes opened wide and she beamed those blues at me. My heartbeat shifted up a notch.

I collected some details from her, fewer than I would have liked. She had recently come to Pulptown from San Francisco, leaving the Bay Area on what she believed were good terms. She was all set to teach literature and fine arts at a local college beginning in the fall. She had planned on reporting to campus early and spending a leisurely summer prepping for her classes. Over the past few weeks, she had met some harmless professors and staff, but no students as of yet. Outside of her acquaintances at work, she hadn't made any friends in town and hadn't knowingly made any enemies.

"Which college?" I asked her.

She waved that off. "No one at the college could be responsible for this."

"How do you know that?"

"I just know."

"Uh huh. Who hates you and knows where you teach?"

"That's what I may be paying you to discover."

"The way to go about this is from the inside out," I said. "Starting with interviews of the people who know you best or at least have the most contact with you. From what you've told me, that would be campus personnel."

"I can't have you asking a lot of invasive questions at my workplace. I'm new there, and if the dean senses anything is amiss, he'll void my contract. That's why I haven't requested a bodyguard. Besides, no one on campus would bother with the U.S. mail when the threats could easily be slid under my office door."

"Maybe whoever wrote them predicted you'd be thinking that way."

"Nevertheless …" Her decision had been made.

I tugged out more snippets of information: Her direct faculty phone number. The fact that she lived alone. The installation of new locks in her apartment. I pressed for a home address and a home phone number but she wouldn't give, citing a longstanding desire for privacy.

"Really?" I asked.

"Really," she answered.

"There are neighbors to be interviewed. And a landlord or a property manager."

"You have the threats. They should suffice."

"You don't want an investigator. You want a clairvoyant."

"Perhaps a little of both," she said as if she were closing the deal. Then she went into her purse and pulled out a small envelope made of ordinary white paper instead of death threat stationery. She sorted through the envelope and drew out some currency, holding the bills tightly.

"Are you bonded?" she asked.

"I am," I said, and pointed toward a framed certificate on the wall.

"Do you carry a gun?"

"If a case gets ticklish, yes."

"And have you ever killed anyone? I mean outside of a racquetball court."

"I've killed a lot of people," I told her, "But I can honestly say that some of them deserved it."

She tilted her head forward and stared at me. The corners of her mouth went up slightly, though not in a smile. She was a little tired of me trying to be funny.

"No, I've never killed anybody. Fired some warning shots, though."

"I just prefer to employ practitioners who are earnest about their work," she said wearily. "Since there's a threat of violence here, I'm looking for a detective with a certain dedication to meeting it."

"I do my job. At times more earnestly than anyone would like."

Somehow she had satisfied herself as to my steadfastness and capacity for gunplay. She placed five bills on the desk — all of them hundreds — and said, "Portraits of Franklin, if you will."

I reached out for the money, but not like a Doberman lunging at raw meat. As I contemplated her story, a good firm voice piped up in the back of my mind. The voice was telling me to maintain an emotional distance. It was challenging everything my potential client had brought to me and it was reeling off some valid points. The trivialized ice pick attack, the screwball threats and the needless evasion were adding up to a fiasco. I knew her vulnerability could have been an illusion, and I knew I could get tripped up in the darkness of what she wasn't telling me.

I ran my fingertips over the texture of the five crisp hundreds and thought about handing them back to her. There were three good reasons for not doing it. First, I needed the payday. Second, I knew I could find out through a skip trace where she lived and where she worked. And third, she had piqued my curiosity.

That was where the good reasons ended and the bad ones began, because she had also piqued something not so cerebral. The simple truth was that I'd never had a woman as enticing as this one walk into my life. And when she did, I wanted to be part of hers. I pocketed the money in spite of the qualms. Maybe that's why I was a private eye, and not a Rotary Club member in some reasonable line of work.

"I'll see what I can do," I told her. "I have a couple of contacts who may be useful. But if you expect me to make any headway, you should stop classifying your whole life as top secret."

"I'll take that under advisement."

She wanted to sign a contract, so I pulled a form out of a drawer and filled in the blanks. Ms. Roxanne Delaplaine signed the contract and so did I. She peeled off her copy, folded it and put it in her purse. The closure snapped and she rose to her feet, signaling that she was through talking.

I stood up. "Better visit a doctor about that wound and my amateur patch."

"We'll see."

With scarcely a goodbye she walked out of my office, leaving the threats behind and the door open. I followed her as far as the threshold and watched her start down the stairs toward the main floor. I walked past the stairwell to a window overlooking the street and saw her stepping out onto the sidewalk in front of the building. If she had parked along the nearby curb, I could at least have gotten a line on her car. She hadn't, which might have been my bad break or her good planning.

She turned to her right and kept walking until she disappeared.

THREE

Fifteen minutes later, I was down the stairs, out of the building and on the same sidewalk. Lousy timing, because the morning breeze had died and left behind a fetid atmosphere that sometimes leaked from the pulp and paper mills that gave the city its name. An unseen cloud of odor hung in the motionless air, but all the mayor would do about it — this time or any time — was hope for a new gust of wind.

Until that came, the stillness would not only hold in the smell but exacerbate the heat and humidity everyone had been yelping about lately. With heat came mosquitos. One landed on my wrist, but I flicked it away before it could draw much blood. By nightfall, plenty more would be out in squadrons, and each outdoor light in town would be swarming with moths and the tiny gnats that flitter around your eyes and ears and nostrils. In six months, though, with the insect populations in stasis for the long winter, the whole state would be frozen stiff and people would be yelping about that too.

I walked by some of the bars that formed the backbone of downtown commerce. Next to the biggest one, The Bottle Cry, the city had reserved a plot of asphalt for free overnight parking. I turned in there to get my car out of the lot.

That year I was driving a 1966 Mustang, which had been a sporty little number long before I bought it used. As it was now, the bumpers and body were scarred and spanked. The color was icy blue — mostly. On the hardtop and hood and rear deck there were pools of exposed gray metal where the sun had gradually inflicted third-degree burns on the paint job. Internally, the old horse was bound to die soon with a whining of the fan belt and a coughing of the exhaust pipe. I got in and moved off toward the exit, thinking my fee from the new batch of trouble could possibly buy a few repairs. I merged into traffic and sifted through it along Vince Lombardi Street, the main drag.

On the way, I glanced between the downtown buildings on my right and at the river running just behind them. Paper mills hunkered along the water's opposite edge. The mills throughout the valley represented the principal economic opportunity for much of the population growing up around here, but to me they were traps. Thousands of guys resigned themselves to sacrificing eight hours a day in them, and hundreds called themselves mill rats with defiant pride in the label. Whether or not they liked their work, they were making union money and spending it on fast cars and booze. After a while, they were spending it on boats and snowmobiles and weekends at their cottages up north. Most of them eventually spent it on mortgages and families. And maybe, on balance, they were contented.

Good for them. I had once given factory life a try and hated every minute of it. I had failed to keep up with the grind and before long, management fired me. The wages would have given me a stable foundation, but in time I considered myself lucky that I hadn't backed into the kind of steady job a good mill employee could hold. The routine was mentally crushing, and I could never get over the feeling that a few years of robotic drudgery would have stunted my brain or dissolved it altogether.

There were times, of course, when an assignment like the one I had accepted that morning made me question whether I was any better off doing what I was doing. Brain or no brain, the P.I. gig was risky and shaky. I had nothing solid under me and no reliable forecast for my future. What I did have was a packet of bombastic death threats, a client who was hiding something and a high likelihood of miring myself in an unresolvable mess. Not much to thrive on, but scenes like the one across the river always put my tottering career in perspective. No matter how many times an investigation got me thumped in the head or kicked in the ribs or bounced off a fender, no matter how many times I came out of a thankless mission without a dollar to the good, at least I had avoided a life sentence of packing napkins or spinning out rolls of toilet paper in one of those industrial dungeons.

At the east end of Lombardi, I turned right onto Ray Nitschke Avenue and took the Jerry Kramer Bridge into a neighborhood of clapboard and brick, oaks and elms. Then it was a left on Hornung and a right on Taylor. Farther down, I veered onto Hawg Hanner Road, an ugly stretch along a railyard dotted with standing boxcars.

Roxanne Delaplaine, if she knew the significance of the street names, would almost certainly be appalled to see these and others like them posted all over town. Years earlier, filled with pigskin patriotism, the local patriarchs had renamed the major streets, some minor ones and all the bridges after the Packer champions from the 1960s. Roxanne was right about the regional obsession, and the renaming seemed excessive even to a fan like me. But a majority of citizens were proud of the results.

The traffic on Hanner Road, and through most of the city, was a slog. It wasn't that we had too many vehicles; it was that our drivers were lethargic, as if they had nowhere to go. They accelerated off green lights like sedated snails and crawled around corners as if they were carrying loads of nitroglycerin. The glut of slowpokes cleared out once I hit Herb Adderley Way, near the city limits. Then it was easy all the way out to the rural route that led south and ran close to the shore of Lake Winnebago.

On my left, the shallow lake lay in the sun. Despite a blue sky, muck circulating from the bottom gave the water a brownish cast. In places, green scum floated thick, and the rank smell of algae came through my open windows to replace the pulp stench that had drifted off. It would have been nice to have a crystal blue lake and cool fresh air. It would have been nice to have a lot of things.

Miles on, angling left off the southbound road onto an unmarked driveway, I pulled up to the gate of what every kid in the old days called *The Nuthouse*. We had been an insensitive bunch, and it never occurred to us to use the hospital's formal name. Not many people used it even now. I knew about a certain psychiatrist working there and about the facility's poor reputation. Nothing else.

At a guard shack, a man poked his greasy head out of a window. "How about those Packers?"

"It's the off-season," I said. "How about those Philadelphia Stars?" No response. "USFL." Still nothing. "I'm here to see Dr. Amanda Foster."

He nodded knowingly and said, "The headshrinker. Got permission?"

"Yes," I lied, hoping to get in on the cheap. He reached for a phone and I said, "I'm the envoy from Bedlam."

The guard eyed my car suspiciously, hanging up. "I don't think so."

"What if I told you I'm here to sell straightjackets?" All I wanted him to do was name a figure.

"Maybe. If I get a finder's fee." For finding what, he didn't say.

"Let's make this easier. I'll buy a ticket." I held out a twenty.

"We can't let just anybody in here, fella."

"Fine," I made it thirty. "One adult, please."

He weighed the offer and took the bills. “I guess that’s all right then.” He pushed a button. The gate opened. The poor reputation was confirmed.

I stepped on the gas, went through to the main property and drove down a long run of gravel. Gnarled old trees formed rows on either side of me, and tangled branches converged overhead to form a green canopy. The trees might have been pretty if they were somewhere else, but here they looked a little foreboding. Then I was up to an institutional building with a mass of brown bricks rising up to a row of barred windows on the third floor.

I parked and reached into the back seat for my sport coat. I put it on and straightened my tie. It was a hot day for the formality but I needed to look somewhat official in case a guard inside got me confused with a restricted inmate.

And why shouldn’t he? Given the documents I was carrying, I could have seemed as delirious as any of them.

FOUR

I cleared a reception desk without any hassles and walked into a wide lobby. I found Dr. Foster's office on the ground floor of a low-security psychiatric ward. Her door was open and she was at her desk, wearing a starchy white smock and tortoise shell glasses that pushed back against a severe hairstyle. She was honing in on a sheet of paper with an inkblot that suggested to me nothing more than an upside-down inkblot. I knocked lightly on the open door and she looked up without interest.

"How about those Packers?" Dr. Foster said mechanically.

"How about those Philadelphia Stars?"

Her eyes were blank for a second, and then they narrowed. If she had never heard of the Philadelphia Stars, it was me she didn't like. As I stepped into her office, she pivoted the sheet of paper. She slid it toward me, out to the corner of her desk. "What do you make of this image?" the doc wanted to know.

"Not much. Thing is, I came in to see if I could get a little information."

"Irrelevant. Go with your first thought," she demanded.

"Sorry, I'm coming up empty. Got a question, though."

"You're suppressing, which is not allowed within these walls." Her tone had become louder and sharper. She must have been great with the patients. Come in looking for counseling and you get a voice as comforting as an air raid siren.

"Okay, it looks like Sam Mills making a tackle," I said. I could tell she didn't like the razzing, but I didn't like the brow-beating. She pulled another sheet of paper out of a folder and laid it down for me. I said, "That one looks like Kelvin Bryant running thirty-seven yards for a touchdown. Against the Oakland Invaders."

Her face was like angry granite. "How did you get in here? No, you would only lie. Normally, a psychiatric evaluation entails a long, painstaking process. But I can diagnose you immediately as a sneak and a cheat."

"I met you at a cocktail party last year," I said, hoping to skip ahead.

"Yes, I remember. Weren't you the private detective who assaulted the city attorney?"

"He was strangling his wife," I said.

"And why was he doing that?"

"Infidelity, I think."

"Facilitated by whom?"

"Well." I shrugged as if a gesture could exonerate me. "Blame me if you want, but I wasn't the only one."

"It is God's place to lay blame," she said. "Although I don't mind making a recommendation."

"The guy's wife was planning for a divorce anyway. And does it make any difference that he turned out to be a serial killer?"

"None of us knew the man's personal history at the time," Foster said. "Lucky for you it turned out that way, since the murder revelations diverted attention from your illicit behavior."

My purpose in coming by had been to ask for help, and already we were going down the wrong path. I thought I could set it right with a little small talk.

"They hit him with life imprisonment just this morning," I said. "You should have been at the sentencing."

"There are much more important events in my life, if not in yours."

"Duly noted," I said.

"State your purpose … Mr. Harbinger, isn't it?"

"Good memory." I set my card down in front of her. "A client of mine has been receiving death threats in the mail. If you can shed any light on who might write that kind of thing, I'd like to know."

"Oh, you would, would you?" She sneered at the card and pushed it away. "I couldn't possibly reveal any confidential information."

"Naturally, but maybe you could give me some hints about the type of person who would come up with these threats. And then, you never know, I may be able to trick you into giving me a suspect's name and address."

"You are not as sidesplitting as you think you are, Mr. Harbinger."

"Thanks. I'll take that as a yes." I reached into my breast pocket, took the threats out and set them in front of her. She glanced at them and then reluctantly motioned for me to sit down. She gave each one a good study.

After some time she said, "Coincidentally, I have extensive experience with death threats. These are extraordinary, the work of a deceptively brilliant mind. Consider the lyrical prose that verges upon poetry. And in the illustrations, note the subtle economy of lines."

"I thought it was just ravings and squiggles."

"As you would," she said condescendingly. "No, it's highly aesthetic, highly literary, with depths of feeling couched in apparent simplicities. The imagery and finely wrought anguish are reminiscent of Poe or perhaps H.P. Lovecraft. And what may appear to you as squiggles … well, would you dismiss Picasso as a common cartoonist?"

"Not at all," I said. "The more eyes in the side of someone's head, the better I like it. But staying with the threats, I thought I noticed a little insane scrawling in there."

"Make up your mind," she barked at me. "Squiggling or scrawling?"

"That's a fine distinction, doc."

"You are naïve," she said with a superior grade of pity. "You fail to recognize that genius and insanity are two sides of the same coin."

"Maybe so, but wasn't Picasso drawing coins with three sides? Where does that leave us?"

"Have it your way. I refuse to debate with a Philistine." She tossed the threats back at me. I gathered them up, stuffed them into their envelope and put them back in my pocket.

"Now that I think of it," I said, "Picasso was a bit of a sadist, wasn't he? Didn't he once burn his wife's face with a cigarette. Maybe the cartoons and the sadism go together."

"That was his girlfriend, not his wife," the doc said. "And he merely held the cigarette close to her cheek."

"By way of a threat, right?"

"Nicely done, but it is irresponsible for you to infer correlations where none exist. Especially since you are grasping for answers from a pit of ignorance."

"Sorry again. But where does all your expertise in art and artists come from? I thought you were just a headshrinker." That got her mouth tightening and her eyes punishing.

"One strives for a well-rounded education," she said with a strain. "In any case, most of us in the mental health disciplines prefer not to use that particular nomenclature."

"Hell, it says you're a headshrinker right next to your door."

Her head dipped and her sigh had some weight on it.

"Unfortunately, I have no control over that," she said. "The so-called officials here have a rather rudimentary sense of humor."

"See? Not my fault. Back to the subject at hand, do any leads other than Edgar Allan Poe and Pablo Picasso come to mind?"

"Everything happens for a reason," she said sternly.

"You mean the threats? I'm thinking the reason is homicidal intent."

"I'm thinking more in terms of what actually brought you in here today. Your client shows you some disturbing correspondence, and you come to me. Could it be that this visit, this transparent display of death threats, is your way of expressing your own all-consuming hostility?"

"You think *I'm* the one who's hostile?"

"Or could it be that God sent you here to my office to obtain the intensive counselling you so desperately need?"

"I don't think so. God never even helped me with my spiral."

"What in heaven's name are you talking about?"

"Flag football," I said. "My passes flutter like a three-winged duck." She frowned at me as if she knew what was coming. "But I shouldn't keep harping on Picasso."

"This flippant attitude of yours is exactly why you are a grubby little man in a sleazy little profession."

"So, which is it, doc? Grubby or sleazy?" She looked at me like a hammer looks at a nail, but I tried once again. "Can you at least help me with some sort of profile? Anything to look for in a person who's likely to pull a gag like this?"

"I can't help you at all, Mr. Harbinger. Beyond the obvious privacy issues, you are far too immature to deal with what you have shown me. I would advise you to recuse yourself from the investigation and pass it up the ladder to a third-rate detective."

She returned to her inkblots as if I were no longer there. I gave her the last word, and hated to do it, but that was better than having someone in a white coat chasing me down the halls of a mental institution.

FIVE

It was the end of the lunch hour when I got back to Pulptown. I stopped for a slice of pepperoni pizza and a beer and felt guilty about it and got an early-bird discount on an autopsy appointment in forty years and told myself not to worry about it yet. Then I drove over to the city administrative offices at Jim Ringo Center. Ringo had been a Packer lineman who had little or nothing to do with the city's history, but nobody could snap a ball and throw a block better than that guy.

The offices were housed in one of those old stone buildings with broad steps, fluted columns, a wide pediment along the roofline and a couple of gargoyles standing guard at the front doors. At first glance, the place looked serious and substantial. But in the extra moment it took to notice the small marquee resting on the sidewalk, the attempt at civic pride fluttered away. The marquee displayed the city's tourism slogan in slightly crooked stick-on lettering:

PULPTOWN. YOU CAN BE HERE TILL NOON
AND STILL NOT SEE EVERYTHING.

The police department took up most of the building's basement. I walked through sterile corridors until I came to Lieutenant Wally Eck's door. I knocked, opened it and found Eck at his desk. He was pumping a wooden paddle and batting a rubber ball at the end of an elastic string. He looked up at me and missed a shot, which didn't make him happy. Eck was as dumb as a post hole and not particularly enthused about his work, but he was fairly honest, which made him a valuable contact on the force. He was also a good man to have on your side in a bar fight because he owned massive chunks of muscle and a jaw like the front bumper of a tow truck. He tolerated me, and that was the extent of our friendship.

"How about them Packers?" he said resentfully.

"It's the off-season. How about those Philadelphia Stars?"

"Ugh, spring football. It ain't natural." He gripped his paddle with one hand and kneaded the ball with the other. "I was going for a hundred, but you broke my concentration. What the hell do you want this time?"

I sat down uninvited and showed him the death threats.

"Does any of this stuff look familiar?" I asked him.

"No. Where did you get them?"

"From a client."

"Why does your client want to kill you?"

"No, Eck, my client received these death threats and hired me to find out who sent them. I'm asking you whether they bring to mind any of the psychopathic killers you deal with on a daily basis."

"Well, that makes more sense, I suppose." He flicked the rubber ball so that the elastic line wound itself around the handle of the paddle. When the ball made its last revolution on its shortening line, he caught it with a finger and held it against the wood. He stared at me.

"And the threats?" I pressed.

"Oh, the threats. No, none of them ring a bell." He put down his gear and shoved the malignant messages back at me.

"Don't you want to keep copies of these on file?" I asked him.

"Nah. By the way, I assume you went down to the sentencing this morning. I didn't even have time to get to the courthouse."

The refolded threats went back in my pocket.

"I can see you're up to your paddle in police work."

"Hey, there's a lot going on here," Eck said defensively. "We've had some missing person reports over the last few months."

"Have you found any of them?"

"Of course not. But that's only because they're not where they're supposed to be. Believe me, they're out there somewhere." He waved a hand toward the door.

"Good point, Eck. Maybe you should be out there looking."

"I gotta be right here, at the nerve center of law enforcement. Hey, one of them is a florist. How could a florist be missing?"

"That's baffling," I said.

A uniformed officer came in with a document and opened a filing cabinet.

"Also," Eck said, "a guy got killed in a boat this morning. Now I gotta deal with that. So, how did the sentencing go?"

"The strangler got life," I told him. "Without parole."

"Really?" the uniform said. "Some of the murders took place when Mercury was in retrograde. I thought that would make the judge loosen up on the sentence."

"Hmmm," Eck said in a tone about halfway to reflective. "How does that retro thing work?"

"Mercury goes backward," the other cop said.

"Does it turn around and fly back the way it came?" Eck asked him.

The officer inserted his document in a file and closed the drawer. He tilted his head and pickled his mouth. "I think it loops off somehow and then it gets on track again."

"It doesn't work at all," I said. "It's an optical illusion."

The uniform smiled at me as if he had mastered something I could never understand. "What sign are you?" he asked.

"Wet paint," I told him.

"Typical." He puffed a contemptuous breath and walked out.

"What's the score on the man in the boat?" I asked Eck.

"He was some faculty guy at the community college," Eck said. "Fishing on the lake out near The Bishop's Retreat. This priest from Saint Opie's is out there at the time to pray with the monks or something. He's walking across the lawn to some shrine or somewhere and he sees the whole thing. The professor is standing alone in his boat, holding up a string of dead fish. A whole schoolroom of muskies leaps out of the water, jumps into the boat and mauls the guy to death. Really rips him up. And then the muskies all jump back into the water, never to be found. What's left of the guy collapses in the bottom of the boat. A wet fishing license in his pocket was the only way of identifying him."

"And that seems plausible to you, Eck?"

"Jeez, Harbinger. You and your damn questions. There was an eye witness there. And the witness was a priest. You think a priest is gonna lie? At least the guy died doing what he loved to do."

"Getting shredded by muskies?"

"No, you numbskull. Holding up a string of dead fish."

"Seems like you'd have a few questions of your own, Eck. In all your years of living around here, have you ever heard of muskies jumping into a boat and eating a fisherman?"

"Yeah. Just this morning."

"I mean *before* this morning."

"Well, no. But hey, muskies have been known to gnaw on people's toes if they're dangling their feet in the water. Maybe the fish are upping the ante. There's no accounting for muskies in the end times."

"That again?"

"Don't laugh, buddy boy."

"So, this happened because the world is coming to an end?"

"If you knew your scripture, you'd see that," Eck told me. "There's all kinds of weird shit going on. The Bible prophesied all of it."

"Like what, for example?"

"War. And talk of war."

"And that's something new?"

"Don't get smart, Harbinger. Open your eyes! This is what you get when you mess with Satan. You start taking dead fish out of their watery tombs and you see what happens."

"You lost me."

"Think about it, peeper." He shook a heavy finger in the air. "All fish are dead. Fish are *born* dead. That's why you need to flirt with the occult to get them out of the water. You ever take a look at the fishing lures they sell over at Squeeze-A-Buck? They got Swedish Pimples, Cajun Crawdads, Whistler Jigs, Fuzzy Grubs, Crappie Queens, Hula Hoppers, Diving Smoos, Deep Pigs, Stinger Flies and a whole pegboard of other crazy shit. Why? All you'd really need to catch a live fish is a worm. But to get these dead fish, you need all them … whatchamacallit?"

"Inducements?"

"Yeah, them. And that's because you're making some shady underhanded deal with the devil. There's a guy in Upper Michigan who figured it all out."

"I need to rotate my tires," I said, getting up from my chair.

"And the whole thing about lures," he went on. "You use the word *lure* when you're trying to *tempt* somebody into doing what just ain't right. You *lure* them in. And it takes some real bad black magic to *lure* these poor dead fish out of their resting places beneath the waves. It's all deviltry."

"I don't know, Eck. I've seen some fish flopping around on a dock. They looked pretty lively to me."

"Oh, they move around and eat stuff, for sure. The guy in Michigan says they're all wound up by Satan. They flop around like that because their springs are too tight. And here's another possibility about the professor and them muskies."

"What's that?"

"Maybe Mercury is in retrograde," he said. "Let me get the clerical gals in on this." He picked up his phone and punched a button. "Hey Martha, is Mercury in retrograde?" He drummed his fingers to recorded music while the clerk checked on it. After a minute the drumming stopped. Eck frowned, shook his head and hung up.

"Well?" I said.

"She says not until the first of September." He dumped himself against the back of his chair, exasperated. "That's a little odd."

"Yeah, that's a sticky one. Hey, I may need you to run some license plates for me later. Can you help me out with that?"

"Nix tricks, Harbinger. For all the plates I already ran, you owe me six beers and a Mexican taco."

"Not a Chinese taco?" I held up two hands to deflect his anger. "Okay, I just got paid. Give me a cash figure and we'll settle up."

"Point is, I ain't your goddamn secretary."

"What do you have against me, Eck?"

"I'll tell you, Harbinger, the one time I got really mixed up with you, I ended up with a million forms to fill out."

"You're still mad about the strangler case? Didn't I help you close it?"

"Yeah, but that was by accident. Only because you were boffing the strangler's wife. And the paperwork turned out to be hell."

"The way I saw it, Eck, I cut your work load by half."

"How do you come up with that?"

"I did the follow-ups on half of your interviews. And without a client."

"Baaghh!" he grunted. "Scram out of here."

"It was nice to see you," I said. "Good luck with that paddle."

SIX

On most investigations there were definite steps you could take to get moving. On this one I was only milling around, going nowhere. Roxanne Delaplaine had taken away my starting blocks with her insistence on privacy, and I knew I'd have to ignore that demand sooner or later. The best I could figure was that her hiring at the college had forced someone out. Maybe the someone was trying to frighten her off. The man who'd been killed in the boat that morning was another professor, and that may have been significant. Or it may have had nothing to do with Roxanne. I didn't even know whether the two of them were linked to the same college.

The public library was next door to the city offices. I walked over and looked up Roxanne's work number in the reverse directory. The number didn't match up with the dead professor's community college in Pulptown, but it traced back to The College of the Immaculate Mind, a small Catholic school in the woods east of the city. That made sense of Roxanne's votive candles, if nothing else about her.

Back behind the wheel of my wreck, I picked my way through the sluggish drivers and eventually took the Boyd Dowler Slant Route out of town. When I had passed a few miles of dairy farms, I entered a thicket and found the side road I wanted. I turned off Dowler and shot a narrow gap between totems of Jesus and Mary. In a clearing at the top of a slight grade, the college complex came into view. Stone architecture with ivy cladding gave it a stately look that didn't fit its weightless reputation. Academic halls, dormitories, athletic facilities and a chapel fanned out from a central administration building. Large and small statues were interspersed among old-growth trees on lush lawns.

There were several scattered parking lots. I chose the one closest to the administration building and walked in. At the front desk, a matronly receptionist burst into a smile.

"And how are you doing this fine day?" she gushed. She apparently didn't care about the Packers.

"Okay," I told her.

"Only okay?" She was suddenly crestfallen, ladling on the sympathy.

"Make it peachy, then. Peachy all day long. How are *you* doing?"

She brightened. "I'm peachy too."

"Good. Got a few questions. My sister is thinking about enrolling, and I was wondering how long it would take to scrub her mind clean so that it's truly immaculate."

The smile didn't break. The sarcasm had passed right through her head, which told me a lot about the place.

"The college offers a two-year associate's degree," she said, "and a four-year bachelor's degree."

"Are you accredited?"

"Heavens no!" She was giddy. "That would mean too much meddling in our curriculum. Did you know that scientists think we come from monkeys?"

"No, I didn't," I told her. "My sister plans on studying the Romantic period. I heard the college is cutting personnel in art and literature."

"Certainly not," she said cheerfully. The phone rang and she excused herself to take the call. While I waited, I picked up a pamphlet called *"The Virgin Birth."* In a minute, the receptionist got off the phone and smiled up at me. "Those departments are actually expanding. The truth is, they recently brought in a new instructor from Milwaukee. A Miss Aeroplane, or something like that."

"That's an unusual name," I said.

"Let me check." She ran her finger down some columns in her directory. "Oops, my boo-boo. That's Miss Delaplaine." Eyeing the pamphlet in my hand, she said, "I see you're interested in the virgin birth."

"There have been some good articles about it in *The Medical Journal*."

"Oh, you're a doctor?"

"A little of this, a little of that," I said. "So, this Ms. Aeroplane. She came here from Milwaukee, not San Francisco?"

"You mean Miss Delaplaine?"

"Either one."

"I'm kinda sure it's Milwaukee, but I don't have all her information yet. She doesn't wear a wedding ring. I know that much." The receptionist winked at me and kept smiling. It was as if she were winning at bingo every five seconds. "I notice you're not wearing a wedding ring, either," she said. "Right now, Miss Delaplaine is in a conference in the Fine Arts Center. Maybe you should go over there and meet her. I have a feeling about these things."

"Maybe so." I tried to smile back. "You wouldn't know if anyone has been angry with her, would you? Maybe angry enough to level a death threat against her?"

"Oh, gracious, no! Why do you ask?"

"Well, if we started dating and there were gunshots."

"My, but you're a prudent person."

"Well, think about this. If I took her home to meet my mom and someone threw a brick through a window …"

"Oh, I get it. Those bricks with the little death threats wrapped around them."

"That's it, exactly."

"Gee, that's thoughtful of you, always looking out for your mom. But I don't think you'd have any problems with bricks. Everybody likes Miss Delaplaine."

More grinning. It was starting to depress me.

"So, I wonder what the two of us might have in common," I said. "Does this Ms. Aeroplane enjoy ice fishing?"

"I don't know." A trace of apprehension crossed her face.

"What about deer hunting?"

"Miss Aeroplane … Delaplaine … hasn't said anything."

"Camping?"

"You know what?" she said, anxious to please. "I've heard her mention bowling!"

"Good. Any other interests? Tennis? Yoga?"

Her face went searching.

"No tennis. But I think yoga is part of the occult."

"Of course, it is," I agreed. "Why do you think I asked?"

"You can't be too careful," she said through another smile, this time a relieved one. "No, I'd say just the bowling."

The information wasn't much, but maybe it could help. I wanted more.

"I also like a woman who knows cars. Does she change her own oil?"

"Sorry, I don't know," the receptionist muttered. She tilted her head and downturned her lips, as if to apologize. "You seem very particular."

"Well, what is she driving right now?"

"I'm sure I don't know, but a few instructors have been talking about it," she said helpfully. "Very hot, so they say. A modern classic or whatever they call it. Let's see. Looking fine in her sixty-nine."

"What was that?"

"Looking fine in her sixty-nine. That's what Mr. Pelton always says about her. He's a poet, you know. So, he does rhymes. And he always draws out the words *sixty-nine*, and then he laughs for some reason. He's a strange fellow. He likes her, but I really don't think the two of them are made for each other."

"Okay, she drives a 1969 something or other. What color?"

"Oh, jeepers, I wouldn't know that."

"Well thanks. Maybe I'll come in and meet her another time. I'm due somewhere in a few minutes."

"I'll pray to the Virgin Mary for you. Maybe she can intercede with Jesus and He'll get the two of you together."

"Worth a try."

"You know, Jesus can hardly refuse a request from the Holy Mother."

"I've heard that," I said. It didn't seem to be enough for her.

"You don't think so?" Now she appeared troubled, maybe sensing the guy in front of her was *one of those*.

I didn't want to annoy her. I said, "I'm just a little skeptical sometimes."

"Skeptical?" She looked at me as if Satan were whispering in my ear.

"It's one of my character defects. Forget I said anything."

"No, really. What it is it?"

"Well, here's the deal. If Jesus already knows what he's going to do and how things will play out, how can it make any difference whether or not his mom asks him to intervene?"

"I don't … get it," she said.

"Well, let's say little Billy has a goiter problem. Mary goes over to Jesus and asks him to make sure the treatment goes well. Now, doesn't Jesus already know ahead of time how he's going to handle the case?"

She leaned forward and spoke as if she were counseling a child.

"But maybe Jesus was going to let the boy wither away and die, and then Mary goes in and asks Him to have a heart, you know? And so Jesus changes His mind and saves little Billy."

"Good thought, but for a guy who's omniscient, didn't Jesus see that one coming?"

"How do you mean?"

"My point is, you can't be persuaded unless you get some new information or somebody makes you look at an issue in a new way. Now, it seems that Jesus would have to be surprised by his mom's request for intervention, and by her argument for it, or he wouldn't be changing his mind at all, right?"

"Lord above, I guess so."

"But he's all-knowing. Don't you think he would have foreseen his mom coming down the hall to nag him? Don't you think he'd foresee her pitch and the answer he'd be giving her? So, why wouldn't he just poke his head out of his office doorway, catch her before she could say three words and tell her he's got the whole thing handled? "

"Jiminy Cricket," she said slowly. "I never in my born days thought about that." Her eyes dropped and went darting all over the reception desk. She looked like she was running a math problem through her head, one of those brain-teasers that take up an entire chalk board. Finally, she spoke: "It must be kind of uncomfortable to have a conversation up there in heaven, what with Jesus reading everybody's mind all the time."

"You're right," I told her. "But I've got the Virgin Mary's pamphlet right here, and maybe that'll clarify everything. Thanks for your help."

"God bless you," she told me. The controversy had somehow washed away and she was beaming again.

I made a move to leave but there was a piddling detail on my mind.

"Let me ask you another question. Has Ms. Aeroplane ever talked about lighting votive candles?"

"Not that I can remember."

"Vespers?"

"I don't think so."

"Any church rituals at all?"

She shook her head. "Uh-uh."

"Anything about Saint Opie's?"

"No, but she's new here and I haven't talked with her a whole bunch. I'll tell you this much, though. I go far out of my way to avoid Saint Opie's."

"Why is that?"

Once more she looked troubled. "I hate to talk out of turn if that's your church."

"I'm from out of the area," I lied.

"Well, people claim there's just something not quite right about that place. And I know you're going to ask me what, but I really don't know. It's just what people say."

"Maybe so, maybe not," I told her. I tapped the virgin birth pamphlet against my palm. "People claim all sorts of crazy things." I turned to leave.

"You seem like a nice young man."

"Thanks. You're pretty nice, yourself."

"You *could* go to hell for asking all those questions about heaven," she said. "But you're very nice, all the same."

She was smiling like a three-year-old with a birthday cake.

SEVEN

I stepped outside. It was late afternoon and still hot, but the air was now stirring and not so heavy.

Where to? I asked myself. The mention of Milwaukee threw me off because Roxanne had told me San Francisco was her last home base before Pulptown. Maybe the Milwaukee reference came out of something the receptionist had misunderstood, the same way she got Delaplaine muddled up with Aeroplane. Assuming the receptionist was right, though, Roxanne had lied to me. And a lie usually had partners. I needed more facts before taking the investigation any further. I wasn't in the habit of dogging my own client, but in this case I thought it would be good to know her address — and whether she was still indulging in those questionable associations of hers. I'd have to follow her home, for a start.

Back in my rickety Mustang, I puttered around and located Fine Arts. I had no idea which door Roxanne would be coming out of. Picking her up as she drove off the grounds wouldn't work because signs told me there were four exits. My best bet would be to identify her car and monitor it. There was a small parking lot in front of her building and a large one behind it. The stalls weren't filled because students were off for the summer, but enough faculty and staff had shown up to leave plenty of cars and trucks scattered around. I went tooling through the two lots.

I saw nothing with a California plate, but spotted two cars that were probably from the late sixties and possibly considered to be modern classics. My Mustang was only a few years older than either of them but it was tired and demoralized and looked like it had been through a mortar attack. The two gems I'd found were in a much different category. They were lovingly preserved or fresh out of restoration and every bit as racy as they had ever been.

One was a Dodge Challenger in black, the other a Pontiac GTO in muscle-car orange with a white convertible top. Both had Wisconsin plates and unnumbered faculty stickers. They were parked on opposite sides of the building, so there was no stakeout position that would allow me to keep both of them in view. I had to choose one classic or the other.

From a distance, I couldn't make the year for either car. I had once kept track of annual design changes in most automotive brands. But when I wasn't twelve anymore my head filled up with more pressing matters.

I steered over to the Challenger, got out and went to the back of it. I bent down and examined a taillight. Raised numerals on the red plastic lens identified it as a 1970 model. My mistake, or maybe Mr. Pelton had gotten his model years mixed up. I drove around to the rear lot, got out and skulked up to the Pontiac. Crouching behind it, I found a small "*69*" stamped on a taillight. This was the one. I made a note of the plate number and with quite a bit of envy returned to the Mustang.

I drove to the edge of the big lot and stopped in the shade of a low-hanging willow tree. Parked with the nose of my car pointing at the GTO, I could peek up at it every few seconds. While I waited for someone to approach it on foot, I amused myself with the pamphlet on the virgin birth.

The document included details on Saint Mary's purity but didn't really explain God's hands-off method of reproduction. There was a bonus in the back pages: a catalogue of the holy virgin's public appearances in recent years. Turns out it wasn't just in Lourdes or Fatima where she was popping in. The gal had also shown up in Bakersfield, California, displaying her face on a screen door. Well, depending on the way the light glinted off the screen at a certain time of day. In Altoona, Pennsylvania, a fan had discovered the Madonna emblazoned on a slice of toast. There were scads of other cameos. However, none of the images were very clear. And without any contemporary portraits of the mother of Christ for comparison, I found it hard to tell whether the vague illustrations on screen doors, toasted bread, wood paneling and damp towels depicted the actual saint or any other woman who had ever draped a shawl over the back of her head.

Within an hour, Roxanne Delaplaine ambled through the rear doorway of the Fine Arts Center, carrying a purse and a soft leather attaché case. She had changed her clothes since her morning visit to my office, and now she looked cool and professional in a navy blouse, a cream skirt and a pair of heels that were fairly down to earth. There were no glances over the shoulder, and her stride was confident and carefree, not the tentative gait of someone worried about a killer.

Maybe hiring a detective had made her feel better.

I slouched in my seat, watching her over the cusp of my dashboard as she walked straight toward the GTO convertible and stepped up to the driver's door. After unlocking and opening it, she slung her lightweight luggage onto the passenger seat. Once at the wheel, she lit up the engine and revved it. She lowered the windows and sent the automatic top peeling back until it folded behind the rear seats. After adjusting a mirror, she took off and made a sweeping turn around a cluster of dormant trucks. In the turbulence behind the windshield, torrents of blond hair danced and whipped against her sunglasses.

I twisted my key in the Mustang's ignition, feeling guilty about my tactics but determined to learn more about my client.

EIGHT

With me following at a safe distance, Roxanne drove out of the campus and turned east onto the Dowler Slant Route. Then she got onto a southbound road cutting straight across level ground. On either side of me as I straggled behind, brown-and-white cattle grazed in pastures fenced off from acres of crops. Most of the farms out this way were carefully maintained, with crisp white houses and neat red barns, but a few of the spreads were unkempt and cluttered with debris. Here and there, derelict cars rusted away on blocks. A gutted tractor sat in weeds that had grown past the hubs of its wheels. A barn sagged as if its loft couldn't support one more bale of hay.

Gradually, the livestock and cornfields and silos phased into native grasslands and the remainders of a forest. The air was now invigorating, laced with an earthy aroma and pine accents that wafted in from the meadows and groves beside the road. Farther along, veteran oaks reached high and wide, and the slim ivory shanks of birches occasionally flashed into view. As I glided through the scents and the scenery, I could recognize something almost idyllic about the place.

My relationship with Wisconsin nature had always been love-and-hate. Autumns were wonderful but brief. Though the winters could be fun in the early stages, the appeal wore off quickly. Snow was fine for Christmas, but as far as I was concerned, they could have packed it away with the yuletide bric-a-brac right after the Rose Bowl. They didn't. What they did was drop the temperatures. In most years, there were too many sub-zero days to make ice skating and cross-country skiing worth all the shivering, and we faced the frequent chores of shoveling drifts from our driveways and scraping frost from our windshields. As we worked, our earlobes would freeze, our lungs would burn and the polar wind would feel like tiny nails driven into our foreheads. By February, it felt like things had always been that way and would always stay that way. March relented but lied to us repeatedly. It told us spring would come after the third week, though by month's end there were seldom any green fields to enjoy. Even the annual thaw had its negatives. The roadside snowbanks that were once clean and fluffy were muddied with slop kicked up by passing tires, and the white blanketing that had once graced our landscapes devolved into gray blobs. Worse, there was often a sleet storm in April, just when we had convinced ourselves that the winter's back had already been broken. Genuine spring — when it finally came — was a halting recovery from arctic fatigue. The clammy cold was gone by early May, but many of the trees were still bare until later in the month, when buds cautiously poked out from branches that had looked dead for half a year.

Then one day you'd find yourself deep into a resplendent summer. Wispy clouds would stream across pale blue skies, the humidity would be carried off by a breeze and the mosquitos would temporarily set aside their bloodlust. When all of that fell together, you had to appreciate how warm and lush and beautiful it could be. This was one of those times.

Roxanne turned east onto the area's main highway. Early evening traffic was light. She passed a few slow drivers, but seemed content to cruise the convertible at a fairly legal pace, letting the flow of fresh air counter the lingering heat. I was able to keep sight of her without ever flooring my gas pedal. And that was fortunate, because I couldn't have matched GTO's full horsepower. The speedometer in my jalopy boasted numbers past 100, but the car was never going to hit the road that fast unless it was dropped out of a cargo plane.

The lady braked and turned right onto one of the fire lanes that led to the northern rim of Lake Winnebago. It was easy to track her, even while hanging back. At the same time, it should have been easy for her to spot a tail, but she showed no signs of being careful about it. She turned left at a *T* intersection and I sped up to keep her in range. By the time I had slowed and carefully retraced her turn, the bright orange car was still rolling.

The houses here were opulent for the local environs. Each one sat on a shoreline lot to my right. Lake views popped up in the gaps between them as I drove by. Ahead of me, Roxanne passed a series of mail boxes and made one more right turn into an oversized property. I stopped and grabbed a pair of binoculars to watch her GTO. It cleared a mechanized gate and approached a garage built for a fleet, then veered across a coachyard to a fair-weather carport. There it tucked in between a red roadster and a silver sedan. The GTO's top rose and clamped into place.

Its windows went up. Roxanne climbed out with her purse and briefcase in hand, walked over to a huge house and went in without ringing a bell.

I drove quietly past the driveway and swung left onto a rutted dirt trail that took me to higher ground. I hid the Mustang behind some foliage and got out. Carrying the binoculars, I hiked through hillside brush until I reached an outcropping of rock. I sat down on that to take a magnified look at the residence across the road.

The mansion was intended to make you think of a castle. A flagstone path led from the carport to a fake drawbridge. A fake moat under that was nothing more than an elongated puddle. Past the bridge, there was an arch of chiseled boulders hulking over the rustic doorway Roxanne had entered. Shiny numerals nailed to the wooden door were gussied up with Olde English flourishes. I wrote the address in a notebook. Rising from the top of the arch was a pike, and hanging from that was a pennant with a gold "*K*" on a field of purple. The building's main façade was rough slate. Along the top of the front wall, there were battlements — notches where imaginary archers could lean in to shoot imaginary arrows at imaginary marauders. At the corners, above the roofline, there were faux turrets.

The whole mockup was ridiculous, an idiot's conception of affluence and prestige.

I trained the binoculars on the two cars parked near the GTO. The roadster was a Porsche, the sedan a Mercedes-Benz. I recorded their plate numbers.

The house below remained unlit for hours, at least the part I could see. Illumination and activity must have been limited to the lakeside rooms. That wasn't a problem because I wasn't there to peep through any windows. The motor pool was in plain sight and I was only interested in any new vehicles coming in or Roxanne's car going somewhere else. None of that happened, and I fought boredom all the way to sunset and an hour past it. With no indications that my client would be leaving, it looked as if she were probably the queen of the castle, at home until morning. If there was a king, odds were he was home as well.

I realized I was assuming too much. And I knew I shouldn't jump to any conclusions just to get the hell out of there, but I couldn't stay all night.

Under stars that were just bright enough, I returned to my car. I got it started but left the headlights off as I descended the dirt trail. Rounding onto the asphalt and aiming for Pulptown, I switched on my lights in time to see a deer scampering across the road. It was a nice moment. At least for one of us.

NINE

Back in the office that night, I checked my answering machine. There was a message from Roxanne, who had called in the late afternoon with questions on the case. It would have been too late to call her back even if I had her home number. Nothing to report anyway, except for some dead ends and me following her. I left the phone alone and went through the connecting door to my apartment.

Ten months earlier, the building's rental value had plummeted so low that the landlord began offering two offices for the price of one. I signed a new lease, and the landlord was supposed to convert the unit next to mine into a domestic space. He missed it badly. A free apartment had sounded like a good deal at the time, but the amenities turned out to be iffy to anyone who hadn't spent most of his years living under a bridge.

The design motif was helter skelter. I had a makeshift kitchen with a toaster oven and the kind of small refrigerator you find in hotel rooms or college dorms. I had a cabinet filled with chipped dishes and branded beer glasses. There was a bathroom with a slow-draining sink and a cramped shower stall. The closet was small enough to leave my shirts and jackets a little stoop-shouldered, and a sock drawer in a clothing chest had been off its rails for weeks. A Murphy bed creaked when I pulled it down, and every time I did, I had to wrangle an easy chair out of the way. On the plus side, the chair and matching couch were fully functional pieces of furniture.

The place's entertainment options were limited: stray books and magazines on a coffee table, a TV with a finicky antenna, an off-brand stereo and some records that were happily out of style. A few personal treasures were set up on tables or pinned up to walls. There were photos and sports mementos and two posters from old noir movies. *Booze, blondes and bullets*, one of the posters promised. The second one featured a buxom actress in a dress that was practically falling off her breasts. The blurb above her explained that loneliness was what made a man go for the wrong woman. Hell, there were better reasons than that.

I fixed a ham sandwich, poured a drink and landed on the couch. I sat wondering what the deal was with Roxanne Delaplaine. She could have received a royal summons for an overnighter at the castle, but if she lived there full-time and not in an apartment, that was another fib she had told me. More complications.

The majority of my cases were straightforward, at least in terms of the background information provided at the outset. Those assignments never got me in any serious danger and I usually got paid on time. They tended to come from lawyers and corporations. Maybe Roxanne was on the level, but the clients who walked in off the street were often trouble. Theirs were the jobs that sometimes left me misled or shortchanged or booted in the muzzle. I knew that one day, one of those jobs might leave me dead.

There was no way to sort it out now, so I tried to forget about it. I turned on the TV and found *"Three Stooges Theater."* The boys had taken over a dentist's office and were having difficulty pulling a tooth. Moe, somehow in possession of dynamite, realized they would have to blast. The episode was instructive and good for the soul, but I had seen it five times.

I turned the channel and found the Reverend Beauregard Pithy. This guy was a crook and a parasite but he was a master showman. He had come to Pulptown to escape the surplus of evangelical preachers in Alabama and was now taping shows from his new church in Green Bay. He looked like a stringent Elvis in horn-rimmed glasses. His wife sat beside him, simpering and nodding. She had a waxy face, heavily reinforced eyelashes and hair like a frozen geyser.

Reverend Pithy was telling his live crowd and his television audience that God whups us upside the head every so often just to get our attention. When we get cocky and start to think we're in control of our own fortunes, that's when the Lord of Riches and Ruin throws economic hardships down upon us. But just as God has the power to bring us to our knees, so God has the power to lift us up again. Reverend Pithy gave us all a reassuring smile. His wife kept grinning like a game-show model. If we will only trust in God, Reverend Pithy was saying, divine prosperity will be delivered unto us. Then Revered Pithy started begging for money to keep his ministry on the air. He covered the myriad excuses people cite to avoid parting with cash, but the excuse he hated the most was abject poverty. When you think you have nothing more to give, Reverend Pithy said, that's the time to gather up every penny you can lay your hands on and send it to the ministry. He reached over toward his wife, who handed him a letter from a viewer. The reverend said the woman who wrote the letter had gotten down to her last six dollars. The power company had turned off her lights, and because of the outage, the poor woman couldn't even watch the ministry on TV anymore. But she remembered Reverend Pithy's pleas. And his mailing address. She sent him the six dollars, along with her wedding ring. Four days later, she went to her mailbox and found a check for eighty thousand dollars.

"It's divine prosperity!" Reverend Pithy shouted. The congregation broke into hosannas as the camera panned over them. Each member had a stupefied face and both hands in the air. That looked about right, since they were all being robbed.

A telephone number flashed on the screen. Reverend Pithy told us that operators were standing by. I called the number.

"I'd like to donate," I said to the operator. "But I'm out of work and my kids are starving and my wife needs surgery."

"Do you have any savings?" the operator said.

"I'm afraid not."

"How about a credit card?"

"I have one of those," I told her.

"Is it maxed out to the limit?"

"I think it has a little more than a thousand dollars in wiggle room."

"Why don't you just give me your credit card number?" she said. "Would you like to donate an even thousand or the whole wad?"

"I don't think I can ever pay it back to the bank," I said.

"The Lord will return your gift ten-fold."

"So that would be about ten thousand dollars," I said. "Reverend Pithy was talking about a woman who laid down only six bucks and got back eighty grand."

"Results may vary," she said. "Past returns are no guarantee of future performance."

"I'm not sure," I said. "Maybe I should take the thousand dollars as a cash advance and go gambling with it."

"Don't do that," she said. "Then the money would just go to Satan. You need to give the money to God. What's the number on the card?"

"Why does God need the money?"

"It takes a ministry to spread the word of God."

"Maybe I could spread the word myself."

"Oh right. Like you have your own TV show."

"How do I get one of those?" I asked her.

"Look," she said with iron shavings in her voice. "If you want divine prosperity delivered unto you, I'll need the number on the card."

"Do you have a pen?" I asked her.

"Of course, I do."

"Can you write this down?"

"I'm waiting!"

"You are so full of crap," I told her.

"But what's the number on the card?"

I hung up the phone and killed the TV.

It was late and I was bushed. I stretched out as much as I could on the couch. After a while, I was only one-tenth awake. I tried convincing myself to get on my feet, take off my clothes, move the easy chair, pull down the Murphy bed and dig my way under the sheets. It was no good. All of that seemed like more work than loading a semi-truck.

I fell asleep without ever getting comfortable.

TEN

The next morning, I woke up scrunched on the couch. My back felt like I had spent the night in an oil drum. I started to get vertical, found my bones and worked out the kinks. My mouth tasted as sour as last night's mood. I brushed my teeth but the mood stayed the same. Then it was a prefabricated breakfast and a shave and a shower and the rest of the daybreak routine. The closet wasn't burgeoning with opportunities, but I picked out a suit with fewer wrinkles than the clothes I had slept in.

The morning paper, the *Pulptown Daily Informer,* was waiting for me on the hallway mat outside my apartment. I always felt a little ashamed when I peeled out the sports section first, but that's what I did. Surprisingly, there was a story on the Philadelphia Stars, who were ripping through the USFL's regular season and heading for the playoffs. Most people didn't care.

On the front page, the lead story carried a photo of a local sculptor, Moot Wankelburg, beaming in front of his latest creation. The guy worked full-time sloshing hot tar on rooftops and roads and parking lots, but he had used his spare moments to carve an approximate replica of *"The Thinker"* out of a huge block of cheese. His piece looked a little mushy and a little lopsided compared to the original Rodin. It was as pointless as any artistic endeavor in human history, but that didn't keep it from being hailed as a cultural milestone for Pulptown. Moot's dream, he said, was to give the people of Wisconsin great art in a medium they could relate to. Cheese was a natural. He had prayed over the daunting project quite a lot, and he gave God credit for guiding his every move. Moot had a point. You couldn't behold his hunk of pensive cheddar without seeing the hand of the highest intelligence in the universe.

There was an article on the strangler sentencing, but I skipped over it because I already knew the details.

The front page also had a story on the strange death Wally Eck had told me about. *Man Killed by Leaping Muskies*. The lead paragraph identified the victim as Harry Armstadt, a local professor. I read through the dry copy without picking up a morsel of skepticism from the reporter. As Eck had said, the witness named in the story was a priest, Father Timothy Mulhooly, now of Saint Opie's but formerly a university official at Notre Dame. The priest was coming out of the chapel at The Bishop's Retreat when he looked out at the lake and happened to see the angler standing in his boat and holding up a string of dead fish. The attack came instantly. According to the eyewitness account, ten or twelve vicious muskies leaped out of the water and gnawed the fisherman to death. Minutes later, his mutilated body was recovered from the bottom of the boat.

Day after day, many of the articles in the *Informer* left a lot of questions unasked. This one certainly did. There was the matter of unprecedented muskie aggression, of course, but there were also some middling details that didn't fit together. The article said there was nobody else in the boat, which made me wonder why the fisherman would be striking the theatrical pose of holding up his string of dead fish. He could have been showing them off to someone on the lake shore, but there were no other witnesses named in the story. Well, it wasn't my case and it wasn't my problem to solve.

I went through the connecting door to my office at about ten o'clock, as bright and early as I could impose on myself. My answering machine sat on my desk and stared at me. Roxanne's message from last night was in there, coiled in a cassette. I stared back at it and won. I wasn't ready to call her yet.

Instead, I got on the phone with a data research company and put in orders for three license plates. I would have liked Eck to run them for free because I couldn't put the searches on my expense account. Clients hated to pay for it when all you were doing was checking out their own stories. On the other hand, I was still on the top end of my five-hundred-dollar retainer. After calling in the plates, I contacted the Winnegamie County tax assessor and gave the clerk the address of the lakeside castle. The clerk traced the property's ownership to something called Terminal, Inc., with the same address as the house. No help there. It would take some time and effort to ferret out who ran the corporation, and then maybe I would only find that it was a subsidiary of some other corporation. I'd have to go that route if the easier search for vehicle information didn't give me what I needed.

I went back to George Orwell's nightmare scenario to wait out the results from the data research outfit.

A little while past noon, the office door opened and a small, bony man walked in. He paused in silence, doped out the room and then focused on me. I placed him somewhere in his seventies. He had closely cropped gray hair, hooded eyes and a raised jaw that more or less pointed toward something above my head. He also had a no-nonsense manner, though I was sure some kind of nonsense was on the way. There were times when I could tell in seconds. He held up an authoritative right index finger and then poked it three times at a manila folder in his left hand. "Crop circles," he said.

I motioned for him to come forward, offered him the client's chair and leaned back to kill some time.

He sat but didn't rest. He was too high-strung for that. "I'm forgetting my manners," he said. "How about those Packers?"

"Quite all right," I said, not even bothering with the USFL. "Training camp coming up in a few weeks. What can I do for you?"

His eyes were fervent. He had the singleness of purpose you find in a great crackpot. He reached into the folder and came out with several sheets of paper. As far as I could tell, they weren't death threats. The drawings on them were circular and intricate, with all sorts of smaller designs worked into the larger ones. There were pentagrams, mazes, keys, webs and swirls. The final drawing showed a succession of circles, each one getting a little smaller than the last, and each with its own pattern inside.

"Very nice," I said.

"And dangerous," he said with gravity. "These are all sketches of crop circles. I also have aerial photographs right here." He rummaged through his folder and dropped a handful of photos on the desk.

The flapping of the photos blew a chemical scent across the desk. My would-be client was wearing either a bargain brand of cologne or a premium brand of insect repellant.

"Some of them are from fields here in America," he said. "Some in Canada, and some are in England."

"You said dangerous. Dangerous how?"

"That should be obvious," he said. "We've got travelers from outer space leaving these messages in our fields and if we don't figure them out soon, our time here on Earth will come to an abrupt end. You can trust me on that."

"I'll try. You said these patterns are messages. What do they mean?"

"The travelers communicate on a subliminal level," he said. "You look at these cosmoglyphs. I call them cosmoglyphs. You look at them and you just get a feeling, don't you? You kind of understand intuitively that they're codes from other worlds orbiting other stars. And they're coming from people who are … well, next to us they're like gods. They're vastly more intelligent than we are. Mostly, they're pure energy, but they can have bodies when they want them. See, they're warning us about something, maybe an invasion, but I can't quite figure out what the warnings mean."

"I imagine that's where I come in," I told him.

"Correct. I need you to investigate these patterns and decode them."

"Where did you get these photos and drawings?" I asked him.

"Oh, I got them," he assured me in a cagey tone of voice.

"Do you have tinfoil pasted up against your ceiling at home?"

The question didn't faze him. "That's affirmative," he said.

"Look, Mr. Morrisey—"

"My name isn't Morrisey."

"Really? Because I got that impression from the crop circle in Devonshire. Sort of a subliminal thing."

"No, I'm Stutzweiler."

"Are you sure?"

"Of course, I'm sure." He was all right until he realized I was yanking his chain. "Hey, watch it," he said. "I'm not some dumb Polack."

"My secretary is from Warsaw."

"I don't see any secretary." He looked around. "What, behind that door?" Then he hesitated, his face reddening. "You mean Wausau, Wisconsin?"

"No, I mean Warsaw. It's the capital of Poland."

"Oh. Sorry. I didn't mean anything by it."

And yet, he did.

The local population was almost entirely made up of Northern European descendants. It was rare to see black people in Pulptown, and those were usually visitors from the southern part of the state. Some Asian refugees had recently moved into the valley, but they were few. Before they arrived, the white population had been so homogenous that the more tribal residents felt it was necessary to emphasize tiny differences. For some reason, the Poles had been cast as the outsiders. And the problem. Almost all of us who were absorbed into that mentality as children had broken out of it by adulthood. But not Mr. Stutzweiler. Whether the source of his discomfort was Poland or Polaris, he had aliens on the brain.

I said, "These cosmoglyphs and emissaries from space. They're not really my specialty. I try to stay out of galactic politics."

"You're a detective, aren't you? What do you do all day, sit in your office? I think you should get out there and do some detecting. Not to mention saving this planet from an interstellar war."

"Have you run this by the Department of Defense?"

"They're the ones who are covering it up," he said.

"And why are they doing that?"

"Who knows? All those Washington types are corrupt. They're probably getting paid off to let the aliens take over."

"In extraterrestrial currency?"

"Nah," he said. "They're taking their bribes in diamonds."

"I'd have to pass," I said. "Anyway, if I'm not mistaken, most of these crop circles are showing up in wheat fields. We don't have many of those around Pulptown. You might look for a detective out in the prairie states."

"Oh, you'd have to take some trips," he said. "Kansas, all the way up to Saskatchewan, over to England. Of course, I couldn't front you the expenses. I've given this a lot of thought and I figure we could work something out. If you can get to the bottom of these cosmoglyphs, and if you can find out where they're coming from and who created them and what they mean, I can sell the story to the *National Embarrasser*. They'll pay a fortune for that kind of scoop. I'll cut you in for half."

"After I do all the work?"

"I'm the one who put you onto it," he said. "Without me, where would you be?"

Good question. And where was I heading? Maybe my mother and father had been right. Maybe I should have studied harder, been more diligent, taken the future more seriously.

Well, I hadn't. And now I was running a half-crazy enterprise out of a frowsy little dump. Looking around the room, I rested my eyes on the pebbled glass window set into my office door. I fixed on its backward stenciled lettering that said to anyone out in the hallway:

Jack Harbinger
Private Investigator

My folks had once dreamed of me getting a master's degree in finance and making good in some metropolitan skyscraper. Maybe I'd even be at the top floor, in a posh executive suite. They could almost see themselves knocking proudly on my office door. They could almost see the door's burnished nameplate with its engraved lettering:

Jackson T. Harbinger
Some Kind of Respectable Businessman

After years of watching me sidestep my way through school, the two of them resigned themselves to the fact that my name would never appear on any brass plate at the peak of any steel tower. They could live with that. But the office door I did end up with was worse than anything they had feared.

"I can see you've been mulling it over," Stutzweiler said. "So, how's about it? Do we have a deal?"

"I'll just say this: These tipsters were smart enough to travel all the way here from Alpha Centauri or the Orion constellation. And yet when they want to plant an idea in our heads, they don't just come and say it out loud. Or even drop us a postcard. If they want us to brace for an invasion or bow down before a golden calf or pass the salt or get out of jail free, why can't they make that clear in plain language without all the rigmarole? What they do instead is show us these enigmatic crop circles. We're supposed to do some interpreting but we can't make heads or tails out of them. The spacemen see the dumbfounded looks on our faces but they keep sending us the same failed messages. Not a good move."

"But they have nearly infinite intelligence," he said. "They have their own ways of conveying ideas. You can't expect them to stoop to our level of communication."

"Not unless they're trying to make themselves understood," I said. "You believe these space travelers are extremely intelligent and that they're trying to tell you something, and yet they apparently don't have the slightest notion of how to get their meaning across. It seems to me that if aliens are really scooting around out there, then the bunch laying down these crop circles would have to be the most inarticulate rubes in the galaxy. Your concept has a few flaws, to put it politely. I wouldn't worry about these things too much."

"But if superbeings didn't create them, how did the crop circles get there?"

I settled back and tried to figure him. He was someone I had met before. Different face, different name, different story. But essentially the same guy. Mr. Stutzweiler seemed sincere enough, in a troubling sort of way. There was just something missing in his eyes, some capacity to ask himself whether what he was saying made any sense. If his mind had an instrument panel, not all the needles would be moving. I tried to tap on his gauges, get them working.

"Ever heard of Occam's razor?"

"No," he said, pitching forward. "Is that a starship?"

"It's a principle. Roughly stated, the simplest explanation is probably the best explanation. Now, which is the simpler explanation? Are geniuses traveling light years to get here only to leave puzzles they realize are *no comprende*? Or are human pranksters driving out to wheat fields in the middle of the night and stamping out these patterns just to laugh at the people who are scratching their heads over them?"

"You're a damn fool," he said. "And ignorant. We don't have the technology to do what you're describing."

"We don't know how to bend wheat stalks?"

"To lay down those patterns!" he shouted. "They're too elaborate, too intricate. Nobody on Earth could pull that off."

"You've seen the logos in the middle of the field at the Super Bowl, haven't you? They're very complicated. Plus, they're in color."

"That's different," Stutzweiler said.

"Not really," I said. "Humans are capable of some fine craftsmanship in that area."

"You think?"

"Somebody has to."

That one didn't sit well. He lifted his jawbone again and went back on the offensive.

"Have you ever been abducted, Mr. Harbinger?"

"By sorority girls, yes. By space aliens, no."

"Well, *I've* been abducted by space aliens. Oodles of times. And you'd never believe the things I could tell you."

"I think we can agree on that," I said. I dug out and searched a medical directory. I wrote down the name and office number of a psychiatrist. Not Amanda Foster, the doc at the mental hospital. She had the bedside manner of a prison camp commandant and I wouldn't have wished her on Stutzweiler or anyone else. Maybe the casually chosen doctor could help him. At least it was something. I slid the paper toward him and said, "Here's someone you may want to discuss your concerns with."

"Who's this?" he sniffed. "Some quack of a headshrinker?"

"I found out yesterday that they really don't like to be called that."

He bubbled and bristled at me, shaking his head and mumbling about how shortsighted and pigheaded people could be. I couldn't argue with him there.

"You have a closed mind," he said angrily. He pushed the note back at me, gathered up his materials and pivoted out of the chair. He stomped toward the door and just before slamming it, he said, "You're not the only private eye in this town."

Actually, I was. Everyone else wanted some dignity.

ELEVEN

After that, nothing much happened until late in the day, when word came back on the license plates. All three cars I'd seen at the castle were registered to Last Chance Mortuary. Like anyone in town who had been bombarded with radio advertising, I knew Last Chance meant Slab Kapowski.

My mind slotted over to the *"K"* pennant at the castle's entrance.

The man behind Last Chance was publicly a funeral tycoon, a wizard at business. The official story on Slab was that he had started as a gravedigger and worked his way up to become a certified mortician. As soon as he could raise a sufficient bankroll, he started his own company. With all-American instincts, he eventually built a commercial empire covering more than twenty cities in our part of the state. So much for the sanitized version. Exactly how he came to dominate the stiffs market was something most people didn't bother about. But in the back rooms downtown, the take on his company's expansion was a little troubling. There were whispers that Slab's ethics were buried deeper than his customers. The hushed word was that he had gotten ahead by intimidating and extorting and maybe even killing off his rivals. It seemed a lot of the established mortuary owners in Slab's crosshairs had poor business sense and sold out to him far too cheaply. Others were holdouts who were suddenly afflicted with rotten luck, dangerous habits or suicidal misery. A hit-and-run car crash took away one of them. An electrocution finished another. Some of them had leaped to their deaths, with a few plunging off the steeple at our own Saint Opie's.

Church was a drag, but it couldn't have been *that* depressing.

There were never any charges, never any arrests. The Pulptown police hadn't turned up anything incriminating on the local fatalities. And in several other jurisdictions throughout the region, quiet inquiries on morticians' deaths had been inconclusive.

But not exculpatory. Not to the guys in those back rooms.

What the hell was Roxanne doing with a guy like Slab? Whatever the reason, I needed to see whether he was showing any violent tendencies toward her. All I had to do was figure out where to find them together.

I knew from an old newspaper profile that Slab was fanatical about bowling. At least that had been the case when the article ran, and maybe he hadn't tired of it yet. Meanwhile, the receptionist at the college had said Roxanne shared the same hobby. It wasn't much of a lead, and trying to catch my client paired with Slab at any given time in any given bowling alley wasn't a promising strategy. But it would be less chancy than following her again.

It was Wednesday, the midpoint in the work week. That was always a heavy night for leagues at Hunchback Lanes, the ten-pin mecca on the northern fringe of town. I called out there and learned that one of the groups on the docket for eight p.m. was the Eternal Peace League. The name could have been chosen by a transcendental meditation society, but it would also be perfect for a merry band of undertakers.

I made my evening plans.

There was still enough time in the afternoon to drop by the church. Roxanne had told me about a nun down there jamming her with an ice pick for flubbing a prayer or folding her hands incorrectly. That sounded plausible. I had spent eight years at Saint Opie's Elementary School and I'd seen worse.

Even so, I had a nagging doubt about the sharp little object I'd pulled out of the lady's back.

TWELVE

I parked in front of Saint Opie's and stood on a street I had crossed more than a thousand times. The church complex — with its rectory, convent and elementary school — was laden with a dour, constricted holiness. In the old days, it weighed on me like a bad report card. A trace of that feeling was still embedded in the structures.

No telling whether a passing demon inspired me, but an impish idea popped into my head. I went over to a Jiffy Cheap convenience store across from the church. I bought cigarettes, a pack of Winstons at random. I also picked up some stray wooden matches from a tray next to the cash register. I went outside, cracked open the pack and ditched the cellophane in a trash can — all the while studying the ecclesiastical façade rising above the opposite curb. The church had been built about sixty years before I was born as a quasi-Baroque throwback. Over the past decade, it had been modernized, which meant blocking over a lot of the Rococo exterior with squared-off planes that created more interior room but killed whatever style the building once had. The resulting hodgepodge was both dull and flamboyant, an eyesore either way. I put the cigarettes and the matches in my coat pocket and walked over to the main entrance.

Above a wide set of stairs, a pair of tall bas-relief doors opened to the vestibule, sort of a shallow lobby, with a gurgling font of holy water, a collection box you couldn't miss and a marble bust of Opius Flavius. Opius was one of the first Roman senators to convert to Christianity and one of the first to be tagged with sainthood. Among the miracles attributed to him was an uncanny ability to pick winners at the chariot races. Historians were pretty much agreed that the fix was in on those races. But when Opie came up for canonization in the Middle Ages, the pope ignored the bad rep and pushed the ancient senator's case until he was a made man. The pontiff may have received a kickback from wealthy Flavius descendants, but hell, he was infallible. Now, almost a thousand years later, Saint Opius of Rome was largely forgotten outside of the Vatican archives and an obscure parish in Pulptown, Wisconsin. His only tangible legacies were this tawdry little church and an old monastery out at the lake shore.

Beyond Opie's bust, heavy oaken doors led into the grand chamber itself. What had they always called it? Not an auditorium. A nave. I went in and leaned against a stone column and took in the view I had known so well as a captive student.

In all the years since grade school, I'd been in here only twice. The first occasion was a morbid wedding with a priest droning about the young bride and groom growing old and decrepit together under God's hand. Happy honeymoon, kids. The second occasion was an oddly upbeat funeral with another priest assuring us that the teenager who had drowned was having a wonderful time in the afterworld. The priest wouldn't have said it out loud, but the corollary to his message was that heaven was all that mattered, and a drowning down here on Earth was no big loss. I never witnessed — before or since — a memorial service that trivialized human life and death more thoroughly.

Sunlight coming through the stained-glass windows cast an eerie glow on the rows of empty pews. On the far wall hung a huge cross, complete with a suffering Christ gazing upward. He was bleeding from his nailed hands and feet and a gash in his side, and more blood trickled down from his crown of thorns. Near the base of the macabre display was an altar draped in gold-trimmed cloth. An ornate pulpit was perched a few paces to one side of it. Gold also trimmed the half-dome overhead. Along the walls, beneath and between the stained glass, there were statues of angels and saints, some of the many deities it apparently took to keep monotheism running. We were always told that the saints were not gods in their own right, and yet they supposedly wielded special powers in heaven and we were sure as hell encouraged to pray to them.

I couldn't always remember what saint ran what concession up there in paradise, but if there was a blaze in the neighborhood, you were supposed to pray to Saint Polycarp. The Romans or some other bunch had once tried to burn the guy at the stake but he wouldn't catch fire. So, this Saint Polycarp might have been able to step in and save your home while the Lutheran house next door went up in flames. If you wanted something sweet, so the playground stories went, you were supposed to pray to Saint John Bosco, the patron saint of chocolate milk. We probably made that one up, but I was sure that if you lost your arithmetic book, you were supposed to pray to Saint Anthony to help you find it. Maybe Saint Anthony had to do some searching, but probably not. And if he already knew where the damn thing was hidden, why didn't he just tell you when you were first looking for it? Was Saint Anthony keeping your arithmetic book on ice until you paid him some attention with your fawning prayers? Don't even ask. Just take off your hat and be quiet. Bow your head. Fold your hands. Kneel down. Stand up. Sit down. And don't forget to leave a donation on your way out. Eternity doesn't come cheap.

I took a step farther inside and heard a rustling behind me. I turned and got a hard slap across the face. It was a shock to my skin cells, but the rest of me wasn't surprised at all.

"Hello, Sister Bludgeonetta," I said, massaging my cheek. "You're still packing a wallop."

She stood there, stern and unyielding, a stalwart with the Sisters of Divine Retribution. Outside of a hockey crowd, they were the most belligerent group of people I had ever been around. Bludgeonetta's expression was as crabbed as ever. The years since I'd seen her hadn't been kind, but as far as I knew, no years had ever been kind to her. She still wore the black medieval robe, the rounded white bib and the stiff white boxwork around the face. There was a plain gold band on the ring finger of her left hand. I remembered that they all wore one of those in the old school. Asking about them had once gotten me in trouble. Maybe the same trouble could help me now.

"Jackson Harbinger," the nun said. Her voice was accusatory, as if I had just thrown a shovelful of dirt on a nativity scene.

"Good memory," I said. "You could make me after all these years?"

"There was always a certain attitude about you," she said. "It's still there. And it's not good."

"Well, anyway, call me Jack."

"Call me accurate," she said. "Your given name is Jackson."

"You've got me on that one," I said. There was a lull.

"Well?" she said.

"How is Jesus doing?" I asked her. Small talk with a nun was always awkward.

"Jesus is doing fine," she said. "He's omnipotent. How else would He be doing?" Now she was ready to start drilling in on my sins. "You were a disrespectful young man in the third grade," she scolded, "and you're still a disrespectful young man today. How come I didn't see you genuflect when you came in?"

"Bum knee?"

"That's a lie. I can read it on your face. And God sees your X-rays. He's listening to your every word, watching your every move."

"He's making a list and checking it twice," I told her.

"What?" The word shot out of her, but instead of taking the Santa Clause bait, she straightened her back, paused and tried to burn a hole in me with her eyes. "Oh, there's a list, all right," she said.

"You've seen it?"

"Never you mind. You haven't been coming in for mass. How long has it been?"

I did a little computing.

"Seventeen years since I was in school here."

"And why do you come here now?"

"Got some questions."

"Ah," she said. "Suddenly you're afraid of going to hell."

"Not exactly. It's business. I'm a private investigator."

"Really. Given your inability to follow rules, I would have thought you'd be on a chain gang by now."

"That pays better, but no."

"Then why the long absence?"

"I just didn't like it here."

"That's blasphemy!" she erupted. She took another swing at my head. I ducked out of the way. She hadn't revealed a weapon yet, but I saw my opportunity.

"What's with the wedding ring?" I asked her.

"You know perfectly well. It means I am a bride of Christ."

"I'm guessing separate bedrooms."

"You vulgar hellion."

"How did *you* get singled out for matrimony?"

"We all wear them."

"So, Christ is a polygamist?"

Her lip curled. "Satan walks in your shadow, young man. Just as when you were a sarcastic little troublemaker years ago." She was mad at me, but not mad enough.

One more card to play. I pulled the pack of cigarettes out of my coat pocket, shook one loose and got it clamped between my lips. I struck a wooden match on the stone column, lit the cigarette, waved out the flame and dropped the dead stick on the floor. Bludgeonetta watched me do all this with horrified eyes and a fallen jaw. She smoldered like the tip of the Winston.

"There's no smoking in here," she said angrily.

"Sure, there is, sister. You ought to be more observant." As I spoke, the cigarette bobbed up and down at the corner of my mouth. It was a nice effect.

"You can't do that, you insolent young …"

I drew in some carcinogens, not deeply enough to make me cough. With the cigarette still stuck in my face, I blew smoke in the general direction of Saint Crispin. That got her boiling.

Bludgeonetta reached into the folds of her robe and came at me with an ice pick. I dodged the point, grabbed her wrist and wrenched the pick out of her hand. She broke free and continued to swing at me until I could catch her right wrist again. While she flailed at me with an empty left hand, I took a good look at the hardware. The distinctive *Cardinal Morelli* logo was etched into its handle. Bludgeonetta slipped out of my grasp a second time as I aimed a question at her.

"Ever get any ice picks from Sears?"

"No!" she said, rubbing her wrist. "We only use the Cardinal Morelli brand."

"Just like the old days," I said.

"Of course. What else? They're made in the Vatican."

"Back in school, there were kids who said the Mafia used the same brand."

"That's another lie!"

She tried again to beat me about the head and shoulders but a male voice from somewhere stopped her cold.

"Come now, sister. We mustn't be pummeling our visitors."

I turned around to see a priest in a prim black suit and a black jersey. There was a little white square peeking out from his black collar.

"He's an insolent young man," Sister Bludgeonetta told him. She looked to the priest for acknowledgement and then glared at me.

"No doubt," the padre said to her. "But each of us has a cross to bear. Now run along."

I could tell Bludgeonetta didn't want to let me off easy. Her eyes wished me streams of molten lava but she said nothing. She was down the chain of command and she went away obediently.

THIRTEEN

"I'm Father Timothy." He produced something like a smile but nothing that placed much of a demand on his facial muscles. His dark eyes, under dense brows, weren't dancing. They were dead on their feet. Above them, an arrowhead hairline jutted into a tapered face. The hair was as black as his clothing. It was combed straight back, flat against his head, and it had a hard luster that made it look like it had been paved with shoe polish. The guy was maybe forty, slight but wiry. Only in his case the wire was wound up a little too tight, so that he had to make a concerted effort to stand up straight. When he forgot himself, his shoulders hunched forward a few degrees. Timothy focused his lifeless eyes on the offending Winston still hanging out over my chin and then glanced down at the ice pick in my left hand. He had no comment on either one.

"My name is Jack Harbinger. I'm a private investigator." I gave him a business card. He stared at it, pinched a wrinkle into it and put it in a pocket inside his lapel.

"We welcome all spiritual pilgrims," he said with his calculating smile, "no matter how noble or abhorrent their professions may be."

"Point taken," I said. I pulled the shortened cigarette out of my mouth. "Got an ashtray in here?"

"It's a … church," he said with overplayed patience. "Most people observe a certain decorum. So … there's really no need."

"Well, I'm not going to stub it out in the palm of my hand."

"You could simply hold on to it until it burns out."

The hell with him. I dropped the butt on the terra cotta floor and ground it under my shoe. Timothy stared at the shredded remains and the black smudge on the tile but didn't squawk. He was a guy who could choose his battles.

"Another question," I said. I held up the ice pick. "An acquaintance of mine recently got stabbed with a tool similar to this one. Name of

Roxanne Delaplaine. Know her?" He pursed his lips, looked down for a second and shrugged emphatically. He didn't ask how the victim was faring, which told me he either knew her condition or he wanted to get off the subject as quickly as possible. I gave him the ice pick, handle first.

He looked it over silently and tried to give it back to me.

"Not mine," I said. "I took it off one of your goons a minute ago. Shouldn't you do some psychological screening before you pass those things out to just anybody?"

"Sister Mary Bludgeonetta becomes overly enthused at times," he said. "But she loves the Lord."

"Tell me, are there any other homicidal maniacs in your flock?"

He scoffed. "I hardly think Sister Bludgeonetta's insistence on discipline would qualify her as homicidal, much less a maniac."

"All right. Bludgeonetta aside, any homicidal maniacs in general?"

His smile hadn't been warm in the first place. Now it carried a frost warning.

"None that I'm at liberty to name," he said. "I'm joking, of course. You ask the strangest questions."

"That's my job. My client has been getting death threats. Some strange ones at that. They could be coming from someone you've counselled, someone who hates women or teachers or outsiders."

"I see, but I'm afraid I can't help you there." His eyes swept the floor. "Half the boys in school hate their teachers, but not to the point of killing them."

"Speaking of death," I said casually. "I read in the paper that you witnessed a gruesome one yesterday."

"Oh my, yes. At the lake shore. The Bishop's Retreat. It was harrowing."

"How did you happen to see it?"

"I was just coming out of worship. Everyone else was still inside, deep in prayer."

"Why didn't you stay in there with them?"

"Oh, pressing church business. I forget exactly what. Anyway, I stepped outside and by chance I saw the man standing in his boat. He was holding up a string of fish he had caught, and he seemed very pleased with them."

"Did he see you?"

"I don't believe so?"

"Who was he showing them off to?"

"No idea. I hadn't thought about that. Perhaps he was only reveling in his own good fortune. Well, suddenly, dozens of muskies jumped out of the water and viciously attacked him."

"It's dozens now? The newspaper said ten or twelve."

"Did it? The details escape me. It all happened so fast."

"How far away were you?"

"I'm not good at distances. Never know which club to choose on the golf course."

"But you were on land and the victim was out on the water, and you could still identify the fish as muskies?"

"I assume they were muskies," he said nervously. "I've heard the lake is full of them. They all jumped back in the water after the attack, so it was hard to be certain. In any case, the poor man succumbed and collapsed. I got in a small boat and, of course, rowed out there to help. I expected him to be chewed up pretty badly, but once I reached him, there was nothing but torn flesh, exposed bone and scraps of clothing. Pulling him out of the water was a horrible task."

"The newspaper said the guy ended up in the bottom of his boat."

"Well, that's where he was when I got there. I grabbed at his boat and almost capsized it by accident. The body started to fall out and I had to push it back in. Push it or pull it, whatever. That's what I meant. That's what happened."

"Sounds complicated," I said.

He nodded and inhaled sharply, more than ready to change course.

"I couldn't help overhearing part of your exchange with Sister Bludgeonetta," he said. "I gather that you had attended school here years ago, but you've fallen away from regular church attendance. Perhaps it would be helpful if I took your confession."

"That won't be necessary," I told him.

"But I'm concerned about your soul," he said.

"So far, so good."

"Your *immortal* soul, that is."

"You mean after I'm dead?"

"Of course."

"I don't know," I said. "Worrying about what's going to happen to me after I die is like regretting all that time I wasted before I was born. It seems like a meaningless concept."

"And yet I'm sensing something else here. You feel indestructible, don't you?"

"I'm afraid to die, like almost everyone else. But I recognize that after it happens, I won't be in any condition to miss the good old days."

"But our souls are *all* immortal," he said. "The only question is whether we will spend eternity in heaven or in damnation."

"Really? I've been wondering. What do people do in heaven, anyway?"

"Mainly, they rejoice in the presence of God and praise His glory."

"Sounds like a rip-roaring good time."

"Many a lost soul eventually comes to prefer praying over carousing," he told me.

"Well, you know what they say, padre. One man's heaven is another man's hell."

"No, I do *not* know what they say. Idle talk is not my forte. For the most part, my thoughts are fixed on the magisterium."

"Some idle talk is pretty interesting," I said.

"And rife with sin, I should think."

"Only if you're lucky."

He was getting nowhere, so he chose another tack.

"You know," Timothy pressed, "we're all sinners but Jesus came down among us to wash our sins away with the blood of His sacrifice." Now the padre seemed proud of himself. He had steered the conversation onto the Jesus tale like a race car driver skidding around a hairpin curve. He downshifted into what he thought was a soothing voice. "It's as if we had been levied a fine that we could never be able to pay on our own, but Jesus graciously paid our fine. Paid the fine for each one of us. All by dying for our sins."

"Do we have to go into this?" I asked.

"What else could be more important?"

"Okay," I said. "Jesus died for our sins. And then what?"

"And then He simply asks us to believe in Him and His plan for our salvation."

"No, I mean what happened after he paid our fine by dying?"

"Well, of course, He was entombed. But He rose from the dead on the third day."

"So, this business about him paying my fine," I said. "What you're telling me is that he wrote a check."

"In a manner of speaking," Timothy agreed.

"But the check bounced."

"Excuse me?" he said.

I leaned on the side panel of a wooden pew and folded my arms. Timothy leaned on another pew across the aisle. This was going to take a while.

"Jesus paid my fine by dying," I said. "But then he snapped back into life. So, he didn't really die, not all the way. Because dead is dead. But that didn't happen. If he sort of died, it was only for part of a weekend. Then — in a manner of speaking, to use your phrase — he put a stop-payment on his check on Sunday by not being dead after all. The check bounced. Jesus was still kicking around, none the worse for wear. So, as far as your story goes, the fine was never covered and we're all indebted just like we were before he ever carried out the whole charade."

"Charade?"

"The charade of ultimate sacrifice on the cross. I know it's your job to keep the fiction in crucifixion, but I'm not buying it."

"I don't think you understand," he said.

"Fill me in."

"Jesus died in His earthly, corporeal manifestation. He now resides in heaven in His spiritual manifestation."

I thought back to the grinning priest at the tasteless funeral.

"An interesting point," I told him. "Let's consider it. I think you'd say our time in this world is more or less a blip compared to the eternity we'll spend in heaven or hell. Is that right?"

"I would agree with that."

"So, for Jesus to lose his corporeal being, his brief time on Earth, was not that big of a deal. Not in the long run. What about the other kind of death, the obliteration of consciousness, of identity, of the self? Fair's fair, padre. That's the real tragedy of the ultimate end, isn't it? The version of death where something precious is lost for all time? But Jesus didn't suffer that kind of irreversible death. So, where's the big sacrifice?"

"Yours is a unique perspective," he said condescendingly.

"And anyway, are you telling me that the spiritual Jesus can't come back as a physical person any time he wants to?"

"I'm … not … sure why He would want to do that," Timothy said.

"But he could. I mean, theoretically."

"Um … theoretically …" He trailed off.

"As Bludgeonetta said, the guy is omnipotent. If he wants to take on human form just to come down here and go waterskiing, he certainly has the power to do it, right?"

"Um … waterskiing? … I suppose so. I've never given that any thought."

Life was probably full of details the holy man hadn't thought about.

"There you go," I said. "Back on the skis in no time. No harm done. What's he lost? Again, where's the sacrifice?"

"But certainly, the suffering."

"The suffering, I'll grant you," I said. "That is, if the story is true. But not the death part of it. That just won't wash."

"You … pose some interesting questions," he said in an oily voice that was supposed to come across as comforting. "But I must say that your way of thinking is something to be avoided."

"I can see why."

"Perhaps it would be helpful if you were to enroll in this Saturday's seminar out at The Bishop's Retreat," he said. "I can't be there myself, but I can make sure the men out there take care of you."

"In what way?" I asked.

"You remember the Opian Monks, don't you?"

"I've heard stories."

"Well, the monks stand ready to counsel you. They are a very traditional order and you may find their verbiage old fashioned. But you'll get used to it. The important thing is that they could take the time to delve into the thoughts that haunt you. They could relieve you of your misconceptions and set your mind on the path to peace." Kind words, but when he said them his smile was crystalizing and his hand was white-knuckling the ice pick.

"I don't think so," I said, straightening up from the pew. "Keep an eye out for murderers, would you? And be careful not to crush that handle."

He looked down at the Cardinal Morelli in his left hand. He used the right one to separate his fingers from the wooden grip as if he were peeling an artichoke. Then he said, "A donation from a former student is always welcome."

"I noticed the collection box on my way in. In the old days, I dropped a nickel in there every week. Ten percent of my allowance, the price of a candy bar. Five cents came dear to me then."

"You have the Lord's appreciation," Timothy said.

"I'd rather have the nickels, plus the compound daily interest."

The padre smiled stiffly. "Be assured, Mr. Harbinger. The Almighty will settle all accounts."

We closed it off at that. I nodded and walked out past the oaken doors. In the vestibule, near the holy water font, I threw the rest of the cigarettes in the trash.

Filthy little things.

FOURTEEN

At a little past eight that night I was in the Mustang, approaching Hunchback Lanes and hoping Slab Kapowski was somewhere inside. With the smell of an alleged crime boss in the air, I had brought along some protection. The shoulder holster and the .38 automatic under my suitcoat wouldn't be the most comfortable gear for knocking down pins, but I hadn't come for the bowling.

Once I passed the overblown sign at the front driveway, I snaked through the parking lot. Tiresome work, scanning row after row of vehicles, but that and my longshot bet on *eternal peace* paid out. I spotted one of the cars I had seen at the Kapowski castle the night before. It was the silver Mercedes, with its plate number matching my notes. I parked a healthy distance from the Benz and walked up to the wide, low building.

The exterior was a plain stretch of cream-colored cement blocks. Above the glass doors there was a blue canvas awning and a neon sign with one of the tubes on the fritz. Inside the doors and a little ways down, there was a pro shop. Across from that, there was a room with lockers for bowling bags and bulky winter jackets when the season demanded them. On a wall just beyond the locker room, a cork bulletin board was pinned with Polaroid prints of customers having a good time, as if management wanted to prove it could be done. Farther down the walkway, things livened up with more neon and a swell of throbbing music, all of it intended for the infantile folds of an adult's brain. At the end of the walkway, the walls opened out to the main desk, where bowlers checked in and clerks picked rental shoes from cubbyholes in a long cabinet. Beyond the desk, more than forty lanes were spread out on a sunken floor. The area down there gave us more stimulants — flashing lights on the overhead scoreboards and the oddly rhythmic percussion of balls dropping onto hard maple. The balls crashed into pins, and the pins went bashing off the side boards like so many heads slapped silly by the nuns at Saint Opie's.

At the foot of each lane, in front of a scorekeeper's desk, a bowler hovered over a whirring ball-return, sorted through to find the right Brunswick or AMF model and then stood tall, anxious to fire at newly set pins. Down the row of lanes, men and women in the ready position bent forward, each cradling a ball in a cupped hand. One by one, they felt around with the opposite hand and buried the tips of three fingers. In a random sequence, they stepped forward, wound up and sent their balls rolling down the smooth wooden tracks.

Behind the players' benches there were banks of ball shelves for the neophytes who hadn't purchased their own equipment. A railing rose above the shelving. On my side of the railing, there was a raised floor with a long row of tables, four chairs to each one. People sat at the tables to watch the competitors from behind or wait their turns to get on the lanes. Some customers sat there just to get drunk and puff on king-size filters and play cards for penny stakes. Alongside the row of tables, the stars and scrubs of the local leagues paraded by in their gaudy team shirts.

In a small room at one end of the promenade, teenagers were packed in tight for foosball, air hockey, video games and pinball. The clattering and bing-bonging in the room clashed with the canned music. The cacophony should have been enough to make everybody in there as crazy as bagpipes, but nobody seemed to mind. At the other end of the building, a barroom with a busy dance floor took up a large wing and offered cocktails and six brands of flavorless American beer.

I never understood the appeal of it all, but the valley supplied enough fans of bowling and drinking and smoking and shimmying to keep the whole operation humming night after night. The crowds fed off the buzz and the low-grade glitz. When I tried to look at the place through their eyes, I could sometimes make out some flecks of excitement in it. I had to consider where we were living, and everything else that was or wasn't available to us. The bottom line was that in our little pocket of the hinterlands, Hunchback Lanes was the closest thing we had to the casino at Monte Carlo.

I went up to the main desk with the intention of asking the clerk where the morticians' league had been assigned. The kid passing out shoes behind the counter was telling a customer that he could improve her luck considerably by selling her a crystal bracelet. A dissatisfied customer horned in, telling the kid she had bought one of his bracelets a week before and had been throwing gutter balls ever since.

"Here's your problem," the kid told her. "You were worried about the gutter. The crystals amplify your thoughts. Your thoughts were negative and the crystals made those negative thoughts a reality. You need to have positive thoughts. Look at me, I don't even know the meaning of the word *negative*. The word *negative* isn't even in my vocabulary."

"Try using it in a sentence," I said.

The two women blinked at me uncomprehendingly. The kid stared at me with annoyance.

"Shoes," he said impatiently. "What size?"

I decided I couldn't trust him enough to keep my questions quiet, and so I waved him off and walked away in my own two loafers.

Slab Kapowski, for all his advertising, had stayed off TV and had almost managed to keep his picture out of the newspapers. I had seen one photo accompanying his profile in the *Daily Informer*, but that was published more than a year earlier and I hadn't memorized the image. My plan was to search out Roxanne. Her looks were unforgettable and I had a pretty good idea that she would be here if she was linked with Slab in the way I thought she was.

I kept my head down and skulked through the crowd, hoping I wouldn't run into her accidentally. If she was around, I wanted to watch her unnoticed, see how closely she was mixed up with the bigtime undertaker. When I found her, she was standing perfectly still at the foot of lane 27.

FIFTEEN

I could only see her from behind and a little to the side, but that was enough. She was wearing a flimsy lavender scarf over a tawny blouse that had "Last Chance Mortuary" stitched across the back. At her waist was a cinched belt, also in lavender. A pair of tight jeans clung to her curves. She had the only pair of high-heeled bowling shoes I had ever seen, and the heels were doing great things for the slope of her back pockets.

Perched in her left palm was an aquamarine bowling ball with lavender swirls that matched her accessories. The fingers of her right hand were searching for the holes almost tenderly. I found a good position along the railing and waited for her to move in toward the pins. She had a tough split in front of her, and she was taking her time. She bent over slightly, leaning out over the floor. A quick thrust of her hip could have banged a bass drum from thirty feet away, but for the moment she was motionless.

She uncoiled slowly, took two steps and swung the ball backward. It froze in the air for a split second and then fell forward in a graceful swoop. She let it go and it hit the lane with a light thump. Her ball traveled straight down the middle, passed idly between the two remaining pins and dropped into an abyss. Roxanne stomped one of the high heels in anger and then stood there with her hands on her belt and her feet set wide apart. It was the most intriguing seven-ten split I had ever seen.

Behind her, on the players' bench, a guy threw a tantrum. He swore, jumped up and went after her, grabbing her by the shoulders and yelling into her face. He was tall and lean, with hollow cheeks and a hawkish nose. The photo from the old newspaper story coalesced in my memory. The man with his hands on Roxanne was the same Slab Kapowski, only a hell of a lot less composed than he'd been in the photograph.

Roxanne fended him off, stepping back as if she were afraid he'd punch her in the nose. The assertive dame I'd met the day before now seemed thoroughly bullied. She grabbed her purse and retreated into the space behind the benches. She climbed a few stairs and headed toward the barroom on the main floor. Nobody stormed after her. Slab kept fuming, as if the missed spare had ruined his life. The other couple in the foursome kept their heads and shoulders low during Slab's rant. Then, as the furor settled down, the second woman in the group got up to take a roll at the pins. I heard Slab say he'd bowl Roxanne's next frame for her, and nobody argued with him.

I moved off my position and followed in Ms. Delaplaine's direction. I couldn't find her in the barroom and leaned on a wall to wait. After five minutes or more, she came out of a ladies' room. Her hair was perfectly whipped and there was a fresh coat of lacquer on her lips. She walked toward the bar and wove her way between the standing drinkers. She found an open slot at the trough and fanned some bills on the bar. The bartender was over there in one quick hurry. He was all toothy smiles and stuttering chitchat. If he had been wearing a bowtie, it would have been spinning.

Roxanne placed her order and the bartender hustled off to make her every wish come true. I came up behind her and tapped her on the shoulder.

She was startled but gathered herself instantly.

"I tried to call you," she said.

"I've been out scouring the city for clues."

"Like where?" she said. "When you didn't return my call, I assumed you'd been frittering away time and money. And now, here you are at a bowling alley."

"Strictly legit," I said. "This place is a gold mine of information on all sorts of criminal activities. Other than that, I've seen a headshrinker, the clergy and the cops."

"You went to the police?"

"Only in a general sort of a way. Your name wasn't mentioned."

"What were you doing with the clergy?"

"I needed to talk with anybody who deals in counseling," I said. "Anybody who might put me onto the nut case behind the death threats."

"Speaking of," she said, "I received this today." She went into her purse and pulled out a sheet of folded brown paper. "I was going to bring it over to your office."

She unfurled the paper for me. Across the top third was the familiar skull-and-crossbones motif, only this time the eyes looked a little more manic. The rest of the page carried another histrionic message.

Even as the sorrowful hound bays at the feckless moon, mindful of its dreadful fate, so too, shall you moan in despair. But no cries in the night can stave off your looming and inevitable erasure. No precaution can shield you, no prayer can yield comfort. For you and your memory shall be expunged. I now grace you with my malevolent eye. Anonymous

"Pretty insane," I said. "But the guy does have a certain panache."

I pocketed the threat.

"Help me," she said with a look that could have melted a tank. "I have to get back to my group."

"Just a minute. One of your colleagues was killed in a small boat yesterday. Maybe there's a connection. Guy by the name of Harry Armstadt. Did you know him?"

"I can't place the name. I haven't read the paper today, and this is the first I've heard of it."

"He was a faculty member at the community college."

"That explains why I haven't heard of him. Wrong college. We'll have to take this up later. If I'm late getting back, I'll be in trouble."

The bartender returned with the goods and looked disappointed to see me standing next to the girl. Roxanne smiled at him and reclaimed some currency from the bar, pushing forward the rest of the bills for the tab and a tip. She nodded at me and took the tray of drinks she had ordered back toward the lanes. The bartender gazed after her as if he were watching his dreams fly away.

I followed Roxanne at a distance. The constant crashing of balls and pins was sounding more and more like gunfire.

I took up a new post behind lane 27 and kept an eye on her. It was easy work until she blew another spare. Slab lost his temper again and went at her. When she tried to pull away from him, he slapped her across the face. That's when I signed up to play.

I bounded down the steps and rushed in behind him. He swung at Roxanne again but she ducked out of reach. I took his arm and spun him around. On reflex, he tried a left to my jaw. I slid away from it and hammered him in the stomach. He didn't go down. He threw a shoulder into me and pushed me back against a rack of balls. I lost my footing and was struggling to get up when he grabbed a black sixteen-pounder. He clawed his fingers into it and used both hands to lift it over his head. Before he could drive the ball downward, I got to my haunches and shoved him off balance. His right hand sunk with the weight of the ball but he held onto it. I rose and landed one hard on his jaw. He went slack for a moment and went down. The ball dumped onto the floor. I'd scored a clean hit, maybe a lucky one, but I knew he'd be up again in ten seconds. I picked up the ball and dropped it eight or nine inches onto his ankle just to dampen his enthusiasm. Slab lay there cursing, grimacing and clutching at the ankle.

The other guy from his bench came at me. I froze him by placing my right hand beneath my left lapel. My gun was riding there against my ribcage but I sure as hell didn't want to shoot up the place. He backed off.

"We need to get out of here," Roxanne said desperately.

She reached for her purse and my left hand and we blew through a gap in the gathering crowd. We ran up the stairs, past the big counter and out the front doors.

We made it halfway across the parking lot before I heard a shot behind us. It missed Roxanne and me but drilled a hole in a Buick's grille. We scrambled down behind an old Chevy. Slab's whole team came running out through the front doors. Guns blasted from a cluster of points in the twilight. Slab's guys weren't splitting up very far from each other, and that was a break. But there were more shots, and heavy thuds when the bullets hit the fenders and doors of the car shielding us.

"What if they hit a fuel line or something?" Roxanne said breathlessly. "We'll never get the car started and we'll be pinned here until they kill us."

"You don't think I'd hide behind my own car in a gunfight, do you?"

"You're a genius."

I sent a bullet back, a warning shot into the air. Slab's boys took cover behind a pickup truck and started firing again. I pumped two rounds toward the truck and sent windshield glass spattering over them. Another bullet came in and zinged off the hood of the Chevy.

Curiosity seekers, most of them in bowling shirts, flowed into the lot to see what was going on. There were twenty or so in the first wave, too many witnesses for Slab's troops to keep up the barrage.

"Here's our chance," I told Roxanne. I tugged at her arm and we ran between rows of parked cars. It seemed like the Mustang was a mile away, but we reached it and tossed ourselves in. I cranked the ignition. "Get down," I said. She slid low in the passenger seat as I hit the clutch and shoved the stick into first. With my lights off, I stepped on the gas and lurched left and right across the lot. In the rearview mirror, I caught sight of someone limping into the open. He leveled a gun at us. I heard two shots, but neither one shattered my rear window or the back of my head. We made it to the road and I wrenched the four-speed into high gear. I pushed hard on the pedal.

Roxanne raised herself in her seat, panting.

"That was Slab Kapowski back there."

"I know. The graveyard guy."

"You've met him before?"

"I recognized him from an old photo."

"Is he dead?"

"No. I don't think anyone was even shot."

I made a sharp turn, then more, shifting brutally and winding my way through a network of lonely roads. There were no headlights or engine noises behind us. I flipped on my lights and took a fast right onto the Fuzzy Thurston Pullway.

Roxanne flattened against the back of her seat, arched her neck and closed her eyes for a few seconds. "You were pretty good in a tough spot," she said.

"Thanks. You were pretty good yourself."

"I've been through shootouts before."

I left that remark alone. The Mustang raced into the directionless night.

"What now?" I asked.

"Slab believes in fasting before a match. We skipped dinner."

"So did I. Let's catch up on it."

SIXTEEN

We walked into The Strong Side Linebacker, one of a glut of restaurants financed by washed-up Packers who were branching out from their usual territory around Green Bay. The place was struggling for business among a few other restaurants on a service road running parallel to Highway 41. It was behind the Defensive End and a short walk from The Left Tackle. Across the highway, the Nickel Cornerback was still under construction.

Inside the restaurant there was the usual collection of blown-up game photographs, almost all of them in grainy black-and white. It was blocking and tackling, running and throwing, one guy's fingers in another guy's facemask. Another photo showed a player with his body caked in mud and his arms raised in triumph. Smaller, similar photos covered the surrounding walls and a few dividing walls within. Over the back bar there was a mural of Vince Lombardi ascending into heaven with a Super Bowl trophy cradled in each arm. The bar was cobbled together from fragments of an old scoreboard at Lambeau Field, and the levers on the beer spigots were end zone pylons. When you dropped your eyes, you could see white yard-lines and hashmarks woven into a green carpet. The motif was as clever as a flea-flicker and as predictable as a punt on fourth and fifty.

A bubbly hostess greeted us with the standard, "How about those Packers?"

"It's the off-season," I answered her. "How about those Philadelphia Stars?" She stared blankly for a moment, and when she decided it was safe to ignore my comment, she reverted to her carbonated grin. She was cute, but next to my date she was only another face on the sidelines.

"Table for two?" she asked, and without waiting for any more trouble from me, she led us to a booth in the back. Roxanne and I settled in, happy to have made it through the night's chaotic crossfire and what turned out to be a one-car chase. The tablecloth between us featured various *X-&-O* formations, with arrows diagramming pass routes, running lanes and blocking schemes. The salt and pepper shakers on the table were figurines of two linemen squaring off. The lighting fixture over our heads was a horizontal wreath made of eleven Packer helmets interlocked at the facemasks.

Roxanne stared up at the chandelier and shook her head.

"At some point, this could get redundant," she said.

After a minute, a waitress trudged over to our table. She was visibly chafing under her genuine game-worn shoulder pads.

"Hut-hut," she said with boredom and a night shift's worth of fatigue in her voice.

"We've reached that point," Roxanne said to me.

"Here are your game plans," the waitress said. She handed us menus that organized drinks, appetizers, entrees and desserts by first down, second down, third down and fourth down.

Roxanne picked whatever brains the waitress had on the intricacies of the menu and the expertise of the chef. Finally, she was satisfied.

"I'll have the balsamic glazed salmon and a glass of Chardonnay."

The waitress shifted her eyes over to me.

"Meat, potatoes, beer," I said. She wrote it down and faded away.

"You certainly make it simple," Roxanne said to me.

"Let's get even simpler right now. You've been lying to me, Roxanne. You've been lying from the start. In fact, I'm surprised you didn't order the red herring."

"How can you say that?" she pouted.

"Don't forget I went to Catholic school. I happen to know that the nuns at Saint Opie's don't get their ice picks from Sears. They use the Cardinal Morelli brand exclusively. Straight from the Vatican."

"Maybe years ago, when you were enrolled," she said.

"Nothing doing. I took one off a nun down there just this afternoon."

"Meaning what?" She was playing innocent.

"Meaning it was not a Saint Opie's nun who stabbed you yesterday morning."

"Maybe the nun had confiscated the Sears model from an aggressive little second-grader," she said. "How am I supposed to know where she got it?"

"That's going to be your story?"

"Back up a minute," she said. "How did you know I'd be at the bowling alley tonight?"

"They told me at the college that you'd mentioned bowling."

"You've been checking on me at the college?"

"At the college and at that counterfeit castle Slab Kapowski calls home. You're cozy with him and he's famous for his bowling obsession. I put two and two together."

"You're being a little pushy, aren't you?"

"And here's another little rocket whistling in on me. I'm told you're in town fresh from Milwaukee, not San Francisco."

A couple of laser beams came out of her eyes, but she calmed herself quickly.

"Well, yes, I'd been staying in Milwaukee for a time, but that sounds so … proletarian. I've also lived in San Francisco, New York, Boston. Also, England and France. That's the tip of it anyway."

"We'll skip over that, but what about your associates? You told me in the car you'd been through some shootouts."

"Maybe one," she said softly. "And that was in the past."

"Everything is in the past a moment after it happens," I said.

"Okay. Years ago. Sectarian violence in Beirut."

"As for recent violence, how come you didn't tell me you were sacking out with a gangster?"

"What are you talking about?"

"Kapowski is a reputed killer," I said.

"Nothing but rumors."

"Maybe, but he nearly took your head off tonight. And his teammates all seem to have guns in their bowling bags. What do you make of that?"

"He can be charming at times," she said, veering off my question.

"You mean when he's not busting you in the mouth?"

"Okay," she said. "He's come at me with blood in his eyes when we argued about the chintzy portrait of the bullfighter he keeps in the bedroom. But the point is, I hired you because of the written threats, which are concrete evidence that my life is in danger. And now I find you've been investigating *me*."

We paused as the drinks came. The waitress set them down slowly, like someone laying flowers on a grave. She went off and I spoke up again:

"You're lucky I *did* investigate you, because if I hadn't, Slab might have stuffed you down the ball return tonight. Admit it. Wasn't he the one who slipped you the ice pick?"

"We've been through that. More than once. Anyway, he has a temper, but that doesn't mean he wants to kill me." She paused for effect. "Does it?"

I didn't answer.

"As it happens," she said, "I couldn't tell you the whole truth and I didn't even want to mention Slab because … well, because …" She looked down and broke off.

"Level with me."

"Because I was having an affair."

"Okay, then. That tells me something about the death threats. Either Slab couldn't stand the idea of you cheating on him or the guy you were having the affair with couldn't stand the idea of you still being with Slab. Easy money, the threats have to be coming from Slab or the other guy."

"But …"

"But what? Spill it."

"I'm a little chagrinned. There wasn't just one affair."

"All right. How many affairs have you had?"

"It seems so callous to put a number on it." She was fidgeting.

"More than two?"

"I'm afraid so."

"This bunch couldn't have been any bigger than a basketball team, could it?"

She nodded weakly.

"Have you been lining up more men than the Milwaukee Brewers?"

"Are we counting relief pitchers?"

"Christ, you actually have to have relievers come in from the bull pen?"

"That's not what I meant," she protested. "You asked me to come up with a number."

"You don't make it easy, do you?"

"Actually …"

"I mean from an investigational standpoint."

She let out a heavy sigh. "Do we have to talk about this right now? I've been slapped and I've been shot at. And I'm so tired."

Even though I had laid it out pretty well, it still didn't pass inspection. If it was Slab sending the threats, and if the guy really wanted to kill her, why didn't he just do it? He had loads of opportunities. Then again, maybe he wanted to inflict a little agonizing first, make her worry over some cat-and-mouse game before he finished her off.

And that was just Slab's part of it. What about all the other guys in her life?

"I'll need names," I said.

"That's out of the question."

"Then I don't see how I can do my job."

"You're getting ahead of yourself," she said. "Those men would be useless leads. They couldn't know who I really was. I gave them all false names and false background stories. They wouldn't even be able to send me a Christmas card, never mind a death threat."

"Was one of them the dead professor?"

"No, I told you already. And I haven't met anyone at all from the community college. Why?"

"He was supposedly mauled by muskies jumping out of the water."

"That's preposterous," the lady said.

"I agree, but the story seems to have pacified the police."

She paused and asked, "Was the professor receiving death threats?"

"The cops didn't say anything about that. The newspaper didn't either."

"Then it's unrelated," she said. "I know you're looking for possible connections to my case, but there aren't any, other than his occupation. And as I mentioned, I'm tired."

I had more questions, but we'd been through a rough night and there were too many possibilities to sort out on the spot. Maybe it was time to let up on the interrogation.

Or almost time.

"One more thing," I said, unable to break the habit.

"No. And if you don't change the subject, one of us will have to eat in the parking lot." Her smile was at ten percent and dropping.

I gave in. The entrees came and over dinner we talked about anything else.

SEVENTEEN

Random chit-chat kept me off my line of inquiry. After a while, Roxanne wanted to hear how I landed in a private eye office in a place like Pulptown.

"I grew up here. Eight years of elementary school at Saint Opie's. My parents wanted me in a Catholic high school but didn't have the money, thank God. I played out the string at the public high school. Then there were a few weeks at a paper mill and a few months at a sporting goods store. After that, a couple of years in college. But I could never get serious about my jobs or my studies."

"Your parents must have been worried."

"They worried that somewhere in the world there might be a grindstone without my nose on it."

"Are they still around?"

"Florida. We don't talk much, and when we do, it's usually about me finding a real job."

"Why don't you?"

"Because it would kill me. What about *your* parents?"

"I never knew them so I don't talk about them."

"Sorry. Where did you grow up?"

"Nowhere for very long." That ended that.

She got the conversation back on my history. I told her about my wastrel years after I dropped out of college. Bouncing around the country, working tedious jobs, ending up selling shoes in Milwaukee, dulling my senses. "Then I saw a want ad from an investigation agency. I'd been watching '*77 Sunset Strip*' and every other private eye show and movie I could find since I was eight years old. I'd also been reading the paperbacks. I figured that stuff had taught me everything I needed to know."

"There is nothing like a solid education," she deadpanned.

"The fact is, I talked my way into the P.I. job based on a few journalism courses and a few published articles in my college newspaper."

"I don't follow," she said.

"They knew I wasn't shy about asking questions and they knew I could write a report."

"I thought all you guys were ex-cops."

"A cop's work is usually different than ours. Most of our cases are civil. And when they're criminal, we don't have the teeth of authority, so we can't approach people the way cops do."

"I suppose."

"It's a funny thing. In the back of my mind, when I was a kid, this is what I wanted to do. But by the time I was in high school and got more realistic — well — who the hell becomes a private eye? Years later, the job more or less fell on top of me. It was unconventional but it felt right. It wasn't often like TV or the movies or the books, but there were moments. As far as my education was concerned, the agency in Milwaukee trained me in skip tracing and I had a knack for it. The objective was to track down deadbeats and uninsured drivers who had run out on their debts or their traffic accidents. I'd have to find out where they were living, where they were working and what kind of assets they had. Preferably without them knowing I'd been snooping around."

"And then?"

"If the deadbeats were worth the trouble, I'd serve them with legal papers. Some of the people I ran down turned out to be too poor to go after in court. But the collectors and insurance companies needed to know which cases were the hopeless ones."

"So, you were playing … what? … cowboys and indigents?"

I laughed at the jab. She had a sardonic streak I liked.

"There was more to it, of course. I got training in fraud detection, workers' comp scams, wrongful death investigations."

"Any homicide cases?"

"Sometimes I had to investigate a murder, but it was never a whodunnit. Once the police had identified an obvious killer, they weren't too concerned about peripheral details. The client would be a life insurance company wanting to pay as little as possible on a claim. The amount sometimes depended on whether the victim had provoked his own death, and that's where I did my digging. It all came down to money."

"As always," the lady said.

"Then there were law suits and the litigators either filing or defending them. The lawyers wanted me to locate witnesses, take statements, find out who was stepping on whose throat. In my spare time, the agency had me untying knots."

She flicked my hand. "Figuratively?"

"Literally. Sometimes a trainer would sit me down in a chair and tie my hands behind my back at nine in the morning. The game was to see if I could wiggle my way out of it by lunch."

"And there I was," Roxanne said, "wasting my time at Harvard."

"I know you don't believe me, but the old-timers told me it was a skill that may come in handy someday. Seemed a little arcane. But what the hell, I was getting paid by the hour."

"Hmmm, if all that is true, it tells me you'll do anything for money."

"What else would you expect from a sleazy detective? Anyway, I gathered a few years of experience there. Less and less of it tied to a chair, if you're asking. When it came time to go out on my own, my first choice would have been Los Angeles. But thousands of other guys had the same idea. In Pulptown I'd be the only shamus around."

"Has returning home been good for you?"

I shrugged. "Don't know yet. Still hoping ..."

"You solved some murders here, didn't you?"

"Well, you probably heard about the Pulptown Strangler."

"The TV news recapped the story the night before the sentencing. They said you cracked it."

"They exaggerated. There was a fluke that gave me a lead, and all I did was follow up on some earlier police results. Things fell together. After that high point, most of my cases were pretty mundane. Then you walked into my office with a minor wound and a major fear. And a whole lot of secrecy."

"Quel dommage," she said.

"Crepe Suzette." I said back at her. She tried to suppress a smile, but a hint of it seeped out. Part of her was exasperated with me but part of her liked me. I was used to that kind of reaction from women. It was the sweet spot between *hello* and their realization that I was never going to change.

I turned the questioning back to her. She told me about her early dedication to art and literature, financed by an inheritance and driven by degrees from Harvard and Oxford. She had published poems in literary magazines. She had worked in a London museum and written a treatise on *"The Fairy Feller's Master-Stroke,"* a nineteenth-century painting by Richard Dadd. She went into some detail on the multitude of tiny, troubling images in the painting. There were grotesque royals, haunted gnomes and a dragonfly playing one of those elongated horns that used to blow fanfare whenever the king made an entrance. In the foreground, a miniature axman was in his backswing, ready to split the hell out of a chestnut.

"Sounds crazy," I said.

"Exactly. The artist murdered his father and did the painting while confined in a lunatic asylum. My treatise examined the relationship between art and insanity."

She told me more. Her life in academia was interrupted from time to time by a dalliance with one bad boy or another. The guys she had been attracted to hadn't gotten caught up in any serious violations, but there were a few dicey situations along the way. None of the bad boys diverted her for very long. Over the years, one thing led to another and she made an impulsive decision to leave San Francisco and accept a position as curator at the Schnubner Beer Art Museum in Milwaukee. After a few weeks there, she met Slab Kapowski at a fundraiser. Disappointed with the museum, she walked off the curator's job so she could move in with him here in Pulptown. Then the college job opened up.

"Seems like a radical departure," I said. "Relegating your career to second place."

"Slab is very powerful. I was swept up."

"Sure, I can understand. When a guy controls every casket moving through Northeastern Wisconsin, it's bound to turn a girl's head."

She smiled grudgingly. "Give me a break, would you? I meant powerful financially. And politically. But he has these rages. More often, lately. As if he's under intense pressure. From what source, I don't know. Some of his rants are directed at me. Life with him has gotten to be part fear and part humiliation, with no hope of getting out."

"How's that?"

"He told me he'd never allow me to leave him," she said. "The affairs were my way of relieving my own stress, but they didn't help. Sometimes I find myself wishing he were dead."

"Maybe you could persuade one of your paramours to knock him off."

"Always something glib," she said. "Is that a defense mechanism?"

"I got bawled out by a headshrinker yesterday," I said. "I can't take another psychiatric session tonight. But if you're not contemplating murder, let's talk about Mr. Kapowski's aptitude for it. Did he ever talk about the morticians he happened to push off the steeple at Saint Opie's?"

"I told you," she said. "Those are just rumors. I can't see him going that far just to win at business. Unless … well … I suppose rumors get started for a reason. But what can anyone do about them?"

I didn't say a thing. All I did was wait.

"I'll be honest with you," she finally said. Now she was looking at me straight in the eyes. "I've had fantasies about him slipping off that steeple himself."

That made it two references to her boyfriend's death in less than a minute, but I let it go. Her eyes fell down and away but she kept talking: "Speaking of the steeple, he seems very committed to Saint Opie's. He donates money to the church and spends an inordinate amount of time down there."

"Doing what?"

"I wish I knew," she said.

"Why don't you forget about that and slip out the back door of the relationship? I know he said he wouldn't let you leave, but that may be nothing more than egotistical rhetoric. From what you've told me, you certainly have the means to succeed on your own somewhere else."

"He'd chase me down. I have no doubts about that." She looked almost resigned. "Now see what you've done? I hadn't wanted to get back to the subject of Slab and my little problems with him, but here we are again. What I'd really like to do is get him out of my hair, teach for a couple of semesters and finish my PhD thesis on modern art and existential dread."

The waitress dragged herself back to our table and offered dessert as if one more order would kill her. Roxanne asked her about the tarts.

"Not so great," the waitress said.

Roxanne smiled gently at her and said, "I think we'll take the check, please." The waitress plodded off again.

"Talk about existential dread," I said to Roxanne.

She gave me the bemused eyes.

"It can be a fascinating subject," she said. "Right now, I'm immersed in Kierkegaard. Sorry, you wouldn't know who that is."

"Wasn't he the fear and trembling guy? Back and forth on God?"

She straightened in her seat and her eyes widened. "How do you know about Kierkegaard?"

"I've walked by a library from time to time," I said. "Stuff rubs off. The leap of faith and all that."

"That's a misconception," she said. "Kierkegaard never used that wording. He wrote about infinite resignation as the last stage before the achievement of faith. But for the sake of argument, consider the phrase in terms of Pascal's wager. If there is a God, then your leap of faith will save you. Meanwhile, your bet on belief makes you feel better. And if it turns out there's no God, then what have you lost?"

"Pascal was hedging his bet," I said. "Let me see your rabbit's foot."

"What? I don't carry a rabbit's foot."

"Why not? If the thing brings you good luck, you're in business. If not, what have you lost?"

"All right, I see what you're saying. When you put it in those terms, the wager is ridiculous."

"Because the concept of a rabbit's foot bringing you luck is too absurd for you to take seriously. That's the way I feel about the concept of God. The whole story folds under questioning. However foolish you'd feel walking around with a rabbit's foot in your purse, that's how foolish I'd feel praying to some father figure in the sky. Anyway, Pascal is being disingenuous. He's not quite out but he's not all the way in, either. He's relying on a hypothetical statement as a metaphysical backstop."

"I've never heard anyone describe it that way," she said. "Still, if blind faith gives people comfort, I don't see the harm."

"Religion is only as comforting as it is plausible," I said. "And it's only plausible as long as we suspend reason. But abandoning reason comes with a cost. People get a few pleasant delusions out of the deal but to make that work, they have to spend decades of their lives in an irrational state of mind. Even if you leave out the Salem Witch Trials, that's a net loss."

"Maybe you're being a little hard on people who are just trying to cope."

"And maybe squandering our intelligence isn't the best way of coping. Look at it this way. I'd like to live among reasonable people, and I expect that you would too. That means there has to be some appreciation for reality, some ability to tell the difference between facts and hallucinations. That goes for the way we run our lives and the way we run the world."

"Well," she said, "I can't argue with that."

"It runs a little deeper," I said. "I'm assuming you wouldn't want your stock broker to pump your money into an investment just because

Mars and Jupiter are aligned. You wouldn't want your doctor to treat an illness by chanting and shaking a rattle at you. By the same token, I'm not enthused about the federal government relying on biblical prophesies to set the course for the country. Right now, we have the president and half of Congress claiming the Bible contains some type of grand plan for America. Hell, the people who wrote the Bible didn't realize there was a goddamn Western Hemisphere, let alone the U.S.A. And we're supposed to run the country on their authority?"

"That's a fair point," she said.

"We stew our brains in religious mumbo-jumbo every day and then wonder why people don't use their heads. My point is that blind faith and wishful mysticism don't stop at the church doors. You can't teach people to think magically on Sunday and then expect them to think rationally on Monday."

She didn't agree; she didn't disagree. She just leaned back, let out one of her microscopic smiles and looked me over for a long time.

"You're not what I expected," she said.

I shrugged at her. "You didn't think I'd be so cynical?"

"I assume cynicism is printed in your job description," she said. She planted her elbow on the table and rested her chin on her fist. Like "*The Thinker*," only not as ponderous as the original Rodin and a damn sight less cheesy than the Wankelburg replica I'd seen in the *Informer*. "What I meant was that you're a very philosophical guy."

"I try to make sense of things," I said. And then right into her eyes: "Sometimes I have trouble with that."

"You're talking about the death threats again," she said.

"What else?"

"You promised to take the rest of the night off."

The waitress broke it up by dropping the check on the table. It landed on a diagram for a play-action pass down the left sideline.

"Two-minute warning," the waitress said glumly.

Roxanne looked puzzled.

"It's another football thing," I told her. "They're closing."

We stood up and I reached for some money.

"Let me," she said, dropping a few bills on the table. "Thanks for the intervention at Hunchback."

We walked along an aisle toward the exit, Roxanne a few paces ahead of me. A guy in a booth watched her go by and leaned out in front of me to study the rhythm of her hips. Slipping out of the booth, drunk and sloppy, he fell to the floor and stalled on the 35-yard line woven into the carpet. He looked up at me like a dazed fullback after a seismic hit to the helmet. I reached out to help him but he rebuffed the offer.

"You think you're such a big ..." He couldn't finish the thought.

I stepped around him, picked up his wallet from the table and handed it off. He clutched it tightly, found his feet and followed my blocking. I knew he wasn't going to make it all the way to the door on this carry, but there was a first-down marker only four yards away.

EIGHTEEN

Roxanne and I walked out to my old beater.

"In all the gunfire," she needled, "I forgot to mention how impressive your car is."

"Try to think of it as a museum piece."

"Fine. One more reason to have it roped off."

I let her in, went around to the driver's seat and asked, "What are you going to do about transportation and somewhere to stay?"

"I could see a brawl coming," she said, "so I have a suite on reserve at one of the hotels not far from here. I have a car there too. Clothes, personal items, even my vital documents. Slab doesn't know about it."

"Not yet. If he has good connections in banking, he can trace credit card transactions."

"I thought of that. A few months ago, I sold two of my paintings. I had cash and I was able to lay it down for the car and an advance on the rent. The seclusion can keep me out of harm's way until Slab cools down. It's the Punt Returner Hotel, just up the highway."

"Is that the one where the bungalows are shaped like footballs?"

"No, but I had to do some redecorating just to tolerate my rooms."

I sputtered the ignition and we rolled out of the lot, along the service road, over to the highway and down a couple of miles to The Punt Returner. Roxanne's place was around the back, where the parking lot was bordered by thick hedgerows.

"It's number 124," she said.

Under a carport and directly in front of the room was a gleaming white Camaro. New, from the looks of it. I memorized the plate number as we got out of the Mustang.

"Nice car," I said. "Is it yours?"

"Thank you. It is. I'm just wondering, though. How do you plan to deal with Slab?"

"I had never met him before tonight," I said. "Same with his bowling buddies. I wouldn't think they'd know who I am. And outside, I had the car lights turned off when we raced away. It would have been difficult for them to read my license plate, so I should be all right."

I walked her to 124. She unlocked her door and opened it. One more step and she'd be safe inside. Before I could back away and wish her a nice long sleep, she looked into my eyes and held them. The eye contact created a sexual vibe in the narrow space between us. That was exactly what I had wanted from the moment we met, and yet I hadn't forgotten that she was a client and that there were rules in place for a good reason. This was my last chance to follow them.

I couldn't. I moved in and kissed her lightly. She didn't set off any alarms. Instead, she ran her fingers through my hair.

"You're almost passable," she said.

"I have another gunfight scheduled in an hour," I told her, "but I can postpone it."

She stood her ground at the threshold.

"Sorry, Jack. I won't be inviting you in. I have obligations first thing in the morning. A faculty meeting on the Romantic poets."

"Can't you blow it off?"

"I'm leading it."

"But you can't go back to the college. Slab or his boys will be looking for you there."

"The meeting is off campus," she said. "Slab wouldn't have any idea where. I'll stay with my normal life as much as possible. I don't want to run away until I see whether this little storm will blow over. What other choice do I have?"

I nibbled at her lips again. She entertained the nibbling for a moment and then leaned in with passion. I took her in my arms and kissed her deeply. She wasn't fighting me but she wasn't pulling me through the doorway, either. This was slow and romantic; we wouldn't be rushing to her bed.

"Next time," she said, teasing me with her voice and her eyes. She withdrew from my arms and slipped into the room. Just inside it she cooed softly, "Now get out of here, ya big lug."

"You stole that line from a movie," I said.

"You stole your whole life from a movie."

She blew a kiss through a tempting smile and closed the door gently. A light went on inside. A hint of her perfume hung in the air, and then it was gone.

I got back in my Mustang and drove at a leisurely pace along the rear of the hotel, around its far wing and then down the driveway to the frontage road. Roxanne had left her scarf on the passenger seat. With the windows open, a soft wind came in and stirred the scarf, sending the scent of her over to my side of the car. It was like having her next to me. I cruised home in a cloud of infatuation — openhearted and free from the slightest trace of common sense.

NINETEEN

Midway into the next morning, I passed from my squalid apartment to my flea-bitten office. I dropped Thursday's edition of the *Informer* on my desk and went over to the main office door. A rolled sheet of brown paper had been stuffed halfway through the mail slot. I pulled it out, sat down at the desk and unfurled the scroll. It wasn't an eviction notice or an advertising flyer.

The usual skull leered from the page with psychotic eyes and clenched teeth. The crossbones were the standard design. But this time the message was directed at me.

She is the summit of seduction, the pinnacle of pulchritude. Her eyes are like tropical pools in the sun, her lips like bonbons, succulent and sweet. You long to kiss her, to caress her orbs of bliss, to mount a lurid expedition into the valley of her forbidden love. But alas, your clock runs down, the hands of time clutching at your throat. Anonymous

That was quick, I told myself. Could have been someone who had been staking out Roxanne's hotel and spotted us together, but it was probably fallout from the fracas at the bowling alley. Maybe I'd been overconfident about my anonymity. Maybe one of Slab's sidekicks had recognized me from somewhere. Maybe my only remaining hope in life was to get Roxanne Delaplaine in bed before I went soaring off the steeple at Saint Opie's.

I filed the death threat under *Death Threats* and picked up the phone.

First things first. No answer at Roxanne's office, which was good. No answer in Room 124 at the Punt Returner. I called my data research people and gave them Roxanne's plate number. Then I called the hardware department at Sears and said I was investigating an assault with an ice pick.

The guy manning the phone told me they had lots of Craftsman ice picks on the shelves but rarely sold one.

"Ice makers right in the refrigerators," he said. "And in nice, neat cubes. Or sometimes in these little crescents." He did remember something odd. One pick had sold two days earlier, on Tuesday morning right after the store had opened. The hardware manager found a barely conscious clerk flat on his back behind the department's cash register. The clerk was a kid just out of high school. He had cash in his grip and there was an ice pick receipt on the floor next to him, but no other clue on what had happened. He apparently hit his head after fainting and couldn't talk much about it afterwards, but he kept smiling and saying he saw God.

"What did God look like?"

"He didn't say," the hardware man told me. "Well, supposedly, the kid saw a goddess. But there's no such thing as a goddess and so I'm assuming he meant God."

"God was buying an ice pick?" I said.

"I assume. Or … God could have popped up behind another customer who was buying an ice pick."

"God was standing in line?"

"Has to. Or the whole system breaks down."

"Okay. Do you have a security camera trained on that cash register?"

"No," he said. "We got a guy who sometimes hides behind a two-way mirror along the wall. But he wasn't there at that hour."

"Did anybody else see God?"

"Well, I wasn't here yet. And no customers came forward."

"What's the kid's name?"

"I only know him as Butch."

"Can I talk to him?"

"He quit the same day to join a monastery."

"The Opian Monks?" I asked. "At The Bishop's Retreat?"

"No. Someplace out of town. He mentioned Las Vegas."

"He joined a monastery in Las Vegas?"

"I assume he went to a monastery. Where else can you go once you've seen God? He said he found his purpose, was all."

"Maybe after he'd seen the goddess," I said, "his purpose was to get a look at the fan dancers at the Flamingo."

"You have a dirty mind, sir."

I thanked him and hung up. To get my dirty mind off my impending doom, I read the newspaper. There was a front-page story about last night's shooting spree in the parking lot at Hunchback Lanes. No injuries were reported, but the article said some vehicles were busted up pretty badly. I felt a tinge of guilt over the bullet holes and the shattered glass and hoped that the vehicle owners were insured.

The participants in the battle hadn't been identified. Good.

In other news, there was a story about a man who had gotten his hand cut off yesterday around noon. The accident happened on a trimming machine at a local paper mill. The guy was making one last pass on the machine before going on his lunch break, and so his work station was almost deserted. Somebody called in to report an emergency, but the medics couldn't get there in time to save the victim. He bled to death on the shop floor.

The coroner hadn't felt it was necessary to run down there in person. He had made inquiries by phone only, and by press time he had already ruled the death a case of bad luck. There's bureaucratic efficiency for you. No wasted time, no pointless questions.

The damage was described by a coworker who also happened to be a volunteer deacon at Saint Opie's. The article wasn't clear on whether the witness saw the accident or just the aftermath. One way or the other, the deacon told the *Informer* he was so traumatized that the Vatican would have to send him on a year-long trip. Destination Borneo. The deacon would be working to enlighten the uninformed in some isolated valley, and he'd be leaving the country in about five minutes. The deacon also told the *Informer* he was glad his coworker died doing what he loved to do.

"Having his hand chopped off?" I said to nobody but me.

Getting ready to go to lunch, the article said.

The newspaper wasted the rest of my time until my own lunch break. I buttoned up the office and walked down to The Pulptown Grill, where a churlish fry cook would be searing hotdogs and slinging hash of questionable pedigree. It was fast and cheap and only three blocks away.

TWENTY

Outside the restaurant, if you could call it that, there were two teenage boys in short-sleeved white shirts, conservative ties, pressed black pants and durable black shoes. Each of them wore a name tag at the shirt pocket. The braver one approached me. He looked to be just out of high school, but his badge identified him as Elder Olsen.

"What have you heard about the Church of Jesus Christ of Latter-Day Saints?"

"You know what?" I said. "I'm just here to get some lunch."

"Have you heard about Joseph Smith?" The other kid asked. He was Elder McKay.

"I have, but I'm a little preoccupied." I moved toward the door.

"Now is a good time to discuss your immortal soul," Elder Olsen said.

"Three years from today would be perfect," I told them.

"We're only here on a two-year mission," Elder McKay said.

"That's what's perfect about it."

The fry cook, who was also the cashier and the company president, came out and tried to scat the Mormons away. "Stop harassing my customers," he said. He raised a spatula as if it were a war mace, but he was wearing an orange apron and a paper hat that made him look as authoritative as a teddy bear. He rushed inside to beat back some flames on the grill.

"Aren't you boys a little afraid of him?" I asked.

"We're trained to overcome adversity," Olsen said.

"Well, come to think of it," I said, "maybe you guys can help me. Follow me in."

There weren't any customers inside, which would have made sense to anyone who had already been through the menu.

"You boys up for some hot dogs?" I asked.

They both sniffed the air and said they'd be fine.

"How about some Cokes?" I offered, just to rib them.

"Can't have any caffeine," McKay said.

"Oh, that's right. Sorry."

At the counter, I placed my order. Payment was required up front in case of a medical emergency. The feast was slapped on a tray almost immediately. The missionaries and I took a corner table near the grill, me sitting where I could keep an eye on the door. The cook cast a disparaging eye on my guests, but for some reason not on my meal. I smiled back and nodded him off.

"The cook doesn't want us here," Olsen said. He was the smarter of the two.

"He'll be okay," I told them. "Have you boys been hawking your wares up and down the street this morning?"

"Well, we've been carrying out our mission, yes." McKay said.

"Been in the big brick office building about three blocks west of here?"

"It's not that big," Olsen said.

"For Pulptown," I said.

"And the bricks are cracking." This was McKay. "There weren't a whole lot of people inside."

"I work there," I told them. "The building is nearly vacant. But here's what I want to know. Did you see anyone kind of shady on the premises? Anyone carrying a scroll of brown paper or fiddling with the mail slots?"

"No, why?" Olsen said.

"Just checking," I said. "If I had any neighbors near my office, I'd be asking them instead of you."

"Now then," McKay pushed in. "You said you wanted some spiritual help."

"I didn't exactly say that."

"Yes, you did," he insisted. He was jousting. All right, he'd get some jousting.

"How are your wives doing?" I asked.

McKay said, "Neither of us is married yet."

"Better get working on it. Think you'll get a quorum, either of you?"

"Well," Olsen hemmed. "That's … that's not really …"

The cook bent over his counter and silently pumped his thumb toward the door.

"It's all right," I told him. "Just three guys talking." He went back to his grill and started scrubbing it with a wire brush.

"A quorum, seven wives each," I said to the missionaries. "That way, you'll get your own planets."

The fry cook looked up. "I thought they couldn't do that anymore."

McKay said, "You seem to be … sort of … that's not us."

"Aren't you boys concerned about going to hell?" I said.

"People have a lot of misconceptions about the church," Olsen said.

"I'm talking about your willingness to follow your own rules," I cut in.

"We try to be righteous," Olsen said. McKay agreed with him.

"So, you both intend to follow the principle, do you?"

"The principle?" McKay said.

"Of plural marriage," I said.

Both of them laughed uncomfortably.

"No, no, no," McKay assured me. "That was changed a long time ago."

"And Wilfred Woodruff," I said. "He was the church leader who dropped the practice, wasn't he? Around 1890?"

"How do you know about Wilfred Woodruff?" Olsen asked.

"The U.S. government was leaning on him pretty heavily, right?"

"No. President Woodruff had a revelation from God," McKay said.

"And the revelation coincided with the firepower of the federal army," I said. "Either Wilfred caved in to the feds or God did."

"God would never cave in," McKay said.

"Okay, then. That leaves Wilfred. He must be in hell right now, don't you think?"

"Certainly not," Olsen said.

"Better check *"The Doctrine and Covenants*," I told them.

"What have you heard about Joseph Smith?" Olsen asked, trying to get me off the track.

"I've heard that God told Smith the rules of conduct," I said. "And that Smith had those rules published. You have your little books with you, don't you?"

"Yes, we do." The missionaries said in unison. They looked nervously at each other.

"Then let's take a look," I said.

They went into their backpacks and brought out their copies of *"The Doctrine and Covenants."*

I said, "Go to Section 132." They ruffled through their pages. "Go to Verse 61 and Verse 62. They're all about the God-given principle of taking multiple wives, aren't they?"

The two of them scanned the verses and went pale. "Shucky darn!" Olsen said to McKay. "He's right. It says here a guy can marry ten virgins and not commit adultery."

"Holy shit," the cook said from the grill.

"Zowie," McKay said.

"Right," I told him. "Now check out Verse 4 in the same section."

"Where are you getting all this?" the cook asked me. He was scratching his head, scraping the wire bristles of the brush over his little paper hat and shredding its tissues.

"Now, about Joseph Smith," Olsen said.

"Focus," I told him. "Verse 4 says this is an everlasting covenant, right?" They read quickly and nodded their heads. "And it says that anyone who rejects it will be damned. Am I right?"

"Yeah," McKay admitted. "That's exactly what it says. But …"

The cook asked, "You mean to tell me this polygamy thing is still okay with God?"

I tried to wave him off, then said to the boys, "I'm surprised they never covered this stuff with you in missionary boot camp."

"Well, I don't know what happened there," McKay said weakly.

"Why do you think they skipped it?" I asked.

"There's only so much time for training," Olsen said.

"Big topic like that, seems like they would have covered it," I said. "Unless they wanted to keep you in the dark about it."

"I'd like to hear more about the virgins," the cook said.

I tried to squelch him with a glare.

"So, now you know," I pressed the boys. "Wilfred Woodruff, the LDS president who overturned polygamy, has been damned according to your own holy scripture. And if you don't get with the principle of plural marriage, what do you think will happen to you? Seems like you'll be damned right alongside of him. Remember, this is an everlasting covenant."

"Maybe we shouldn't fool with everlasting orders from God," the cook said.

McKay brightened up. "It depends on what you mean by *everlasting*," he said.

"Let's not mince words," I told him. "I think we all know what *everlasting* means. Come on, boys. Either God was lying when he said plural marriage was an everlasting covenant, or your scripture got it wrong. It's got to be one or the other."

"That's not really LDS," Olsen protested. "It's the fundamentalists who still practice plural marriage. But they've been excommunicated."

"For following the rules in *your* little book?" I said.

The cook piped up: "You can't fault them for that."

"Well … how many wives do you have?" McKay asked me.

"I don't think he has a lot of wives," Olsen told his partner. "And he doesn't really think we're going to hell, either. He's only sowing the seeds of doubt."

"Nice grab," I told him. "Makes you think, though, doesn't it? Maybe the whole damn thing is a fraud."

"Ten virgins," the cook said dreamily. "I wonder what that's like in bed."

"I don't think we can help you there," Olsen told him.

"How many converts you guys got so far?" the cook wanted to know.

"None," McKay said.

"Well, I'll be your first!" The cook beat his wire brush on the counter like a judge's gavel. "Where do I sign up?"

"Oh, my heck!" McKay said. "This is getting kind of weird."

"Maybe we better get out of here," Olsen said.

"Not so fast," the cook pleaded.

The two juvenile elders got up from the table without another word, picked up their gear and went out the door. The cook hurried around his counter and followed them onto the sidewalk. "What can you tell me about Joseph Smith?" he shouted after them. They got out into the street and broke into a trot to the opposite curb. The cook came back in, gently rapping the back of the brush against his knuckles. "Ten wives … ten wives," he muttered to himself.

"Of course, you know how brutal that is for the women," I said to him.

"I never heard there was any problem," he said, now reflexively defending the faith.

"And you know they all wear canvas nightgowns," I lied.

"Really? Well, shit, ain't that the way? Anything nice, always a catch."

I ate my hot dog and drank my Coke and left.

A little before one o'clock, I was back at my desk. I tried calling Roxanne Delaplaine again. No success at either number. I sat there skimming

George Orwell, waiting for news on Roxanne's license plate and thinking every few seconds about my life expectancy. I figured the hot dog may have set it back a few ticks, but that wouldn't matter if the guy behind the death threat could get to me first.

Before I could check the actuarial tables, the office door banged open. In my trade, big entrances were usually a bad sign.

TWENTY-ONE

A behemoth stood silently in the doorway. His head, almost the size of a basketball, blocked the light from the bare bulb out in the hall. He stared at me for a good long while, breathing hard. The breathing wasn't the snorting of a beast in a bullring. It was more of a passive gasping caused by a trek up the stairs and the pressure that three hundred and fifty pounds will put on the lungs. In his lumpy hand there was a .44 Mag revolver.

Both of his flanks rubbed against the doorframe as he squeezed his bulk into my sanctum. He had arms like culverts and legs like construction pilings and it would take an old man a whole minute to walk around his beltline. When the labored breathing subsided, there was hardly any personality left in him. His face was empty of expression and his eyes were as bright as an abandoned coal mine. A mustache was rooted sparsely across his upper lip and his hair looked like it had been matted down with a garage rag. His clothes were dirty but his gun was gleaming. He slammed the door behind him.

"Jack," he said gigantically. He had a voice like a fog horn with bronchitis.

"Don't tell me," I said. "You've climbed down the beanstalk because you think I've made off with the golden goose."

He grunted at me.

I laid my book on the desk, careful not to make any sudden moves. I leaned back in my sprung chair, turned slightly to my left and slowly put my feet up on the desk, sliding one heel forward to carve a trail through several weeks' worth of dust. The other foot cradled in comfortably. The shift in position put my right hand within striking distance of the middle drawer. Inside the drawer was my best friend.

The thug made the arduous calculations necessary to form a few more words in his mind and get them into the air. "How about them Packers?" he said. Each word came through as if he were clearing sludge out of his throat. With the usual courtesies covered, he added, "You gonna be a dead man."

I knew this guy. His name was Flunk Vanderhovel. I had gone to school with him, but it seemed he had flunked so often that at one time or another he had been in school with half the population of Pulptown. It wasn't just his ineptitude that kept him behind. He was always getting taken out of class for police questioning or court appearances or stints in the juvenile clink. It happened so often that he couldn't possibly keep up with the work. People said it took him thirteen years to get through all eight grades at Saint Opie's and another seven years to get through the public high school. During his academic ascent, he had beaten me up a few times. But that was our only socializing. Rumor had it he was now running interference for Slab Kapowski.

"Never mind the Packers," I said. "You playing quarterback at Princeton this fall?"

"Huh? No. Dead."

"I figured that," I said. "I got your mail this morning."

"What mail?" His bloated face screwed up as if I had given him a complex puzzle to solve.

"You didn't stuff a death threat into my mail slot?"

He shook his head and I saw an opening.

"Somebody put a lot of effort into that document," I told him. "Don't you think you should give me a little more time to be terrorized by it before you kill me?"

"Huh?"

"Look, pal, why don't you let this go for a couple of days? I'll be here quaking in fear over the death threat and then you can come back and kill me later."

He thought it through with all the brain power of a termite mound. He apparently had no idea what I was talking about. But if he didn't deliver the death threat, who did?

"Um," he said.

"Who sent you over here?" I asked him.

"I ain't tellin you nothin' about it. Usually, I kill people in the dark so they don't even know who killed 'em. But here we are in the daytime at, what the …" He stared at his watch and shook it at his ear. "Crumps," he said.

"A little after one," I said.

"Thank you. Here we are a little after one and I gotta kill you anyway."

"Let me ask you something," I said. "If you're killing these people, how could it possibly matter whether they know who did the killing?"

Obviously, the question disoriented him. He paused for a long time, his eyebrows pulling down the lower regions of his forehead. He looked as if all of his thoughts had been shaken up and now he was trying to let the sediments in his brain resettle. At last he decided.

"You and me could meet up in heaven one day, and then if you knew who killed you, you could get the drop on me. You know, revenge."

"Been reading Saint Augustine, have you?"

He stared blankly with his brows laid low and his mouth looped in a little circle. The gun waved aimlessly in his hand.

There was a knock on the door. The big man glanced over, worried, not knowing what to do. The lapse in his concentration wasn't long enough for me to spring for the desk drawer in front of me. Then, in one-second intervals, his eyes bounced between the door and my face. I hoped it wasn't Roxanne out there, possibly another target if Slab Kapowski was the boss who had sent this guy over. But I figured if it was her, she would have just walked in without rapping. If it was anyone else, fine. Flunk had probably been told to limit his targets to Roxanne and me. I had to use whatever opportunity I could.

"Go ahead and open it," I said. "Might be important."

"There could be people," Flunk said brilliantly.

"Well, then you should put the gun away."

"Why?"

"You keep wagging that barrel around and you could poke somebody's eye out."

"No," he corrected me. "I always use a sharp stick for that."

That line of conversation wasn't working out for me, but a second set of knocks had the big guy looking flustered. I tried another tack: "Could be some free samples for you."

"Of what?"

"Find out."

That did it. Keeping the gun and one eye on me, he opened the door to a dowdy woman carrying an armful of pamphlets. Nothing of any value to a man like Flunk.

"Nobody home," he told her.

"Wait a second," I said. "Jehovah's Witness, right?"

The woman gave me a bland smile and nodded. "Do you think the world is getting better or worse?" she said from the hallway.

"Since eternity is right around the corner," I said to Flunk, "maybe I ought to hear what this lady has to offer."

"Not the true religion," Flunk said. "Bad voodoo."

I gave him one of those *gimme-a-break* looks and said, "It's my funeral, isn't it?"

"Well, I guess so, yeah."

He reluctantly let the woman in. She stepped toward the desk and Flunk closed the door behind her.

"Do you think the world is getting better or worse?" she asked again.

The question was aimed at me and not at Flunk. He tilted his head and dimmed his eyes and let his mind go off to some fish pond.

"Well," I said. "On one hand there's professional football in the spring, which is good. On the other hand, there's a professional killer standing here holding a gun on me, which is bad."

She considered the heater in Flunk's mitt.

"Why do you think people are so violent?" she asked me. I tried to convey the idea — just by looking at her — that maybe she should excuse herself and sound an alarm. She wasn't picking up on it.

"I figure it's because we're evolved to cooperate in some instances and compete in others. And then there are those times when we're supposed to call the cops."

Flunk wasn't listening, which was a break, but Jehovah's Witness didn't catch on.

"Evolved!" she said derisively. "If there was such a thing as evolution, then why don't some people have arms coming out of their heads or something?"

"I imagine you've heard about birth defects."

"That's different," she said.

"Not really."

"Well, Jesus is sitting at the right hand of His Father and they're ruling the world. And Charles Darwin is dead. So, who are you going to believe?"

Flunk stared at something out the window, but he was still pretty good about holding the gat on me. I kept at the Witness.

"You really don't understand the theory of natural selection, do you?"

"That's the devil's work," she said. "I don't need to understand it."

"Still," I said, "let me explain it to you just so you can argue against it more effectively. You'll get more converts that way,"

"I suppose," she said. "Shoot."

"Huh?" Flunk said, jostled into alertness.

"Not what she meant," I said. "But listen up, Flunk. This is good for you to know."

"I can't remember now," he said lethargically. "Either I'm suppos'ta kill you or just break your face. Is it all right if I use your phone?"

"Make it quick," I said. "And no long-distance calls."

He lumbered up close to the desk and picked up the handset. I watched him closely to memorize the numbers he was punching in at the base. He kept the gun on me, propped the phone against his shoulder and used his free hand to shield his lips from view. He mumbled into the mouthpiece. For a few seconds he was on hold. Then someone came on the line and there was more mumbling from Flunk. He listened with a pained expression to a muffled male voice and then hung up the phone.

"Thanks," he said to me. "I'm suppos'ta kill you."

The Jehovah's Witness had me tabbed as the main prospect and was obviously tuning out anything Flunk said. She sat down in the client's chair while Flunk stood, letting his burdensome weight shift from one foot to the other.

I didn't bicker with Flunk. All I did was go into lecture mode, still leaning back in my chair. With any luck, I could keep talking long enough to lull him into a mistake.

"In any species," I said, "there may be genetic mutations."

"Caused by Satan," the Jehovah's Witness said.

Flunk said nothing. He backed slowly into his old position near the door. The gun held steady in his hand but his eyes wavered around the ceiling, as if he were watching for spiders.

"Hear me out," I said. "If a random mutation happens to provide a survival advantage, then the individual who carries it will generally have more opportunity to reproduce. Isn't that right, Flunk?"

"Huh?" he said again. His mouth hung loose and his features were almost emptied out, but I had what little there was of his attention.

"And if the mutation can be inherited as a dominant gene," I went on slowly, "then the individual's descendants will carry that trait as well. Over a long period of time, their greater survival rates allow them to reproduce more often through subsequent generations." I was letting my voice get more monotonous as I went along. "Greater birth rates will gradually result in the new trait spreading throughout the larger population, ultimately throughout the species. Are you getting this, Flunk?"

He stared at me. My summary was as dry and technical as I could make it, and it was working. I could see a numbing boredom coming down over his face like a curtain.

"And in that way," I said, "the species gradually changes, or evolves." Flunk's eyes were getting more distant by the second. Maybe on some reptilian level of memory, he was reliving his catatonic reaction to a classroom lesson long ago. In a low, lazy voice, I said, "Think back, Flunk, to when you heard all this in sophomore biology. That's right, sophomore biology … year … after year … after year."

Every fact Flunk heard now would pack one more layer of gauze around his brain. His mind was back in high school. I was sure of it. Life in that world had no meaning for him, and getting a dose of scientific instruction was like being fed a pair of sleeping pills.

"Remember all that talk from your teacher," I said softly. "Think of all those long … complicated … explanations." Flunk's consciousness was sinking and his neck was going slack. He jiggled himself half-awake for a moment.

The Jehovah's Witness spoke, but her muted voice imitated mine. "If all that's true," she whispered, "then why don't we have pencils built into our fingers?"

"Suppose you met a guy," I whispered back, "who actually had pencils growing out of his fingers. Not to be indelicate, but this is all about reproduction. Would the pencil fingers make you more or less likely to, let's say, marry him?"

She looked closely at my hands. "You're not proposing, are you?"

"You're missing the … forget it."

I held up a hand to quiet her and then pointed at Flunk. He was going under again. He lifted his pistol absentmindedly and started picking his teeth with the gunsight. His legs wobbled and his body swayed. I could sense his brain activity dissolving under the tedium of my voice.

"You remember all this from your homework, Flunk. Hours and hours of endless homework."

The light in his left eye was doomed — like a dwarf star spiraling into a black hole. Then his right eye went out, though both lids remained open. The gun weighed on his hand. Then he was no longer chewing on the sight and the barrel began to slide down a rivulet of drool on his chin. The hand and gun slowly descended to hip level.

Like a cobra, I went for the desk drawer. I whipped out my .38 and leveled it at him.

"Oh, my goodness!" the Witness said.

Flunk was startled but groggy. Recognition of his plight worked its way across his face. The hand with the pistol hung at his side.

"Drop it," I said.

"Drop what?"

"The gun, stupid."

"Oh."

He let it go and it went off when it hit with the floor. The Jehovah's Witness screamed at the crack of gunfire. A bullet zapped against the filing cabinet and ricocheted into the bookcase, where it lodged in the binding of "*A History of Western Philosophy*" by Bertrand Russell.

The Witness propelled herself out of her chair and went running for the door. She clawed it open and escaped into the hall. I heard her heels clacking on the tile floor and then down the stairs.

"Thank God the bullet didn't hit the water cooler," Flunk said. "That would be a mess. Everything happens for a reason."

"Empty your pockets," I told him. He started whining but I brandished my gun. It was time to establish who was boss.

Item by item, he dumped bullets, keys and miscellaneous junk on the worn carpet.

"No wallet?" I said.

"I'm not suppos'ta carry my wallet when I'm killing people."

"Where do you keep your money?"

"I lost it all at the lawnmower races."

"Any other weapons?"

He whined about that too. I wiggled the gun to keep his attention. After what seemed like five minutes of prodding, Flunk had dropped a knife, a blackjack and a slingshot.

"Punch yourself in the mouth," I said firmly.

He rammed a hammy fist into his own teeth.

"Ouch," he said.

"Now break your trigger finger," I told him.

"No way, hey."

"Don't be like that, Flunk." I shook the gun barrel at him as if I were shaking my finger. "Don't make me shoot you." He resigned himself to my authority, and used his left hand to bend back the index finger of his right. He pushed hard, and a nauseating *crack* echoed through the office.

"Ouch," he said again.

I got up from the desk and flicked the gun to spur him toward the open door. I glanced at his pile of debris and picked up a set of keys without sorting through the rest of it. "We're going down to the street," I told him. "You first."

TWENTY-TWO

I followed Flunk Vanderhovel down the single flight of stairs, holding my gun on him. On the first floor, we crossed the deserted lobby and stepped out onto the sidewalk. There were no pedestrians nearby.

Flunk stared at his right hand. His trigger finger was badly swollen. It looked like a bratwurst with knuckles.

"In a few minutes," I told him, "the cops are going to be all over you."

"What'd I do?" he said in an abrasive whine. "I didn't even kill you."

"It's what you're about to do. The question is, what are you going to tell the cops when they grill you about it?"

"I don't never tell the cops nothin' they ask," he said.

"That's a double-negative," I told him. "Maybe a triple negative. You should say you don't ever tell the cops anything. That way, the plusses and minuses all work out."

"I flunked plusses and minuses."

"I know. I was there." I pointed to a small business across the street. "Go over to that shop and kick in the biggest window, the one with all the writing on it. I'll have the gun trained on you, so no monkeyshines."

Flunk let his head slump in defeat. He traipsed halfway across the street but stopped in traffic to look back at me. An Oldsmobile swung around him, but he hardly seemed to notice. I saluted him with the barrel of my .38 and waved him on his way. He turned forward again and continued to the opposite curb, nearly hit by a passing truck. Flunk seemed to have accepted the basic idea now, so I slipped into the shadow of my office building's doorway and tucked my gun out of sight.

All alone, like a big boy, he walked up to the shop and stood before the four-color masterpiece painted on the broad front window. The words *"Downtime Donuts"* were rendered in a flowing script drawn to look like icing with sprinkles. Flunk reached up to the glass and gave it a little push, as if measuring its resistance. I was impressed; he had done this before.

He retreated a few steps and set himself. Then he took two long strides toward the window and kicked it into shards. It was an awkward maneuver for him and he fell backward onto the sidewalk. He crawled out into the street, the first phase of his getaway. A driver screeched his brakes to keep from running him over.

Nine or ten cops, jolted at the counter inside the donut shop, scrambled from their stools. They streamed out the door and gang-tackled Flunk on the pavement. They couldn't get their handcuffs around his thick wrists, so one of the cops went into the trunk of a squad car parked at the curb. The cop came out with a hefty length of rope. It took most of the police force to hold Flunk down and cinch his arms behind his back. Then they manhandled him to his feet and got him up against another squad car. He squirmed and fought so hard that they couldn't stuff him into the back seat. They had to get more rope and tie him down onto the hood like a dead deer fresh from his last innocent romp in the north woods. By the time they got Flunk battened down, the older and heavier cops were sweating and wheezing. The whole bunch of them drove off in five cruisers, including the trophy car. I figured that would hold the would-be killer for a while.

Leaning in the doorway, I pulled Flunk's keys from my pocket. None of them bore the mark of any automotive make or model. On the keychain was a little plastic gravestone with no logo or inscription other than *"R.I.P."* The gravestone made me think of Slab Kapowski's death mills, but it could just as easily have come from a box of Count Chocula cereal.

I walked up and down the street looking for a vehicle big enough to hold Flunk. In the lot next to The Bottle Cry, I found an old armored truck with a brushed-on coat of flat gray paint. The slathered gray was blistered over what was probably deep rust on the left rocker panel and the hinges of the driver's door. Pressed unevenly in white applique letters across the top of the windshield was a misspelled slogan: *"Loosing is not an option."* This had to be the one.

If there were one person in town who would leave an armored truck unlocked, it would be Flunk. Sure enough, the door opened. I climbed into the driver's seat. Glued to the dashboard was a dusty figurine of Jesus, with the Saint Opie's brand pasted on its base. Christ had the lead spot, but he shared the dashboard with a supporting cast of biblical characters. Each of the other figurines had a Saint Opie's decal on its foundation. The cab also held a landfill's worth of food wrappers, empty cans and crumpled cigarette packs. An overflowing ashtray smelled like a garbage fire. In a long box I found a thumbscrew, a garrote for choking a medium-sized neck and a baseball bat with a six-inch nail driven through the business end. I tried the largest of the keys in the ignition. The truck rumbled to a start. I cut the motor, jumped out and left the keys on the floormat. The driver's door clapped shut as if it couldn't take much more of the same.

TWENTY-THREE

Back at my desk, I laid my gun where I could reach it more easily in case another assassin decided to stop by.

I tried to call Roxanne at her office on campus but there was no answer. I tried the main number for the college and got the same impossibly sunny woman I had met the other day. I asked about Ms. Delaplaine and was told that her off-campus meeting had broken up. The receptionist also said Ms. Delaplaine hadn't yet checked in at the administration building.

"Has anybody been out there looking for her?"

"Not here at *my* station, no. Have we met before? I hope so, because you just really sound familiar."

"I imagine it's hard to keep track of all the people you meet," I said. "Have you seen any characters out there who looked a little suspicious?"

"We can't see Satan, but he's always lurking. Don't you agree?"

"I meant more earthly types. Guys with scars on their cheeks."

"Gee, I don't think so," she said cheerfully.

"Thanks."

I hung up and called the Punt Returner Hotel, getting a disinterested clerk. Whatever he'd been doing or not doing, he seemed to resent the interruption. I asked for Room 124 and got rings but no answer. I called the front desk again and asked the clerk to clip a written message to the guest's door. He made it sound like I was asking him to come over and wax my car.

"So, you want her to be careful," he said mockingly. "Could you be a little less vague?"

"She'll know what I mean."

Next, I tried the number Flunk had punched out when he had forgotten his instructions.

"Last Chance Mortuary," an operator said. She was trying to sound sweet but her voice had been worn down by repetition. "Caskets for every budget. You rate 'em, we crate 'em. How may I direct your call?"

"Never mind," I told her. "Mom is feeling better now."

"Call again soon," she said.

That settled that. Flunk was just the kind of dolt Slab would use for rough stuff.

I went through the pile of debris Flunk had left on the carpet. Along with the weapons and the bullets, there were a few stones, some pennies, two bent cigarettes, matches, a wrapped mint and a Batman ring. There was also a rosary. The religious gizmo had a small oval of silvery metal strung among the black beads. The oval was engraved with "*Saint Opie's Church*" on one side. The back of it was engraved with a slogan: "*Let us do your thinking.*"

I gathered up Flunk's gun, the ammo, the slingshot, the blackjack and the knife. I put them into my safe and spun the dial. The rest of his possessions went in the trash.

Like most of my life, it seemed.

And yet I took a certain pride in having a folder of death threats locked in my filing cabinet and the arsenal of a hit man locked in my safe. What mill rat or shoe salesman could say the same? And how could anyone ever think I'd been making the wrong choices all these years?

I knew that sooner or later I'd have to head down to the mortuary and have a little talk with Slab Kapowski. But in the meantime, there were links to Saint Opie's I couldn't ignore. Besides everything I had found in Flunk's pockets and vehicle, I had a bad feeling about Father Timothy. I decided to go down to the church again and try to wring more information out of him.

Before leaving, I called a private investigator I knew in Chicago. Directory assistance down there had nothing under his real name, Leslie Flimphorst, but they had a business number for the name he had adopted and made official through the courts.

"Eddie Trouble," he said when he came on the line. "Difficulty is my business." Eddie used to tell people that *trouble* was his business, but the estate of Raymond Chandler had obtained a restraining order against him.

"Jack Harbinger here."

"Hey, Jackie Boy! How's it going up there on the Frozen Tundra?" He laughed for a few seconds at his own joke.

When he regained his composure, I said, "Actually, things are getting overheated."

"Can't believe it."

"How about you?"

"The usual," Eddie said. "Blackmail and bloodshed. Slow day right now, though."

"You have some contacts over at Notre Dame, don't you?"

"Sure thing. All levels. Past and present."

"Good. I'd like you to run a check on a priest by the name of Timothy Mulhooly." I spelled the last name for him. "He used to work at the university, right there in the Catholic big time, and he somehow ended up in a dead-end post like Pulptown. I'm thinking there must be a reason."

"Gotcha," Eddie told me. "Professional discount, but I'll have to grease a few palms. That would tabulate out to a C-note to cover the grease and a few calls from my office."

"I'll write you a check for a hundred dollars."

"C-note," he insisted.

Whenever you talked fees with Eddie, you had to put all the figures in the private eye patter that he seemed to live for. A main point of reference was the sawbuck, so twenty-five dollars — or twenty-five smackers if he was in the mood — would work out to two sawbucks and a fiver. Everybody got used to it.

"How am I supposed to write out a check for a C-note?"

"Good question."

"Never mind," I said. "I'll send cash."

"Better make that greenbacks."

"Whatever it takes," I said.

"I should have something for you by tomorrow."

We left it at that. I got ready to leave. I checked my own ammo, strapped on my shoulder holster and slid my .38 into the leather.

TWENTY-FOUR

I walked into the vestibule at Saint Opie's. Somewhere between the holy-water font and the hymnal racks I bent down to pick up a dime. When I rose again, I got smacked in the back of the head. I turned around to see Sister Mary Pugnacia glaring at me. I handed her the dime and she dropped it into the collection box.

"Probably somebody's last one," I teased her.

"You walked right by the holy water without even dipping your fingers in it," she said sternly.

"I'm trying to cut back," I said.

"And wet or dry, you failed to make the sign of the cross."

She was angry, which had been her natural state when I'd known her years ago. I could see veins bulging at the edges of the white linen frame around her face. I rubbed the back of my head.

"Quite a stroke you have there," I told her. "Your handball game must be coming along great."

"We don't have time for useless folly here," she scolded me.

"Depends on how you define it, I guess."

"You were an impudent young man in the fifth grade and you're still an impudent young man."

"Nice of you to remember."

She slapped my face straight on.

"And that's for not showing up at church in … how many years?"

"Seventeen, I think."

"Seventeen years wasted," Pugnacia said with slow, metered condemnation. "Seventeen years of debauchery and depravity. And for what?"

"Well," I said, "there was the debauchery."

She slapped me again.

"You've fallen away from the Church." I could practically hear the bile in her throat.

"More like escaped," I said.

She tried to slug me again, crossing with her right, but this time I grabbed her wrist. She threw a left at me but I grabbed that wrist as well. She looked at me as if I had cut the Shroud of Turin into dishrags. After a second, she pulled out of my grasp and backed away.

"You will surely burn in hell," Pugnacia said.

"That's my understanding," I said. "By the way, I got a visit this morning from Flunk Vanderhovel."

"I don't know any Flunk Vanderhovel. So what?"

"He's a thug. A hired killer."

"Never heard of him."

"Big guy," I reminded her. "Voice like a bulldozer in first gear."

"Don't recall."

"Dumb as a housefly."

"Why would I even know such a person?"

"He spent three years in your fifth-grade class."

"Oh, you mean *Clarence* Vanderhovel. I haven't seen him since then."

"That's funny," I said. "Because it took him quite a while to get through elementary school after you advanced him to grade six. He plugged away for several more years right down the hall from you."

"I was totally immersed in my own classes."

"And from what I can tell, he's still hanging around. The guy is up to his bandolero in Saint Opie's gear."

"I can't possibly keep track of everyone in this whole congregation!"

Her fists were clenched. She was seething now, and maybe a second away from spitting at me.

"How about Slab Kapowski?" I said.

"He hasn't been in his office for days."

"What office is that?" I asked her.

Her eyes dove to the floor. She pursed her thin lips as if a secret had gotten loose.

"No office at all," Pugnacia said.

"Yeah, well, I need to find Father Timothy."

"To confess your countless sins, I assume."

"Maybe to go over some other people's sins," I told her.

"Find him yourself," she said with finality. "God help you, But *I* won't."

She spun in her black, dreary cloak and walked away, leaving me with the pounding of her heels. She was probably off to string a cat o' nine tails.

I passed through the double doorway and between rows of unoccupied pews in the nave. Alone in the place, I approached a stage, though no one in the church business would have called it that. On the stage was an altar where at each mass a priest would turn flavorless little wafers into Jesus. During most of my childhood years here, the priest recited something in Latin while he was doing it. I didn't follow the Latin text at the time and never studied the language later, but the key passage must have been roughly equivalent to *abracadabra.*

To the right of the stage, and down a narrow hallway, I came across an alcove crowded with two life-sized statues. Saint John the Baptist was pouring water over a woman's head, and she seemed to be enjoying it. I had never seen these two figures, but I had never explored the innards of the church before, and so they could have been there for decades. At an angle across the hallway was what I took to be the vestry, which was a dressing room for the priests. From the open entrance to the vestry, I saw a second door at the back wall of the small room. That door was opened to an inner chamber, and Father Timothy was barely visible inside. He was sitting sideways at a massive mahogany desk and leaning back in a padded chair. I walked into the vestry and rested a shoulder against the frame of the connecting door. Timothy didn't notice me because all his attention was focused on a human skull he held in his left hand.

"Alas, poor Yorick," I said.

TWENTY-FIVE

Timothy was surprised for a moment. Turning a stony gaze my way, he smiled unpleasantly. He seemed at ease with the skull, as if time or indifference had blunted its tragedy. He held it up in my direction.

"This could be a reasonable facsimile of you, soon enough." It was said in a tone of counseling, but it came off as a little spiteful. He brought Shakespeare back into play: "Where be your gibes then?"

"All dried up, I guess. But why so ominous today? Anything I should know about my life span being cut short?"

"Oh, it's just a standard approach," he said with a smarmy reassurance. He set the skull aside. I couldn't tell how recently it had been scraped and buffed as a collector's item. "People need to be reminded of the fragility of life. You have to scare the hell out of them to make them appreciate the value of heaven."

"Very comforting," I said.

"Comfort is sometimes overrated. Especially if it leads to spiritual complacency. I only meant to say that poor Yorick, as you call him, makes an excellent prop for a sermon. Don't you agree?"

"Sounds as if a good sermon is a lot like a good death threat," I said. "Could be I'm not too far off the scent."

"Ah, your death threat investigation. I had forgotten. But I can assure you that a priest is not in the habit of making threats via sermon or any other means."

"People fall into bad habits all the time, padre. Anyway, you're missing the whole point of hell, aren't you?"

"I'm sure I don't know what you mean."

"What is hell but a coercive threat?"

"Oh, Lord," he said. "You are indeed a hard case."

He invited me to sit down in a stuffed chair facing his desk. The deep cushion under me seemed bottomless and left my knees pointing at the ceiling. It gave me the strange feeling that my tailbone had foundered lower than the floor. The thickly upholstered arms were too high and constricting, looming up to my shoulders and forcing me to keep my elbows pinched inward. The sagging confines kept me in an awkward posture and put me on a level below Timothy's as he sat high and unhindered in the captain's chair. All for effect, I told myself, a clumsy trick used by executives and politicians trying to signify dominance.

"I trust you're comfortable," he said.

"I'll be fine as long as you throw me a rope when I want to get up again."

He sniffed at me.

Around the room there were shelves holding ornately bound books. The shelves also displayed ceramic vases, a small marble pieta and a plaster version of "*The Last Supper.*" On one wall there was an oversized crucifix. On another, a number of photos memorialized the padre shaking hands with the pope and some cardinals at the Vatican. Potted plants had grown tall at either end of Timothy's desk. Behind it there was a well-appointed bar. Liquor bottles and highball glasses weren't what most people would expect to see in a church's office, but to me they were no stranger than anything else in the building.

"I hadn't even known this room existed," I said.

"I take it, then, that you were not an altar boy during the years you attended elementary school here."

"No, I wasn't. Must have been fate. A wise man once told me everything happens for a reason. Guy by the name of Flunk Vanderhovel. Maybe you know him."

He bent the corners of his mouth downward, looked off to one side and shook his head. "Can't say that I do," he said.

Timothy had been careful about his wording. Lying is nervous work, even to liars, and so they often couch their denials in technically correct wording just to slide by the stress of deceit. Timothy couldn't say he knew Flunk, and that could have been because he really didn't. Or it could have been because he couldn't afford to get *caught* knowing Flunk.

"He's a thug," I said. "You probably don't hang around the criminal element enough to have met him,"

"Actually, I do a bit of counselling down at the jail. I can tell you that the unsavory are often housed there because they've strayed from the grace of God." He gave me the slippery smile.

"Well, Flunk was in my office this afternoon. As a matter of fact, he came over to kill me."

I expected a big reaction from Father Timothy but didn't get one.

"Oh, really?" he said.

"Yeah, Slab Kapowski sent him."

"Come now," Timothy scoffed.

"You have your goons and Slab has his."

"You do have an imagination," Timothy said. "Mr. Kapowski is one of the church's most ardent supporters. He donated the new fountain out at The Bishop's Retreat. He even handled the construction details. There was a wonderful dedication ceremony out there just last week, and Mr. Kapowski gave up his valuable time to attend."

"Does Slab have an office on church grounds?"

He ignored the question and went on to something else.

"Supposing for a second that Mr. Kapowski had sent this Flunk person over to kill you, then why are you still with us?"

"I outsmarted him."

"Of course, you did." All smiles again. "I suppose that in Mr. Kapowski's case, one must choose one's goons more carefully."

"You mentioned the unsavory," I said, "I see that Sister Pugnacia is still around, right in there with Sister Bludgeonetta. It's nice to see that nothing ever changes."

"And yet change is inevitable. Most of the old guard from your time are now deceased, as you may have heard."

"How about Sister Inflexia?

"Passed away."

"Well, she was the oldest," I said. "Sister Scorpia? Sister Recriminata?"

"Also dead. I'm afraid it's a sad inventory."

"Plus, you lost a deacon."

"A simple administrative matter."

"And Sister Fracturina?"

"Happily, she's still here."

"Is she still practicing karate?" I asked.

"Pardon me?"

"Years ago, I saw her give my pal a karate chop in church. She couldn't tolerate his slouching. The violence was typical, but that karate chop really surprised me. I wouldn't have thought the influence of Odd

Job from the '*Goldfinger'* movie would have extended all the way into the nuns' convent."

"Well, I don't know much about karate, but the sisters have often been faced with unruly children."

"Ever wonder about the names they all chose for themselves? A bit combative, don't you think?"

"Scrappy, I'd say. Our nuns have mounted some fierce attacks on Satan."

"Him and a few kids. Whatever happened to Sister Invincia?"

He shuddered almost imperceptibly when I mentioned the name.

"She gave me the willies too," I sympathized.

"That's hardly …" He let up, but flashed irritation.

I said, "Invincia always looked like she was standing in a darkened room and holding a flashlight under her chin. Is she still the principal here?"

"Accurate memories are elusive," Timothy said weakly. "Sister Mary Invincia is no longer the principal at the school. Regrettably, that job has now gone to a lay person. As have many of the teaching positions. But she's still here, upholding the strict standards of her order. She now heads up the nuns' convent."

"Kicked upstairs?" I asked.

"I don't think you understand who does the kicking around here," he said, then looked as if he wished he hadn't.

"Maybe I do understand. Sister Invincia was a tough broad. Almost twenty years ago, I caught her threatening to throw a kindergartener into a trash compactor."

"Oh, please."

"True story. I had left my classroom on some errand and thought I was alone in the halls. I heard a small child crying as I started down a stairway. I saw what was happening below and stopped dead. Invincia didn't see me up there. Her hand was like a vice grip around this little guy's forearm. He looked to be five years old. He must have been up to no good, acting like a kindergartner or something. There happened to be a garbage truck just outside. The thing was huge. It had one of those overhead compactors. The mechanism was grinding away, loud as hell, and pressing down to crush a load of trash. Sister Invincia saw her chance to teach the kid a lesson and told him she was going to throw him in there. He was screaming for his life and trying desperately to pull free. The kid might have been five, but he was damn close to a coronary seizure. She kept threatening him anyway, and yanking him toward the truck. I guess she assumed that no one was watching her. When I showed myself and stared her down, she was spooked and lost her grip on the kid's arm. He ran shrieking down the hall in absolute terror. I was only a sixth-grader and wasn't sure what I could do about it. There was nobody to report it to at school because Invincia was the goddamn principal. She never said anything to me about it then or later. I'm still not sure whether she was embarrassed at what she'd done or just pissed off at me for catching her."

Father Timothy let all that soak in. He didn't defend Mother Superior. He didn't tell me I was lying or crazy. There was nothing he could say, and he spent a long time not saying it.

TWENTY-SIX

"But it occurs to me that you have a poor attitude," he finally offered. "You tend to dwell on the negative. What about the fine Catholic education you received here?"

"When I finally entered public school, I was pretty far behind everybody else, especially in the science classes."

He frowned and said, "Well, we can't always afford test tubes and cathodes and anodes. But schooling aside, what about everything that the Church of Saint Opius represents? What about all the people who find relief from their suffering in the holy mass every Sunday?"

"Yeah, I know. The masses at Opie's are the opiate of the masses."

He couldn't keep from smirking. "There's a symmetry in there you kind of have to admire," he admitted. "Nevertheless, you would do better paraphrasing the Bible rather than Karl Marx."

"Let's paraphrase the part about God wanting to rub out the Canaanites."

"Well." He manufactured a diffident smile. "You can pick apart anything."

"Ever read *'The Book of Revelation,'* padre? Something about killing a woman's children so that all the churches will know that your God is the one who searches minds and hearts. Touching, isn't it?"

"You're taking that out of context," Timothy said. "The offending woman was Jezebel, a pagan who tried to beguile the nation of Israel into worshipping Baal."

"In what context is it okay to kill children?"

"I'm sure …" He couldn't finish his answer.

"You're sure everything was on the up and up? You're probably right. Maybe that passage was what gave Sister Invincia the idea to throw the kid in the trash."

Timothy cocked his head and looked away momentarily, maybe formulating a response and maybe hoping another garbage truck would come by to dispose of me quickly. At last, he came up with something.

"But you're discounting the New Testament and its message of love and forgiveness and redemption."

"Different God, different message," I said.

"No, you misunderstand. Jesus is one with God, not a different God."

"Come on, padre. One is gentle and the other is cruel. Good cop, bad cop."

"Upon a superficial reading. But God's nature is actually unchanging, immutable."

"You mean Christ is the same guy who turned Lot's wife into a pillar of salt? Just because she was homesick or maybe looked in the wrong direction?"

He exhaled, tilted forward and rubbed his temples. "You seem fixated on these things."

"Professional interest only," I said, brushing him off. "In my line, it's a good practice to keep tabs on who's murdering who."

"Whom," he corrected. "I'm reluctant to criticize, Mr. Harbinger, but your humor can be a tad off-putting."

"My way of coping with claptrap."

"And with your guilt, I suspect. Very well. The Bible does contain some seemingly incongruous material. No use getting bogged down in it. There's a measure of symbolic language that shouldn't be taken literally."

"But the Bible is God's word, isn't it?"

"Certainly," Timothy said.

"He dictated it to the authors of the various books?"

"Through divine inspiration, yes."

"Why didn't God just say what he meant?"

"Well, He chose … to … what are you getting at?"

"Why so obscure?" I said. "Why all the symbolic language? Why all the vague prophesies and the hokey miracles? Why didn't God lay it all out clearly? And if he wanted to certify his legitimacy, why didn't he cite facts that nobody in the ancient world could have known? If his Bible had described DNA sequences or the half-life of uranium, then we'd have to take it seriously today."

"Do you presume to tell God His business?"

"I'm saying there would have been any number of reasonable, efficient ways for God to get his ideas and his credentials across but he didn't use them. If the guy you're describing really wanted us to know he was the genuine article, he obviously wasn't very smart about selling himself."

A barely veiled contempt crept over Timothy's features.

"You have to remember," he said, "that the Bible was written for simple, uneducated people. God had to use language and stories that they would understand."

"Why didn't God simply educate them? I mean, so he could make his case."

"But … these people were farmers and shepherds. They would have been overwhelmed if God had thrown modern scientific theories at them."

"So, what you're telling me is that the almighty did the best he could, given the limitations he had to work under."

"Well … I wouldn't … limitations …" He let it go. "But let's talk about you. I've been worried about your immortal soul since our earlier encounter. I think I'd better hear your confession."

"You seem awfully intent on that," I said. "But what I'd really like to do is collect information, not confess it. Especially information about Slab Kapowski. My fault for getting sidetracked on grave matters of theology."

"What would you like to know?"

"What kind of business does he conduct down here?"

"I told you," Timothy said. "It's strictly charitable. There's the fountain at The Bishop's Retreat, and then there are other improvements throughout the church grounds."

"Where is his office?"

"Out at his mortuary, I presume."

"I'm talking about the office here on the premises."

"I'm not sure why you think there's any such thing," he said without a denial. "But you seem to have so little faith. And I'm wondering why. I really think it would be helpful if you declared that weakness in the confessional."

"You're tenacious," I said.

"Unswerving," he said.

"I can see we'll have to step through your little ritual in order to move the conversation forward."

"Sounds equitable, doesn't it?"

"One thing, though," I said. "I won't be kneeling in one of those confessional booths."

"Fine," he said. "Tell me your sins right here."

"All right, I'll play your game. First off, I'm not all that obedient. Or humble. I don't go to church. I don't say my prayers. And about an hour ago, I threw a rosary into a waste basket. Most of my other sins involve cocktail waitresses, but I don't know whether you want to hear about those."

"The details won't be necessary. Any other sins?"

"I guess the big one is that I'm an atheist."

"Not surprising to hear you say so. And yet, I can't believe you mean that."

"I'm a nonbeliever, all right. Heretic, infidel, heathen. Whatever you like."

"Certainly not deep down inside."

I raised my right hand like a witness in a courtroom. "May God strike me dead."

Something small and quick passed behind his eyes. It may have been resentment or revulsion or combativeness.

"So, you *can* cite the Bible after all," he said. "The Book of Samuel, no less, though once again out of context. But if you don't believe in God, where will you turn when trouble comes?"

"Trouble is already here," I told him. "Remember the big bad man in my office today? He was pointing a gun at me."

"The gun should have clarified things for you. Maybe next time it *will*. No doubt you've heard there are no atheists in foxholes." He leaned back and made a pup tent out of his fingers, as if he had really laid one on me.

"And when you're scared shitless in a shallow pit with bullets whizzing by," I said, "is that when you're doing your clearest theoretical thinking?"

"Fear can be the mother of spiritual epiphany," he insisted. "The moral of the foxhole aphorism is that people often find their ecstasy while under duress."

"Well, sure. A guy can find some pretty exciting stuff under a dress."

He tightened the cords in his neck, but didn't lose his temper.

"I'll overlook your quippery for now," he said. "Your other remarks indicate that you're a philosophical man. Are you familiar with the Five Ways of Saint Thomas Aquinas?"

"Proofs of God," I said. "Supposedly."

"Impeccably reasoned," he said.

"I forget the details," I said. "I think he said everything needs to have a cause except for that which doesn't need to have a cause. And that's God.

The rest of it is similar. He makes a universal assumption, finds an exception to it and then hypes the exception as if it proves his point."

"A summary flawed by your rather slapstick oversimplifying," he said. "Thomas Aquinas also tells us that the first cause must inevitably be perfect, and thus constant, benevolent and omnipotent."

"That's totally arbitrary," I said. "And anyway, maybe this God character of yours had just enough benevolence or power to create the universe as it is, but not enough to create the universe as it might have been."

"You may indulge in philosophical maneuverings, Mr. Harbinger. But God remains the utmost goodness."

"And therefore, he would necessarily come up with genocide and hellfire, plagues and pestilence. I'm not quoting Thomas Aquinas now. I'm just editorializing."

"I should say," Timothy scolded me. "You seem very bitter."

"Just exasperated. I hear doubletalk every day. It comes with the job. In your case, it's all word play and tautologies."

"Such a big word, Mr. Harbinger."

"It means your conclusion is simply a restatement of your premise."

"I'm perfectly aware of what a tautology is," he said. "But you're missing the point. As Saint Anselm tells us, God is a being so great that no greater being can be conceived."

"That doesn't necessarily mean this being is as great as he *could* be. What if our conception of greatness is limited? And anyway, are we really *conceiving* anything with any clarity? Do we really have any idea what constitutes this greatness? Or are we simply floating the notion that some undefined greatness may be out there somewhere?"

"God is the sum of all things, physical, intellectual and spiritual."

"Including evil?"

"No," he said. "Evil is the absence of God."

"And evil exists?"

"Of course, it does."

"So, there's existence outside of God."

"You're twisting things again."

"No, padre, they're twisted up all by themselves. I'm trying to untwist them."

He took a deep breath and let it out slowly. I could tell this whole conversation was wearing thin for him.

"But," he said, holding up a finger to bolster one more point. "How could the world, the universe, even exist as it is without God? Surely, the ingenious system of it all could not have happened by mere accident. It must have been the design of a supreme intelligence."

"That's another conclusion that restates your premise. Come on, padre. You call the universe ingenious and then insist that there must have been some kind of a genius behind it. But from everything we can observe, every scientific theory we can verify, you've got it backwards. Intelligence is a product of evolution, not the other way around."

"You were an obstinate young man in elementary school," he said. "And you're still an obstinate young man."

"You didn't know me then," I said.

"I'm extrapolating."

"Fair enough."

He lightly slapped both palms on the desktop.

"In any case," he said, "although you are clearly in the bondage of sin, and although it is clearly my job to free you, I'll have to excuse myself. I've had a particularly rough day and I need some rest and recuperation. The altar boys are having a pool party and I thought I might surprise them."

"What about the Kapowski dossier?"

"I owe you some cooperation," he said. "I won't deny it. But I'm afraid the conclusion of our little talk will have to wait."

He had begun to stir out of his chair when the phone rang. He picked it up and I could hear a muffled female voice on the line. Timothy went pale as the voice got louder.

"Just a moment," he said into the phone. He placed a hand over the mouthpiece, leaned toward me and smiled without a trace of friendliness. "Just a call about a fundraising effort that's gone sour," he told me. "These bake sale ladies. I'll only be a minute." He went back to the phone, said, "Now then," and listened.

The voice from the other end crackled and wasn't very concise about the crackling. I couldn't hear a word clearly, but this must have been the most contentious bake sale in history.

Finally, Timothy swiveled away from me and spoke into the mouthpiece. "Yes, I've been dealing with it today … I've tried everything I know … I'm afraid it's a lost cause … Yes … You're correct … I'll try a different tack … Yes, and I can certainly use all the help I can get … In a little while, then. Yes. Goodbye."

He hung up and turned back to me.

"Sorry for the interruption."

"The business of business is business," I said.

"Forgive me for being so distracted and so rushed. I've been under a lot of pressure these past weeks. Perhaps we should talk more about the case you're investigating."

"Good. So just level with me. Does your Mr. Kapowski keep an office on church grounds?"

"Before we go into all that, let me pour you a drink as a peace offering."

I wondered what the hell was going on.

TWENTY-SEVEN

Father Timothy got up from his desk, went to the bar behind it and reached into a lower cabinet. He straightened and with his back to me, worked on a couple of drinks for a long time. Too long. He turned around, holding two gold chalices. There were two fresh-looking overturned glasses on the bar but for some reason he hadn't poured the drinks into them.

"Aren't these chalices supposed to be for sacred rituals?" I asked.

"Don't worry," he said. "Call them goblets if you like. I bring these out for special guests like yourself." He handed down a full one to me and went back to the superior position of his desk chair.

"I guess it's better than a lead mug," I said. I passed it under my nose and watched the liquor swirl inside of it. I couldn't smell anything but bourbon, and the opaque vessel obscured any foreign substance I might have seen through glass. It could have been just a drink, but I hadn't studied all those detective movies for nothing. When I tilted the goblet to my lips, I kept them clamped down on the rim. Nothing was swallowed, but I couldn't help tasting a drop or two.

"One more thing before we move on," Timothy said, stalling.

I was tired of arguing and tired of wasting my time. If I had been polite to him, I would have been tired of that too. "Let's get it over with," I said, hoping he would answer my questions about Slab Kapowski before an hour went by.

"I've noticed that your arguments are more fitting for a debate with a Protestant," he said. "You'd fare much better sparring with Reverend Pithy, who's now in Green Bay. He's well-meaning, but academically unsophisticated."

"I've seen his TV show," I said. "He's a moneygrubbing liar, but what bothers you is his lack of sophistication?"

"We differ on our appeals to the faithful. More importantly, we also disagree on matters of doctrine. And some of his opinions are rather quaint. For example, he thinks pedophilia causes earthquakes."

I gave Timothy a look through my eyebrows and said, "Catholics think pedophilia causes transfers."

"Vicious, unsubstantiated lies!" He gathered himself and dropped back into low gear. "The truth will vindicate the Church."

I made another feint at drinking. A drop of the bourbon-and-whatever remained on my upper lip. Father Timothy was in no hurry, and there hadn't been just one more thing. He plowed ahead with efforts to reacquaint me with the One True Church. Though I tried hard to keep up with him, it was getting difficult to concentrate.

"Plates and tonic," I said, not sure why. My thoughts were getting foamy and the goblet was getting wobbly. I put it down and said, "I mean plate tectonics. Earthquakes. But … where was I? Pithy … is … um. Oh, yeah. What about Slam's office? Slab's office."

He told me that was a good question but left it hanging. He went on with more sloppy reasoning. I couldn't stay ahead of it. All I could do was wonder why the room was spinning. Timothy was saying something about … something.

Cockamamie daydreams played havoc with my head.

Roxanne was the gunnery officer on a ferry crossing the Detroit River. I was coming on to her but her pet tiger threw me overboard. The tiger wore a catcher's mitt and used it to wave bye-bye from the railing.

Then I was a quarterback in a USFL game and Roxanne was in the Michigan Panthers' locker room, making pudding out of their plum-colored jerseys. Detroit again. Panthers and Tigers. Where were the Lions? Cats everywhere. Catnip in my drink. There's your problem, son.

Then I was a lion tamer in the Pontiac Division of General Motors and Roxanne was my charming assistant. She drove onto the stage in Slab's GTO, got ahold of my whip and cracked it. She made me jump through hoops of fire but my legs fell off and the audience laughed at me. The lions attacked the audience. Not so funny anymore. Better watch out for the lions.

"Wash out the limes," I said to Timothy. "Eskurz me, I muss hab a speesh imperdiber."

"Please, tell me," he said patiently.

"I doe wanna." My eyelids weighed in at about eighty pounds each. "I wanna go seep."

"Relax, my son." He was moving, coming around the desk. "Sleep in the arms of the Lord."

I was in limbo for a few seconds, on the edge of a blackout. I couldn't really focus, but I saw Father Timothy standing over me. No, this isn't. This can't ...

Like a guy nodding off on a late-night drive, I worked up the willpower to bite down hard on my lip. I shouted something nonsensical just to wake myself up. I rattled my head and popped my eyes wide open.

The priest backed away. His own eyes bulged and his mouth gaped, as if he were surprised that I had regained consciousness. His hand went for a stapler on the desk and I got the feeling he was going to hurl it at my head. I pulled my gun on him and struggled with its heft. I let the thing wave in the wind long enough for him to get the point. He set the stapler down before my gun could go off. Good boy. I was dopey, my lips were numb and my tongue was thick. But I could speak:

"Yo gonna missile pole partum." Well, I *thought* I could.

"Now, close your eyes," he said soothingly.

"No ... you ... you're going to miss your ... pool party."

That was more like it.

"Have a drink," he said, backing himself into safety behind his desk.

He wasn't going to throw me a rope and pull me out of the sunken chair. I had to climb out of it like a zombie clawing his way out of a grave. I grabbed the chalice I'd been given and held it up. Hands not too steady. Mouth getting better. Brain clearing up.

"Nice try, padre." I poured the mickey into one of the pots next to his desk. "Sorry. Your fern is going to be a lot less articulate for a while."

I let the sacred cup drop to the floor. Timothy stammered without speaking any actual words.

"Slab's office," I said. "Where is it?" I twitched the gun at him, now with a tighter grip on its weight.

"Mr. Kapowski doesn't have an office in the church!" The priest looked terrified, but a sudden hint of optimism flashed across his face.

There was motion behind me. In my peripheral vision I picked up a glimpse of Bludgeonetta and Pugnacia rushing in from the vestry. Bludgeonetta ripped the big metal crucifix off the wall. The heavyset nun came at me fast, swinging the cross at my face. I turned my back on Timothy and leaned away from Bludgeonetta's swipe. I felt a blow to my kidney. My gun fell to the floor. I whirled to land one on Timothy but Pugnacia came at me from the side, slamming me in the mouth. I was off guard and Bludgeonetta's next fling with the crucifix caught me on the cheek bone.

I was woozy and on the boards. Timothy kicked me, but I grabbed his foot and wrenched him off his stance. He hit bottom and whined about his hip. I got to my feet.

Pugnacia came at me again. She threw her arms free from the folds of her cloak, drove a left into my stomach and tried a flashing right that went nowhere. I blocked her swing and pushed her back. She tripped into a bookcase. A delicate vase toppled from a shelf and shattered over her head. Pugnacia swooned onto the floor, sitting upright. A thin line of blood dripped from the rim of her black and white linen headgear. An ice pick lay next to her motionless fingers. She was breathing, but in no shape to get up.

Timothy got to his feet and reached for the marble pieta, but I heard Bludgeonetta coming in behind me. I turned.

Her face was red and feral. She gripped the crucifix like a battle axe and took a level swung at me. I deflected the blow, throwing her off balance. She raised the big cross overhead and came down with it like a mauler driving a railroad spike. I ducked in close under the downward force and let her mass fall onto my shoulders. I straightened, leveraging her weight and flipping her over. Her momentum cartwheeled her into Timothy and blew him backward. He bobbled the pieta. The heavy dingus dropped onto Bludgeonetta's knee as she fell beside him. She squealed and lay there, writhing in pain. Timothy groped for the big crucifix but it had bounced out of his reach.

He charged at me anyway, punching in a fury. He landed a fist in my ribs but I rammed one into his belly and that one made the difference. He doubled over, sucking hard for oxygen. I pushed him away from me and he crashed into his shelves. An avalanche of books fell on his head. He lay flattened and still.

The chaos in the room froze for a moment. I looked around, regaining my breath and my bearings. Father Timothy and the nuns were temporarily out of commission. They moved sluggishly, testing their arms, legs and necks.

Bending over was dizzying, but I picked up my gun from the floor and put it away in my shoulder holster.

I stood there rubbing my cheek where the crucifix had cut me. So that was what it felt like to be touched by Jesus.

I stepped over the nuns and went out through the vestry. In the hallway, there was a louvered door directly across from the vestry's entrance.

I poked the slats open and saw that it was only a supply closet. Deeper into the hallway, I found an unlocked door. The room behind it held a bare conference table and empty chairs. Not anyone's office.

As I walked back down the cramped hallway, groggy voices began to float out of Timothy's office. The three divinities were regaining their faculties. I wanted no part of them.

I walked quickly down the hall and out into the big empty nave. I threaded my way between the rows of pews and slipped out through the oaken doors at the rear. In the vestibule, I went over to a staircase that wound upward into the dusty narrows of the steeple. I wondered how many chumps had been herded up there at gunpoint. I climbed the stairs. High up, I found a hatch on an inward-sloping wall. I pried the hatch open and saw clouds and blue sky. The aperture was just large enough to shove a man through. Nothing more up there.

I went back down the stairs to the vestibule and continued searching for Slab's office. If there was one more room or passageway at this end of the building, I couldn't find it. I checked for hidden doors and knocked on paneling, listening for the resonance of a secret recess. Nothing. Time to get out.

The tall front doors opened to a sunlit landing and a bank of broad steps dropping to the familiar sidewalk and street. I made for my car.

TWENTY-EIGHT

I drove toward Slab Kapowski's mortuary, intending to question him, but the developments at Saint Opie's made me rethink my plans. So did the pain in my back and ribs. And the burning red cut on my cheek. I turned for home.

In the lot at The Bottle Cry, Flunk Vanderhovel's truck was being towed. Across the street from my building, the donut shop window was being boarded up. In my apartment, the air of success was escaping through cracks in the walls. I flopped onto the couch and took stock of a hard day. The investigation was going nowhere. I was mentally and physically depleted. My brain had residual effects from the dope and the rest of me felt like a tackling dummy on the last day of training camp. I stood up, sponged off my face, took a shower and put on a suit that wasn't spattered with blood.

I went through the connecting door to my office. There was nobody waiting to shoot me, so things were improving. Momentarily anyway, because there was another scroll of rough brown paper stuffed halfway into the mail slot. I unpeeled it and felt the familiar cold flutter in my stomach as I looked it over. This time, across the top of the page, there were two of the little skull-and-crossbones guys grinning fiendishly at each other. The scrawled message below was simpler than usual.

As befitting your duplicity, I shall kill you twice. Anonymous

The brevity was a nice change. I filed the threat with the rest of my collection.

I sat down at my desk and left the .38 in the ready position just off the blotter. A light was flashing on my answering machine. I punched a button and an efficient voice told me the plate on the new Camaro had come out to someone named Rebecca Chatterton. That set me back even more, because if Roxanne hadn't borrowed the car, she had given me or the DMV a fake name. Why? Rebecca Chatterton was both the registered owner and the legal owner, meaning there wasn't any bank loan involved. The purchase date was only three months ago. The owner's listed address was on Stowell Avenue in Shorewood, about a hundred miles south of Pulptown and just outside of Milwaukee on the banks of Lake Michigan. I pulled out a map of the greater Milwaukee metro area and looked up the street. It was a stone's throw from Lake Drive, and the stone in that neighborhood could easily have been an emerald. Not every house there was a mansion, but there were some that made Slab Kapowski's castle look like a blacksmith's hut. So, Rebecca Chatterton was probably well off. Or she had a wealthy benefactor. And maybe she and Roxanne were the same person.

There was still enough time left in the afternoon to do a little business. I got on the phone to a reliable investigation agency in Milwaukee and put in a request for searches of criminal and civil court records under the names Roxanne Delaplaine and Rebecca Chatterton. If it was just a matter of looking through microfiche index logs down at the county courthouse, it would be fast and cheap. If there were hits on the names, and if there were paper files for the researchers to track down and summarize, then my client was going to cost me half my fee just by playing coy.

I tried calling Roxanne, or Rebecca, or whatever her real name was. No luck at the college or the hotel.

A few minutes later, the phone rang and I grabbed it. The caller started off in a mumble and I wasn't sure I caught his last name.

"Is that Newton?" I asked. "As in Isaac?"

There was a long pause. "Newton … as in fig."

This was going to be another one.

"What can I do for you, Mr. Newton?"

"I came to your office and you weren't there," he said sluggishly. "I've been calling every half hour."

"Didn't my recording invite you to leave a message?"

"I don't trust disembodied voices."

"Right now, our voices are electronic signals," I pointed out.

"That's different. You're really talking and so am I."

"Do you ever listen to the radio?"

"Same difference," he said. "That's people talking live."

"And what if they're playing a pre-recorded commercial?"

"Well … that's … I didn't call you to nitpick me," he said. "I called you to do an investigation. But you're never in your office."

"I was working," I told him. "To tell you the truth, I was out getting beaten up."

There was another long pause. "I guess that's okay, then."

"How can I help you?" I said. Not that I thought I could.

"I just bought a new house," Mr. Newton said. "Well, it's an old house but new to me. There's a ghost moping around in it."

"And you're sure whoever's in there is a dead person?"

"Well, she's a ghost. So … yeah, dead."

"And she's moping? How about sulking?"

"Could be either one," he said. "Moping or sulking. Hard to tell. But she seems very unhappy."

"Sounds like post-mortem depression," I told him. "It's very common." Stone silence. I was hoping he'd swear at me and get off the line, but he didn't.

"Yeah, probably," he said. "I'm thinking that, maybe, she got murdered and she never got over it. She's from, like, 1880 or something. That much I know."

"How can you tell?"

"Um, aah, from the dress she's wearing. It has a bustle. Like the old schoolmarms wore. I also seen 'em in those Victorian movies from London where people are always walking around in a fog."

"Just like they do in Pulptown," I said wearily. "So, what would you like me to do?"

"Obviously, I'd like you to investigate her."

"She owes you money?"

"Of course not! She's a ghost, for crying out loud."

"I guess what I'm asking is why you want her investigated."

"Because," he said slowly, spacing out every syllable. "She … is … a … ghost. Do I have to spell it out for you?"

"P – O – I – N – T," I said. "Get to it."

"Hey, watch yourself. You're kind of rude. How can you even stay in business?"

"I have no idea," I said. "But let me ask you this. What kind of entity can come back as a ghost?"

"Well, it has to have a soul."

"So, it can't be a rock," I said, "Or a pocket watch or a serving dish."

"That's right. It has to be a living spirit."

"What about an orange?"

"Hmmm," he said. "An orange would have been a living thing at some point, but it still wouldn't have a soul because it's only a piece of fruit. And even if it did have a soul, I don't think an old orange peel would be able to hang on to it for very long. Do you?"

"How about a cotton ball?"

"Same thing," he said. "Not fruit, but pretty much the same. I don't think you're very smart about these things."

"Then how come these ghosts that people see are always wearing clothes?"

"Huh?" He couldn't follow me.

"The ghosts are always wearing clothes," I pressed. "Why is that?"

He let out a breath slowly, as if he couldn't believe the guy on my end of the line could be such a blockhead. He answered with drawn-out condescension. "Is it because? … could it be? … because? … maybe? … the ghosts are modest?"

"You're missing it," I said. "Take a piece of cotton clothing that fell apart or got ripped up for rags a hundred years ago. Did that clothing ever have a spirit that could come back now as a ghost?"

"No," he answered. "I already told you. Only a living soul can do that."

"Then how did the bustle get here?"

"The bustle?" He said.

"The ghost you saw was wearing clothes. She had a bustle. If she was naked, that's one thing. But somehow the ghost of her clothing came back along with her. By your own description of the way all this works, how could that happen?"

"I don't see what that has to do with anything," he said.

"It's simple," I told him. "You're seeing what you want to see, or what stories have conditioned you to see. You buy into the idea that a ghost would come here from another century, so you not only conjure a woman, but you dress her up in appropriate clothing. You subconsciously want to place her in the year 1880 or whenever, so your mind pins a bustle on her. You just got through telling me that clothing doesn't have a soul and can't travel through time. So, I'm asking you, how did the goddamn bustle get here?"

His silence went the full eight-count.

"Maybe it was an *enchanted* bustle," he said.

I hung up on him. The phone rang immediately. I picked it up and practically yelled into the transmitter:

"There's no such thing as an enchanted bustle!"

Roxanne said calmly, "How do you come up with these keen insights?"

TWENTY-NINE

"Sorry," I told her. "I thought that was another client calling back. Are you okay?"

"And how many of your cases involve ladies' undergarments?"

"Not as many as I'd like. But I need to know whether you're okay."

"I'm fine. The faculty meeting took place over breakfast at the Left Tackle, and I haven't been on campus all day. After the mess last night, it seemed a wise policy to stay away for a while. I just got your message on my door, assuming that was you."

"It was, via the desk clerk."

"What's been happening?"

I knew I'd have to ask her about Rebecca Chatterton before long, but I decided to hold back on what I'd learned. No good reason; just instinct. I did ask her whether she'd ever met a guy named Flunk Vanderhovel.

"He's a flunky for Slab," she said. "Thus, the name, I imagine."

"Actually, it has more to do with his academic accomplishments."

"What about him?"

"Early this afternoon, he stopped by my office to shoot me."

"What? Are you all right?" There was real concern in her voice.

"I'm not shot. Or otherwise dead. I tricked him into dropping his gun. Do you know whether Slab has Flunk doing errands at Saint Opie's?"

"He has Flunk deliver envelopes and packages to the church from time to time. Anticipating your next question, I don't know what's in them."

"The priest at Saint Opie's denied knowing Flunk. Do you think that's credible?"

"I couldn't judge, but I'd think the priest would have met him by now. Mostly, and this is just barroom talk, Slab uses Flunk when he needs to intimidate a city councilman or scare an embalming fluid salesman. As far as Flunk executing people, I haven't heard anything like that. Why did he want to kill you?"

"He wouldn't say, but I know it was Slab who put him up to it. I'm not sure how Slab found out about me. One of his cronies at the bowling alley must have recognized my face. Another thug may be bearing down on you right now."

"I wouldn't be shocked."

"Maybe it's time to go to the police," I said.

"Absolutely not," she said forcefully. "I thought I made that clear."

"You did, but things change, don't they?"

She left that one unanswered. A few beats went by.

"There's another wrinkle here," I told her. "I've received two death threats, definitely targeting me and not you."

"Oh, no. How did they get to you? What did they say?"

"They were stuffed into the mail slot at my office. It appears I'm about to suffer lethal consequences for getting tangled up with you. Funny thing is, the first threat was here a few hours before Flunk Vanderhovel came over to whack me. But the way it turned out, I don't think he was the one who had delivered it."

"Why not?"

"Because he denied it even when he had no reason to. Might have been a habit of denying everything, I suppose."

"And there was a second threat?"

"That one came in hours later, after Flunk had been arrested for vandalism."

"Wait, I would have thought attempted homicide."

"To keep things confidential, I had to get him out of the way without leaking the whole story." I explained about Flunk shattering a shop window and getting hauled off by the cops. "My point is that while he was in custody, another threat found its way into my mail slot."

"That does seem odd," she said. "Unless Slab delivered the death threats himself. Or he had one man deliver them and another man try to kill you."

"Are you assuming now that the threats are coming from Slab?"

"Who else?"

"He seems like the top candidate. He's violent and he's jealous. But I'd like to be certain. I'm told Slab has an office on church premises. Did he mention that to you?"

"No," Roxanne said. "He didn't discuss business with me."

"Is he very religious?"

"I never got that impression. Could be that he maintains ties at Saint Opie's just for the funerals. I've heard him schmoozing about dead people going to heaven, but it might have been lip service."

"Well, he's basing some type of operation at the church. I was there today and when I grilled the priest about it, he tried to drug me. Then he and his troops tried to smash my brains."

"Come on, Jack. That seems extreme, even for them."

"Trust me. They really don't like brains down there."

"So, they're covering up for Slab?"

"Feels like it. And I'm wondering whether his church hideaway is holding some secrets. If I can find it, maybe I'll come across a clue linking him to the death threats."

"Such as?"

"I don't know yet. The same rough paper? The same manic doodling? Notes on the sorrowful hound and the feckless moon?"

"You may get lucky," Roxanne said. "I'd be interested in seeing what other transgressions he's up to. Tax evasion, money laundering, anything illegal."

"Now you *want* the law involved?"

"In Slab's life, not in mine. He can't hurt me while he's under a close watch by the police. Question: If there's no damning evidence in his office, will you confront him directly?"

"You mean show him the threats?"

"I mean show him your gun. And tell him you're onto him."

I gave it some consideration. "You're right about contacting him, although he'd answer vague accusations with vague denials. I could try to finesse him instead, maybe get an unintentional admission out of him. But not on his turf at the castle or the mortuary."

"This confrontation — is it going to be in some dark alley?" She was a girl who liked drama.

"No. I'm hoping to catch him where there are plenty of people around. That should make him less trigger-happy."

"Hmmm." She sounded a little disappointed. "It didn't work that way at Hunchback Lanes."

"It did when the crowd spilled into the parking lot. After that, only two shots were fired. Incidentally, it would be helpful to have you along while I'm looking for Slab."

"Are you out of your mind? The man is obsessed with murdering me!"

"I'm not talking about setting you up in front of him. You know his patterns, his haunts. I'd like to keep you close enough to guide a search. If he's not in the first place we check, he could be in the second or third."

"I suppose that makes sense."

"For starters, where is Slab likely to be this evening?"

"Oh, God," she said. "You want to drag me to the lawnmower races?"

"It's not the Royal Ascot, but it's perfect for what we need."

"I thought you were planning to search his covert office."

"Locating it could take days, but after tonight that may not be necessary. If I can wheedle Slab into making the wrong remark, he'll realize he's incriminating himself. He'll have to back off."

"That's pretty optimistic," she said. "He's not the most reasonable guy."

"How else can I end this quickly?"

"You got rid of one killer. Can't you get rid of another?"

"Sure, I could always take him out with a sniper's rifle."

She was quiet for a long time. I tapped on the handset.

"Roxanne?"

"I was waiting for the details," the lady said.

"We're both playing cute and we probably shouldn't. Are you available?"

"For tonight? I'll be ready at my hotel by eight, but you shouldn't rely too much on negotiations with Slab. Once anyone crosses him, he never lets it pass. Whichever way your powwow goes, I'll still be at risk. And even if you can avoid a shootout, you won't be free from the trouble he can stir up for you."

"Are you saying a shootout is my best option?"

"I'm saying Slab has a lot of connections. And influence with people who can inflict economic damage. I've seen him ruin people's careers."

I sent an audible shrug through the phone.

"In my case," I said, "that's already been taken care of."

THIRTY

With some spare time and an appetite, I got my bucket of bolts out of the lot and let it wander over to a roadhouse across town. Dinner was better than lunch, but it would have had to be. Back in the car, I looped around a few blocks in a figure eight to make sure I wasn't being tailed. Then I headed in the direction of the Punt Returner.

On the car radio, a commercial featured the shrill voice of a local retailer who would have us believe he was operating on a colossal scale. To hear him tell it, he bought stereos, TVs and major appliances at tremendous volume and sold below cost. He didn't care if his business plan was bound to plunge him into bankruptcy. All he cared about was passing the savings on to us. As loudly as possible.

I switched the channel and found some news. There was a story on another odd death, a millworker run through by a forklift. This one had taken place first thing in the morning, when a priest was down at the mill to bless the machine. The unidentified priest told the station that the forklift inexplicably lunged at its driver just after he had climbed down from it to kneel in prayer. Somehow one of the forks ran the driver through. Well, I asked myself, was the forklift idling at the time? And if it was, did someone or something bump it into gear? Were there other witnesses? The radio announcer apparently didn't think those issues were important. He did report that church officials believed the forklift was possessed by demons. The name of the victim was withheld, pending notification of family travelling overseas.

Earlier, Father Timothy had mentioned having a rough day without offering any details. He'd been stalling me every way he could, and if he had seen a fatality that morning, you'd think he would have told me the story just to kill time. He didn't. The witness was probably some other priest from some other parish.

At the Punt Returner, I drove to the rear of the building and coasted past Roxanne's room. I ducked the Mustang under a carport and watched.

Nobody came driving in behind me. I puttered away from the port and parked in an outlying stall, walked over to Unit 124 and rang the bell.

Roxanne opened the door. The sight of her hit me like a shock wave.

She wore a thin, airy blouse in hot pink, with a chasm of a neckline and a sash knotted loosely at the midriff. There was a silver chain with turquoise gemstones hanging between the contours of her breasts. Below all that was pair of white shorts that barely fulfilled their legal responsibilities. She wore tan shoes with high heels and a latticework of straps laced up over the ankles. Her blond hair was fluffed out, her red lipstick matched her nails and her eyeshadow was a pre-coital shade of blue. When she got a good look at me, her hand went to her mouth and her eyes got wide.

"My God, what happened to your face?"

"Crucifix across the cheekbone," I said. "This afternoon at Saint Opie's. Like I said, the people down there mean business."

She pulled the door farther back and invited me into her suite.

"Can I get you anything for it?" she said sweetly.

"No, I'll be fine."

"Somebody at Saint Opie's hit you with a crucifix?"

"I got into a skirmish over Thomas Aquinas and his five proofs."

"Really?"

"It's a rough place. Always has been. But that's a long story." I reached into my coat pocket and came out with her scarf. "You left this in my car the other night."

"Sorry about that."

"I was glad you did. On the way home, the scent of it made me feel like you were still with me."

She gave me an affectionate smile and thanked me. I gestured toward her outfit.

"Is this what you wear when you want to go unnoticed?" She was as understated as a riot.

"Do you think I should tone it down?"

"It may not matter," I told her. "You'd get undivided attention even if you were wearing camouflage."

"Nice of you," she smiled.

There was no reason to assume she had been thinking of me when she picked out her clothes for the evening, but I couldn't help feeling that she was working me again. Why, I didn't know. My job now was to persuade Slab Kapowski to leave her alone. I could have asked her what else she wanted from me, but I figured she wouldn't give me a straight answer anyway.

"If everything goes well," I said, "you'll be in the car with the doors locked when I'm talking with Slab."

That was true, but the other truth was that I didn't want her to change a thing. Too much of her was just right for me.

"Sit down for a minute," she said.

She had eliminated the usual Packer themes from the suite's living room and customized it with archeological curiosities on the tables and paintings you would never see on the walls of the standard hotel. There was a tidy kitchenette and a compact dining area. In another room, behind a nearly closed door, I could see a bedspread so soft and sumptuous that I wanted to dive into it.

"You put a lot of effort into this place," I said, "especially for an emergency hideout."

"It got to be a hobby for me. Anyway, I wanted it to be comfortable in case I ever needed to spend much time here. And I was almost sure I would."

"Some of these paintings belong in a modern art museum. They couldn't have been here when you checked in."

"They're my own work." She blushed a little.

One of her larger paintings had a tropical motif. In the foreground, there were flat green silhouettes of bamboo stalks crossing each other. The focal point knifed into darkness. Just short of the darkness there was a monolithic stone face, almost obscured by leafy vines. To the side of the stone face a light glinted in the eye of some amorphous animal lying in wait. The work was done in a primitive style, but it wasn't merely a cartoon version of a rain forest.

"This reminds me of Rousseau," I said. "Only more emotional."

She looked a little surprised, though not impressed.

"I would have thought your knowledge of art was limited to a rack of comic books. How did you know about Henri Rousseau?"

"I was being chased by assassins one day and I ducked into an art gallery."

"Is it asking too much to have a serious conversation with you?"

"I thought we were having one. Look, if Slab is at the races tonight, you may be waiting in the car for a fairly long time while I go into the stands. You may want to bring something to read."

She took a volume of Kierkegaard off a shelf, dropped it into her purse and she was ready. I stood and walked out into the heat as she locked up. The white Camaro was parked in front of her suite, but I didn't say anything about the Rebecca Chatterton registration. Another topic for another day.

We walked out to my car. I was watchful as we drove off. We got onto Highway 41 and stayed on that until we hit Kostelnik Road, bearing north toward the race track at the county fairgrounds. Roxanne didn't talk much on the way, and I could feel her brooding about the prospect of being anywhere near Slab.

Farms and woodland slipped by in the evening light. I tried to soften the mood by pointing out the tall sumac growing beside the road. "There are miles of this stuff. The leaves get to be a deep red when the colors change in late September and early October. You'll enjoy it."

She said, "We can enjoy it together if we live that long."

THIRTY-ONE

As we approached Bovine Downs, Roxanne snickered at the sign arching over the entrance. "What's with the name?"

"Haven't you seen that sign before?"

"No, I was always able to talk my way out of coming here with Slab."

"The name was somebody's notion of a tribute because the fairgrounds used to be a cow pasture."

"That's the dumbest business decision I've ever heard," she said.

"The public proved you right. When the track and stadium opened decades ago, the builders wanted to race greyhounds. The name of the place made people think they were racing cows instead. Nobody showed up for that in spite of the advertising, and the investors lost their shirts. The bleachers rotted under the sun and snow, but they were never torn down. A few years ago, somebody re-opened the track with a different scheme in mind. The new promoters tried to call it something else, but the old name stuck anyway. One of those historical insults or embarrassments that people celebrate after a while. Now they have riding-lawnmower races in the summer and snowmobile races in the winter."

"Just like they do on the front lawn at Versailles," she said under her breath.

There were hundreds of cars in the lot and hundreds of people walking toward the ticket windows. I swung wide of the parking attendants funneling cars into neat rows and circled into a vendor's stall near the grandstand. I parked the car and dug into my trunk to pull out one of the magnetic signs I had stashed there. I chose *"ACME SPECIAL EVENTS"* because the moniker was meaningless enough to cover any number of things. With the sign slapped onto the driver's door, I was hopeful that the security people wouldn't get huffy about where I'd parked. I reached in to plug my key in the ignition and invited Roxanne to slide over into the bucket seat at the controls.

I said, "Are you okay with a manual?"

"Of course." She was limber enough to get over the gear shifter easily.

"Drive out of here the moment you sense any trouble."

"I'm not going to leave you behind," she said.

"But you should. I have a gun and I don't think you brought one."

"Good point." She told me she'd be fine and pulled the Kierkegaard out of her bag.

The heat was wearing off but the air was still sticky. Clouds of tiny insects swirled in shafts of slanting light. I looked up at the rear of the stadium. Green polyethylene tarpaulins rose at least thirty feet, covering the bones of the structure. Breaking over its upper rim were strains of country music, with twanging guitars and a mush-mouthed vocal.

Bubba turns on the TV and sets hisself down,
Watchin' Fords and Chevies go 'round and 'round.
He's a left-turn junkie, he's a hardcore fan.
Hell, he's found hog heaven, he's a NASCAR man.

Leaving Roxanne in the car, I walked over to the ticket sellers, laid out a few dollars and went in at the turnstiles. The country song was louder now.

Bubba sure loves watchin' guys changin' them tahrs.
He loves cripplin' crashes and disfigurin' fahrs.
And he loves them drivers 'cause they got enough balls
To go a hundred and ninety right into them walls.

Inside the gates and under the slanting framework of the stands, a gaggle of gearheads milled around a monster truck on display. The vehicle's body sat high over enormous tires, a rugged chassis, a big-block engine and eight chrome exhaust pipes. The lower half of the rig was caked with dried muck from the previous night's festivities. Apparently, its driver had won a contest to see who could pull the heaviest load of logs through a muddy bog, the truest test of a man and his creations. On the sides of the huge truck, brash lettering touted it as "*The Colossus of Roads.*" I assumed the joke slid by nine out of ten onlookers. Maybe it had also gone past the guy who did the lettering.

The majority of the surrounding crowd fell into an older demographic. Many of the women had pear-shaped haircuts that left stubble at the back of the neck. They'd tell you the style was easy to take care of, though there wasn't any point in taking care of a style like that. Down from the hair, there were ill-advised halter tops or nylon pullovers with their seams under pressure. There were khaki shorts in billows or spandex pants that were stretched beyond reason. Below puffy legs, there were mostly plastic sandals or canvas slip-ons fraying at the knuckles of the toes.

Most of the men wore baseball caps with logos advertising the Packers, hardware stores, gasoline additives or tractor companies. Some guys had buttoned shirts fighting to contain bellies that ballooned out over smothered belt buckles. Others had loose tee shirts with garish graphics or inane slogans. Across the gamut, they wore faded blue jeans. They stood in dirty sneakers or rough clodhoppers with knobby treads.

Me, I was wearing a gray suit, a burgundy tie and polished black shoes. In this bunch, that made me stick out like the Chancellor of the Exchequer.

Above us, the grandstands were showing their age. They had been built quickly and cheaply in the 1950s. I had been up top two summers earlier on a case, and I noticed at the time that the wooden benches were disintegrating. Flaking green paint hadn't covered their jagged edges even then. I estimated that half the seats in the stadium were now ready to spall off a sharp splinter.

I walked between two tiers of bleachers and then through a tunnel to the infield of the track. On a stage facing the banked seating, the country band was wrapping up their stock car song. The rest of their playlist was certain to touch upon hoedowns, honkytonks, hootin' and hollerin' and girls in skimpy cutoffs. And probably a shotgun in the rear window of a big ol' pickup.

About twenty yards from that, there was a mechanical bull surrounded by a bed of sawdust and a ring of drinkers urging each other to get on the thing's back. I watched the show for a few minutes. The bull took on all comers, with an operator off to one side starting each ride slowly. Every time a new rider looked like he had things under control, the operator gradually amped up the power. The bull thrashed and spun until it threw the pretender onto the sawdust. Some of the thrown riders jumped up. Some stayed limp as friends dragged them off.

I couldn't figure the wild west fetish in this area, four states north of Texas and two east of the Badlands. It wasn't just the usual myths of Americana. Or the television reruns of *"Rawhide"* and *"Wagon Train."* It was the fake rodeo here at the fairgrounds, the buckeroo music galloping through the radio waves, the dancers in fancy boots two-stepping their way through the rustic saloons, the cowboy hats that — judging from the yahoos who wore them — could suck the brain cells right out of your head. The local economy was dominated by factories, urban construction and service industries. Sure, there were wide open spaces. But the rural countryside was gridded with dairy farms and agricultural fields, not horse ranches. Life on the outskirts was strictly about milking Holsteins and raising corn, and there might not have been any call for a bronco buster within five hundred miles.

Of course, I had to admit this was no place for a private eye, either.

I walked back through the tunnel and went up a long flight of stairs into the growing, chattering mob. I kept climbing to a walkway at the top of the bleachers. On my way along the length of it I carefully scanned the rows below me. There was no sign of Slab Kapowski, but the first race was still a while off and the seats hadn't filled up yet.

At the far upper corner of the stands, I spotted Betty Betz, whose real name I never knew. She was middle-aged and squared off. Above a plain frock, she sported a wide-brimmed scarlet hat with a twelve-inch ostrich feather dyed the same color. The showy headdress didn't reflect her taste. It was a practical trademark, a beacon for customers trying to find her among the rabble.

I was lucky the red hat caught my eye, because good bookies always had inside information.

THIRTY-TWO

Betting on the lawnmower races was prohibited, but thousands of dollars were wagered anyway. Betty Betz was the one to give you the straight line. She could handle your action herself or pipe you through to a high roller in Milwaukee. She carried some clout — and a code of ethics. It wasn't wise for losers to run out on Betty, but if her clientele won, their winnings were as safe with her as they would have been in the First National Bank.

She was writing something in a notebook and wishing good luck to a big farmer in denim overalls and a John Deere hat that roughly matched the green paint on the bleachers. The dirty cap was tilted back on the farmer's head. The front of it was pitched high enough for me to see the sweat stains on the underside of the bill. The stains were darkest along the inner curve and receded out to the brim like the rings on a tree stump. The farmer tucked his betting slip into a pocket and puffed hard on a cigar the size of a torpedo. He blew tobacco exhaust into the thick air above some spectators. As the smoke settled over them, they coughed and winced. The sodbuster stirred and hauled his weight down an aisle, leaving a plume of Dutch Masters stink behind him. I walked over to Betty, who was waving the notebook to give her lungs a little relief.

"You should get yourself a gas mask," I said as I approached.

She looked up at me with a discounted smile.

"Yeah," she said. "The cigar wasn't the worst of it. That guy's been in the barn too long. But there's always a chance a tornado could come through and clear the air before the last race. Good to see you, Harbinger. How about those Packers?"

"How about those Philadelphia Stars?"

"I guess it's been a while since we talked. You're into the USFL, are you?"

"Religiously."

She laughed and shook her head.

"So, you pray for the Stars to win," she said, "and curse God's cruelty when they lose."

"You know me."

"Nobody's more devout. But I actually see people praying about football, basketball, even these lawnmower races. Here I am, looking at the money and the elbow grease that goes into setting up a suspension or tuning up a motor for maximum performance. Some riders insist on quality. Others don't. And then, of course, I'm looking at the nerve of the riders and which one of them woke up this morning with a hangover. The knothead players in the stands aren't thinking about any of that. Then they lose their money and wonder what went wrong. Christ, what I do for a living is not only illegal, it's almost dishonest."

"As they say, Betty, you're preaching to the choir."

"Not that you're a betting man," she said, "but you wouldn't want to abandon your scruples and lay something down, would you?"

"Nah. Hardly a dollar to spare. Speaking of changing the subject, what are you hearing about death threats?"

"Not a thing," she said, frowning. "Although some of the rodents I know are squeaking about fatalities that don't smell right. I imagine you've heard."

"They're supposedly explainable," I said.

"That's what we're being told. One guy gets eaten by muskies. Not a chance. Another guy gets his hand cut off in a paper mill accident. Maybe. These things happen. Then a third guy gets run through by his own forklift. That one's a howler."

"I agree," I said. "But they're not my cases. I'm working on something else."

Betty gave me a level look. "The cops don't seem to be working on anything at all. As far as what *you're* working on, your case is whatever's under the rotten logs you turn over."

"What do you mean by that?"

"I couldn't stay in business if I betrayed a confidence."

"I'm still in the dark," I said.

"I hear you've been mixing it up with some pretty nasty people. Why do you think they're so mad at you?"

"Slab Kapowski thinks I stole his girlfriend. He sent his trigger man over to kill me, but it didn't work out that way."

"And the others? The ones down at Saint Opie's?"

"You're good, Betty. You do keep your ear to the ground."

"I hear things. So, what about Opie's?"

"I'm not sure. They didn't like me asking about Slab. That much was obvious. But who knows? Maybe they were pounding my head just because of the way I misbehaved in school years ago."

"Could be," she said. "But you wouldn't want to find that head of yours rolling around on the floor."

"Well, that goes without saying, Betty. Or at least it goes without clarifying."

"Another thing that's gone without saying is the name of the third corpse, the forklift driver."

"The last I heard on the radio," I said, "the authorities weren't releasing the identity of the victim."

"I hear it was Pete Pulaski."

The words hit me like a punch in the stomach.

"Jesus," I said. "I knew that guy fairly well back in grade school."

Betty pulled down her brim and looked around to make sure no one was listening. "And what were Pete's religious convictions?"

"He never believed any of it."

Betty nodded her agreement. I was surprised that she knew anything at all about Pete. "If you heard the story on the radio, you heard the statement the priest gave to the reporter. Makes you scratch your head a little, doesn't it?"

"It does," I said. "What the hell was Pete Pulaski doing kneeling in prayer during the blessing of a goddamn forklift?"

"There you go," she said.

"The radio newscast didn't identify the priest. I suppose you're going to tell me it was Father Timothy from Saint Opie's."

"That would be an assumption a lot of smart people would make," Betty said carefully.

"Holy Christ."

"Look, half of what I hear is insinuation, and most of that comes from outright speculation. The only confirmed fact I can give you is the name of the guy who got his guts run through. And that part, you'd get in tomorrow's newspaper anyway. But no matter when that little piece of information leaks, doesn't it make you wonder how the Pulptown Police Department could leave this alone?"

"They wouldn't if you were the one behind the big desk," I said. "But there's a case I have to take care of first. Do you know where Slab sits in the stands? I need to talk with him face to face."

"Talk him out of having you killed?"

"Maybe trick him into an admission. If that fails, try to make nice."

"Front box, middle section," she told me. "Good luck."

"Thanks, Betty. I'll knock out my business with Slab and then I'll ask around on the other thing. What do I owe you?"

"Zilch. But take care when you do the asking. On all of them."

"I get the feeling you know something more about this," I said.

"Only what I told you about Pete. I knew him because he was a player. A smart one. I don't know a thing about the other guys who turned up dead."

"Then why the cautionary note?"

"General principles when people are dropping. If you don't push, questions get you nowhere. If you push too hard, questions get you killed."

THIRTY-THREE

I left Betty and went back to the middle of the high walkway. I descended a stairway almost to the bottom of the bleachers and spotted Slab Kapowski's hawklike profile. He was on his feet and leaning forward on a railing to watch the lawnmower drivers rev their engines at the starting line. He breathed in deeply through a cigarette and expelled a dirty cloud through his nose. There wasn't any substitute for Roxanne Delaplaine by his side. There wasn't any Flunk Vanderhovel, either, but there was another bruiser in his place. This one was smaller than Flunk because almost everyone was smaller than Flunk. But he was younger, leaner, more muscular, and his eyes appeared to be operating at a somewhat higher level. I sidled up behind Slab and said hello.

He turned around and his bland curiosity hardened into hatred. I could tell he wanted to lash out, but not in public. His lips had a tight grip on the cigarette. The tip of the butt smoldered, and Slab's gray, metallic eyes squinted behind the rising vapors. He took a long draw and pulled the little white tube away from his face in a careful, deliberate motion. He blew smoke at me, then casually flicked an ash in my direction. The ash didn't hit me but he knew the gesture would.

"You abdicated my girlfriend," he said in a restrained growl.

He must have meant *abducted*. "I knew you'd say that," I told him.

"You sucker punched me and then you dropped a bowling ball on my ankle and then you got my best guy locked up."

"I thought *I* was your best guy," the muscle said.

Slab blinked hard and turned to him.

"You're new, Rance. We don't even know about you yet."

"How's Flunk doing?" I asked the undertaker. "Did the cops have to knock out a wall to fit him in a cell?"

"I liberated him out already," Slab said impatiently. He dropped the cigarette butt and crushed it dead under his shoe. "Never mind about Flunk. Where's Roxanne?"

"How would I know? After I got her out of the bowling alley, I drove her to the Greyhound station and dropped her off. They have buses leaving in all directions at all hours. By now she could be heading anywhere from the Yukon to the Yucatan."

The big roughneck stepped forward eagerly.

"This guy's a pipsqueak," he told Slab. "I could go take her back real quick,"

"Shut up, Rance."

"That's a slick name," I said to the muscle. "Is it short for Rancid?"

The thug leaned in toward me but Slab held him back.

"Not here," Slab told him in a subdued voice. "Too many people around." Then he bored in on me again. His voice was quiet but serrated. "Why did you infiltrate your probiscis into my affairs?"

"What else could I do?" I said, not as quietly. "It looked to me like you were going to kill her."

Slab twisted his face, looked around and pressed his open palms downward against the air, trying to lower the volume of the conversation.

"I'll extradite that girl back here, one way or the other," he said.

"One way or the other," Rance parroted.

His boss drilled him a look. "Zip it, Rance."

Slab aimed his flinty eyes at me and whispered straight from the spleen.

"As far as you're concerned, Harbinger, you're deceased, disoperational. The spectrum of death lays dark across your path."

Specter of death? I didn't correct him. "That was some nice phrasing, Slab. You ever consider the literary life?"

"Don't try to obliterate," he said.

"Because you'll come after me, right? After all, you're in the same America as me."

Once again, Slab whispered savagely.

"What the hell are you uttering about? Of course, I'm in the same America as you! How many Americas are there?"

"There's North America and South America," Rance pointed out impressively.

"I told you to shut up." Slab said to him.

"There you have it," I said. "North America and South America. Don't you despise that kind of duplicity?"

The last word held him up for a second.

"Indelibly," he said, one-upping me. "As in you stop breathing."

"Calm down a minute, Slab. You don't have any beef with me. If I had let you haul off and smash her head in, she'd be dead and you wouldn't have her anyway. And in the middle of a bowling alley filled with solid citizens? No police connections in this country could have gotten you out of it. I actually did you a favor."

"And that's why you came here? To tell me what a pal you are?"

"More or less," I said. "I know you sent Flunk over to my office to kill me and I thought you and I should talk it out before something like that happens again."

"Very mentalistic, Harbinger. But you're dead anyway. The cloud of mortality rains hard on your picnic. Even now, the vultures gather."

"You should really write this stuff down in your diary."

"Don't try to flatter me up," he said.

"Although it would have been better for you to say the *ants* gather."

"What?"

"Ants, not vultures," I said. Goes with the picnic. Makes a tighter metaphor."

"Oh yeah? Well, why don't you forget about a tighter metal floor and pay me for your funeral right now?"

Below us, the lawnmowers were chomping at their chain drives, making a raucous nuisance. Rance leaned in toward Slab.

"Hey, Mr. Kapowski, you think we should say a prayer to Saint Opie so he can make sure our guy wins the first race?"

"Don't be lugubrious," Slab bullied him. "Go out and have a cigarette."

"I don't smoke," Rance told him.

Slab gave him the big stare. He reached into a pocket and came out with a pack of Chesterfields. He shook one out and handed it to Rance.

"Then go out and give it to somebody who *does* smoke."

For a moment, Rance looked puzzled.

"Can you handle that?" Slab asked him.

A spark of recognition lit up Rance's face. "Is the pope Italian?" he answered reassuringly. He smirked at me, then went out into the aisle and up the stairs toward the nearest exit.

I felt as if those picnic ants were crawling up my spine. The cigarette was probably meant for someone else I knew. When Flunk Vanderhovel wasn't holding a gun, he was holding a cancer stick. He'd been that way since his third try at fifth grade. I hadn't counted on Flunk getting sprung this soon. Or being on duty with a broken trigger finger. He probably knew my car, and if he could find that, he'd find Roxanne.

Slab eyed me closely, looking for a reaction. I blanked out my face as best I could. What I had going for me was a little time. If Rance could locate Flunk down there somewhere in the huge lot, it would take Flunk a while to find my Mustang. I squelched the urge to get out of there quickly and run down to where I'd left it parked.

On stanchions high above us, lights woke up, glowed faintly and then brightened. Spectators near us yipped and clamored, even though in another minute they'd be wishing they had gone bowling instead. Down on the track, the gates opened and the mowers moved out slowly.

"They're off, and chugging," I said to Slab. "How can you watch this stuff?"

He ignored me as the lead drivers rambled down the dirt and kicked up dust for the trailing drivers to swallow. The crowd noise bumped up a smidge, but within the first hundred yards the fans were grumbling. The mowers rounded the first turn like arthritic possums. Out beyond the infield, the machines dragged their way down the back-stretch and the audience got even more surly. As the mowers came around the second turn, one of them blew a gasket. It spewed black smoke and the throngs cheered for the smoke because it was the next best thing to a pileup. This went on for three laps without even one crash to keep the crowd engaged. Then the leaders plodded into the home stretch and finally crossed the finish line. The public-address announcer said it was a photo finish, but he was overstating the suspense by half a length. When it was done, Slab cursed his luck and ripped a betting slip into shreds.

"You should have tried the prayer," I told him.

"Mutate yourself," he said angrily. "That means *shut up*, if you don't happen to be assimilated."

"You're blaming the wrong person for your girlfriend running out."

"Yeah, well, evacuate your ass away from here," he said. "And spend every second worrying about getting shot through the head."

"You're a real sweetheart, Slab."

"Fuck off, Harbinger. Go quiet into that nocturnal night, from which no man can escape the … what is it? … Christ, I had this a second ago. Anyway, get lost."

I'd been dismissed without rushing off on my own, and that was good. I backed onto the steps of the main aisle, climbed to a portal in the stands and then descended a connecting stairway to ground level. I moved as casually as I could before stopping and turning quickly at the bottom of the stairs. I couldn't see anyone following me. I picked up my pace, found my exit and walked out.

THIRTY-FOUR

My car was still there and Flunk's oversized vehicle was nowhere in sight. Roxanne was in the driver's seat, alive and reading Kierkegaard. She was a little alarmed when I rushed up and pulled the magnetic sign off the car door. She handed me the keys and I opened the trunk to stow the sign. I slammed the lid and got in behind the wheel as she slid over. I cranked the ignition and moved out into the lot.

"Keep an eye out for an old gray armored truck," I told her.

"I didn't hear any shots," Roxanne said.

"Maybe you will now."

"What happened up there?"

"Like I told you" I said, "I tried to reason with him."

"And how did that work out?"

"Not so well," I admitted. "We've got another problem."

We neared the lone exit. I asked her to keep her head down, and she scrunched down in her seat. Once I was through the open gate, I stepped harder on the gas. I thought we were all right until I picked up a glimpse of the armored truck in my rearview mirror. Flunk must have been hiding behind a billboard at the gate, waiting for my Mustang to pass by. Now he was pulling away from there and racing up behind us on the gravel driveway that led out to the paved road. It was getting darker, but I could see in my mirror that he was alone. I turned onto the pavement at Kostelnik and forced whatever power my heap could muster. The first exit from Kostelnik was a left at Bart Starr Pass. I took it in a headlong downshift with the back of my car skidding badly. The road curved around some shallow mounds and then got us into the woods. More curves hugged the bank of a winding creek. I could see the armored truck chasing us, now with its headlights in my mirrors.

"What's going on?" Roxanne asked me from down in her seat.

"Flunk's been bailed out of jail and he's on the job again. He's back there in his truck."

"How far back?"

I didn't answer. I felt a thump against the car as I heard a gunshot.

"Nothing serious," I told Roxanne, hoping it was true.

"Can't you get any more speed out of this thing?" she demanded.

"Sure, all we have to do is get the engine rebuilt."

There was a second shot, but it wasn't on target. I raced through an S-curve and braked where the road dipped toward the edge of a ravine. I hit a sharp right turn and almost lost it in the opposing lane. I steadied the car and flicked my eyes up to the mirror for a moment. Flunk was coming fast. A sharper left surprised me. I charged into the breakneck curve in second gear, held it and upshifted for a straightaway. Behind us, there was screeching and shredding and then something like a crack of thunder. I checked the mirrors again. There were no headlights. I slowed and took a longer look into the darkness of where we'd been.

"Why are we stopping?" Roxanne wanted to know.

"He didn't manage that last turn," I said. "I think he crashed into the trees."

I made a U-turn, headed back and found a gash in the thickets where the big truck had apparently blasted through. I couldn't see the truck from the road, and I realized it must have gone down an embankment.

I parked on the shoulder. "I'm going in," I told Roxanne.

"Right behind you," she said.

I ran across the pavement carrying my gun and a flashlight. Once I was into the trees, I saw a pool of light from a single headlight down the slope, near a creek. I went stumbling and sliding through low brush and toward the truck. The grille and a front fender were mangled around the broad base of an immovable tree. In the flashlight beam, I could see that the driver's door had been blown away from its rusted hinges. Nobody in the cab. Flunk wouldn't have been the type to wear a seatbelt. He must have been thrown against that door and all the way through the opening when if broke off. My flashlight searched the area. Near the vehicle, there were broken branches protruding like spears from a fallen tree. A couple of the sharp limbs were wet with blood, and a fragment of clothing clung to one of them. The flashlight beam finally landed on Flunk.

He had tumbled farther into the weeds. His back rested against the mossy, decomposing trunk of another grounded tree. I went down to him. He was looking my way but not focusing. Blood dripped from his nostrils onto his patchy mustache. My vision instinctively went to his hands. The left one was empty. On the right one, a large cast wrapped around his index finger and extended past the base of his thumb. He'd been driving and shooting one-handed. His gun lay a few feet away from him, out of reach. I dropped mine into my shoulder holster.

A bone had poked through one of his sleeves. A swatch of his shirt had been ripped away and what remained was soaked with blood. His legs were splayed at the wrong angles, and more dark liquid squirted from a slash in one of them. The blood was draining into a puddle where he sat. Too much of a puddle. There was nothing any makeshift bandages or even a tourniquet could do. He had seconds at most.

I bent down beside him and tried to lock in on his eyes.

"Flunk, it's Jack Harbinger."

"Yeah. I was … suppos'ta … shoot you." His voice was sputtering.

"Someone is getting help," I lied. Lying was the one thing I could do for him.

"She's gonna kill me," he said.

"Who's going to kill you?"

He looked terrified. "Mother," was the only word he could get out clearly. The rest of it was a stretched-out, agonized hiss. He coughed up blood. His head slumped and after a moment Flunk Vanderhovel wasn't there anymore.

Maybe it was fitting that his resting place was one of the rotten logs Betty Betz had talked about.

The ravine was silent in the thick night air. Not a burble from the slow-moving creek, not a chirp from a cricket. I straightened up and stood over the body, reflecting on what little I knew of the guy — mostly his career preparation at Saint Opie's. One day, during a classroom uprising, Sister Pugnacia had him thwack a kid who was too big for the nun to handle by herself. Flunk hit the kid with a wooden chair and then expressed his disappointment that the chair hadn't splintered into pieces like the ones in the cowboy shows on TV. Even then, he was displaying the abundance of malice and the deficit of smarts you look for in a good henchman. How could his later life have been any different?

Now there was a faint, rough noise in the brush above me. I moved a few steps away from the husk of the man. Roxanne came inching down the embankment, careful not to trip in her high heels. She stopped beside me, clutching my arm and reaching for the flashlight. She shined it over the scene and drew a loud breath.

"He's dead, isn't he?"

"When I got to him, he was bleeding from multiple wounds. There was no way to plug them all. He was gone in no time."

"My God, his arm." she said. "The bone … and he's all … bent out of shape. He must have broken a leg."

I nodded. "No telling what else."

"At least he died doing what he loved to do," she said.

"Getting torn up in a crash?"

"No, silly. Trying to kill people."

THIRTY-FIVE

My footing was better than Roxanne's, and I more or less pulled her up the embankment. We got into the car, turned around and headed away from the fairgrounds again.

"Did Flunk say anything down there?" Roxanne asked.

"Something about his mother, which is strange because I always heard he was an orphan."

"He was probably hallucinating," she told me.

"That must have been it. Right now, we have to find a phone."

"You're not going to call the police!"

"Has to be done," I told her. "I'll keep your name out of it. And mine."

We drove a couple of miles before we came to a small gas station that had closed for the night. There was a phone booth up against the front wall. I called the county sheriff's department and kept talking when the dispatcher tried to get some identification. I told her I'd seen what might have been a car crashing into the woods along Bart Starr Pass, two or three miles east of Gas Guzzle. I hung up before she could ask any more questions.

I sped off with Roxanne and took the first side road I could find. By the time we heard sirens, they were far behind us. I slowed down and took a meandering drive past farms and groves, circling clear of the race track and the accident site.

"That's twice you've saved my life," she said as we drove through the darkness. The windows were open and the warm, heavy air was running its fingers through her hair.

"I'm not so sure about that," I said. "Maybe I only endangered your life by bringing you along tonight. It was pretty clear back there that Slab wanted me dead, but I didn't pick up any sign that he wanted you dead as well. I told Slab that you had already gotten out of town. Maybe he bought the story. Maybe he didn't."

"He lies all the time," she said. "And so he assumes everyone else is lying."

"There was a new sidekick with him," I said. "Have you met a piece of muscle by the name of Rance?"

"No."

"That means Rance wouldn't have recognized you outside the stadium even if he saw you. Unless he'd seen a photograph. He apparently got a message to Flunk, and that's why Flunk was waiting for my Mustang at the gate. When we passed by, you were burrowed down in my passenger seat. Flunk probably wouldn't have seen you or known you were with me."

"So, are you saying the gunshots were for you only?"

"I think so. And I think Slab just wants you back."

"In a box lined with velvet," she said. "He and his men were definitely shooting at both of us outside the bowling alley last night."

"Reflex," I said. "Slab was already angry about your bowling and then you ran out on him. All the shooting went on before any of them had time to think it through."

"No, I'm more and more convinced that Slab intended to kill me a lot earlier."

"Well," I offered, "the way he talks may be one more reason to suspect him. His lingo has the same overwrought quality as the death threats."

"I hadn't noticed."

"Really? It was obvious."

"I suppose I was too upset to be analytical. But you may have something."

"Trouble is," I said, "some of his vocabulary doesn't match. And by the way, is it probiscis or proboscis?"

"What? Do you mean the monkey?"

"Could be the monkey," I said. "Could be long, intruding noses in general."

"It's proboscis. What does that have to do with anything?"

"Something Slab mentioned. Maybe nothing. But I've asked myself a question, and now I'll put it to you. If he wanted to kill you, why hasn't he done it already?"

"Maybe he's getting off on taunting me like a cat playing with a mouse."

"That's the same answer I came up with," I said. "It seemed a little far-fetched when I thought of it, but you're the one who knows him."

We made it from the sticks onto Highway 41 and after a few miles I got off onto the frontage road leading to the Punt Returner. By the time we stopped near her suite and got out of the Mustang, I was satisfied that nobody was tailing us. On a few other counts, I wasn't satisfied at all, but I couldn't make myself talk about them yet. Maybe I was hoping they'd all go away if I ignored them.

"It's still hot," Roxanne said.

"Humid," I said meaninglessly.

I had my mind on something more sultry than the night air, something like what had happened at her threshold the night before. But I was only a guy she had hired. I had been out of line when I'd kissed her, and she might have reconsidered her signals and her response by now. If anything from last night was about to go further, she'd have to be the one to restart it. I walked her to her door, readying myself to endure a frustrated drive back home, back to nothing.

"I'd feel better if you didn't leave me here alone," she said. And in a snap, life was good.

"I suppose I could sleep on your doorstep," I said.

"You can sleep when I'm done with you."

THIRTY-SIX

Roxanne moved in close and laid a kiss on me that accelerated every blood cell in my body. Her tongue touched mine and then probed deeper. My hand pressed against the small of her back and drifted down past the cuffs of her shorts. Her breathing perked up and so did I.

She broke away long enough to dip into her purse, dig below the Kierkegaard and come out with a set of keys. She unlocked the door and let it swing open. Then she took me by a lapel and led me in after her. Letting go, she closed the door behind us, flipped the lock and dropped her purse on a chair.

Outdoor lamps glimmered through sheer curtains, the softened light making her even more beautiful. Anticipation heightened my senses and blotted out most of my foresight.

"There's something I'm not telling you," she said.

"No kidding."

"It's important. And I don't want any secrets between us."

"It'll keep," I said.

"Maybe it will." She smiled like a conspirator and plucked a bottle from a liquor cabinet. She splashed whiskey into two glasses and handed one to me. "Here, you'll need this."

I started on my medicine slowly. She threw hers back in one swoop and set her glass on the cabinet.

When she had first come to my office — not exactly dressed for business but dressed all the same — she had thrilled me just by standing there. Now, impossibly, she was peeling away her pink blouse. Beneath it was a matching bra that was pretty much a launch code in lace. She unbuttoned her white shorts and let them drop to the floor, revealing more pink lace coming up from a deep *V* and riding high over her hips. One foot stepped out of the fallen shorts and the other kicked them across the room. Finally, she undid her ankle straps and shook both shoes loose. She paused, letting her performance take its full effect. Never mind stopping traffic; the girl could have stopped the bull run in Pamplona.

I bottomed out my whiskey and tried to place the tumbler on a table without taking my eyes off her. The empty glass tipped off the table's edge and fell unbroken onto the carpet.

"If I were more secure," I said, "I'd think you were flirting with me."

"Shut up and take off your coat. And your shoulder holster."

I threw them on the couch.

Roxanne grabbed my tie and dragged me into the bedroom, barely giving me time to jettison my loafers. Loosening her grip on me, she tossed the bedspread to the floor. Then she turned on a nightstand lamp and draped something in chiffon over the shade.

Suddenly we were mauling each other. We grappled ourselves onto the bed and melded into a long, feverish kiss. I ran my hands lightly across her back and up to her bra. It took all my training and experience to pop the tiny hooks in one smooth motion.

She burst out of the cups, her nipples on high alert. My heartbeat and respiration were racing toward the red line. I pulled the last wisp of lace down from her hips and threw it aside. The vision of her almost blew the retinas out of my head.

She ripped the tie off my neck and clawed her way through the buttons of my shirt. The shirt and the rest of my clothes flew off in a storm. I gathered her in and kissed her desperately. My mouth went to the warmth of her neck and her breasts. My hand slid down her belly. She was undulating and flowering under my touch.

She rolled me over and looked me in the eyes, letting her hair dangle in my face. Her lips kissed mine and then fluttered down my torso. I was as volatile as a pipe bomb. When she had played me just enough, she raised her head and sassed a smile.

I flipped her onto her back and went in low. I was insane with the scent and the taste of her, and there was a moment when I knew I had every sensation in her body tuned to the tip of my tongue. She arched and tightened and lost herself in waves of tremors before settling in softly. I moved up into her embrace, and when the thrill of entry came it felt like I had never done it before.

It was the height of glory and the depth of depravity. We tore up the sheets and punched holes in the blankets. We were clenching and writhing, bouncing off the bed and doing stunts that should have landed us in traction. A pounding rhythm overtook everything and everyone else in the world, and if there were people in the next room banging back at us and yapping about the noise, we wouldn't have noticed.

A cool surge of lightning ran through me and forced me into my last ecstatic lunges. Then, if she had asked me to wiggle my toes, I couldn't have done it. I was as spent as a drunk's paycheck.

THIRTY-SEVEN

A few minutes later, I was trying to read the currents in her eyes, wondering where all this might go. She closed her lovely blues before I could find any answers.

My motor skills gradually returned. I shifted myself aside and looked around the room. A mirror was fogged, the plaster above the bed was cracked and the mattress had jumped six inches away from the headboard. The nightstand lamp had fallen, so I returned it to its place and turned off the switch. My head plopped onto a pillow. The explosive passion had calmed into a blissed-out equilibrium.

Roxanne was on her back, glowing sunny side up in the faintest of light. She nestled her neck into the crook of my arm and lay there without speaking. Her eyes remained closed but she wasn't asleep. She was squeezing my hand and there was contentment on her face. I listened to her taking deep breaths and letting them out slowly.

Sighs matter.

After a long while I touched her, more gently than before, and she finally broke the silence. "Does '*The Inca Dinca*' mean anything to you?"

"Something they sang in Vaudeville?"

"No," she said, looking over at me. "It's kind of the ancient Andean version of '*The Kama Sutra,*' only less inhibited."

"Never heard of it."

"Few people have," she said. "It was an oral tradition. A Spanish conquistador heard courtesans reciting it and wrote it down in French to hide what he was doing. His manuscript was lost for centuries. A Canadian archeologist discovered it in the 1920s and immediately had a heart attack. It was suppressed on moral grounds, but eccentric collectors passed it around. About fifty years later, it surfaced in Marseilles. That's where I read it. We just went through the first five chapters. Next time we'll do chapters six through ten."

"Christ," I said. "I'll have to get a whole new set of nerves installed."

"You're so sweet."

I ransacked my memory banks for the ups and downs of Inca rituals.

"Is any of this going to involve a sacrifice?" I asked her.

"Every relationship does."

"What I mean is, what happens when '*The Inca Dinca*' hits the last chapter?"

"Well, I'm not going to rip your heart out, if that's what you mean."

"The thought occurred to me."

"That was more of an Aztec thing," she said. "Anyway, I'm beginning to feel a certain fondness for you."

"I don't mind you either."

"Just wait," she cooed. "Chapters six through ten." She yawned, gave me the dreamy eyes and kissed me again. Her lips were warm and soft. She laid her head on her pillow and said, "Do you feel bad about Flunk?"

"Strangely enough, in spite of the fact that he was trying to kill me, I do. It wasn't his fault that he was a big dumb lummox."

"I feel bad too," she said. "If he had a soul and if there's a hell, I wonder if he's there now. He did enjoy terrorizing people."

"So do the nuns."

"Hmmm," she said. "And they're supposed to go straight to heaven."

We were both too tired to go on talking. I reached over to caress her face and kiss her one more time. She had put me in a spell and I would have liked to stay in the moment forever. But it wasn't long until the spell gave way to a deep sleep.

THIRTY-EIGHT

In the morning, sunshine tickled my eyelids. I heard Roxanne setting up camp in the bathroom. The shower started running, and I felt a strong compulsion to search through her desk and her cabinets. I overcame it. I wrestled the mattress into place and pounded three pillows into a backrest against the headboard. Lounging there, I reached for a remote on the nightstand, brought the bedroom TV to life and thumbed into a local news program. On the screen, a man-and-woman tag team recited a script that was supposed to sound conversational but didn't. The segment was midway into a follow-up on yesterday's story about a man getting stabbed to death by a warehouse forklift. They were no longer withholding names. Besides identifying Pete Pulaski as the victim, they had Father Timothy on tape talking about what a nice forklift he'd been blessing and what a fine and reverent person Pete had been. The hell with that. A fine person, I could go with. But reverent — not likely. As long as I had known Pete, he had been a skeptic. And a thorny one at that.

One day back in grade school, a priest made an appearance in class and explained how God had drowned millions of people in The Great Flood because they were wicked. Pete wanted to know why God had hauled off and drowned millions of innocent dogs and cats at the same time. When Pete got around to mentioning all the children God drowned, Sister Fracturina whipped him across the back with a yardstick. This was the way theological debates were sorted out at Saint Opie's.

Pete had been brilliant, but he couldn't tolerate anything his parents would have called formal education. Saint Opie's Elementary School and Holy Sorrows High School across town left such a bad taste in his mouth that he never wanted anything to do with college. At eighteen, he fell into employment as a mule at the Pulptown Supply warehouse. Over the years, he worked his way up to be a forklift driver. He was the kind of guy who read books on archeology just for fun, and forklift pilot seemed like a poor fit for his life's work. But he once told me that all he wanted from a job was a living wage and a chance to be left alone with his thoughts. I wondered what he was thinking in his final moments, and how he found himself on his knees at the wrong end of his machinery.

Now, on the video tape, the priest was saying Pete had finally accepted all the tenets of Catholicism just before his death. "At least he died doing what he loved to do," Father Timothy said to the TV reporter on the scene.

"Getting punctured by a forklift?' the reporter asked.

"No, you idiot, kneeling in prayer."

The circumstances of Pete's death were still unclear, the reporter told us. There was apparently a lot of confusion at the time and the initial news broadcast on the radio had been rushed. As it stood now, nobody was sure whether someone had been driving the forklift or whether it had somehow lurched out on its own.

The program jerked away from the accidental death story and without a moment of respect changed over to sports. There was an interview with a baseball player who said his late mother in heaven had magically lifted the ball over the right field stands, helping him hit that game-winning home run. No interview with the pitcher, who must have resented the dead woman for messing with his earned run average. I nixed the TV.

The shower turned off and after a minute Roxanne came out in a plush white bathrobe. There was a towel turbaned on her head and she got it unfurled. She gave me a few hundred watts of her smile and flicked her robe open for a moment, teasing me. I grabbed at her on my way to the bathroom. When I got out, she was dressed in a breezy white blouse, blue twill shorts and a pair of wedges with ropey trim around the soles. I got dressed and made the bed as she sat down at a vanity to work on her makeup.

"I'll have to head back to my office," I said. "And I'll need a change of clothes."

"Are you going to confront Slab again?"

"No. I've got some checking to do."

"What kind of checking?"

"A bookie at the races last night put me onto something, or at least got my conscience working."

"What about Slab?" she said. "I mean, he sent Flunk out to kill us, didn't he? Or at least to kill *you*." She looked worried, but whether she was worried about me, I couldn't tell.

"There's been a rash of oddball deaths lately," I told her. "They're supposed to be accidental but that's quite a strain when you add them all up. Slab comes into play, if only because he'll profit from the funerals. And he could be involved more aggressively. I get the feeling he's helping to produce the bodies."

"With Slab, you never know," she said.

I sat down in an easy chair across the bedroom and watched her work in the glow of a domestic serenity that I knew would be gone in the next few minutes.

"Last night," I said, "you mentioned there was something you weren't telling me. As I recall, I was too preoccupied to listen."

"I remember it that way too," she said with a sly smile.

"Let's have it."

"Nothing really." She looked away and went back to her eye shadow.

"I've shown some of the death threats to a psychiatrist who also happens to be a connoisseur of the fine arts. The doc said the economy of line in the images is right up there with Picasso."

"Oh, really," Roxanne said. She paused with her makeup brush in the air.

"Not only that, but the headshrinker said the wording is lyrical. Pure poetry."

"What a nice thing to say," she murmured. "I mean, a nice thing to say about Slab."

"The death threats didn't come from Slab," I said.

"But you pointed out the way he speaks. Everything is, sort of, grandiloquence with him. Overwrought, as you put it. Just like the death threats."

"He doesn't have the goods."

"What do you mean?" She wrapped up the makeup and swiveled to face me.

"Probiscis, proboscis," I said.

"Monkeys again?"

"The monkeys and the noses and all the rest of it," I said. "The nomenclature, the lexicon, the vernacular. He uses a lot of 50-cent words but he's getting them all wrong."

"Using them all incorrectly," she said.

"Stay with me here. The death threats had everything right. They would have made it through any copy editor in the Ivy League."

"So, maybe he had some help."

"Who's he going to run it by? Flunk Vanderhovel?"

"Well, I don't know!" Now she was miffed. Her eyes were as beautiful as ever, but they had cooled a few degrees.

"Then there's the artistic flair on top of it."

"Where are you going with this?"

"At first, I blew off what the shrink told me. But the more I thought about her take on it, the more it gnawed at me. And the more right she got."

"Became," Roxanne said.

"The more right she *became*, then. Are you trying to lose your own argument?"

"What argument? What are you driving at?"

"It was you who wrote the death threats, baby."

THIRTY-NINE

"That's ridiculous!" Roxanne said.

"First of all, your story about the church was a little off the rails. You're either the type to light votive candles or the type to take up Kierkegaard and existentialism. Not both."

"You know nothing about the power of ritual," she protested.

"Maybe not, but that's only part of it. There's also the nun who stabbed you with an ice pick because you hadn't folded your hands correctly. I've told you before. The nuns at Saint Opie's don't use Sears Craftsman ice picks."

"Ever?"

"The attack story was a strategy, a way to throw me off or maybe a way to lead me somewhere. Damned if I know why."

"You're not making any sense," the lady shot at me. She got up from the vanity and began pacing. "A nun stabbed me with an ice pick. You've been to Catholic school. I don't know why you find that so hard to believe."

"I wouldn't put it past any of them," I said. "But that won't work."

"Okay then, it was Slab who attacked me. At first, it didn't seem like anything serious. I thought you'd be wasting your time investigating him, so I lied. Then it was too late to go back on my first explanation."

"That won't work either. You bought the ice pick Tuesday morning, just before you hired me. Somebody at Sears took note of the sale because there was a receipt left on the floor. A clerk on his first job out of high school was lying next to it. He was found unconscious behind the cash register after fainting and hitting his head. When he came to, he said he'd seen a goddess. The goddess was you, Roxanne."

"You can't prove that."

"You were on a security camera," I lied. She didn't challenge me. "What did you do, tell him he was handsome?"

She stopped her pacing, glared at me, then softened. She fell theatrically onto the edge of the bed but I didn't go for the bait.

"Oh, all right," she admitted. She sat upright. "I bought an ice pick. So what?"

"And the kid?"

"I didn't flirt with him. I smiled and maybe leaned forward a little."

That would have done the trick. She had more cleavage than the San Andreas Fault.

"Didn't you notice the kid passing out?"

"It happens to me all the time. What am I supposed to do? I can't call an ambulance every time I go shopping."

"The question is *why*," I said.

"Why did he faint?"

"Why the whole ruse with the ice pick?"

"I don't know what you're talking about."

"The second floor in my building is practically unpopulated," I said. "Whatever you did there, you wouldn't have to worry about being seen. I think you stuck the pick in your own back while you were in the hall outside my office."

"Why would I do that?"

"The jab wasn't deep enough to cause any real injury, but it was real enough to draw an emotional reaction. Maybe it was supposed to make me feel sorry for you. Maybe it was intended to enhance the tale of woe you were laying on me."

"I never said the ice pick had anything to do with the death threats."

"That's true. But look at the peril of the attack and the pathos of the wound and the gravity of the threats. Poor little you, beleaguered on all sides. You wanted me to pull the thing out. Doing that and wiping the blood away had me right up next to you. Close enough to get me hooked on your body chemistry alone."

"I needed some first aid. That's all."

"You needed help with something a lot more serious. And more aggressive. The first three death threats were meant to convince me that you were a victim. The others were metered out along the way, just to keep me interested. You had one ready in your purse and stuffed two more into my mail slot."

"But ..."

"You cooked them up yourself, and there's no use dithering about it. Slab wasn't capable. I go back to what the headshrinker said and I see it's true. Only someone with your literary and artistic background could have come up with that level of genius."

Her eyes started to get damp, but she held herself well short of crying. "That's the nicest thing anyone has ever said to me. To be honest, the death threats were adaptations of Gothic poems I wrote in freshman English."

"Harvard?"

"Illinois Central. It's a two-year college in East Peoria."

"Now we're talking," I said. "The death threats gave you an in. You knew I'd poke around enough to figure out that you were seeing Slab Kapowski. And you knew I'd realize that Slab is a dangerous man. When you first came to me, you wanted to know whether I had ever killed anybody. Why was that?"

"Isn't that a standard question?"

"It isn't. I think you wanted to know whether I'd be willing to mix it up with a suspected murderer. You wanted me to get in the middle, right between you and Slab. You wanted me to lose my cool and shoot him just to protect you. That way, I'd either get away with it or I'd go to jail. But Slab would be dead."

"All this is …"

"Or maybe I'd try to stand up to him and fail. Maybe I'd get myself killed in the effort. If that happened, you could tip off the police on my assignment. Even Pulptown cops can put two and two together. They'd trace my killing to Slab and he'd get locked up for life."

"But I told you I didn't want to go anywhere near the police."

"Not until you could use them. Not until somebody was already dead."

"That's just …"

"Any way you look at it, you'd be rid of Slab and you'd be in the clear. Hell, you even wanted to make sure I was bonded and you wanted to make sure we signed a contract. You wanted to have something legal to hide behind in case the plan backfired and somebody tried to pin you with a murder by proxy."

She got up nervously, went to the dresser and stood there fiddling aimlessly with the jewelry arrayed in a shallow silver box.

"I'm a respectable college professor," she said defiantly. "Why would I go to such lengths?"

"Because you knew you'd never shake Slab," I said. "You told me that yourself. And as for you being a professor, I'm wondering whether you're faking that too."

Her breathing got harsh and there were creases between her brows. She went back to her pacing. Maybe she suspected I was making it up as I went along. But she had nothing to counter me when I kept at her.

"The college isn't even accredited," I said, "so you knew they might be a little sloppy on vetting your resume. Maybe you used a fake name. Maybe you forged your credentials and had the rubes in the college personnel office route their reference calls to your shills in Boston or wherever. You could have hired some fop of an actor in England to pose on the phone as Lord Uppercrust from Oxford. In Paris, you'd be covered because all the French officials who answer phones over there claim they can't speak English anyway."

"You can be very ruthless," Roxanne said.

"You're changing the subject."

She slumped on her feet, went back to the vanity and sat on the cushioned bench in front of it.

"All right," she said with resignation. "You have the gist of it. Only it wasn't an actor in England. It was Lord Hoghound. His estate taxes were overdue and he was susceptible to a cash offer."

"Why go through all the trouble for a job you didn't need?"

"Because Slab said he wanted me to play the part of a respectable consort. Or as he put it, a respectable *concert*. I really did go to several colleges but I never got a degree. I was largely self-taught. I had innate talent, if I may brag a little. I've sold sketches for thousands and I've published poetry. I knew I could wing it in a hayseed town like this. As for teaching, I can deconstruct T.S. Eliot in my sleep."

"Who is Rebecca Chatterton?"

She caught her breath, but her eyes weren't throwing accusations anymore.

"The Camaro," she said. "My, but you *have* done your homework."

"I do my job, as you should have known I would."

"All right," she relented. "Rebecca Chatterton is my real name."

"And you have a house in Shorewood?"

"Hardly. The museum job paid well and I got a good deal on a rental because the owners were traveling abroad for a year. I was still staying there when I bought the car. Satisfied?"

"Not yet. When you gave me the ice pick story, it wasn't only to gain sympathy. You knew I'd start nosing around at Saint Opie's. Tell me why."

"Slab supposedly spends a lot of time over there. I guess I wanted to know what he's been involved with, and whether that was really where he was going every night. He was always so secretive about it."

"You were jealous? You wanted him rubbed out but you still wanted to make sure he wasn't cheating on you?"

"A girl has her pride."

"And maybe a girl — a woman of the world — wants to know more about Slab's business dealings, church included. Just in case there's a quickie marriage in the offing and a tragic widowhood right behind it, courtesy of a lovestruck private eye by the name of Jack Harbinger."

"You're reaching," she said.

"Am I? Let's say the quickie marriage has the name Roxanne Delaplaine on the license. Slab goes under, and anyone who wants to recoup what Slab has stolen or extorted starts looking for his widow. But there's no traceable person under that name. And after an inheritance is liquidated, after a little cash is laundered, Rebecca Chatterton makes off with all that money. There's no record of her ever being associated with Slab Kapowski at all."

"You didn't seem to mind my foibles when you were making love to me last night."

"That was a runaway train," I said.

"You weren't jumping off."

"True enough," I said. "Maybe I did lose my head. But not all the way. And not in the way you wanted me to. The fact is, I was hoping that when morning came you would have a reasonable explanation for all this."

She pivoted toward me, her eyes pleading and penetrating.

"You were partly right about me," she said. "But things have changed. The false name is there because of something I can't explain now, something very tragic that happened to me years ago."

"I'm guessing a criminal conviction."

"No," she said. "My record is clean. It was about a man, the wrong kind of man. Anyway, it's true that I wanted to know where Slab's money was coming from and where he was hiding it. That was just a matter of security. It was never about any kind of a shakedown."

"What do you mean by *security*?

"We were supposed to be married in Las Vegas."

"What did I tell you?"

"Just listen. It would have happened in a week or ten days after I came to your office."

"I didn't see any engagement ring," I said.

"Slab was too mercurial for that. He had just dropped the news on me the night before. It wasn't so much a proposal as a unilateral declaration. I agreed, but mainly out of fear. Inside I was wavering, not just about the wedding but about the whole relationship. I didn't know what to do, whether I should go through with it or how I could possibly get out of it."

"You could have walked out on him."

"It wasn't as simple as walking away. With Slab, nothing is simple. By the time I admitted to myself what kind of a man he actually is, I realized I needed help from someone."

"Why me?"

"I wasn't sure what kind of help it would be, but I knew I needed it. And you, well, you have a reputation for being … irreverent. That made me think you might be willing to step outside of the law if you felt you had a good reason."

"Stepping outside of the law means what?"

Her head turned to the side and her palms turned upward. "Everything you said about me wanting Slab dead … maybe that was true. Although it wasn't the cold calculation you described. I was deceiving myself, as if the idea were only there on a subliminal level, but of course I was consciously entertaining the thought. Believe me, Jack, I was only thinking that way because I couldn't escape him."

"And you knew that if you laid it out bare at the beginning, I wouldn't touch it. You wanted to pull me in slowly. You couldn't have known I'd find you at Hunchback Lanes on Wednesday night, but when I did, the slap from your boyfriend and the rescue and the gunfire couldn't have fallen together any better if you had planned it that way. You also knew that I'd be emotionally involved only if I spent more time with you. And my ego would be invested only if I had to pry open a mystery on my own."

"It … it sounds so conniving."

"Yeah, it kind of does, doesn't it?"

The undercurrent of the conversation had shifted from resentful to poignant and back again. I wanted to talk it out but clarity had become difficult. I wanted to touch her but there was something stopping me. It was almost like a prison visit, with a scratchy phone line connecting us and a plate-glass partition separating us. She was silent for a long time, and then I knew she'd be walking right through that barrier.

She got up from the vanity and came over to my chair. She sat on my lap and ran a finger down my cheek.

"I was discouraged and confused," she said, still campaigning.

"You appeared pretty damn steady to me. With or without an ice pick in your back."

"That was just an act. I'll admit I was using you, and I'm sorry. But as I said, things are different now. All of that was before I got to know you." She tilted her head and kissed me. "And last night, I had a pretty good ride on that train, too. Anyway, the danger from Slab is very real. If he can't have me back, he's not going to let me move on. I'm still afraid of him. All that's really changed is that I don't want you to end up with a bullet in your belly."

"And that's the nicest thing anyone's ever said to *me*," I told her. "Just the same, I can't trust you now. You gave me five hundred and I was on the case for three days. That's a standard fee of three hundred. And then there was mileage, bloody clothing for the cleaners, a bribe, data searches and a gun blast in my left rear fender."

I didn't count Eddie Trouble's fee for the Notre Dame fishing trip because for all I knew, that was only a net tossed into a dry lake.

"Why are you talking this way?" she demanded.

"Forget the sheet metal work on the car," I went on. "What would be the point? But with everything else on the tab, I'll keep four hundred and we can call it even. I'll give you back the other hundred as soon as I can take it out of my safe."

"No," she finally said. "I'll still need a bodyguard."

"I'm not in the bodyguard business, lady. You hired me to investigate death threats, and that's a done deal."

"Then I'll hire you to … I don't know, but I'll hire you."

"I've got things to do," I said.

"Where are we going?"

"It's where *I'm* going."

"Wait," she said. "You told me Slab is probably up to his neck in a series of deaths. If that's true, I need to know. I'm hiring you to investigate those. And I don't want to be left alone for Slab to find me. If you think you can get rid of me, you're wrong." She laid a long, deep kiss on me. "I told you, I'm starting to warm up to you."

"A couple of degrees warmer and the whole bedroom is going to burst into flames."

"Then you can't refuse me. I'm going with you."

My resolve was dissipating. Christ, I was half ready to run out and get her a dozen red roses.

I could hear the warning again, the one coming from the back of my mind. She'd been lying to me, all right, and maybe putting me smack between her and a mortal threat — a real one this time. Still, no amount of logic or experience or simple self-preservation could have outweighed the fact that I was falling hard. Sex had obviously amplified and complicated things, as it always does. But now I sat there looking into her eyes and I knew what my feelings for her would have been even if we hadn't crossed that line.

"All right," I agreed, not really surprising myself. "We'll stop for a little while at my office. But first, you'll have to change into something less casual. We'll be talking with people who are in a deep state of mourning. You won't have to wear a black veil, but you know the drill. It'll be a long day and it won't be any fun."

"But I'll be with *you*."

She gave me a reassuring look to go with her healing voice. She knew what to say and how to say it. Maybe she was being sincere and maybe she was conning me again — tightening her hold.

I could be reasonably certain of two things. My judgment was now shot full of holes. And Rebecca Chatterton was now the name of the girl with her finger on the trigger.

FORTY

We rode the Mustang to a little breakfast café along the highway, then headed back into town and cruised along the street that ran by my office building. It didn't look as if anyone had followed us along the way. I planted the car in front of the same donut shop the late Flunk Vanderhovel had attacked. The establishment was again doing business as if the dust-up between Flunk and the Pulptown P.D. had never happened. The broken glass from Flunk's vandalism had been cleared away. A new plate glass window had been set in place and a sign painter was busy recapitulating the original lettering.

I asked Roxanne — Rebecca — to wait for me in the car. I figured if Slab's new gorilla was watching the area, the cops hanging around the donut shop would dissuade him from kidnapping her. I asked her to look for my signal in the largest window on the second floor. I crossed the street, went into the building and climbed the stairs with my gun at the ready.

The hallway was deserted. A newspaper lay on the floor just outside my apartment. I left it alone and went over to my office door. I unlocked it and threw it open quickly. Nobody jumped at me or aimed a Glock automatic at me.

I went back down the hall to pick up the paper and then re-entered the office. Laying the paper silently on my desk, I walked over to unlock the connecting door to my apartment. Opening the door fast, I scanned the small studio. No one was in there swinging a Louisville Slugger at my head. I went inside and pushed the bathroom door open. No one was even lurking behind the shower curtain. My gun went back into its holster.

I stepped back into the world headquarters of the Jackson T. Harbinger organization and sat down to play the messages on my machine. The first was from the detective agency in Milwaukee. Their research on criminal and civil court records had turned up empty for both Roxanne Delaplaine and Rebecca Chatterton. That was a good sign, although the girl's actual name could have been Rapunzel Towers. Hell, I couldn't account for everything.

The second message was from Eddie Trouble, who wanted me to call him back in Chicago.

I went into my floor's main hallway and stood at the big window. I waved at Rebecca, letting her know she could come up. She got out of the car and crossed the street toward me. She was wearing black shoes with reasonable heels, a pair of black slacks that weren't too tight and a mauve blouse with a bit of breathing room. Slung over her shoulder was a black leather bag. On anyone else, the outfit would have looked demure.

When Rebecca walked cautiously into my office, I said, "You'll be more comfortable in my apartment. Barely." I opened the connecting door.

"Your apartment?" She walked up to my bookcase, surveyed it, did a double-take and then went into what passed for my domicile. She took a quick inventory. "Isn't this place a little depressing?"

I shrugged at her. "Anywhere I hang my head is home."

She frowned and picked up Carl Sagan's "*Cosmos*" from the coffee table. "By the way," she said, "I noticed something odd in your office. Did you know there's a bullet in one of Bertrand Russell's books?"

"That's the handywork of your friend Flunk Vanderhovel," I said. "I told you, he barged in with some notion of shooting me. His gun went off, the bullet bounced around and Bertrand Russell took it in the spine. Philosophy is a tough business."

"What an insane line of work you're in. And all to live like this?"

"It's a sacred mission," I told her. "I had to take a vow of poverty. You can have the easy chair in the corner." I walked over to it and slapped it with a small pillow, knocking a puff of dust onto the floor.

"Very classy."

"Sorry," I told her. "It's the maid's year off."

I left her in the apartment and went back into my office, closing the connecting door behind me and locking up the hallway door while I was at it. I sat down at the desk and dialed up Eddie Trouble.

After the opening banter he said, "I've been busy picking brains. One of my sources will cost you an extra sawbuck, unless it comes out of my hide."

"You're covered," I told him. "Any information on our boy from Notre Dame?"

"Boxcars of it, but no caboose."

"No end in sight?"

"No closure," he said.

"Closure for what?"

"We'll come to that. This Father Timothy character really had it sussed in the bosom of Catholic scholarship in America. He spent some prime years there as the Dean of Intellectual Compartmentalization."

"What the hell is that?" I asked.

"Cognitive dissonance, pal. Say they're teaching science courses and at the same time they believe in the biblical story of creation. They have their faith, but the university has to maintain a decent level of education in biology, geology, physics … you get my drift. They can't ignore what we know in those fields, but they can't allow facts to blow the Bible out of the water. They have to find a way to maintain their academic standards but still prop up the old fairy tales."

"I get it," I said.

"That's where Father Timothy Mulhooly came in. He was in charge of twisting and filtering holy scripture so that it seemed to make sense even when it didn't. Or, he'd try to poke holes in scientific theories that weren't really pokable. When worse came to worst, he'd fall back on the argument that scripture is a matter of interpretation."

"That must have gummed up the works," I said.

"Right you are, pal. It was a sore spot because it undermined the absolute authority of the Catholic Church."

"What else?"

"The university's take on history was also filled with bugaboos. So, somebody had to take it all apart and cobble it back together to fit the times. For example, they had Father Timothy sweating to wrench anti-slavery sentiment out of a Bible that clearly didn't have any objection to slavery. That way, they tried to make it look like the Bible had been right all along. And on and on. Anyway, Mulhooly was kind of like a criminal defense attorney. The point of his job wasn't to get at the truth, but to muddy the waters."

"So, he was an apologist for the church."

"Exactly, only this guy really had some apologizing to do. It seems he was dancing around his vow of celibacy. Well, what does that word really mean, technically? How should he define it? Loosely, as it turns out. I've put in calls to a janitor and a secretary and two assistant professors. Here's the skinny. At some point, something rotten crawled out from the ooze of Father Timothy's libido. As we speak, nothing's been proven. But the rumors are that if you're an eight-year-old, you don't want to let him get behind you."

"That fits with something he said just before he slipped me a mickey and had his goons work me over. He told me he wanted to surprise the altar boys at their pool party."

"Probably not to make balloon animals," Eddie said.

"How many eight-year-olds are there at Notre Dame?"

"Not many, but he was big in the surrounding community. Summer camp, Sunday school. Loved the kids, hardy-har-har. Rumors flew. The guy became an embarrassment and he got pushed out. There was a series of reassignments to small colleges. More rumors. More exits. He tumbled all the way down to a string of parishes in rinky-dink towns like yours. No offense. The reassignments have gotten more frequent as the years have gone by. We're talking more transfers than a bus ride from Wrigley Field to Rio de Janeiro."

"Any criminal convictions?"

"Nah. Hot potato. Nobody was willing to press charges and put their kids on the stand. And civil suits were killed off in confidential settlements. The Church has a crusade's worth of lawyers covering Mulhooly's tracks. The way they figure it, they can't let their reputation be soiled by a scandal. Better to let the joker run amok in one new town after another. How come he's on your radar?"

"Could be an accessory to murder," I said.

"Hmmm. Nothing here under that category. But it looks like you're dug in against a real scumbag up there."

"One or two. Thanks, Eddie. I'll put your greenbacks in the mail, extra sawbuck and all."

"Just don't get yourself snuffed out before you do," he said. "I got bills to pay." He recited his address and we hung up.

Eddie had brought up a fair point. I raided my safe and stuffed bills into an envelope, prepping and stamping it. Then I thumbed through a phone book, finding an entry for Pete Pulaski's mother and father. The white pages listed them at the same old Lincoln Street address where Pete had grown up.

The phone book also came through with a number for Harry Armstadt, the guy who had died in his boat off The Bishop's Retreat. The address for Harry and his wife Ellen was unlisted, which crimped my plans because I wanted to make an unannounced call at their door if possible. I phoned the county assessor and gave the clerk the two names. The couple had paid property taxes on a parcel of land along the lake shore, not far from where Harry died. There was a homeowners' exemption for the parcel, meaning they'd been residing there. I jotted down the street address that corresponded to the parcel number and checked off another box on my list.

Next, I scanned the morning's edition of the *Informer* and found an article identifying the machine operator whose hand had been chopped off. The guy's name was Norman Lumm. I couldn't find a phone listing for that name or for any Lumm in town. Nothing in the article pointed to a home address or any next of kin, but for now that didn't matter. The article named the paper mill where the death occurred, and that was good enough. It was a place I knew fairly well because I'd been there months earlier on a liability case. Someone I met during that investigation later became a client. And a long time ago, I had worked there as an apprentice mill rat for a brief but miserable stretch.

I clamped down the office windows and went back into the apartment, locking the connecting door behind me. Rebecca was curled up in the easy chair, engrossed in Carl Sagan's commentaries on distant stars. I showered and shaved. I treated myself to a clean white shirt and a striped tie, along with a freshly loaded gun. There was one more acceptable suit in the closet and I put it on.

"I'm ready," I told Rebecca. She held up a finger and finished a page while I lowered the shades. I left one of the apartment windows unlocked. That would allow a prowler to get in, but I did it in case the prowler turned out to be me.

Rebecca slapped the book shut and returned it to its place on the coffee table.

"Where first?" she asked.

"Into the depths of parental grief," I said.

FORTY-ONE

On the way to Lincoln Street I made sure to drop Eddie Trouble's greenbacks in the mail while I still could. I found Pete Pulaski's old house and parked at the curb, just behind a blue Corvette. Rebecca looked at me nervously. Neither of us wanted to be there, but she was game.

I could tell at a glance that the phone listing was up to date. Pete's parents were the only ones who would have had it looking the way it did. The aluminum siding had once been a woodsy green but it was now faded to the color of peas. Shrubs along the foundation were losing their own shade of green for lack of care and water. Much of the front yard's grass had yellowed. A line of cement stepping stones led from the sidewalk to the door. On one side of the path, there was a shrine with a two-foot statue of the Virgin Mary. "Our Lady of the Bathtub," I said to Rebecca. "You used to see these things all over town." Rising behind and arching over the virgin was one end of an antique porcelain tub. Painted a light blue, it was either half-buried or cut to size. It was supposed to look like the grotto where the long-dead virgin had reportedly appeared to some peasants. The half-tub actually looked more like a band shell, and if someone had put a miniature microphone stand in front of Mary, the whole tableau would have made more sense.

In front of Our Lady, there were two indentations in the dirt, probably evidence of Pete's mother kneeling there day after day. Near the indentations there was a collection of other statues. Saint Francis of Assisi was bending over to pet a lamb. A yellow canary was perched on his shoulder. Next to the saint and his passive animals, martyrs were standing tall before hungry lions that Francis had never bothered to tame. A floating angel was wired to a wicket stuck in the ground. And a pudgy friar was either gazing heavenward or rolling his eyes at all the clutter around him.

Sadness hung in the air as we walked up the path to ring the bell. Pete's dad came to the door. He had aged, of course, and he was stooped, but he still had the same suspicious, confrontational look in his eyes. I remembered him having the personality of a hacksaw when Pete and I were kids, and the saw's teeth hadn't dulled any since then. I couldn't tell whether he recognized me.

"State your business," he said.

"Mr. Pulaski, this is Rebecca Chatterton. My name is Jack Harbinger. I used to know Pete."

"So what?" he said. "Are you two from the warehouse?"

"No, I haven't seen Pete in a long time," I told him. "Is it all right if we come in?"

Mr. Pulaski stepped aside and with some annoyance reached out to push the screen door open. We walked into a stuffy living room full of elderly furniture and sacred portraits. Some of the picture frames had gold or silver sunbeams lancing out from the edges. In one corner of the room there was another shrine to the Virgin Mary. I remembered it from long ago, but there were now a lot more prayer cards and rosaries nailed to Mary's pedestal. Mr. Pulaski saw me eyeing the display.

"My wife is devoted to Our Lady," he said.

"Yeah, we noticed when we pulled up," I told him

"The shrines are nice," Rebecca lied.

"Humph."

Mr. Pulaski settled himself into a wooden chair. He pointed at a couch with badly worn cushions that must have been sinking into the frame since the Second World War. We sat down. Way down.

"I'm a private investigator," I told him, laying a business card on a small table. "I know it's difficult for you to talk about Pete so soon after the incident at work. But we'd like to ask you a few questions."

"Private investigators, bah," he said, including Rebecca in his condemnation. "Who's your client?"

"That's confidential, but unfortunately, there are always liability issues in cases like your son's. I'm interested in … confirming whether Pete's death was purely accidental."

"I should hope not," he said with a sting. "That boy was a disrespectful little shit as far back as I can remember."

Rebecca met my eyes and shook her head slightly.

"I'm sorry if I was being too abrupt," I said.

"I'm thinking you're with some bloodsucking lawyer looking to sue somebody," he said. "It won't work. You can't sue God."

"You think God made the accident happen?" Rebecca asked.

"God is in control of all things," the old man said. "They said Pete was … injured … killed … while kneeling in prayer. I can't tell you how much I wish that was true, but I know my son."

"Tell me more about that," I said.

"Pete was an unbeliever," he said. "Well, that's putting it politely. Fact is, he was a goddamn atheist. Questioned everything. Even back in elementary school at Saint Opie's. I kept after him about it. We both did, the missus and me. Didn't do any good. Believe me, I tried to do right by Pete. Must have given him the strap a hundred times."

"You'd think that would clear his mind," I said flatly.

"But it didn't," Pulaski said. "The people at the church and the school, they just wrote him off after a few years. We enrolled him in the Catholic high school anyway, just to try and pound some sense into him, but that didn't do any good either. They damn near threw him out. After a while, Pete grew up and got married, but sure enough, that broke up. I finally had to bring in Father Timothy from Saint Opie's. He was here night after night, battling it out with Pete. But Pete was beyond reach."

"Wait a second," I said. "This was here at your house? Didn't Pete have his own place?"

"Not after his wife tossed him out." The old man's voice was acidic. "The marriage was annulled. By the Church, mind you. They were never really married, not in the eyes of God. A nice girl, too. A servant of the Lord. Pete wasn't good enough for her. He lived here the last few months, trying to get back on his feet. That's only because his mother took pity on him."

"Is your wife here now?" Rebecca asked.

"She's over at Saint Opie's, praying for Pete's immortal soul. Good luck with that."

"You told us Father Timothy was here night after night," I said. "What were he and Pete talking about?"

"Dirty mouth blasphemy," Pulaski said.

"How's that?"

"Pete used to tell Father Timothy that if Jesus really was God the Son, then He must have come down to this earth to lighten up on the bullying of God the Father. He said Jesus must have been doing some kind of damage control for all the mistakes God made in the Old Testament. I couldn't believe what I was hearing."

"Like what mistakes?" I asked him.

"Oh, Pete liked to point to a passage in the Old Testament where God said anyone working on the Sabbath has to be put to death."

"That's definitely in there," Rebecca said.

"You bet it is," the old man told her. "Exodus, Chapter 31, Verse 15. That's why I never worked on the Sabbath in my life."

"Never worked on a Saturday?" I said.

"Sunday," he said.

"In the Old Testament, it was a Saturday."

"Jesus changed it to Sunday."

"To correct his father?"

"No, not to correct anything. You're as bad as Pete was. The point is that we don't make the rules, God makes the rules. Or Jesus makes the rules. Same thing, even if it's different rules. And if some people don't like it, too bad. Pete found out the hard way."

"So how did Father Timothy react when Pete told him all this?"

"He was calm about it at first, and he read scripture to Pete, tried to reason with the boy."

"By quoting passages from a book that Pete thought was nonsense?"

"Well, yes. Pete picked apart everything the Bible said, and Father Timothy got madder and madder by the day. He warned Pete that he was endangering his immortal soul. Pete just laughed at him. And then one day, all of a sudden, Father Timothy got real calm again. I suppose God spoke to him in some way. To comfort him in the face of Pete's devil talk."

"Sometimes people feel relief when they decide to take drastic action," I said.

"What kind of drastic action?" he wanted to know.

"At this point, we're just looking for possibilities. When was the last time Father Timothy was here?"

"Just the other night. The night before Pete got killed. That's when Father Timothy finally got himself calmed down."

"What else do you remember about that last conversation?"

"I couldn't hear the words clear. Just the tone."

"Do you have any details on how Pete died?"

"It was an act of God, I'm sure."

"An act of God? You mean forces of nature? You don't think human error, maybe a mechanical malfunction, might have had anything to do with it?"

"And who has dominion over errors and malfunctions?" Pulaski said. "God does, that's who. Here you are, the Supreme Being, the Creator of Heaven and Earth, and you have a guy, Pete, who doesn't even believe in you. Your own priest is trying to bless this forklift and this unbeliever is right there thinking this is all a bunch of hooey. What an insult! Well, if you're God Almighty, then maybe it's time to unleash a little righteous indignation."

"Through the machine?" Rebecca said.

"Well, if one of the forks goes right through Pete's chest, who's fault is that? It's not the machine's fault and it's not God's fault. It's Pete's fault."

I broke in: "Are you saying there was no driver?"

"I have no way of knowing," he said. "Except for a revelation, and I ain't had one of those. But if there wasn't a driver, then the forklift took off on its own. Or it was steered by the Holy Ghost. Same thing, really. It was fate, pure and simple."

"And there was no way to prevent it?" I asked.

"That's what Father Timothy told me. Anyway, the Lord works in mysterious ways, and I certainly can't blame Him for doing what needed to be done."

"That's ... maybe a little cold," Rebecca said.

Pulaski ignored her, keeping his eyes on me as he spoke:

"Let me turn this around and ask *you* something, Mr. Harbinger. What would you do if people denied that you even exist?"

"I'm not sure I'd kill them," I said. "But that's a tough call."

"Where do you get these ideas?" Rebecca said to the old man.

He flared back at her.

"Vengeance is mine, sayeth the Lord. If Pete went around spouting all kinds of blasphemy, then he got what he deserved."

"Was there a police report?" I asked, trying to stay on track.

"No. It was all pretty straightforward."

"Was there a report from OSHA?"

"What's that?"

"Occupational Safety and Health Administration. It's federal."

"Communist bastards! No, nothing from them."

"Then how do you know it was straightforward?"

"Because Father Timothy was right there doing the blessing. He saw the whole thing and called me afterward."

"And what did he tell you?"

"Just that Pete took the right fork through the chest."

"But what else did he tell you about why and how it happened? Why was Pete positioned in front of the forks?"

"I don't know. I didn't ask," he said.

"Okay," I said slowly. "Was this a new forklift? Or an old one?"

"I don't know. Father Timothy just told me he thought it might help if he blessed the forklift Pete was driving every day."

"And Father Timothy told you this before or after the accident?"

"Before," he said. "It was the night before. Father Timothy told me he'd go down there and bless the forklift the next morning. He told me this on the sly, because he didn't even want Pete to know ahead of time. He said he was afraid Pete would call in sick just to avoid the ceremony."

"And you didn't tell Pete about Timothy's plan to bless the forklift?"

"Hell, no. I can keep a secret."

"Did Pete or Father Timothy ever tell you about any other machinery being blessed down at the warehouse?"

"No," he said. "I never heard anything about that."

"So, let me see if I'm getting this right. Father Timothy comes in out of nowhere and blesses the forklift. Pete is there, and he's kneeling down, supposedly in prayer. The forklift had to have been running, or the accident wouldn't have happened."

"Unless there was a miracle," Pulaski said.

"Unless there was a miracle," I humored him. "But let's say the machine was turned on and idling. Are you saying it slipped into gear or something? It just took off by itself and headed straight for Pete?"

"I didn't say there was no driver. I just said *maybe* there was no driver."

"But Pete was the usual driver," I said. "Why wasn't he up in the driver's seat instead of down on the floor?"

"Well, maybe Father Timothy brought in his own forklift operator. I suppose the driver has to know all the ins and outs of the blessing ceremony or everything gets all fucked up."

"And you didn't take these issues up with Father Timothy?"

"Why should I? It was the hand of God that killed my son. What good would it do to fire off a lot of pointless questions all over the place?"

Rebecca and I gave each other a quick look.

"And given everything you knew about Pete's outlook on religion, didn't it seem odd to you that he would have been kneeling at the time?"

"Well, the story is, he was kneeling in prayer. The news on TV said Pete converted right before he died. Father Timothy said so too. But I ain't sure. I think Pete was probably just kneeling down to tie his shoe or something. Can you imagine the disrespect? Tying his shoe right there in the middle of a blessing? The point is, God decided to take him then and there before he could get himself into any more trouble."

"More trouble than getting run through with a forklift?" Rebecca said.

"I'm talking about Pete's immortal soul," Pulaski said. "Everything happens for a reason. Maybe God saw something redeemable in Pete. Maybe Pete could have burned off his sins in the fires of Purgatory."

Rebecca barely kept herself from blowing up at him. "You're talking about God killing your son? And then throwing what remains of your son's consciousness into a fire?"

"That's kind of the way it works, little lady. Don't blame me. I didn't write the Bible."

"That sounds kind of merciless," Rebecca said.

"You can't question the ways of God," he told her. "Is God's right of vengeance going to be suspended just because it makes somebody feel bad? It is not!"

"You have a point there," I said with a poker face.

"I see you're a God-fearing man," Pulaski said.

"He's a frightening figure," I answered. God or Godzilla, I was thinking.

"That's fine, then," he said. "That's the way it's supposed to be. I've just about had it with skeptics."

Rebecca dipped her head and put her fingers to her brow.

"Did you get a call from the management at the warehouse?" I asked.

"No, I think they just decided to let Father Timothy handle all that."

"Did you get a call from the police?"

"No. what would the police have to do with it?"

"I've outlined some questionable circumstances," I told him.

"Well, not everybody is as suspicious as you are," Pulaski said.

"Let me ask you something else," I said. "Did Father Timothy mention Slab Kapowski to you?"

"The guy that owns all the mortuaries? Yeah, he said Mr. Kapowski was there when my son got killed, and he said Mr. Kapowski felt real bad about it and hoped we'd use his funeral services."

"Slab was there? How come you didn't tell me that before?"

"You didn't ask."

"I'm asking you now. Could Kapowski have been driving the forklift?"

"I already told you. I don't know."

"Okay, Mr. Pulaski. Think now, because this is crucial. Did Father Timothy say anyone else was there? That could be anyone, whether you think the person was important or not."

"Nah."

"Did you speak with Slab Kapowski?"

"No, but we got a call from Last Chance Mortuary."

"When was that?"

"Last night," he said. "They say in their commercials that they have funerals for all budgets, but the woman on the line went on and on about cheap wooden caskets and how water seeps in and how they get moldy, and how worms burrow in to get at the bodies. Didn't bother me much, but it made the missus cry. The woman on the phone kept trying to sell us the deluxe casket, stainless steel. But the money was out of the question. She tried to make us feel guilty for scrimping, and she told us we ought to take out a second mortgage. We're on pensions. We can't take out a second mortgage. And then the Lord put an idea in my head. Why not sell Pete's car? It's the Corvette out front." He pointed vaguely at the world outside his window.

"Sure, we saw it," I said. "Pete always told me he wanted a sports car someday."

"It was an abomination before the Lord," Pulaski said. "Self-puffery, thy name is Corvette. But it just goes to show that the Lord was looking out for the missus and me. We needed money for the funeral. And damned if what they say isn't true. The Lord will provide. So, we went ahead and ordered up the deluxe casket and the big funeral. I'll put the Corvette up for sale today. Hopefully, we'll get a buyer before the funeral bill comes in. How about you, Mr. Harbinger? Are you in the market for a car?"

"I'm good."

He turned toward the window again and trained his eyes for a few seconds on the dilapidated Mustang parked at the curb.

"Doesn't look like it," he said.

FORTY-TWO

I drove through Pulptown and then skimmed the western banks of our secondary lake, which was only a bulge in the river running north toward Green Bay. Rebecca, beside me, was hushed. No surprise. We had just been through a depressing interview and we were probably on our way to more of the same.

Veering away from the lake, we took side roads leading us to the sprawling parking lot of Great Wisconsin Paper Mills. The huge building beyond the lot was windowless, utilitarian, mostly hard angles and unbroken planes. Steam rose from stacks topping a three-story tower on the left side of the structure. To the right of that section, wall panels in corrugated metal stretched more than a hundred yards out toward the woods. I followed the property's long perimeter fence and chose an out-of-the-way parking stall at the far corner of the plant. Near us, a train spur ended at a loading dock.

"Why are we parking way back here?" Rebecca said.

"We can walk right through the mill if we look sanctioned," I said. "But if management catches on to us, we won't want to go back the way we came. Better to slip out through the rear doors if possible and make it to the car quickly."

"Do you know your way around in there?"

"Roughly," I told her. "I've been here for an insurance investigation. And just out of high school, they hired me as a bottom-level mill worker. I got fired after three weeks."

"For insubordination, I would guess."

"They told me I had a bad attitude, and they were right. I packed napkins coming off an assembly line. I was a mindless robot, and maybe the worst employee in the history of the company. The best thing that ever happened to me was that they tossed me out before I could get acclimated to it. You'll see what I mean when you're inside. Let's get some props ready."

Once we were out of the car, I opened the trunk and went into a small box. I flipped through a collection of fake business cards and stuffed three of a kind into my wallet.

"What about my cover story?" she asked.

"Just build off whatever I tell them and bluff your way through. If anybody can do that, it's you. We want to come off as bureaucratic types. Can you tie your hair back?"

She reached into her purse and came up with an elastic loop. She funneled her hair into a ponytail that toned down some of her pizzazz. For my part, I threw my jacket into the back seat, loosened my tie, rolled up my sleeves and affixed the logo of a fictitious government agency to my shirt pocket. I went back into the trunk and pulled out a clipboard with an attached pen and legal pad. I handed all that to Rebecca and she stowed her bag.

"Make it look like you're taking notes," I said. "Or checking off boxes, but don't let anyone see what you're writing."

"Okay."

"When we go in, you'll smell pulp and ink and solvent. Try not to give a reaction anyone can see."

"Got it," she said. "Make them think I do this kind of thing every day."

As we took the long walk to the building's main entrance, the afternoon heat gave us a double dose, radiating from the sun and bouncing off the metal exterior of the building. We were glad to see shade under a canopy at the front doors. On a wall next to them there was a payphone. I dropped a quarter into the slot and went through directory assistance to the administrative offices above us. A receptionist connected me with a guy I knew in payroll.

"Vern Griesbach here," he said.

"Vern, this is Jack Harbinger."

"Aw, hell."

"Remember that time I got you out of a jam?"

"I guess …"

"That wrestling promoter never broke your legs, did he?"

"Yeah, true," he said suspiciously. "I can see where this is going. What do you need from me?"

"I'm at the payphone right downstairs from your office. I need you to show me where Norman Lumm got his hand cut off."

"Jesus, you're not going to open *that* can of worms."

"I am," I told him. "I need you to walk me through the mill. It'll look official. I even have an assistant who's carrying a clipboard."

"A clipboard? Well, you can't get more official than that. Look, Harbinger, I could get fired."

"We can get through the entrance without any problem," I said. "For the rest of it, you'll be walking in front of us. You don't have to acknowledge our presence. To anyone who glances up, it'll look like we're being escorted. But if any management types ask, you didn't know we were following you. And we'll dummy up, guaranteed. All you need is some pretext for coming down to where we can spot you and then for going back into the mill to where the accident happened."

"All right," he said with a quiet groan. "But don't even speak to me once I get down there. Look for me near the time card racks. We'll walk through the plant and get into the offset press room. You'll know we're there because that printing requires air conditioning. Once we get inside, you're on your own. Lumm got killed on a trimming machine. It's the tall one in the back of the room. Just leave my name out of it when you question the machine operator."

"Agreed. By the way, you said this accident is a can of worms. How come?"

"I shouldn't have said that. Look, I'm in payroll. I'm not involved. I don't know what went on down there."

"Except for what, Vern?"

"You'll see," he said flatly.

"All right. I'll make sure your name stays out of it. And thanks."

"Then we're even, right?"

"All square."

I hung up and we gave it a minute before we went in. When we did, the sapping heat, the choking chemicals and the pall of monotony hit me hard. All of it put me right back to the time I had dragged my feet down the same corridor day after day for three long weeks. Where the corridor widened into the factory floor there was no gatekeeper, but a few men loitering nearby gave us a double-take. That could have been because we were unfamiliar or because Rebecca was Rebecca. I avoided eye contact with the employees and pretended to go over something she was writing on her clipboard. Vern came down a stairway and the idle shop men went back to what they had been doing. Without glancing at us, Vern stopped to pull a couple of time cards from a rack a few feet from where we were standing.

He put one of the cards back in its slot, studied the other one and carried it off toward the heart of the mill. We followed a few steps behind him.

Past a storage depot, we got into an open space and walked by rows of green machines half-covered by fine white dust. The machinery put out a thumping roar, pulling endless streams of unprocessed paper from huge rolls and wrenching it into finished products. Alongside a machine close to us, men and women moved like automatons and sweated like plow horses. They grabbed handfuls of napkins that were spit out by rapid-fire mechanisms. They inserted each batch between brackets. Another mechanism automatically wrapped the napkins and popped up packages that had to be caught by hand and packed in boxes. Once filled, the boxes had to be sealed and labelled. The whole career took about five minutes to learn, and the workers repeated the routine for years on end.

For a short time, that was my life eight hours a day. Better to be picking a slug out of my shoulder every now and then.

After passing an acre of tireless machines and exhausted laborers on the big shop floor, we reached the offset press room and trailed our escort inside. The temperature and humidity dropped sharply, as Vern had told us it would. The noise level didn't improve much; it was almost as loud as it had been out in the main factory. Vern showed his time card to a guy behind a desk.

Rebecca and I peeled off.

FORTY-THREE

In the far corner was a machine I had seen years earlier but had never operated. I knew it trimmed paper placemats after they had rolled out of the offset presses. The man currently working on it stood with his back to us. I studied his actions.

The operator placed a stack of printed placemats into guides on a thick metal tray and then slid the tray under four blades poised above. He pulled a lever. The blades came down with a heavy pneumatic punch that cut scalloped edges on hundreds of sheets in a single chomp. The blades retracted. The guy grabbed a wooden stick and reached in with it to pull out scraps of paper that clung to the blades or dropped below them. He drew the tray back and set the trimmed placemats aside, dumping the scraps into a large box. He repeated the process.

As we walked up behind the machine operator, he duplicated the steps for the third time — up to the point where the stick went in to clear the scraps. Suddenly the blades chomped down without anyone touching the lever. The shocking force jarred the operator and cut the stick in two. If the operator had reached in with his hand, he would have lost it.

We approached him with a soft word, careful not to startle him. The guy wasn't shaken by us or even by the misfire. His anxious eyes squinted at me as if I could only cause him trouble.

"Terry Lennox," I introduced myself. "This is Linda Loring. We're from the National Safety Authority." I showed him a business card with a fake address in Washington, D.C. and a telephone number that would lead a tracer to the dark side of the moon. He didn't take the card but shook my hand, staring at Rebecca.

"I'm Junior," he said. "If you're here about Norm getting himself killed, we already had a safety inspector in here. I got a production quota to meet. You're not gonna shut the machine down again, are you?"

"Not at all," I told him. "But we do have some questions about Mr. Lumm's accident. There are layers of overlapping responsibility for these things. You know how the federal government can be." He looked relieved, though still somewhat irked. We got his actual name and some other personal information and Rebecca wrote it down. "Just a few details. First of all, it looked like the machine gave you a scare a minute ago."

"The machine'll repeat even when you don't pull the lever," Junior said. "The blades'll just come down on their own for no reason. That's why we have to gather up the broke with a stick."

"The broke?"

"The leftover paper. It's called broke. Don't ask me why. You pull the leftovers out from under those big teeth after they bite down. Hopefully you remember to use the stick so you never get your fingers chopped off. And then you throw the waste paper in the broke box. Poor Norm, he must have reached in there with his hand. You know, in a hurry."

"How often do the blades go out of control that way?"

"Sometimes not for an hour. Sometimes every two or three whacks. You can never tell when it's going to happen. Or stop. But you kinda get used to it after a while."

"How much experience did Norm have on this machine?"

"Years."

"And Norm should have known better than to reach in there with his hand?"

"Seems like he would," Junior said.

"How long has the punch been repeating?"

"Months."

"Why didn't anybody fix it?"

"Well, that's the thing. On Wednesday, Norm was the machine operator and I was just a helper. My job was to box the placemats after they were trimmed. We were working as usual. The machine wasn't acting up just then, but a new mechanic came in to try and fix it anyway."

"Had you and Norm put in a request?"

"No, the mechanic just showed up."

"Were you here when the mechanic's work was being done?"

"Not really," he said.

"That could mean anything."

"Well, I was around, I guess, at first."

"What time was that?"

"Around eleven in the morning. That's the lunch break for the a.m. shift."

"Go on," I said.

"When the mechanic told Norm to stay and help him, I figured I'd hang around too, just to watch."

"You gave up your lunch break just to watch the mechanic?"

"Sure. I like to keep an eye on the pits during the lawnmower races. Same thing."

"Who else was here at the time?"

"Only Dennis and the mechanic's helper."

"Who's Dennis?"

"A press operator."

"You just told me the mechanic brought his own assistant. But he still wanted Norm to help him?"

"Doesn't make sense," Junior said. "Now that you mention it."

"Right now, this room is full of offset press operators," I said. "How come only one of them was here at the time?"

"They all went out on their lunch break. Almost all. They can get away with leaving a couple minutes early."

"But *you* stayed behind."

"Until the mechanic sent me off on an errand. He wanted me to go find a three-quarter synchronized hex cropper."

"What's a synchronized hex cropper?"

"Heck if I know. I was just supposed to find one. The guy at the maintenance shop didn't know what it was, either."

"Did you get the feeling that the mechanic was just trying to get rid of you?"

"Yeah, I kinda do now," he said. "But I didn't think about it at the time."

"And the other guy, Dennis," I said. "Why did he hang around?"

"Don't ask me."

"You mean you don't want me to ask? Or you don't know the answer."

"I mean, I don't know why. None of this was my fault."

"I get that," I said. "Who was the mechanic?"

"I never seen him before. I'm sure he was the manufacturer's own guy."

"What makes you sure of that?"

"I don't know. I assumed. Am I under suspicion here?"

"Not at all. What did the mechanic look like?"

"Well … um … kind of tall and thin. He was wearing a baseball hat and goggles, so I didn't get a clear look at his face. He had a beak on him, though."

"A prominent nose?"

"Yeah, like a bald eagle or something."

Rebecca gave me an almost imperceptible nod.

"Are you getting this, Miss Loring?"

"Check," she said.

I turned back to Junior.

"What did the mechanic's helper look like?"

"Big," he said. "Really big. Later thirties. Dark hair. Sort of a half-ass mustache."

Rebecca caught my glance again and threw in a question: "Did the mechanic's helper say anything?"

"Not much. I can't remember what, exactly. His voice was kind of funny though. It sounded like it was coming out of a garbage disposal."

"What was the helper doing?" she asked.

"Just standing there holding a big long tool box. Waiting, I guess."

"All right," I said. "You told us Dennis was here. What's his last name?"

"Canfield. But he doesn't work here anymore. He left for Borneo right after the accident. He said he was going there to repent."

"Repent for what?"

"I'm not sure," Junior said.

"You mean you have some idea but you're not certain?"

"I feel like you think I'm responsible for all this."

"Try to get past that," I told him. "I'm just looking for clear answers. If anyone was responsible, maybe it was the guy who thought he needed to repent. I'd like to know why he felt that way."

"I never gave that any thought," Junior said. "He just said he felt bad, is all. Maybe he felt like he should have prayed harder or something."

"Was Dennis a deacon?"

"Yeah. Down at Saint Opie's. He used to get into arguments with Norm all the time."

"So," I said. "Do you know whether Dennis saw the accident itself?"

"That, I couldn't say."

"You mean you can't reveal that information to me? Or you just don't *have* the information?"

"I mean I don't know if Dennis was here."

"Let's back up a little bit. What kind of arguments did Norm and Dennis have?"

"Religious. Dennis would try to tell Norm what was what. Then Norm would say oh yeah? And he'd ask Dennis all kinds of questions he couldn't answer."

"That Dennis couldn't answer?"

"Right, but then Dennis would tell him he'd pray for him. Norm laughed about that. But Dennis was always trying to convince Norm that the Bible was a true story. They would get all tied up in knots. Dennis would tell Norm that Jesus was either lying or crazy or the Son of God like he said he was."

"The old C.S. Lewis thing," Rebecca said.

"Whoever," Junior said. "Anyway, Dennis said Jesus couldn't have been a liar or a lunatic so he had to be divine. Norm said not so fast, Jesus was a nut like any other nut walking around saying he's God. That's Norm talking. Not me. Norm was on the fringes that way. Dennis got mad at him and told him he'd be filing a report."

"A report with the management here at the plant?"

"I don't think so," Junior said. "Just a report. I didn't know to who."

"And were they arguing like this any time close to the accident?"

"Yeah, the day before."

"So," I said, "let's go back to the time when the mechanic came in. What was he supposed to fix?"

"That repeating thing, the blade coming down all by itself."

"And why did the mechanic come in to fix it on that particular day as opposed to several months earlier?"

"I don't make those decisions."

"I'm not asking you whether you're the president of the company," I said. "Do you have any idea why the repair was delayed for a matter of months?"

"No, sorry. All's I know is, I came back, kind of sheepish because I couldn't find that hex cropper, and there was blood all over the place. Norm was laying across the machine with his chopped arm dangling and his cut-off hand under the blades."

"What time was that?"

"I didn't look. But everybody was still on their lunch break."

"Was Norm already dead by the time you saw him?"

"I'm not a doctor."

"I figured that. You're not wearing a stethoscope. What I'm asking is, did he appear to be dead?"

"He coulda been passed out, but he looked dead to me. He was pale, almost white. He already lost a ton of blood. He wasn't moving and he wasn't breathing. I shook him but he didn't flinch. I guess that's pretty dead. Dennis was just standing there next to him, sort of helpless, with an awful look on his face. He might have been the one who called the paramedics."

"The mechanic," I said. "Where was he when you got back to the machine and saw Norm?"

"I couldn't tell you."

"You can't tell me? Or you just don't know the answer?"

"I have no idea where the mechanic was. Or where he went."

"That's better," I said. "And the mechanic's assistant?"

"Same thing. Gone."

"Did anyone ever get a name for either of them?"

"I'm sure they … well, not that I know of," he said.

"Did you ever see either of them again?"

"No. Why? Is that important?"

I said, "Did Dennis know, maybe only hear, how the hand got chopped off?"

"Don't ask, I mean I don't know. Maybe Dennis found him like that."

Rebecca jumped in. "You must have been concerned enough to ask the deacon how the accident happened."

"Yup," Junior told her. "But he didn't want to talk about it."

"Did you tell all this to the police?" I asked.

"The police never came down here. Why would they? It was an accident."

"And the safety inspector," I said. "Who was that?"

"I don't know. He didn't talk to me. Mostly he talked to Dennis. Maybe that's what made Dennis feel so bad that he had to quit and go to Borneo."

"Did the safety inspector know that a mechanic had been here?"

"I'm sure he did," Junior said.

"And what makes you so sure?"

"Well, why wouldn't he?"

"So, Junior, when you say you're *sure* the inspector knew about the mechanic, do you only mean you *assume* he knew?"

"More or less."

"It was a *yes-or-no* question."

"Yes," Junior said reluctantly. "I assume he knew."

"And nobody else ever questioned you?" I said to Junior. "None of the managers upstairs? Nobody from the union?"

"Not me. Dennis told them everything, as far as I know. I guess they took his word for it, him being a deacon and all."

A man in a button-down shirt and business slacks entered the offset press room through the doors where Rebecca and I had come in. He didn't look our way, but I knew he'd be over as soon as he noticed us taking up the machine operator's time. I took a chance with one more question.

"Have you reported to management that the blades are still punching down on their own?"

"Nah," Junior said. "Whenever we did, they always told us to keep a good supply of sticks around."

"Did management even care about the problem?" Rebecca said.

"I'm sure … I assume … heck, I don't really know. But you can't blame me for that."

I didn't want to deal with upper echelons yet, so I thanked Junior and nudged Rebecca toward the rear door of the offset press room.

We got out of the air conditioning and into the heat of the shipping department without being detained or followed. We crossed quickly through a maze of stacked boxes and found an exit at the loading dock. We went out that door, down some stairs and across the railroad tracks.

When we were back in the car, Rebecca pulled her hair loose, took a deep breath and asked me a sharp question. "What do you think was in that long toolbox?"

I started up the motor and headed out through the lot.

"You first," I said.

"An axe. They cut Lumm's hand off and blamed it on the machinery."

"We're on the same page," I told her. "Save it with a bookmark. One more stop, and then we can regroup to count up what we believe and what we know."

FORTY-FOUR

Harry Armstadt had lived in a pared-down version of a Gallic chateau on the north shore of Lake Winnebago. A black mansard roof topped two stories of carefully distressed white brick. Around French doors and leaded windows, the walls were strapped with vines. In the front yard, a willow tree's branches dropped to the grass. The house had been set back from a narrow road running between the lake and a small inlet of still water. On the inlet side, three or four linked ponds were thick with reeds and lily pads and algae. The location would have been great most of the year, but right now it was swampy, with the algae's odor hanging in the late afternoon air. Rebecca and I walked up to the chateau's entrance, trying not to inhale too deeply. I hoped we would catch Harry's widow at home. More than that, I hoped she would let us inside, where an air conditioner's filter would allow us all to breathe easy.

I was spiffed up again. Coat, tie, professional demeanor. Ready to make a good impression. Rebecca was still perfect.

One of the twin doors was opened by a tall, gracefully dressed woman on the far side of fifty. I said, "Mrs. Armstadt?" She nodded at me with a distance in her bearing. "I'm Jack Harbinger." I gave her my condolences and one of my legitimate business cards. "This is my associate, Rebecca Chatterton. We're here to discuss your husband's incident in his boat off The Bishop's Retreat."

She gave me the usual put-off: the police had already told her all the facts and asked her all the questions.

"We're not covering the same ground as the police," I said.

"Is this about the life insurance policy?"

"No, it's more about safety issues on the lake, fish attacks, that sort of thing."

"Why doesn't the county send out their own employees?"

"Normally, it would, but the regular staff is tied up with vector control after the heavy lake fly invasion this year. Sometimes they're so busy they have to farm these things out to private agencies like ours."

It was quality flapdoodle. Rebecca was visibly impressed by it and Mrs. Armstadt accepted it rather than calling to verify credentials.

The widow moved aside, inviting us into the house and its refreshing air. She led us through a foyer and into a room that would have been elegant and comfortable if it hadn't been so large. Jumbo seascapes and full-length portraits of eighteenth-century aristocrats filled the side walls. Picture windows in three enormous frames cut out a good part of the back wall and displayed a panoramic view. Outside, past a patio, there was an immense lawn. At the end of that, beyond a dock, the lake extended southward as far as I could see. On its eastern rim, to my left, bluffs lined the water. The bluffs gradually shrank in perspective until they became a thin green line that disappeared in the distance.

On the dock there was a wide and airy boat shelter — a slanted roof supported by six metal posts. A motorized fishing skiff and a simple rowboat were suspended on slings. There was no sailing sloop or cabin cruiser tied up out there, and that surprised me.

Inside the large room, furniture was arranged in a conversational grouping between two spaces that could have accommodated a dance floor and an orchestra. Ellen Armstadt sat in an overstuffed chair and cast her eyes toward the placid water on her right. In spite of her height, the wings of the chair dwarfed her. Rebecca and I sat opposite her, close together on a sofa that might have fit both of us end-to-end. The widow looked at us across a marble table loaded with books and magazines and pamphlets. Like everything else in the room, the table was too big. It was wide enough to park a Volkswagen Beetle and seemed long enough to land a Piper Cub.

"May I get you something?" Mrs. Armstadt said. "Coffee?"

"Very nice of you," I said, "But no, thanks."

"Harry still speaks to me," Ellen Armstadt told us. "He came to me last night when I was in bed and trying to fall asleep. He told me he wants me to cash out our energy portfolio but he doesn't want me to sell the house." She waved a hand out toward the water. "He knows I love it here."

"Harry must have been a skillful investor," Rebecca said to her. "You have a fabulous home." I couldn't tell whether she was just being polite.

"Thank you," Ellen said. "My husband's father had been one of the moguls of the paper industry in the valley, and Harry always handled his inheritance very well. He followed the stock market and made quite a lot of money in it. People said he had a great deal of foresight. Of course, he now has visions of the future he could only guess at during his time on this planet."

I broke in: "Harry can tell the future?"

"The past, the present and the future are one, Mr. Harbinger. You would know that if your body could release your soul. Suffice it to say, Harry's financial acumen is such that it speaks from beyond."

My mind squibbed an image of a Ouija board chuttering out Wall Street ticker tape a week in advance.

Ellen went on: "I think he would have done even better if he had taken the advice of my astrologer, but Harry wouldn't have any of that. He was the linear inflexible type."

"I've been called that myself," I said. "Maybe Harry and I would have gotten along."

The widow's smile was just short of tolerant. "Perhaps not," she said.

"It's a difficult thing to deal with," I said, trying to sound respectful, "but I wanted to ask you about the day … the last day your husband took the rowboat out onto the lake."

"Nothing unusual," she said. "He liked to go fishing right off the point."

"Near The Bishop's Retreat?"

"Yes, anywhere along in here, just a short distance from the shore. He didn't like to go out too far in the rowboat."

"Who brought the news to you when Harry's … remains were found?"

"A police officer came to the door. He told me there had been a terrible fish attack, which made sense to me because Harry had taken so many fish out of the lake over the years. I knew that nature was bound to even things out."

"Even things out? How do you mean that, exactly?"

"I can see the skepticism in your face, Mr. Harbinger. Do you know what karma is?"

"I think it means that if I step on an ant, some day that same ant will step on me."

Rebecca surreptitiously kicked my ankle under the massive table. Karma was starting already.

"I'm not sure you grasp the subtleties of the concept," Ellen said. "I always told Harry the universe would take care of him, but not if he kept going on these rampant killing sprees."

"Killing sprees?"

"The fish." Ellen said.

"You don't enjoy fish?" Rebecca asked.

"I enjoy them in the lake, where they belong. I don't eat them, if that's what you mean. You see before you a strict vegetarian."

"Very humane," Rebecca said.

Me, I was thinking of terrified carrots trembling on a dinner plate.

"Look at that monstrosity out there," Ellen said. She gestured toward a broad, bricked-in grill on the patio. "Harry was out there grilling nearly every day when the weather would permit. Either fish or steaks or hamburgers. He fully comprehends the horror of that now."

"Good," I said.

"He told me this morning, just as I was waking up."

"Right. If I understand this correctly, Harry's body was found in the bottom of the boat after the fish had attacked him."

"Yes, his body," Ellen said. "But his head must have fallen into the lake."

"The fish bit right through his neck?"

"Apparently. As you can imagine, Mr. Harbinger, I didn't ask for details."

"That's to be expected," I said. "Sounds like Harry still has a head for business, though."

"Excuse me?" Ellen said.

Rebecca's eyes threw a couple of darts at me.

"You said Harry is still advising you on your stock portfolio."

"Oh, that," Ellen said calmly. "Yes, he does."

"I imagine that's very helpful," I said.

The flashpoint had passed, but Rebecca secretly stepped on my foot anyway, grinding her heel on my toes. She was right. Sometimes I had fun when and where there was no place for it.

I moved on. "Have the remains been interred?"

"No. The body was cremated soon after I identified it through a birth defect. Last Chance Mortuary called within hours of the tragedy. They were gracious enough to take care of everything for me. For a fee, of course."

"This may be a little indelicate, but did anyone ever send a diver down to recover the head?"

"Yes, but the diver was unsuccessful."

"How do you know that?"

"The young woman from Last Chance told me. But that's all right. Harry is now a spirit on the astral plane. He doesn't need his flesh and bone anymore."

"Do you remember the name of the woman from the mortuary? And did you ever meet with any representatives in person?"

"No. And no. Everything was arranged over the telephone. The mortuary performed the cremation and scattered the ashes. Rapidly, per my request. They wanted to make a huge production of a funeral with a gold-plated casket, but I refused. There was no formal ceremony. I forbid it. It seemed irrelevant when the essential Harry would never be lying in some grave. His soul is all around us."

She didn't seem upset about losing her husband. For her, mysticism was one big tranquilizer, a drug she could take to dull the pain of reality.

"Did Harry seem troubled by anything in his last few days?"

"What does this have to do with safety on the lake?" Ellen said.

"Just trying to rule out any aggravating factors on land, any contributing causes outside of the lake itself. If you could bear with me for a minute, were there any squabbles or frictions between Harry and anyone else?"

"Well, the Knights of Columbus were trying to get his philosophy course canceled."

"What course was that?"

"Harry taught philosophy at Pulptown Community College. It was his avocation. Let's see. It's hard to remember the exact name of the objectionable course."

Rebecca pitched in: "Fallacies of the Ontological and Cosmological Arguments?" She held up a brochure. "The course outline was right here on the table."

"Yes, I remember now," Ellen said. "My husband had a problem with those arguments for the existence of God. It was a shame, really, because Harry failed to recognize that there are innumerable ways of receiving and interpreting truth."

"Why did the Knights of Columbus get involved?" I asked.

"They felt Harry was doing a disservice to God. By questioning doctrine and planting the seeds of doubt. One of their men was here shortly before Harry's death. The two of them went into Harry's study and had a terrible battle over Alvin Plantinga. They were quite loud and I could hear every word."

"Who is Alvin Plantinga?" I asked.

"He's a noted scholar, a theological philosopher," Ellen said. "Plantinga's ontological position is that there is a possible world in which there exists an entity of ultimate greatness. Therefore, there must necessarily be such an entity, which is God. So, of course, God by his nature exhibits ultimate greatness in every conceivable way."

"Sure, why not?" I said.

Ellen said, "Sadly, Harry dismissed the insight out of hand. He told the man from the Knights of Columbus that Plantinga's premise was an arbitrary assumption, and that Plantinga's conclusion merely repeated the absurd ideas of Rene Descartes."

"Let's go with that," I said, reaching back to Bertrand Russel and some other philosophers I had read. "Descartes argued that existence is perfection, and that the idea of God is one of a supremely perfect being. He said that if God didn't actually exist, then God would be less than perfect. But because God *is* perfect, then he has to exist."

"A bit redundant, but yes, that's basically it," Ellen said.

"Did Harry and the guy from the Knights of Columbus talk about that argument?"

"They did, and Harry was very derisive about it. He said the logic was circular, and the philosophy was gibberish."

"I don't suppose Harry's comment went over very well with his visitor."

"It definitely did not." Ellen said. "How can any of this be significant?"

"Maybe I'm putting Descartes before the horse," I said. "But these philosophical battles could be the aggravating factors I was talking about. Please indulge me a bit longer. If I'm reading Harry's take on things correctly, he would have said the real question here is why existence itself should be considered as perfection. Besides that, why is it necessary that the universe would include an entity of ultimate greatness, as Plantinga seems to assume?"

"Yes, that's almost literally what Harry said. And all the man from the Knights could do was hem and haw. Rather weakly, I must say." Ellen looked down uncomfortably. "And then Harry went for the jugular. He could be very cruel that way."

"What do you mean?"

"Harry told the man that he was shallow and stupid. He said what Descartes and Plantinga were actually postulating was the idea that any phenomenon we can possibly imagine must necessarily exist in reality."

"And then?"

"And then the man, the Knights of Columbus man, accused Harry of restricting himself, thinking in terms of limits. And I can see the poor man's point. He said if a perfect being is possible, then an infinite universe containing all possibilities would necessarily contain such a being."

"Where did it go from there?" I asked.

"Harry told him to look at it logically. Harry always relied too heavily on logic."

"And …? What else did Harry tell him?"

"Harry told him that in a universe infinite in variety and containing all possibilities, two of those possibilities would be an all-encompassing God and a limited God. And Harry told the Knights of Columbus man that these two versions of God were mutually exclusive. He told the man that he couldn't have it both ways, and that the concept of an infinite-variety universe is self-contradictory and incoherent. Those were Harry's exact words. He also told the man that even if the universe is infinite in size, it doesn't necessarily follow that it is infinite in variety."

"So," I said, "Harry painted Sir Knight into a corner. And I'd bet the guy wasn't happy about it."

"Harry's debating style could be extremely aggressive at times."

"But he was right," I said. "Harry pointed out the knight's inconsistency and made him look silly."

She looked at me with pity in her eyes and spoke slowly. "Ralph Waldo Emerson said a foolish consistency is the hobgoblin of little minds."

"I'm guessing that Harry would have called Emerson's mind a foolish hobgoblin of little consistency."

Now the pity was becoming something else.

"I will assume you do not believe in reincarnation," the widow sniffed at me. "But perhaps you and Harry *did* get along in your past lives."

"I think we served together in the First Bengal Lancers."

Rebecca dug her fingernails into my leg. She was right again, but I couldn't take much more blather.

"You are hopelessly sarcastic, Mr. Harbinger. Just like Harry. And, like Harry, you are indeed linear inflexible."

"Maybe that's why I feel for him, ma'am. The guy from the Knights of Columbus, was he local or sent by the diocese executives in Green Bay?"

"He mentioned Saint Opie's a few times."

"Did you catch the knight's name?"

"He introduced himself to me, but it was one of those names you forget instantly."

"Can you describe him for me?"

"I didn't pay close attention," Ellen said.

"Anything at all?"

"Middle aged. Balding. That's all I can recall. When I sensed a worsening conflict, I tried to put the man out of my mind. I went upstairs and left the two of them to their arguing."

"So, Harry and the other guy went over all this for how long?"

"For more than an hour. And from what I could still overhear, the man from the Knights of Columbus got more irritated with Harry by the minute. He started shouting at Harry about the vengeance of the Lord. Harry finally threw him out of the house. Figuratively threw him out, but I'm sure Harry felt insulted enough to do it physically."

"Philosophical double-talk will do that to a person," I told her.

"You have a closed mind, Mr. Harbinger."

"That may be, Mrs. Armstadt, but there are people who won't wait for the Lord's vengeance. I'm suggesting that your husband was murdered."

"That's unthinkable!"

"It's part of a pattern."

"Then this interview doesn't really have anything to do with safety on the lake," she said indignantly.

"You're right, and I apologize. I was playing a little loose. No, that's not fair. I was lying like hell. But if I'm onto something, if Harry was in fact murdered, wouldn't you want to know about it?"

"Certainly, I would. But the police never said anything about murder. They had a witness from the church."

"I've spoken with that witness," I said. "He's isn't exactly solid. And the police around here don't have the best reputation for thoroughness."

She considered what I said for a long time. Then she checked with Rebecca, who gave her a pair of sincere and reassuring eyes.

"Do you truthfully think there could have been foul play?" Ellen asked her.

"That makes more sense than muskies." Rebecca confirmed.

"Is it all right if we borrow your rowboat?" I said to Ellen.

"I suppose so. But why?"

"To test a theory, more of a hunch. You said Harry liked to grill burgers out there on the patio. Did he possibly leave any unfrozen meat in your refrigerator?"

"I think there's some ground beef in there," Ellen said tentatively. "I would have thrown it out but I hate to even touch it."

"The rowboat and a pound of hamburger would go a long way toward clearing this up," I told her.

"That's a very strange request, young man."

"Again, please indulge me."

FORTY-FIVE

When we got out to the car with the package of hamburger meat, I stowed my coat and tie in the trunk but left my gun and shoulder holster strapped on.

Rebecca said, "You're flaunting your weapon. That's a bad sign. What's happening?"

"Like I said, I'm following a hunch."

"What hunch is that?"

"Just help me get Harry's boat in the water." With the pound of flesh in my grip, we walked beside the house and out toward the dock.

"At least tell me where we're going," she demanded.

"The monastery. The Bishop's Retreat."

"Why don't we drive there like everybody else?"

"Because everybody else has to pass by the guard shack. And get permission to enter."

"What's so important about the monastery?"

"Slab donated a fountain there, right?"

"I guess so."

"Did you go with him to the dedication ceremony?"

"No," she said. "I begged off."

"Well, the fountain is what I want to see."

"And you'll need a gun for that?"

"Not if we're careful." We got under the shelter. "Quick, help me with this." We pulled a blue tarp off the suspended aluminum rowboat.

"What's the rush?" Rebecca said.

"I don't know how long our reconnaissance mission will take. There are stagnant ponds across the street from here and by dusk a million mosquitos will be in the air. I want to get the boat back in place before the little bloodsuckers come down on us like vampire bats."

She gave me one of her looks but rolled up the tarp as I cranked a manual winch to lower the boat. When the hull was afloat, I tossed Harry Armstadt's package of cold but pliable hamburger into it.

"That meat will spoil down there," Rebecca said.

I went aboard. "Trust me. It won't matter."

"Why don't we use the motorboat?" Rebecca said.

"It's too noisy."

"Seriously? The monks are going to shoo you away if they hear a motor on the lake?"

"Could happen," I told her. "The main thing is that I want to look around without being watched. I can't afford to have a reception committee on the shore."

She gave up on the questions and joined me. Along the length of the boat, under the seats, there was a pole covered at one end with dried scum and weeds from the lake bed. Two oars were also stowed there. We pulled those out and clipped them into the oarlocks. I sat on the middle bench with my back to the bow. Rebecca took the bench at the stern, facing me. She twisted around to push the boat away from the dock and I dipped the oars into the water.

"I'll need you to navigate," I said. "From what I hear, there's no sign for the place. But look for a stone shrine. And let me know if you see any security personnel."

"You're paranoid."

"Maybe, but where Slab has been, I don't want to take chances. If there are guards on the premises, I want to avoid them."

I rowed east from the Armstadt manor. We crossed the mouth of a small channel and skirted a blunt peninsula. Rebecca straightened her back and pointed.

"Avast ye, matey" she said in a quiet, snarky voice. "I can see the shrine."

"Any activity?"

"Not yet."

"All right," I said. "Guide me in."

I rowed toward the shore until she told me to raise the oars. I tucked them inside the gunwales as we drifted in. Rebecca took the long pole from under the seats and stood up to drive the scummy end of it into the underwater muck. I pivoted to face forward. From a thicket of trees, a sturdy branch hung out over the water. Rebecca pushed the boat close enough for me to grab the branch and pull us into the thicket. At the bow, one end of a rope was looped into an eyehook. I tied its loose end to a sapling and Rebecca stowed the pole.

I grabbed the package of meat and we got out. We stepped from sandy pebbles onto a rough-cut lawn. The turf gradually pitched upward, and we climbed the incline to where it leveled off at a group of buildings. We stopped at a stone shed.

"Even if we find a grill, we don't have any hamburger buns," Rebecca said. "You want me to steal some from the pantry?"

"Keep it down," I told her as we eased along the rear wall of the shed. "This job isn't supposed to be fun."

"You should talk."

I poked my head around a corner of the structure. The fountain was in a courtyard formed by a surrounding colonnade. No one was visible there. We moved out from our position and walked cautiously toward the new installation.

The fountain's pompous vulgarity was outdated by a few centuries. In its center, metal cherubs huddled around the feet of a stone Jesus. Water streamed out of the cherubs in urinary arcs, and the streams poured into a wide surrounding moat. The water in the moat looked to be two or three feet deep. A school of fish, each of them six or seven inches long, swam through it aimlessly.

I used my car key to slit open the package of raw hamburger and then pinched the contents from the cellophane into the moat.

"What the hell are you doing?" Rebecca said in a loud whisper. After a couple of seconds, the water started roiling. Suddenly it was churning violently. "Oh my God," Rebecca said. "They're piranhas!"

"My hunch was right," I told her.

One of the fish came vaulting out of the water and landed on the flat stone rim of the moat. The thing flopped wildly, gasping for water. It was tiny, but the rows of teeth in its gaping mouth were as cute as barbed wire. I reached down, intending to brush the piranha onto the grass, but it launched itself off the rim and back into the drink. Probably a lucky break for my finger.

After a few more seconds, the feeding frenzy was over and the roiling stopped.

"This is what happened to Harry Armstadt," I said. "Somehow, they lured him onto shore when they spotted him fishing."

"Who's they?"

"Father Timothy from Saint Opie's and the monks or acolytes or whoever else might live out here. They must have gotten him all the way up to the fountain and thrown him into the moat. When the piranhas were finished with him, Timothy and the others must have used grappling hooks or rakes to pull his body out. And then they threw the remains in the bottom of Harry's rowboat. They pushed the boat out into the lake and called the police. Some idiot patrolmen came out here and bought their story about man-eating muskies."

"How did you know the piranhas were in there?"

"Lucky guess, except that muskies don't go in for this line of work. They're nibblers but they're not going to leap out of the lake and tear a grown man to shreds. Apart from that, Father Timothy was fudging on his details when I questioned him."

"What details?"

"The number of fish, the type of fish and the body going overboard. He was supposedly an eye witness to the muskie attack, but his story didn't make any sense. When I found out that Slab had donated the fountain out here, I wondered how he and Timothy were putting it to use."

"Mrs. Armstadt said the head was never recovered," Rebecca said in a low, tight voice. " I wonder whether it's in here."

We walked around the moat. No heads in the clear water.

Rebecca said, "What do you suppose happened to it?"

"When I walked in on Father Timothy yesterday, I caught him contemplating a skull, like Hamlet contemplating Yorick in the graveyard. All I have is suspicion. Maybe it was Harry's skull Timothy was playing with."

She pulled up her shoulders and shuddered. "Good thought," she said. "But it couldn't be. From what I've been told, it takes weeks and weeks to strip the flesh off a skull."

"Really? Why so long?"

"They can't simply scrub it. Mostly, they apply tiny maggots that slowly eat away at the muscle and cartilage and whatever else is attached."

"And this just comes up in conversation? Damn, Rebecca, who the hell do you hang around with?"

"Don't bother yourself about that. You should try to catch one of these fish."

"I had my chance and missed it. You want me to stick my hand in there and grab one?"

"You'll still have your other hand," she said.

"You want a lot for a hundred dollars a day. But even if I could produce a piranha in a Mason jar, I couldn't prove it came from here. What I'd like is for the cops — some smarter cops this time — to show up unannounced and inspect the place."

"All right, be that way," she said. "We're going to tell the widow about this, right?"

"Not yet," I said. "She's liable to come storming down here on her own, and if she does, they can distract her and delay her at the gate until the monks remove the piranhas. Then we'll be left with nothing more than a crazy story. Let's get back to the boat."

A door opened in a building beyond the colonnade. Three figures came out, each one in a brown hooded robe. The lady and I hid low behind Jesus and the pissing cherubs. We could hear tones of conversation in the still air, but nobody looked in our direction. One of the monks went back into the building, and the two remaining figures walked on, heading farther away from us. When it was all clear, Rebecca and I left the fountain and the courtyard and started back down the grassy slope. I kept hold of the meat packaging, not wanting to leave behind any sign of outsiders.

We were fifty or sixty feet from the boat when another figure in a brown robe came out of a dense grove near the water. He set himself to face us, blocking our path. His eyes were hidden by the robe's floppy hood. A thousand years behind the times, he would have been laughable if not for the long, curved blade on the scythe he was brandishing.

FORTY-SIX

"Who goeth there?" the monk challenged.

"He's got to be kidding," Rebecca said softly.

"We came to grill some burgers," I answered.

"Didst thou come through the gate?" His voice was gritty.

"Sure," I said. "We got dropped off and we walked in."

"Where art thy identification passes, hanging heavy on thy lanyards, as behooveth thine unholy state?"

"The guard must have forgotten about them."

"Nay, for Brother Bartholomew standeth guard. He doth not miss a squirrel. Nor wouldst he countenance the firearm upon thy sacrilegious rib."

Rebecca gave me a bewildered look. "Is there a time warp out here?"

"Seems that way," I told her. "Let's try to slide by."

"How say you now, vile trespassers?"

"Someone's going to pick us up in a boat," I called out to the monk. "We'll be on our way as soon as we can get down to the water."

As we started moving again, the monk raised the scythe to halt us.

"Methinks not. The wheel of justice doth not grind so lightly."

"Are you with security?" I asked him.

"None but an Opian monk, charged at this hour to harvest the grass as a service to the Lord in Heaven."

"Boy, they have you working pretty late," I said, trying to be friendly.

"The obedient monk cutteth and prayeth. Mine own purpose is thus. But thou hast no purpose here before the Lord. Indeed, he who cometh unwelcomed upon this hallowed ground giveth need for the judgment that passeth his soul into the depth of hell."

Rebecca barely opened the corner of her mouth. "Maybe he's their public relations guy," she said.

The hood loomed over the monk's face. He bent forward and walked slowly up the slope toward our position. He wielded the scythe with authority, then stopped and set himself firmly on the uneven turf.

"Sorry for the intrusion, Mr. Reaper," I said to him. "May I call you Grim?"

"Thou art a million laughs," he said in a monotone.

I decided to goad him a little more, get him off his train of thought. "Didn't I meet you at the Flat Earth Society?"

"Thy jest be noted," he said. "I get thy reference. Thou thinkest of me as an antiquarian. Verily, for the old ways are at last the best ways, and the earth shall prove to be flat indeed, as Scripture hath made manifest. Mark thee, thy rash and careless japes carry no mirth within the bounds of this sacred place."

"That's fair," I said. "Maybe another time, then."

We moved once more toward the water but the monk stepped in our way again. He held out the scythe like a roadblock.

"Time hath run out for thee in this base and earthly realm," he said. He repositioned the scythe — blade up — with a little more intimidation.

I dropped the cellophane packaging and rested my right hand on the grip of my gun.

"Back off," I said.

The threat of bullets didn't seem to mean anything to him.

"Huzzah!" he cried out. "An Opian monk welcometh death as the gateway to everlasting paradise. If thou should let fly thy ignoble projectiles, then thou wouldst only quicken the advent of mine own salvation."

"Well, you got me there," I said. I had counted on him being afraid to die, but he wasn't. I couldn't shoot him because a gun versus a scythe would have been murder in any court. Even if I fired a warning shot over his head it might not get him to stand down. Besides, the noise would bring every one of his brethren swarming down the hill. I left the .38 in its holster.

He approached again, then stopped a few feet away from us and widened his stance. His weapon was poised over his right shoulder.

"The interlopers must needs die as the errant weeds must needs be slain beneath a righteous blade."

"He's crazy," Rebecca said. She stepped in close to me.

"Get to the boat," I whispered to her.

"I heard thee," the monk said. "Move not an inch."

She moved anyway, stepping to her left and toward the trees. I sloughed over to my right into the open lawn to draw him toward me. The monk measured both of us and made his choice. He turned to me and crouched into combat position. Menacing and determined, he shifted his weight and extended the scythe. I didn't let my eyes track Rebecca, but I knew she was running for the water.

"You looketh a little comical in that get-up," I said.

"Thou speakest with the tongue of Beelzebub."

"Yeah, nuns have been telling me that since I was ten."

"Hark! By thine own account, thou hast been diabolical as a child. Even today, thou art like unto the devil. Hast thee not perpetuated thy impiety?"

"Don't get yourself too worked up here, Grim."

"The obedient monk must needs destroy the offender."

He came toward me, his eyes now visible and burning under the hood. I inched backward up the slope. He kept coming, the scythe getting more and more dangerous. He closed both hands around the base of the shaft and thrust himself forward. He took a swipe at me, the sharp edge of the tool whipping like a scimitar inches away from my stomach. I was terrified but I kept talking.

"You misseth me," I said.

"No, no, no," he said. "That's twice you've gotten it wrong."

"What?"

He took another swing at me. I leaned backward and almost lost my footing on the slippery grass.

"Everybody gets it wrong," he said. "It's more like *he looketh comical* in the third person, like he looks comical. Or *he misseth me* in the present tense. Like he misses me, only it's *misseth*."

"What?"

He took another roundhouse whiff at my stomach as I backed my way up the incline. He kept advancing.

"Present tense and the third person," he said again. "Not *you misseth me*, but *he misseth me*."

"You mean it's kind of a lisp?" I said.

"We don't like to call it that, but I suppose it operates the same way."

We went slowly up the grade, the monk matching me step for step. There was a hint of movement behind him. I worked like hell to keep my eyes off the movement and on the monk's face.

"That's really interesting," I said. "I never would have known."

He stopped. "Anyway, that's the way I *think* it operates. I'm not sure." He was almost friendly now. "I oughta check the manual. I transferred over to the Opians only a few days ago."

"A few days!" I said. "Maybe you should reconsider. Are you sure you're supposed to slice up anyone who wanders onto the premises?"

"Forsooth." He was back to his medieval playacting. And not so chummy anymore. "The obedient monk doth not question, lest evil find its way through doubts that be as cracks in the ramparts of his faith. Mine own orders be clear."

"Orders be clear? Now you're sounding more like a pirate."

"What? A pirate? No, that's not …"

"Next you'll be telling me you'll scuttle my bones in the briny deeps."

He started to lose his temper but took a deep breath and stayed in character.

"Thou wouldst jest and play the fool until thy death and damnation!"

"Why not?" I said. It all theems a little thilly."

"No! It's not a lisp all the way through, you idiot! Just at the end of the word! And then only … aagh! Why do I even bother?" He stepped forward again.

"Nevertheleth," I prodded him.

Now the monk was enraged and paying no attention to the stirring behind him. His face twisted into a grimace and his voice went into a wail. "I shall cleave thee in twain!"

My feet caught against a tuft behind me and I tripped. He cocked the scythe like a hockey player about to try a slap shot. My insides went cold.

A length of wood crashed into the side of his neck and green slop flicked off the end of it. The monk went down in a heap of brown cloth. His grip went slack and the scythe fell to the turf. His left hand went to his neck.

"Zounds!" he swore. "From whence did *that* come?"

He started to get up but Rebecca lifted her push-pole again. She brought it down like a sledgehammer on the monk's right collar bone.

The monk flattened, moaning and writhing on the ground.

Before he could recover, Rebecca picked up the scythe beside him and threw it like a javelin into a patch of tall grass. She kept hold of the pole. I got to my feet and we ran down to the shore. We hit the waterline and scrambled into the boat.

At the bow, I pulled the rope loose from the sapling. I reached out for the big overhanging branch and pivoted the boat away from the thicket. At the stern, Rebecca drove one end of the pole into the muck and pushed us out. I took the oars amidships and started rowing as Rebecca sat down and put the pole away.

When we were a few strokes offshore, I saw a couple of men in brown robes run downhill to the fallen monk and lay their hands on his elbows. They helped him to his feet. He was wobbly but able to stand on his own. There was some conversation between the three of them, but I couldn't make out any words. One of the able monks walked downhill and picked up the cellophane wrapper I had lost in the grass. Then he and his partner ran down to the waterline and stood staring in our direction.

"Hamburgers, verily," one of them said. The calm surface of the lake now carried his voice out to us. "Yet their grill hath vanished. Nor doth a solitary hot coal glow beneath the sweep of mine eyes."

"Aye, 'tis black magic," the other monk said. "Beware the sorcery of Satan. Let us pray."

The two of them knelt and the first one spoke loud enough for God to hear him. I stilled the oars to listen.

"Oh Lord, Thou hast delivered us from the thralls of Satan, even as the devil's foul vessel doth recede upon the dark and mysterious waters. But if the dread enemy in the persons of them, the one and the other, should return to our midst, we pray Thee, silence the vexing tongues of them. And by Thine infinite power, constrict and otherwise fetter the demons' wanton smitings upon Thy faithful servants, the Monks of Saint Opius."

"Amen."

The last of it was barely audible as we drifted away in the current. The two figures stood up, turned and started walking up the grassy slope toward their stricken brother. The monks' prayer hadn't mentioned the fountain, so they probably hadn't realized that Rebecca and I knew about the piranhas. That was a break. I pumped hard at the oars.

"I don't think they're coming after us," I whispered to Rebecca.

Neither of us said another word until I had rowed us all the way around the point. By the time we made it back to the Armstadt property, there was no flotilla chasing us.

We maneuvered the boat to the shelter and the underwater slings, then climbed up onto the dock. I ratcheted the lightweight hull above the surface and locked the crank. Rebecca replaced the tarp across the seats, leaving everything as we had found it.

We walked up a path to the driveway and my Mustang. We got in and closed the doors as quietly as we could, not wanting to alert the widow and owe her an explanation. I gave the key a half-turn, stepped on the clutch and took the transmission out of gear. The car rolled backward down the driveway and I started the engine when we hit the road. I drove off slowly.

"Thanks," I told her. "You were damn impressive."

"I told you I'd been in scrapes before," she said.

"Yeah, you told me all kinds of things. Anyway, one more swing of that scythe and I might have been bleeding all over the lawn."

"Why didn't you just shoot him?"

"Too much noise and too much legal trouble."

"I guess. That was a lot of fun, in spite of what you told me. Is every day like this for a private eye?"

"No. Most days are all about law suits and indemnity clauses."

We rode through town, both of us trying to come down off the flow of adrenalin.

"Where are we going now?" Rebecca wanted to know.

"We'll get dinner."

"Could we go to a restaurant where they don't have Packer memorabilia on the walls?"

"We'll try to locate one." I told her. "Then we need to find a guy who likes to play pool at a downtown bar. I'd like to run all this by him and see what he thinks."

"He's a confidante?"

"Something like that."

If I had told her anything more, she would have jumped out of the car.

FORTY-SEVEN

During dinner we went over the interviews. Later, back in the Mustang, we joined some dawdling downtown traffic. I said, "Did Slab ever mention anything related to what we heard today?"

"He never talked about names or unusual deaths or even funerals," Rebecca said. "I tried to draw him out, but he clearly *did not* want to discuss business."

"Well, my friend's hangout is up here on the right. I'm sorry if it doesn't meet your standards."

I parked behind The Drunk Tank, the last watering hole on the commercial strip of Lombardi Street. We were blocks from my office building — and anyone watching it — but not far enough away to feel safe. It wasn't just the case; it was the venue. The Drunk Tank was the kind of bar where you could get a fat lip as easily as a stiff drink. According to local folklore, nearly a hundred brawlers had been carried out of there on stretchers. Two of them dead. In remembrance, I kept my .38 close to my heart.

As soon as we walked in, the smell of spilled beer hit us. The floor was sticky with it. Smoke dimmed the overhead lights. The air tasted like it had already been through three or four sets of lungs. Every few seconds, antagonistic voices rose over the general din. A bartender in a flak jacket had a Camel or a Marlboro dangling from his lip. The timing of his cigarette maintenance was a little off, and a drooping arm of ash fell into the drink he was mixing. He used an index finger to swirl the ash into whatever liquor was in the glass.

"Very swanky," Rebecca said. "I assume they have a direct shuttle to the hospital."

Waitresses fended off macho hotshots while circulating among tables and chairs. Beyond them, resolute pool players chalked their sticks and lined up shots. There was an open booth at the rear wall. I ushered the lady into an inside seat, telling her I'd need to spring to my feet in case there was a ruckus. But that wasn't what I was thinking. Before long she'd realize who I was there to see. And when she did, she'd have to climb over my lap to escape the booth.

A familiar waitress came by, took our orders and returned with our beers. We were drinking Schnubners out of bottles.

"This beer is dreadful," Rebecca said.

"I know it is, but it's the best brand they serve. I thought you would have tasted it before."

"I worked in Schnubner's museum." She paused and studied the label. "But I never drank their beer." She smiled. "Anyway, what a remarkable day we had."

"You never know what to expect in this job. Some of it is awful. I'll tell you, though. Besides the fact that you saved my life, it felt good to have you with me."

"Thanks. I felt the same."

Petty conversation filled the next quarter-hour and then I said, "Here's my contact. He's heading straight for the pool tables, as always."

The imposing Wally Eck — in his civilian tee shirt, jeans and sneakers — carried a narrow case that would have contained his custom pool cue in two pieces. He took long strides through the gaps between customers until he saw me waiting for him. He stopped short, shaking his head and pushing his mouth over to one side, the way people do when they're disgusted. He came up to our booth, ready to warn me off his turf, but when he got an eyeful of Rebecca he went bleary. It was as if someone had tossed a cold drink in his face. After a few seconds, he took his eyes off her and got ahold of himself. He bore down on me.

"How about them Packers? And what the hell are you doing in here?"

"This is a friend of yours?" Rebecca said to me quietly.

Eck locked on her again and breathed in deeply.

"Sit down," I said to him. "You'll find it's easier to stare when you're at eye level." He slid his big frame onto the bench opposite ours and laid his case on the table. "Eck, say hello to Rene Antolini. She's an accident reconstruction expert over here from Deadwood, South Dakota. Emphasis on *dead.* Rene, this is Lieutenant Eck, the finest man in Pulptown's crack police department."

Rebecca tensed. If I hadn't been blocking her way, she would have run out on me in a second. She gave me an angry look, but instantly put on a pleasant face for Eck. "Nice to meet you," she told him politely.

Eck mumbled something in return, transfixed by her.

I snapped my fingers and waved a hand through Eck's line of vision.

"There's police business," I told him.

He turned back to me, barely regaining his strength.

"It's Friday night," he moaned. "If you have police business, why not come into the station on Monday morning?"

"Because this won't wait," I said.

He slumped against the back of the bench and let out an exasperated breath.

"This is about them death threats, right?"

Rebecca's knee bumped hard into mine.

"I solved that one," I told him. "New case, new client."

"Okay, Harbinger. But this better be good."

FORTY-EIGHT

"Any news on your muskie investigation?" I asked the lieutenant.

"What investigation? I told you, the priest from Saint Opie's was down there at The Bishops' Retreat and he saw the whole thing. What am I gonna do, bring in a bunch of fish for questioning? And anyways, I also told you fish are born dead."

"Jack?" Rebecca said. "Is there something …?"

"Just roll with it," I answered her. I turned back to the lieutenant. "Look, Eck. Let's suppose you're right and fish are born dead. They still bite, don't they?"

"I suppose so." Eck picked up on the music that leaked from a jukebox at the other side of the bar. He absentmindedly drummed the edge of the table.

"How is forensics doing at identifying the type of dead fish that bit Harry Armstadt?"

"What forensics?" he said. "There wasn't much left of the guy."

"His bones could have shown teeth marks," I said.

"I heard the mortuary already burned up the bones." The music stopped and so did Eck's unconscious drumming.

"And the warehouse fatality," I said. "Any breaks on that?"

"Who, the forklift guy? Father Timothy saw that one too."

"Third thing," I told Eck. "The machine operator who got his hand cut off in the paper mill."

"What about him?"

"That's what I'd like to know. Weren't there any questions asked?"

"Donkey's ass, Harbinger. It was an accident. We can't go around interviewing a slew of mill rats every time somebody gets his hand cut off. Besides, I heard that somebody already knew everything about it. That deacon who moved away to Tahiti."

"Dennis Canfield," I said. "And it was Borneo."

"Borneo? Tahiti? What's the difference?"

"At least five thousand miles," Rebecca said.

"Ms. Antolini here has done some extensive research," I said, though I knew she wouldn't be pleased. "And she says none of the stories on these deaths hold up under scrutiny."

Eck stared at her again. For a long time.

"That's right," she said, playing her role. "In each case, there were suspicious circumstances."

Eck was virtually paralyzed by her attention. He garbled some words. I had to shake him out of it.

"You can't keep her, Eck. She has to go back to Deadwood."

"Hey, shut up, Harbinger."

"There's a pattern to all three deaths," I told him. "A thread running through them. Don't you want to hear about it?"

"Maybe on Monday," he fired back at me. "This is my pool night."

"Yeah, that's how I knew we'd find you here. But like I said, there's a certain urgency to this."

"Aw Jeez," he whined.

The same waitress came back to the booth. Eck was antsy, rubbing his forehead, tenting his eyes to avoid hers. She was probably in her twenties but weathered by something more than time. She had a straw-stack of yellowish hair, dark at the roots. Teeth not so straight. The black outlines around her eyes looked like they'd been drawn with a crayon. Her skin was pasty and her expression was blank, except for a little umbrage aimed at Eck. I knew he dated her off and on — whenever she and her husband were fighting.

"Hi Connie," Eck finally said to her. "You know what I'm drinking."

"The lady and I are set," I told the waitress.

When she was gone, I asked Eck, "How are you two crazy kids doing?"

"Stuff it, Harbinger."

"So, about the series of homicides," I said.

"Oh, now they're homicides?" he snarled. "Really?"

I turned back to Rebecca and said, "The thing about Eck is, he's not very dedicated."

"The hell with you, Harbinger."

The waitress was back in less than a minute. She held Eck's beer bottle tightly and plunked it down, not hard enough to break it but hard enough to make suds climb up the neck and spill over. Eck took it quietly. He wouldn't even look up at her. I laid down some bills and signaled for her to keep the change. She nodded at me, sneered at Eck and walked away.

"All right," Eck said. "What's so goddamn important that it can't wait for a few games of pool?"

"Back to front," I said. "The papermill killing."

"You mean accident."

"I mean killing. Father Timothy wasn't there but the deacon, tied in with Saint Opie's, was right on the scene. And the deacon had been badgering Norman Lumm about religion."

"Who's Norman Lumm?"

"The guy who got his hand cut off. Don't you read the newspaper?"

"Okay, I forgot." He threw down a swig of beer.

"Lumm was making fun of the deacon's arguments and the deacon threatened to report him to the authorities. Soon enough, a mechanic showed up at the mill to work on Lumm's machine."

"What's unusual about that?"

"Nobody knew who he was," Rebecca put in. "He wasn't an employee of the mill. The strange thing is that the mechanic looked like Slab Kapowski."

"And here's something else," I said. "He showed up with a helper who looked and even sounded a lot like Flunk Vanderhovel."

Eck tilted his head and did some heavy concentrating.

"Wasn't he the guy who smashed a window and then crashed his truck out in the woods?"

"That's the one," I said.

"What's the connection?"

"Flunk was Slab's enforcer. You really ought to keep an eye on the underworld around here."

"I got a lot on my mind," Eck said.

Rebecca said, "The mechanic got Lumm to help him repair a malfunction while almost everyone else in the area was on a break. A few minutes later, Lumm was missing a hand and bleeding to death."

"But the deacon," Eck said.

I cut in on him. "Damn convenient that the deacon got shunted off to Borneo before he could provide any formal testimony. He didn't even give a clear account to the reporters."

"I guess you're right about that," Eck said. "What did the mechanic say about it?"

"We don't know," Rebecca said. "The mechanic and his helper vanished."

"Then there's the forklift victim," I said. "Pete Pulaski was his name if you don't remember."

"Hey, I don't have to memorize the name of everybody who dies around here."

"For one thing," I said, "Father Timothy had been badgering the warehouse victim about religion right up until the night before the death. On the morning it happened, the padre was at the facility to bless the victim's forklift. For another thing, Father Timothy may have brought his own forklift driver to the warehouse that day, even though he wouldn't have needed to. Slab Kapowski was on the scene and I'm betting he was the one driving the machine when the victim was killed. At this point that's only speculation."

"It's *all* speculation," Eck said.

"But listen to this. The victim was supposedly kneeling in prayer when the forklift skewered him. I knew that guy for years. Pete never knelt in prayer in his life unless a nun was there to horsewhip him if he didn't."

"Maybe there was a nun at the warehouse," Eck said.

"No such report," Rebecca told him.

"And you want me to believe," Eck said, "that Father Timothy brought Slab Kapowski down there to kill a guy? Kapowski is a big wheel businessman, for chrissake."

"His business is funerals," I said. "Necessary and unnecessary. In a lot of the recent ones, the guest of honor didn't exactly die of old age."

"That don't mean Kapowski killed them," Eck said. He took another swig. "And that still don't explain the guy who got ate up by the muskies."

"Piranhas," I told him.

Eck braced upright up in his seat.

"In Lake Winnebago?" he said. "I didn't even know we *had* piranhas. Could be an end times thing, though."

"They're not in the lake," I said. "They're in a fountain at The Bishop's Retreat."

"Now you're going batty," Eck said. He took a long pull on his beer.

"I've seen them," Rebecca said. Eck seemed to take her word for it.

"How did you two get past the guard?" he wanted to know.

"We bribed him with a chocolate cake," I said.

He nodded seriously, not catching my tone. "Good idea. I bet those guys don't see many of those."

"And by the way, Eck, it was Slab Kapowski who funded the fountain. He oversaw construction and was there at the dedication ceremony. I suppose that would have given him the right to choose koi or catfish or anything else he wanted to put in there. It certainly gave him the opportunity to plant the piranhas."

Eck worked on it awhile but came up short. "How the hell did the college professor get his boat into the fountain?"

"Think about it, Eck. They obviously lured him onto shore near the spot where he was fishing. They threw him in the fountain moat and when the piranhas were done with him, they pulled out what was left of his body and his clothes. Then they dumped the whole package into the bottom of his boat and set it adrift on the lake. All to make it look like he was killed out there."

"But the priest saw it," Eck protested.

"I questioned Father Timothy," I said. "His story doesn't hold together."

"Remember the missing piece," Rebecca said to me.

"Right," I said. "The widow told us that her husband's head was never recovered. She assumed it was lost at the bottom of the lake. But I'm wondering whether someone is collecting skulls."

"Come on, Harbinger! Why would anybody do that?"

"Hell, I don't know. But I saw Father Timothy playing with one."

"Perhaps an old trophy," Rebecca said.

"Now we're dealing with head hunters?" Eck asked.

"I'm not sure exactly *what* we're dealing with," I told him. "But Ms. Antolini may be right. Who knows where the rest of the skulls ended up after Slab got ahold of them? Trophies or no trophies, there's something here that can't be written off as accidents or the feeding habits of dead fish."

Eck went for his beer again. "I can't see people getting murdered over a religious disagreement. If we had that, the Catholics and Lutherans and Presbyterians and Methodists would be sending hit squads all over the valley."

"It goes deeper than that," I told him. "I don't think it has anything to do with clashing denominations. The victims were nonbelievers. They weren't just quibbling over details. They were rejecting faith in God altogether. They were shooting big holes in religious thinking itself and asking a lot of embarrassing questions. And yesterday, at the church, I told Father Timothy I'm an atheist. He and two of his nuns tried to pulverize my brains."

"So now you're saying the nuns are involved in all this mayhem?"

"That shouldn't surprise you," I told him. "You went to Catholic school."

"Sure, I did. And I seen a nun knock the freckles off a fourth grader just for getting an arithmetic problem wrong. You gotta expect violence from nuns."

"The point is that the people who run Saint Opie's can't tolerate any unorthodox thinking."

"All this is a little far-fetched, Harbinger."

"So is a school of killer muskies."

"Uh, maybe."

Eck downed the rest of his beer and thumped the empty bottle on the table.

"You mean this is something like the Spanish Inquisition?" he said.

"All I know is this, Eck. The religious outlaws in this town have a funny way of dying violently."

"Yeah, but," Eck said, "what does Slab get out of it?"

"More stiffs to hold expensive services for," I said. "His people have been calling the next of kin in two out of the three cases. They've been laying on some high-pressure sales tactics to pump up the funeral bills. There may have been similar calls to Norman Lumm's family, but I haven't questioned any of them. Another angle for Slab is this: Maybe he plays ball with church personnel in exchange for them keeping quiet about his business rivals flying off the steeple."

"*Now* what's bothering you?" Eck exploded. "All them guys were depressed. Hey, I'd be depressed too if I was a mortician. No wonder they jumped."

"One of them had his hands tied behind his back!"

"Okay," he said. "That guy was a mortician, plus his hands were tied behind his back. That's double the reason for being depressed."

"Come on, Eck. Even with your brain in storage, you should be able to understand what I'm getting at."

"Okay, okay, I get it," Eck relented. "But you haven't proved anything that could stand up in court."

"Of course not," I told him. "I've only been on this for a few days. But it reeks of serial murder. That's why we're bringing it to you. The whole mess begs for a detailed police investigation."

"Why can't you keep investigating it yourself?"

"Because murder seems to be an industry with these fanatics. I don't have your department's resources. Or your files on those missing persons."

He tried his bottle, remembered that it was empty and ruefully laid it on its side. He scrunched his lips, sunk into his bench and grumbled: "More victims? Do you realize how much paper shuffling this is gonna cause?"

"You'll get promoted," Rebecca told him. "With a raise."

He shrugged. "How many pool cues can one man buy?"

"Eck," I butted in. "It didn't take any brilliant detective work to see what's been happening. There are facts in plain sight, plain enough for anyone who bothers to check. If the *Informer* has one decent reporter, the first article in a series could hit the front page any day. How are you going to look then?"

"That's a good point," he said. "I guess I'll open a case on Monday."

"How do we know they're not targeting somebody right now?" I asked him.

"Like who?"

"Like me, for one."

"Hell, I don't know," he waffled. "Maybe Slab has an explanation for everything. And Father Timothy, he's kind of creepy, but so what?"

"My sources tell me he's even creepier than you think. He's been transferred all over the map during the past few years and there are plenty of dirty rumors about why."

"Dirty like what?"

"Child molestation."

"No shit?" Eck said. "Well, that puts a new worm in the tequila."

"Mezcal," Rebecca said. "The worm actually goes in mezcal."

"Don't mind her," I told Eck. "She knows a lot about a lot."

"So," Eck said with a strain. "You're saying we can't be sure what they're capable of?"

"Exactly," Rebecca said.

"If you say so," Eck responded. He pried his eyes away from her and turned back to me. "Well," he said. "If this is everything you two claim, it just ain't right." He came up with two of his cards and a pen. "Here, I'm passing these out to both of you. And I'm writing down my home phone number on them. Which I never do. If the bad guys come after you, give me a call. Other than that, I got my weekend. I'll take this up on Monday. And since it's now a police matter, stay out of it."

"Starting Monday?" I said.

"Starting now, smart guy."

FORTY-NINE

When we were back in the car and rolling, Rebecca let me have it.

"What kind of a stunt was that?" she demanded.

"I know you wanted to keep the cops out of your life," I said. "But there's something going on here that's bigger than you. Anyway, I left out the part about Flunk Vanderhovel trying to kill me. I couldn't explain any of that without bringing up the connections between him and Slab, and between Slab and you."

She let that simmer for a while.

"Well, maybe," she said. "I still don't like it. Why did you have to tell Eck that I'm an accident reconstruction expert? That puts me right in the middle of your investigation."

"I was improvising a little, and it seemed to me that your presence as an expert helped to reinforce what I was telling him. Besides, I thought it was a matter of respect. I didn't want to go behind your back when I let the police in on this. And I didn't want to leave you sitting there silently."

"Well, aren't you the gentleman?" I could tell that her anger was breaking down into forgiveness.

"You're not under any police microscope," I said. "I went to the trouble of giving you a fake name, which you ought to be pretty comfortable with by now."

"Thanks a lot."

"And I landed you in South Dakota, which I imagine you'll have no trouble staying out of over the next few weeks. Eck is probably kicking himself right now because he forgot to ask you for your business card."

"He may try to locate me through you," she said.

"I'll tell him I only bumped into you at one of the accident sites and now we've lost touch. If he calls directory assistance in Deadwood, barring an incredible coincidence, there won't be any Rene Antolini in their listings."

"Thin ice, Mr. Harbinger."

"As usual."

Soon I was driving down peaceful streets with Rebecca mellowing beside me. The warm night air held her fragrance in spite of a breeze at our windows. Nice — until I ruined it.

"Why so hinky about the police, anyway?" I asked her.

"Isn't it obvious?"

"Nothing about you is obvious," I said. "I get the part about your fraudulent identity down at the college. And you've hinted about your involvement with some iffy characters, even before you coupled up with Slab Kapowski. Also, I suppose you'd rather hide the fact that you hired me to knock off Slab for you. Is there anything more?"

"Now you're embarrassing me," she said.

"Are you on a wanted poster somewhere?"

"Of course not."

"Insider trading? Art forgery?"

"Please."

"Okay, another thing I don't get is this idea that Slab would track you halfway across the world if you skipped out on him. Say you went to Paris. Can you imagine him sending a sharpie like Flunk Vanderhovel all the way over there to look for you? The guy would mill around aimlessly until he bumped his head on the Eiffel Tower."

"Flunk is dead."

"But you see what I'm getting at," I said. "The next guy, then. Rancid P. Happenstance or whatever his name is. Slab's new hatchet man out at the fairgrounds."

We passed quiet houses where, as far as I knew, no one was hiding from killers or cops.

"Don't sell Slab short," Rebecca said. "Some of his contacts are far more sophisticated."

"Maybe, but you're twice as smart as he is. Someone with your knowledge and skills could find a way to live incognito almost anywhere in this country. Or France or New Zealand or wherever. This claim that Slab could find you in any city in the world is nuts. Christ, he hasn't even found your hotel room in Pulptown."

"Well," she said, tapping the dashboard. "Not yet, he hasn't."

We rode in silence for a minute, leaving the residential streets behind and accelerating along a wide curve onto Highway 41. The wind coming through the windows kicked up and when she finally spoke, her voice was a little louder.

"So, I suppose you're done with the case now."

"Why? You figure there's still time for me to go down to the mortuary and shoot it out with Slab?"

"Look, I told you I was sorry about that." She leaned over and touched my cheek. If she meant to calm my nerves, it wasn't working. Her perfume and the nearness of her filled my consciousness. She spoke softly, her lips close to my ear. "I understand why you felt you had to go to the police. You're trying to do the right thing. I just want to know what you plan to do next. In fact, I'd like to know what *anyone* is planning to do. It doesn't appear that Lieutenant Eck is very tuned in to his duties."

"Eck may push it or drop it."

"Leaving matters to him seems like forgetting any of it ever happened," she said.

"But I'm not the police force around here."

Now her hand was on my knee. And drifting inward a sixteenth of an inch at a time.

"Perhaps you could help move things along," she said.

"Jeez, Rebecca, you really *do* want me to kill Slab for you."

"I just thought if you gather more evidence against him, something the police can't ignore, then they'll have to arrest him. He'll be in jail. Or even if he gets out on bail, he'll be immersed in his criminal defense case. One way or the other, he'll be off my back."

"I'm not sure," I said.

Her fingers lightly kneaded my thigh. "It's a simple matter of you helping your client."

"I guess if I were bonkers, I could look at it that way." My mind clicked through my options. The worst one was never seeing her again. Her hand slid a little closer to the red zone. She had me jumpier than a kangaroo. Reluctantly, I said, "Your retainer *did* buy my time up through tomorrow. Maybe I can scare something up."

"Thanks, baby," she cooed. "It's been a long day. Is there anywhere you need to be in the morning?"

"No."

"Good," she said. "Then we can sleep late."

"I think I need a full psychiatric work-up."

"I know what you need." She had made her point, so she lifted her hand away from my thigh, laughing. "For now, try not to drive off the road."

FIFTY

A couple of hours later, we lay in the near-darkness of her bedroom. I was in a post-orgasmic stupor, unable to move and barely able to speak. An aftershock of euphoria swept through my bloodstream, but the drug that was Rebecca Chatterton was beginning to level off. "Whah wi the thpinna?" I mumbled.

"What's with the spinning? Is that what you asked?"

"Prethethly."

"Don't worry," she said, cuddling into me. "The paralysis will go away after a few seconds."

"Tha's gooh," I said.

Chapter six of *"The Inca Dinca"* had started out with a lesson on centrifugal force. By chapter ten, I was screaming into my pillow. The ones in between had explored the ins and outs of the oral tradition, and those were the chapters that had nearly shut down my communications.

"The whirling dervishes in Turkey spun themselves to achieve spiritual elation," she said. "For the ancient Incas, spinning was a means of sexual foreplay."

"Whah … abou … chapper …" I tried to flex my tonsils. "What … about chapter … nine? How did the ancient Incas … get access to electrical wires?"

"I don't know what you mean."

"The part where I was blindfolded. Weren't you using jumper cables on me?"

"No, silly. Those were just my fingers."

"Holy Christ, Rebecca."

"Has it worn off yet?"

"My whole body is still tingling. And you?"

"Absolutely wonderful," she told me, melding closer. "You did better this time, especially the last forty-five minutes." She winked at me across the pillows. "How is your tongue feeling?"

"Like it's been carrying a suitcase through an airport."

"Poor darling." She feathered a comforting hand over my forehead, clearing away a tousled lock of hair. "You'll be fine in the morning."

I found I could move again. I rolled toward her and ran my hand over her hip. "It's going to be pretty rough on me when you move to Paris."

"Who says I'm moving to Paris?"

"Istanbul, then. To keep an eye on the whirling dervishes. I don't think you can sustain your fictional identity at the college, no matter how slapdash they are. And I don't know what else a woman like you is going to do around here. It's a cinch you wouldn't be satisfied checking groceries at Piggly Wiggly."

"You have a hospital," she said. "Maybe I could hire on as a brain surgeon."

"I already looked into that when my caseload was getting low. They'd prefer someone with a medical degree."

"Sticklers."

"Honestly, though, you'd go insane if you tried to live in Pulptown for any length of time."

"You live here and *you're* not insane," she said.

"Sometimes I think I'd have to be."

She reached over and tapped me on the nose. "You *did* volunteer for a psychiatric evaluation."

"There's a pesky question somewhere in my head, but I can't remember what it is."

"Don't talk now" she said with a yawn. "It's late, and you've been through a lot."

FIFTY-ONE

It was almost nine o'clock by the time I woke up fully. Ideas on the case had been passing in and out of my dreams, but I had lost any chance of concentrating on them during my hours of intermittent snoozing. I got out of the sack, and at the bathroom mirror I caught a reflection of my face. I couldn't see any signs of intelligence until that lost question bubbled up from the dregs of my memory. I knew I was going to need a private phone.

In the bedroom, Rebecca was still enfolded in the sheets and deep in Saturday slumber. She was silent and motionless as I got dressed and stood looking at her. The girl was lascivious — even in her sleep. I wanted to hold her again, hold her and more, but shook off my baser inclinations. I picked up a pen and a pad from her nightstand and left a note saying I'd get a newspaper. I was quiet going out the door.

The Punt Returner's lobby was all the way around Roxanne's wing, at the front of the complex. Nearby, there was a hotel restaurant and a swimming pool glistening in blue. Kids were splashing in the chlorine. A few adults were close to them, lounging in deck chairs and munching on the donuts that somehow counted as a complimentary breakfast.

Beside the lobby entrance a phone booth was lodged against a stone wall. It had gone a thousand and one nights without cleaning. Its cobwebs clogging the vents and its glass walls trapping the direct sunrays were creating a greenhouse effect even this early. I had enough heat tolerance and enough change for a brief long-distance call to Shorewood. I dialed information and asked whether there was any listing for Rebecca Chatterton.

There were two entries under Chatterton, neither one citing Rebecca. The first listing was for Gary on Larkin Street and the second was for Kenneth on Stowell Avenue.

"Stowell, that's the one," I told the operator.

She gave me the number and I wrote it down. I dropped coins into the slot and called the number. A woman's voice came on the line and I asked for Rebecca Chatterton.

"This is Rebecca."

"I'm calling about your Chevrolet Camaro."

"That's the strangest thing," she said. "I got a new car service coupon in the mail a couple of months ago. It was for a Chevrolet Camaro, but I hadn't bought a Camaro or any other car lately, so I thought it was a mistake. I threw the coupon away. Who is this?"

"I'm with the Department of Motor Vehicles," I said. "I'm checking on some anomalies in our registration records. Dealerships get these records mixed up all the time, and that's why you received the promotional material. I apologize for the confusion."

"You're calling on a Saturday?"

"Evenings and weekends are when you find people at home, ma'am. It's all part of being a public servant."

"I suppose so. Should I be concerned?"

"Not at all. We can straighten this out on our end."

"Maybe I should get your name," she said.

"Anyone here can help you, but I'm already filing the correction. Thanks, and goodbye." I hung up before she could say another word. With any luck, she wouldn't call the DMV.

I was glad to get out of the hot, dirty phone booth but not so happy about what I'd learned there. I leaned on the stone wall and took stock of what I could dope out.

Rebecca — not the actual Rebecca Chatterton but I had to call her *something* — had obviously bought the car for cash and had it registered under the real person's name and address. Then she may have used a fake driver's license to pick up the car's license plates at a DMV office. But why would she have gone to all that trouble? Maybe she was worried that the hotel up here might flag the plate number for a parking miscue or some other trifling reason. If that were to happen, she'd want the car's registration info to match the name she provided at the desk. Good to cover contingencies. But why sign in with a phony name to begin with?

I needed a lead from her transactions at the hotel. Anything pointing to a true name and a true address, or a specific bank in a specific town. Probably, she had linked her key accounts to her alias, but she could have missed a trick. Maybe she had mistakenly written an old check for rent.

Maybe she had carelessly submitted the wrong credit card for room service. Odds against, but I had to give it a try. I opened the big glass door to the lobby and walked in.

The hotel's reception area was done in pallid woodgrains and innocuous wallpaper, backdrop to images of assorted Packers running with the ball. There were black and white photos of Willie Wood and Elijah Pitts. Farther along there were bright color shots of Jon Staggers and Willard Harrell and a few other punt returners I'd lost track of over the years. The desk was broad and chest-high and painted in forest green. A kid in a green and gold shirt stood behind it and greeted me with enough cheer to make me feel welcome but not enough to make me wince.

"How about those Packers?" he said affably.

"It's the off-season," I said. "How about those Philadelphia Stars?"

The kid stiffened a little and looked from side to side, as if he wanted to make sure there were no higher-ups listening.

"You're into the USFL?" he asked.

"A big fan," I told him.

"No fooling," he said with some relief. He kept his voice low and his eyes scanning the lobby. "Hey, look at this," he whispered. He reached into his pocket and came out with a Tampa Bay Bandits helmet logo on a key chain. He flashed it and put it away quickly.

"Banditball," I said. Sympatico.

The kid was gratified to meet someone who could talk about the new league's teams. At the same time, he looked a little fearful that supervisors might find out his attention had deviated from the Packers.

I said, "We're not under a security camera, are we?"

"Nope."

"Then relax," I told him. "Your secret is safe with me."

"Thanks. I can't wait for that game against Birmingham tonight on ESPN."

"You and me both," I said.

"The snag is that I don't have a video cassette recorder. I'm supposed to come back here tonight and work another shift. But I'm going home sick if it kills me."

"Good luck. Do you have a sub lined up?"

"They'll find somebody," he said.

"On a Saturday night? Not necessarily. If management comes up empty after a few calls, they may get you a stool and make you stay behind that desk until you drop. And if you take a dive, they'll call for an ambulance. Then you'll have some explaining to do after the paramedics get a good look at you."

"Really?" He looked deeply worried.

"Better call around to your coworkers and have a plan ready."

"Then the other clerks will know what I'm up to."

"This is why we have bribery," I said. "While you're cogitating on that, I need to ask you about the account for room 124."

"Ms. Chatterton," the kid said reverently. And there was something besides reverence in his face. He took a deep breath and let it out in as if the thought of her had winded him.

"I know the feeling," I told him. "Thing is, she's misplaced her checkbook."

"Oh, no."

"Probably nothing. I think she left it at my office. But she said her account is on the edge. She hates math and doesn't always keep up very well with balancing her logs. She may need to pump in some money from savings to cover a big check she wrote last week."

"That sounds like a hassle."

"I'm concerned that any recent check she's written to the hotel may bounce. I'm wondering whether you have a check that hasn't been deposited yet."

"Are you … a friend of hers?" He was hesitant, and careful. Not the dullard I had hoped for.

"Yes, I am. I'm trying to save her some embarrassment. I don't want to see her evicted from here because of a bookkeeping error."

"I can understand," he said.

"Has she paid for the next few days or weeks in advance?"

"Well," the kid said. "She doesn't really use checks or credit cards for incidentals. Always cash whenever I'm here. As for major stuff, she doesn't pay directly for the suite."

"Who does?"

Now the kid looked apprehensive.

"To tell you the truth," he said, "I'm not sure I'm supposed to be talking with anyone about this."

"Let me have today's *Informer*, would you?"

"Sure thing." He turned and pulled a newspaper off a shelf behind the desk. "That'll be a quarter."

I dropped a twenty-dollar bill on the counter.

"Keep the change," I said.

"Mister?"

"You remember what I told you about paying off one of your co-workers? Here's your way of financing it."

He bit his lip for a second, then tilted his head and raised his eyebrows. "I don't know about this," he said with a pained look.

"It's all right," I told him. I handed him one of my business cards.

"You're a private investigator?" he said. "I thought you said you were a friend of Ms. Chatterton's"

"I'm both. A detective working on her behalf and a friend looking out for her welfare. The lady has her secrets, even from me, but my questions could be very important for her case. And believe me, nobody else needs to know about them."

"Um … if you say so."

"You were telling me about the rent payments," I said.

"Checks come in from Mr. Tombstone once a week."

"Mr. Tombstone?"

"Yeah. Regular, as far as I know. I don't always see the checks but there's never been a problem with Ms. Chatterton's account."

"Do you have any copies of Mr. Tombstone's checks?"

"No, they go to the bank as soon as we get them. And we don't make duplicates."

"Do you remember what his first name is?"

"No, the last name jumped out at me, so I remembered it. The first name was kind of goofy, but I didn't pay enough attention to it."

"Do you remember which bank the checks came from?"

"No. To me, a check is just a check. The bookkeeper might know, but she's off on weekends."

"Do you remember the city?"

"Sorry."

I asked for the local phone book and the Yellow Pages. No Mr. Tombstone in either volume. The kid let me use the desk phone, but calls to directory assistance in Green Bay, Oshkosh, Madison and Milwaukee drew four blanks.

Next, I asked him to show me Ms. Chatterton's registration card. He was wary, but there was that twenty-dollar bill on the counter.

The card was dated in early April. It showed a P.O. Box in Milwaukee as a permanent address, but that was probably a gag. No credit card number shown.

"Nothing here that helps," I said. "I know the room's been paid straight through, but has she actually been here all the while?"

"Steady at first. Lately not as much." He eyed the money.

"Keep it," I said. "You've told me plenty. No need to talk about this with Ms. Chatterton or Mr. Tombstone, though."

"Believe me, I won't," he said.

"I hope you enjoy the game tonight."

I pushed the twenty a bit closer to his hand. He palmed it furtively, succumbing to the plot.

"Thanks," he said.

"Do me a favor and call me if you see another check from this Tombstone guy. And here's a quarter for the *Informer*."

I spun the coin on the counter. He slapped it flat and picked it up. A guilty smile surfaced for a moment.

FIFTY-TWO

She was waking up when I got back to the suite with my newspaper.

"Jack?" she said in a groggy voice.

"It's only me," I assured her. I crossed the small living room and went into the bedroom. She scooted over and I sat next to her on the bed. She was soft and drowsy under the sheets. It was already warm in the room and there was the slightest mist on her skin.

"What are you up to now?" she said, coming out of it.

"I have a lead to check," I said.

"I'll go with you."

"No, you take the day off. All I'll be doing this afternoon is going over some dull stuff. Newspaper clippings, that kind of thing."

"Looking for what?"

"I won't be sure until I find it. Things might get more interesting tonight."

"Then you have to bring me along for that," she said.

"It could be dangerous."

"I'm up to the challenge."

"I'm sure you are, but right now I can't tell where this is going. What if I come back here about seven? We can talk about it then."

"Maybe we should meet somewhere for dinner," she said. "I'll go stir crazy in this hotel, and I don't want to be waiting around here if you're delayed. There has to be one more restaurant in town that doesn't have a football motif."

"And one where Slab doesn't go. I suppose eating beef jerky and peanuts at The Drunk Tank is out."

"You suppose correctly."

"Has he ever taken you to Range Wars?"

"No. Do they have cowboy shootouts?"

"You're supposed to think of chefs battling it out at their kitchen ranges."

"Jesus. Really?"

"Hey, it isn't bad food and it isn't about the Packers. Look for it about three miles north, just off the highway."

"What's the atmosphere like?"

I shrugged. "Seventy-eight percent nitrogen. Twenty-one percent oxygen."

"I liked you better when your tongue was paralyzed."

"One percent trace gasses," I finished.

"You're terrible," she said.

"It's a steakhouse. What can I tell you?"

"Do they have a bar?"

"They do."

"All right," she said. "I'll meet you in the bar at seven. Or sevenish, if you can't be there on the dot."

Her lips kissed the air in my direction. She rested her head on her pillow, closed her eyes and snuggled back into the sheets. Every fiber of me from the neck down wanted to crawl in there with her, but my head was learning to take charge. It was tough standing up from the bed and walking out the door, no matter what her game might have been.

FIFTY-THREE

Pulptown didn't have the resources I needed, so I decided to make the thirty-five-mile trip to Green Bay. A few blocks up the frontage road from the Punt Returner, I stopped at a gas station. As I stood at the fuel pump with my hand on the nozzle, another loose end from my troubled sleep practically poked me in the eye. It was something my artful client had said the night before at The Drunk Tank. The pump clicked off. Back in the station, I got my change in quarters for another long-distance call, this one from the phone booth outside the service garage.

I called directory assistance in Milwaukee and eventually got through to the Schnubner Beer Art Museum. The receptionist told me the curator for the past four years was a man by the name of Leonard Pitworth, and there hadn't been any short-term curators to cover his vacations. She had never heard of Roxanne Delaplaine or Rebecca Chatterton. So, the museum story was one more lie in a bundle of them. One more disappointment, and probably not the last.

Back at the wheel, I coaxed the engine up the entry ramp onto U.S. Route 41. I cruised north as the four-lane highway bent away from Pulptown and passed farms and granaries. There were several implement supply stores on the way, and their tractors and graders and skip loaders were displayed out front. In the distance, there were groves of trees. But sometimes you had to peek between billboards to see them.

My windows were open and the scent of the countryside was blowing in. On the tinny speakers of my stereo, oldies from Radio Pavlov fought against the road noise until a segment of Packerland News broke in. There had been a fire during the Saturday morning shift at a garment factory in Oshkosh. Four workers had been trapped and killed where they were crammed into a line of sewing machines. The good news was that an unidentified woman had pulled a wheezing old pattern cutter out of the fire just in time. In a recorded interview, the old man said the woman who saved him was an angel. Instead of thanking her, he gave full credit to God, who had very thoughtfully sent her in.

"Everything happens for a reason," the pattern cutter told the radio audience. "God still has a purpose for me on this earth, even though I'm a sinner." After answering some questions about falling beams and toxic smoke, the old man went off again about celestial clemency. "The Lord threw quite a scare into me," he said. "And I deserved it. But God doesn't give us anything we can't handle."

The statement was as brutally insensitive as any I had ever heard. Obviously, the four terrified, dying employees had been given more than they could handle. What was it about disaster survivors that so often made them excrete that kind of numbing stupidity?

Corky Williams, the station's reporter on the scene, gave us more details on the catastrophe. Then she got on a verbal teeter-totter with the anchorman in the studio.

"Well, Corky," the anchor said, "sounds like there was a tragic shortage of angels at the factory."

"That's right, Larry. But it's hard to imagine four more guardian angels trying to elbow their way into an already crowded work space. The weather was pretty darn tragic too. Witnesses said a sudden cloudburst might well have doused the fire."

"Well, Corky, under the blue skies we've been having lately, a thunderstorm would have been God's welcome miracle."

I shook my head and exhaled a long, disgusted breath. At least they weren't bringing up Saint Polycarp.

"What about Saint Polycarp, Corky?"

"Yes, the patron saint of fire dodgers. Sad to say, Larry, but he's one of the lesser known saints."

"Apparently, Corky, none of the four burn victims knew enough to invoke Polycarp's considerable influence with the Lord, especially where matters of combustion are concerned."

"That's right, Larry. But authorities say there wouldn't have been any point in that level of divine intervention in this case."

"Why is that, Corky?"

"Well, Larry, as we've heard, God clearly has a purpose for the old man who was saved. No one has been able to determine whether God had any further use for the four people who died."

"Looks like they were collateral damage in a heavenly plan that we can't even comprehend, Corky."

"That's right, Larry."

"God's plan worked out perfectly," Larry said. "That's a wonderful thing for Packerland. Thanks, Corky Williams, for some excellent reporting."

Great. Now I had helpless burn victims and infuriating news commentators to feel bad about on top of everything else. I switched off the radio and made a mental note to kick Larry in the shins if I ever got the chance. It wouldn't have been right to lay a foot on Corky.

I turned my attention back to the road in front of me. Once I approached the comparative metropolis of Green Bay, I went a bit out of my way, staying on Highway 41 long enough to exit onto Lombardi Avenue — a street name that actually made sense. I drove east through a few blocks peppered with nondescript stores and chain restaurants and gas stations. After that, I was gliding past the shrine of Lambeau Field. No particular reason for following this route, except for the chance to get a glimpse and a feel of the 1960s again. Beyond the stadium, I zigged and zagged north and east across the city.

Green Bay had seemed like the big time to many of us growing up in the outlying areas, but that was mainly because it had the Packers and three television stations. Truthfully, the place was only a larger version of Pulptown. Like home, it was a city with pleasant neighborhoods interspersed with tracts of dog-eared housing. Much of it was made up of strip malls, humdrum commercial zones and wide swaths of industrial grunge. The river running through the city was wider than it was in Pulptown, but the waterfront views were often marred by slag heaps, cranes and warehouses.

I drove up to a drawbridge that had just been raised to let a tugboat and a barge pass by. On my left, at the mouth of the river, there were cargo ships that might have come in from the northeastern states or Canada or Europe and would soon be on their way home. Once unloaded and reloaded, the ships would follow a passage up the bay, out past the Door County Peninsula and into the expanse of Lake Michigan. Unless they were heading farther north to Lake Superior, they would sail into the lower Great Lakes. Some would cruise the Saint Lawrence Seaway and fewer would continue all the way to the Atlantic Ocean. Along the way there would be ports of call that were bigger and more exciting than this one. I suspected that when the time came to cast off from the docks at Green Bay, the ships' foreign or domestic crews would be happy to get out of town.

Green Bay's main appeal for me now was its library that held many more Midwestern advertising volumes than the smaller library in Pulptown could stock. I gambled on Mr. Tombstone being my client's employer, not her sugar daddy. I also gambled on him plastering that catchy name — real or assumed — on whatever company he might have owned. If I was right, a Yellow Pages ad would probably tell me more about him than I'd get from directory assistance.

Once across the lowered drawbridge, I was in a civic section of the downtown grid and looking for a place to park.

FIFTY-FOUR

I corralled the Mustang in a public lot and went into the Brown County Central Library. Close to the reference desk, a bank of shelving held phone books and advertising directories from nearby towns and the larger cities in the surrounding states. Double-checking, I started with the slim local volumes and spread my search outward from there. Nothing in my quadrant of Wisconsin. I combed through the thick publications for Milwaukee, then Madison. Nothing there, either. I widened the field to take in Detroit, Indianapolis, Chicago, Des Moines and Iowa's Quad Cities. It was tedious work, with none of it paying off. I was close to extending my radius or trying to cover a multitude of small towns when I hit something in the Yellow Pages for Minneapolis and Saint Paul.

Tubby Tombstone's Mortuary Mania jumped out at me in full-page glory. An ad with a two-tone photo showed the proprietor with his hand on a coffin the way a used car salesman poses with his hand on a Cadillac's fender. The playful first name didn't give him his due. Tubby's jowls billowed from under his chin and ears, piling multiple layers of weight and volume onto a torso that just about dwarfed the coffin he was promoting. Anything behind or below his eyes, nose and mouth blended into the huge, indistinct mass that was his body. Three more faces and he'd be Mount Rushmore.

The ad trumpeted Tubby's fabulous selection of coffins in outlets serving the Land of Ten Thousand Lakes and beyond. Bargains were also available on the most beautiful burial plots a body could ever hope to occupy. I made a photocopy of the ad and then took down some phone numbers for the area's largest newspapers.

I walked a block or so from the building's rear exit, went into a Jiffy Cheap and hooked the clerk on my second bribe of the morning. Twelve bucks for a ten-dollar roll of quarters. Once I was back in the library, the coins had me ready for a phone booth. I sat on a fixed metal stool and arranged the quarters into neat one-dollar piles on a shelf below the base of the phone. I untwisted a ribbed metal cable connecting the handset to a bulky box on a wall and tried the administrative number for Tubby Tombstone's Mortuary Mania. The phone company's long-distance operator butted in with a demand. I pumped in the required number of quarters and got a ring tone. Since it was a Saturday, I was only able to get a recording, but I hoped that would be enough.

A dry male voice gave me a menu of department heads and the numbers I should press to get messages to any of them. No executive mentioned on the recording was familiar to me but I had a queasy feeling about the only woman's name on the list. I punched in the number for *Rhonda McKinnon, Research and Acquisitions,* and dropped more quarters down the slot.

Another recorded greeting came on, this one in melodic feminine tones. Ms. McKinnon was letting us know that she would be out of the office indefinitely but would be checking for messages and returning calls at her earliest opportunity. The timbre and inflections on the recording were easy to place. Something cold and invisible grabbed at my gut, and it took me several seconds to recover. The voice was Roxanne Delaplaine's, Rebecca Chatterton's. Even Rene Antolini's if you wanted to count that one. I hung up without saying a word.

I pulled out my notes and called the editorial division at the *Minneapolis Star Tribune,* pumping in another batch of quarters. A receptionist picked up and I asked for the city desk. A couple of ring tones later, a new voice came through.

"Nancy Nordgren, city desk."

"This is Jack Harbinger. I'm calling from Green Bay, Wisconsin. I'm looking into the mortuary business here and I'm following up on a lead. I'm wondering whether someone there can help me."

"The *Green Bay Press-Gazette,* huh?"

"You know your newspapers," I said vaguely. We made some small talk about the weather. We agreed that it was hot on both ends of the line but at least it wasn't twenty degrees below zero like it was last January. Same old stuff.

"What can I do for you?" she said.

"I'm looking for information on Tubby Tombstone."

Nancy laughed and said, "He's making his presence felt all the way over there?"

"Possibly," I told her. "Just a little shop talk from insiders. I don't think anyone outside of the cadaver business around here has ever heard of him."

"They probably will before too long," she said. "Tubby Tombstone's real name is Einar Thordahl. He's from Duluth. Came to the Twin Cities — what is it? — ten or twelve years ago. After he bought out a mortuary in Minneapolis, he changed his name legally as a marketing gimmick. Got his commercials all over the radio and local television. He's kind of a merchandizing nut. He was successful and started buying up other mortuaries in the area. Over the years, he's gobbled up half the competitors in Minnesota. And he's taken his act out of state, mainly to the west."

"All on the up and up?"

"That's the big question. Some people say he's built his empire at any cost."

"Are any of his former employees talking?"

"No, they won't say a word. That could mean allegiance or fear. We don't know which."

"You mentioned that he's built his empire at any cost," I said. "Does that include murder?"

"Nothing quite so dramatic," she said. "Word is, he likes to make generous offers to competing mortuaries. If they don't bite, he tries to find weak spots in the potential sellers. The suspicion is that he uses blackmail and other strongarm ploys to force his competitors to sell. But those are just rumors. Nothing we can print and nothing you should take as anything but background."

"Got it," I said. "And the former competitors never talk?"

"Not so far," she said. "We still don't know why. Maybe it's because the sellers are scared or because Tubby has something on them. Or maybe it's just because the dollars were so good that the sellers went away happy."

The operator broke in and told me to plug in more quarters.

"Sounds like you're calling from a payphone," she said.

"You know how it is. Always on the run."

"Been there."

"Can you tell me anything about Tubby's key executives?"

"No, they're low profile. Tubby is the face of the organization. The face and much more."

"So, is Tubby expanding this way? Into Wisconsin?"

"Funny you should use the word *expanding*," Nancy said. "If you were in a room with him, you couldn't imagine him expanding any more than he already has. To say he's obese would be a gross understatement."

"I've seen his picture," I said.

"Well, to answer your question, he's trying to move into Wisconsin. For a long time, he hadn't branched out eastward, but that's changed over the past year. Tubby is now set up in La Crosse and Chippewa Falls and a couple of other places. Otto Lindstrom, another reporter, knows more about it than I do. He'll be in on Monday. I could ask him to give you a call."

"I'll try calling him next week," I said. "One more thing. Ever heard of a mortuary tycoon named Slab Kapowski?"

"I don't think I have."

"He's a local bigshot," I said. "Maybe not as big as he thinks, and maybe only a midnight snack for Tubby Tombstone."

Nancy laughed again. "Could be," she said. "Tubby seems to have quite an appetite. In every sense of the word."

"Thanks for all your information. You've been very kind."

"Glad to help a colleague," she said.

I hung up and scooped the last of the quarters into my pocket. I felt bad about misleading Ms. Nancy Nordgren. Then again, I felt bad about damn near everything.

FIFTY-FIVE

It was past noon and getting hot. I didn't know whether it would be safe to go home, not that I wanted to go there anyway. I drove over the Walnut Street Bridge to the west side of the Fox River, got onto Broadway and parked in a lot between Titletown Plumbing and Titletown Wire Stripping. Across the street there was a bar called Titletown Tap.

After the Packers had won a couple of NFL championships in the early sixties, the city of Green Bay branded itself as Titletown, USA. Over the following years, the moniker got pinned onto countless local businesses. I figured a tavern called Titletown Tap would be so steeped in the Packers that the bartender wouldn't have a baseball game on his TV. I went in there in search of a beer and some grub.

The bar had Packer helmet cutouts and Packer pennants and Packer posters on the interior walls, more than enough of it to clog the senses. But there were also some nods to the Milwaukee Brewers, and that made me uneasy. If they were playing a day game, the lone TV in the place would be locked onto it. Right now, it was showing beer commercials, as if that were necessary. I sat on a stool at the far end of the bar, where I could keep a distant eye on the door. Although I was a long way from home, it was conceivable that Slab Kapowski's death squad could have followed me. And since paranoid was better than pickled, my .38 was closely tucked in.

The joint was narrow to the point of claustrophobic and dim to the point of mournful. On the back wall, beside a window into a cramped kitchen, there was a silent juke box with some of its lights burned out. Next to that was a lonely pool table in such poor condition that even Wally Eck wouldn't have considered it. There were a few male customers slouched on stools at the bar. Despite the early hour, the guy two spots down from me was soaking up beer like a sand pit. A number of men and women were planted in booths along the side wall, hands on their glasses or bottles. Every face in the dive was as somber as the lighting. Hell, I knew I wasn't looking all that frolicsome myself.

The bartender was a big husky guy with a big friendly attitude. "Packers," he said. He assessed my mood and didn't push the topic. "How are you doing, there, buddy?"

I frowned and pushed away some air with the back of my hand. "I'm soaring through clouds of joy on gossamer wings."

My sarcasm didn't put him off. "Yeah, you look a little down in the mouth. It was serious with her?" He had nailed it.

"No reason I should have thought so, but you know how it goes."

He nodded with all the wisdom of the ages, the way the best of them do.

"Well," he said, "sometimes a broken dream is better than no dream at all."

I spread some bills on the bar, surveyed my choices and ordered a Leinenkugel, which was about ten grades above a Schnubner. With no breakfast in me, I also ordered a burger. The bartender set the beer in front of me and told me the food would be up in a few minutes. He slid down the bar to counsel some other hapless patron. The TV screen, high on my left, popped onto baseball, the dullest form of entertainment ever devised by humankind.

It wasn't the Brewers and it wasn't anything close to home. It was a National League game from the East Coast. The score was 0-0 in the bottom of the fourth and the game had all the urgency of a death march. The pitcher lobbed the ball to first base to hold a runner. Then he lobbed it to first again. The pitching coach walked out to the mound with his hands in his back pockets. A toe in the dirt and a little small talk and then the coach sauntered back to the dugout. Then there was a foul into the stands. The pitcher shook off a sign. He shook off another sign before consenting to throw the damn thing. One more foul ball looped into the seats behind the plate. Another lob to first. The pitcher leaned forward. The hitter called timeout. He stepped back, flexed his shoulders and returned to the batter's box. The pitcher stared at him and then stepped off the rubber. Eons dragged by until the pitcher finally threw ball four. The manager lazily walked out to the mound with his hands in his back pockets.

"For the love of sanity," I said to the bartender. "Can't we watch a Bugs Bunny cartoon or something?"

"We'd watch the Packers," he said. "But it's the off-season."

He went to the kitchen portal and came back with my burger and a free side of shoestring fries.

"Ever watch the USFL?" I asked him. He didn't have time to answer.

"That ain't real football," a Budweiser man said from down the bar.

No point in arguing. The unreal teams weren't playing this afternoon anyway. I took a bite of the burger and labored over the quasi-potatoes. The burger was burned, which was better than undercooked. The shoestring fries tasted like they had just come off an old pair of wingtips. It was a pretty standard meal for a pretty standard bar, and it bolstered my strength.

"That league's got a team down in Chicago," somebody called out.

Everyone agreed; they hated Chicago.

"What are the Chicagos called?" a stout woman wanted to know.

"They're the Chicago Blitz," I told her.

"What's a blit?"

"No, no, no," someone corrected her. "It's a blitz. You know, like when the defense sends in a couple of linebackers to sack the quarterback."

"Oh, blitz," the stout woman said. "Like a blitz."

"Yeah. Blitz like a blitz."

The bartender caught my brow sagging and gave me a sympathetic look.

"Sorry," he told me. "This ain't exactly the Round Table at the Algonquin."

"Why don't you give this new guy the riddle?" somebody called out from a booth.

"That's a great idea," the bartender said to the room. He turned to me. "Tell you what. If you get this right, I'll switch the channel. If not, you'll stay and watch at least three innings."

"Hit me," I told the barkeep.

He rose to the enormity of the occasion. "Answer me this," he said. "Can God create a rock so heavy that even He can't lift it?"

"The short answer is *no*," I said. "Let's watch a rerun."

The bartender gave me a knowing smile.

"But," he said dramatically, "if God is all-powerful, then He can create a rock as heavy as He wants it to be."

The customers murmured.

"So, it's like this," the sand pit guy slurred at me. I was surprised that he had been paying attention. "God could always make the rock heavier than any weight you could think of. And if He wants a rock so heavy that even He can't lift it, no problem. God can make it, plus heavier if He wants."

"But even so …" the bartender said. He paused for effect, leaning in with an assured air like a lawyer addressing a jury. "If God is all-powerful, then He'd certainly have the ability to lift any weight in the universe."

"Such as that rock that's supposed to be too heavy for Him," someone said from a booth. Murmurings turned into a collective snicker.

"So, we're stuck," Sand Pit said.

On the TV, an umpire was checking for spitballs.

"Okay," I said. "Sounds like you'll need the long answer."

"Have a go at it," the bartender said behind a grin.

"God can't create anything," I said. Somebody gasped. "Any more than Huckleberry Finn can build a raft."

"Huckleberry Finn built a fine raft," a man said.

The other customers jabbered their approval. The bartender withheld his judgment.

"No, he didn't," I said. "A book *said* Huck Finn built a raft. But think about it. There was no such person. He was only a fictional character. He was the product of Mark Twain's imagination."

"You have something there," Sand Pit said. "But I don't know what it is."

"So," I said, "If Huck Finn isn't a real person, then he can't make a raft or anything else. As far as your riddle goes, he can't *lift* anything either. Neither can God. Not even a beer bottle." I lifted mine to demonstrate my power. "Can't do it any more than Paul Bunyan can lift an axe. There's no such being as Paul Bunyan. He's only a storybook figure and so he can't lift *anything*. And he can't cut down a tree. Can't even break a twig."

"I knew a kid named Paul Bunyan," a drunk said from down the bar. "I seen him pick up a stick."

"Come on, Hubert. That's not what this guy means," the bartender told the drunk. "He's not talking about some normal boy whose parents, Mr. and Mrs. Bunyan, thought it would be cute to name their son Paul. He's referring to Paul Bunyan the legend."

Hubert grunted. He seemed to be turning that over in his mind.

The bartender went on: "Now, this is pure conjecture, Hubert, but I'd say the kid you knew didn't walk around with Babe the Blue Ox."

"No, I never seen that," Hubert admitted.

"My point," I said, "is that these so-called people are imaginary portrayals. They have no power. Same with God. God can't actually make a rock or lift a rock because God is only a fictional character. And when we describe that character, we're not very careful. One part of the portrait cancels out another part. But we don't bother to think about that. The question itself — the riddle you guys posed — points up the fact that our descriptions of God are self-contradictory. They make no sense. They depict a being who doesn't exist, and could never exist."

"Look at that!" the barkeep said. "I've been posing the same damn riddle for years and he's the first person who's gotten it right."

"Wait a second," Sand Pit said to him. "That's the right answer? You mean there's no God?"

"The guy aced it," the bartender told Sand Pit. "I have to give him credit."

"Well," somebody said. "If there's no God, that would explain just about everything."

The bartender picked up a remote and pointed it at the TV. He paused for no apparent reason. On the screen, a right-handed relief pitcher leaned forward on the mound. He froze, waiting for inspiration. Then he took a short stretch while looking over his left shoulder at the new runner leading off first base. The pitcher held the ball. He held it longer. He wheeled and lobbed it to second as the runner nearby tiptoed to the bag.

"Oh, just kill it," Sand Pit said.

The bartender hit a button and the screen went to another channel. Then another and another and so on. None of it was worth watching, but on the other hand, nobody in the place was clamoring for a blank screen. With my reluctant okay, the bartender switched back to baseball. I thought it would kill me. That and some other things. My soul was draining out through my shoes and clotting on the floor under my bar stool. I stuck around anyway, not wanting to go back to my doghouse any earlier than necessary.

Hours later, I had downed one more beer, about fifty fewer than Sand Pit. I had played a dozen pool games against drunken opponents and dealt bravely with warped cues, a chipped seven-ball, torn felt and dead cushions. When the sheer exhilaration of that got old, I went out to my car across the street and slid in behind the wheel.

I started the engine and tried Radio Pavlov. They were playing a heartbreak ballad. The song made me think about the girl. I was saturated with self-pity all the way home.

FIFTY-SIX

When I got back to the center of Pulptown, I was still ruminating about Rhonda McKinnon, formerly a couple of other women I thought I knew. I should have seen through her early on. Hell, I *had* seen through her, but what I sensed at the time hadn't made enough difference. Caution had given way to lust and all the softer names that lust goes by. I'd been shunning forethought and making lousy decisions. I'd been snookered and I'd been used. My self-respect was just about ready to hand in its resignation.

The rest of me probably should have done the same, but I couldn't let go of the case or the woman that easily. The big question was whether I could see things through without losing too much blood.

Driving slowly down the street in front of the building where I lived and worked, I scanned for surveillance operatives and didn't spot any in doorways or in the cars parked along the curb. Even the donut shop was empty. I took the safe route anyway. Once I had parked in the lot at The Bottle Cry, I passed through a pedestrian gate near the river. I walked down a stretch of crumbling asphalt between the concrete riverbank and the backsides of several bars, skirting trash cans and litter and a thousand drops of motor oil. At the rear wall of my building, I stepped up onto a pile of broken machine parts, hopped onto the lid of a dumpster and then up to the top of an out-of-work boiler. From there I climbed a fire escape's ladder to the platform outside my office windows. I peeked in there and saw no one inside, though I couldn't see the whole room without exposing myself too much. I made it over to the apartment window I had left unlocked the day before. With my gun in one hand, I gingerly lifted the window's lower sash. I reached over the sill and pulled a cord to raise the shade. I crawled through the opening. Nobody shot at me or clubbed me over the head.

Inside the apartment, it was all clear. I set down my gun, took off my coat and laid it over the back of the easy chair. It was almost nice to be home.

My peace of mind lasted for about a second.

There was a noise from the other side of the adjoining door to my office. I picked up the gun again and stepped silently to the door. I held my ear to it. A faint sound of rummaging leaked through. It probably wasn't my faithful client in there, pining for my return. More likely it was a rat. Or a man. Or a combination of both.

I thought whoever it was must have been waiting for me to open the main door, the one off the hallway. The intruder probably wouldn't have expected me to come in through the side door. I pressed my ear to that one again. The office was now soundless. With the gun in my right hand, I used my left to release the door's lock. Quietly. I laid my fingers lightly on the doorknob and worked it with an agonizingly slow rotation.

I threw the door open and instantly knew I hadn't fooled anyone. Slab's man Rance came at me from the left. I ducked but a glancing blow put me down.

My gun fell and skidded along the carpet. I rolled and got to my feet as the thug came at me again. He raised a revolver and smacked the barrel across my cheek. The impact threw me against a wall. I bounced off it and barely kept my balance. He charged in with a left but I blocked it. I clipped his jaw with an uppercut and that stopped him for a moment. I took advantage and slugged him in the stomach. He hunched forward, huffing and coughing. His right arm hung low and the gun wobbled loosely in his hand. I got a grip on his wrist and pried at his fingers. The revolver dropped to the floor. As I kicked it aside, he heaved me away. I went after him again, but he had a longer reach and more weight. He blocked a punch and pounded me in the face with some tonnage behind his fist.

The blow drove me into my desk. I slid across the top of it. The Rolodex and the pens and the other stuff got snowplowed off the surface. I dropped over the edge and collapsed against the credenza. My knees went to the floor and my right hand knocked over the racquetball trophy. I got halfway up on one leg. I could hear him behind me, coming around the desk, yanking my chair out of his way. I grabbed the racquetball player's metal body as the thug charged in. I spun around and whipped a backhand, smashing him in the mouth with the trophy's heavy base.

Everything stopped.

My backhand kill shot hadn't killed him, but it left him stunned on the dirty carpet. Blood dribbled from his lips and his nostrils. He tried to get up but I regained my footing before he did. I clutched the trophy tighter and broke it against the back of his head. He was out and I checked to make sure he was still alive. I found my gun, picked it up and slipped it into my shoulder holster.

On the floor next to the desk was a pair of handcuffs I had never seen before. A key protruded from one of the manacles. I withdrew the key and pocketed it, leaving the open cuffs on the desk. The goon was coming to — just barely. I tugged at him and got him to his knees. His higher functions were obviously muddled, but he had enough automatic reflexes to move with me when I wrangled him toward a large window overlooking the fire escape. I unlocked and opened the window, then managed to push him through the opening and dump him on the iron landing. Then I grabbed the cuffs from the desk and climbed out after him. While he was still groggy, I wrestled his hands up to a railing. I slapped the cuffs on him so that its chain and his arms were looped around a strong, solid length of metal. His face leaned insensibly against a vertical bar.

He came out of it slowly and produced a few blinks. His eyes were muddy. He sat there looking up at me like a dog that had gotten its leash wrapped around a post.

"Well, if it isn't Rancid P. Happenstance," I said.

He shook his head, as if trying to remember how to think.

"Why do you call me Rancid?" he mumbled through bloody gums.

"Because I don't think you know what *loathsome* means."

"I ain't lonesome," he insisted. "I got season tickets down at the whorehouse."

"Case in point," I said. "Did you come over here to run an errand for Slab Kapowski?"

"Is the pope Italian?"

"Actually," I told him, "the pope is Polish."

"You know what I'm saying. Jeez, how come you snuck in through the side door? If you'd a come in by the front door like you're supposed to, I'd a had you cold. But the side door? I had to get over there fast when I saw the knob turn."

"You weren't fast enough," I told him.

"Where did you come from? You got two offices or something?"

"I run a talent agency on the side," I said. "Mostly carnival acts."

"Really? The bearded lady and all that junk?"

"Sure."

"Sounds pretty stupid. By the way, what the hell did you hit me with?"

"Past glory," I said.

"Huh?"

"A trophy."

"From a bearded lady contest?"

"Racquetball," I said.

"Oh, pfffff. I saw it sitting there. Second place. Pretty stupid."

"Speaking of stupid, you should have shot me dead while you had the opportunity."

"I wasn't ordered to kill you," he said. "I was just ordered to beat you up and put you in handcuffs and haul you off. I think you were gonna get killed later."

"Haul me off to where?"

"I ain't saying."

"To Slab's mortuary?"

"Ha!" he said sharply. "You don't even know what you're dealing with."

"Suppose you tell me."

"Ha!" he said again.

"You're tight-lipped, is that it?"

"Does a bear shit in the woods?"

"Look, Rancid, you may as well tell me now."

"I ain't saying nothing."

"So, if you're not saying *nothing*, then you must be saying *something*."

"Huh?"

"What is it with you gangsters and the double negatives?" I said. "Didn't you ever go to school?"

"Eleven years at Saint Opie's," he said proudly.

"Good. Then you made it through all eight grades quicker than Flunk Vanderhovel did."

"He was older than me. I never even seen him there."

"Well, you won't be able to visit his grave tonight, either. I'm going to call the cops in a while and tell them there's been a break-in. They'll find you handcuffed out here and they'll throw you in the hoosegow. If I were you, I wouldn't call Slab to bail you out. He won't be too happy about you muffing this one."

Rance looked frightened. He tried to kick me, so I pressed my shoe hard against his kneecap to tamp him down. He groaned and shook his head in frustration.

"Asshole," was the worst he could do.

"In fact, I'd say you and Slab are pretty much through. You need to look out for yourself now. Starting with some answers. Where were you supposed to take me tonight?"

"Go to hell."

"Two syllables," I prompted him.

"What?"

"It's a game. Two syllables, right?"

"No, three."

"You actually know what a syllable is?"

"Of course, I do!"

"Prove it," I said. "First syllable. Sounds like."

"Huh?" he said. "I don't know. What rhymes with …? I know! Paint!"

"Ain't? Faint?"

"No, you stupid fuck."

"Saint? Saint Opie's?" I said.

He was shocked. "How did you guess that?"

I let up on his knee and stood back, moving out of his kicking range.

"Exactly where at Saint Opie's?" I said. "Where is Slab's office?"

"I ain't telling you nothing."

"You're not telling me *anything*."

"That's what I just said!"

"And what was supposed to happen once you had dragged me to Saint Opie's?"

He snarled at me and rattled his handcuffs before he spoke.

"You think you can get away with all your blasphemy?"

"Does the pope shit in the woods?" I said.

"Oh boy!" he said, thrown back a little. "Oh boy, oh boy. Just you wait till they get ahold of you."

"Wait till *who* gets ahold of me? Who's *they*? Are you talking about Slab and Father Timothy?"

"I'm not saying nothing! I can't even hear you with all your stupid questions. Blah blah blah blah. See? I can't even hear you!"

"Goodnight," I told him.

"Hey, you're not gonna leave me up here!"

"Why not?" I said. "All the other businesses in the building are closed for the weekend. So is the paper mill across the drink. There won't be anybody around to hear you holler."

"Asshole," he said again.

"Come on, Rancid. You'll have peace and quiet and a nice view of the river."

"The cops'll get me off this thing before dark, right?"

"If they don't, you'll also have the twinkling of the heavens."

He furiously scraped the short chain of the handcuffs along the railing. The cuffs were holding. So was the railing in spite of its rust.

"That's not fair!" he said angrily.

"You came here to kidnap me," I said. "What do you expect?"

"I was just following orders."

"That doesn't make you a good boy," I told him.

Once more, he raged against the cuffs. Finally convinced of his captivity, he gave up his frantic attempt at freedom. He laid himself the best he could on the iron honeycomb of the landing. He had nothing more to try and there wasn't any point in yowling about it.

I climbed back in through the window, closed it and latched it. I picked up the Rolodex and the rest of the stuff from my desk and put it all back where it belonged. Then I picked up the pieces of the trophy and laid them on the credenza. Rance's pistol went into the safe along with Flunk Vanderhovel's weapons. A smart man would get rid of the whole arsenal before a grand jury could get their hands on him. No time right now. At the main door to the hallway, I examined the lock. It had been picked but not jimmied and broken. I closed the door from inside, secured it as much as possible and wedged the client's chair under the knob. I went out of the office through the adjoining door to my apartment and clicked that lock behind me.

FIFTY-SEVEN

Inside my apartment, I closed and sealed the window leading to the fire escape. I tested the other windows and then went over to the bathroom mirror to check my face. It didn't look so good. Neither did the existence behind it. I was depressed and tired and falling into a bad habit of getting drubbed in the head every so often. And for what? A bogus assignment. Worse than that, I was running a two-bit racket in a hick town. I was inconsequential, even by local standards, and that was probably why Lieutenant Eck had put me off. I looked for a bright spot and found half a flicker: I was important enough that a few people wanted me killed.

I wondered where I had strayed off course, but in fact I'd been loyal to the course I had chosen. Maybe too loyal. Maybe the path of a P.I. was inherently a dead end and I wasn't able to admit it.

And maybe I had started misleading myself long before I ever got into the business — cheating myself with the aspirations I had taken on during my formative years. Television shows, movies and paperbacks were laying out their glorified detective adventures all the while I was growing up. Naturally, I knew those narratives were only fables. And yet they were working their way into my impressionable subconscious. Eventually, almost by luck, and in spite of the commonplace careers all around me, I actually became a private eye. *That's great, Jack. Now don't expect too much.* Good advice. But it never got through, and I always had the feeling that I could capture the essence of those old stories.

My ideal adventures weren't supposed to unfold like the current one. Or any of my other debacles in Pulptown. Somehow, I was supposed to be in California — like most of the TV detectives — driving a snazzy red convertible down Pacific Coast Highway, passing romantic palm trees, scanning for danger, protecting the lost and lonely princess beside me and guarding the diamond necklace at her lovely throat. The sun would set beautifully, but sinister types would loiter in the shadows. The girl and I would head inland for the cover of the crowded nightclubs on Sunset Boulevard. Dodging felons between drinks, we'd feel too exposed among the hipsters and hustlers. We'd slip into an alley, finding its doorways infested with spies. Back in my car, we'd zoom into the hills and lose our pursuers on dark, winding roads. Our hearts pounding, we'd park at a mountaintop viewpoint, rest briefly and gaze out over the vast, vibrant city shimmering with Hollywood searchlights. From there, we'd speed along Mulholland Drive and then cruise down to Malibu to spend the rest of the night outwitting jewel thieves and kissing under the stars.

Well, there would never be any such mission. For that matter, there would never be any red convertible in any race across a glamorous landscape. Life had put me in a stripped-down junker and my world was a demolition derby.

Only one remaining part of my real mission fit into the old paradigm, and that was my upcoming dinner date with a femme fatale. She was the most alluring woman I'd ever held in my arms, a woman who had made love to me with an implied option on more to come. And true to form, a woman who had brought me lies and manipulation and gunshots. Amazingly, I still wanted her to explain it all away, to show me I was wrong about what I'd uncovered and what I'd surmised. That was a slim hope, though, and any conversation we might hold instead was likely to blow up our relationship before the main course could make it to the table.

Excuse me, waiter, but there's a hand grenade in my soup.

I shaved carefully, tracking lightly over my abrasions and swelling. Then I showered and took out the darkest clothes I owned, thinking I would do a little snooping before the night was through. I dressed in a black polo shirt, black jeans and a pair of black shoes with rubber soles. I strapped on my shoulder holster and put on a black nylon windbreaker. I grabbed some bullets and topped off the magazine for my gun. The loaded rod went in the holster and the key to the handcuffs went in a pocket.

Whatever I had told Rancid P. Happenstance, it would be useless to call the cops and report him for breaking in. Sure, the police would arrest him, but I couldn't afford the possibility that he'd get bailed out within hours. So, nix to the proper procedures. My best option was to leave him chained outside until morning.

If that led to a charge of unlawful imprisonment, I could emphasize to a jury that Rance had a scenic place to relax and hundreds of mosquitos to keep him company.

In the hallway, I secured my apartment door — as if the cheap lock were strong enough — and then went downstairs to the sidewalk. The bars I trudged by were already making their quorums for the evening. One block up and a dogleg at The Bottle Cry and I was in my wreck, starting to roll through the lot. On Lombardi Street, traffic lagged. That was fine with me because I didn't really want to get where I was going.

FIFTY-EIGHT

I pulled up to the restaurant about twenty minutes late and drove around to the back of the building. The white Camaro was there, discreetly parked behind a supply van. I stayed clear of it, kept moving to the congested front lot and parked on a gravel extension beyond the blacktop. It was a warm evening, but I walked to the entrance with a chill in my stomach. Inside the front doors, a sign pointed to the bar.

My date was sitting in a corner booth. The ones near hers were unoccupied, which was a break because I needed some privacy.

She was wearing black, as I was. On another night we might have made a nice couple. In front of her, there was a highball glass holding ice cubes and an inch of amber liquid glowing in a soft wash of light. Close to her right hand, there was a silver purse. It was just big enough to hold a makeup kit and a .22 caliber pistol. What a suspicious mind I had.

"Sorry I'm so late," I said, sitting down opposite her. "I'm glad you waited for me."

She was jarred at the sight of my face.

"I keep asking you what the hell happened to you," she said. "But what the hell happened to you?"

"A little dabbling from Slab Kapowski's new hooligan."

"Are you okay?" she said. "Cancel that. I can see you're not okay. Any broken ribs? Do you have a head injury?"

"Not that I can diagnose. My racquetball trophy was more busted up than I was. I had to hit him in the mouth with it."

"So, how did this get started?"

"He was in my office when I got back late this afternoon," I said.

"He, meaning Slab?"

"No. He, meaning the hooligan. He had picked the lock on the hall door and was waiting for me inside. When I went in there from my apartment, I got clobbered. My mistake."

"You poor guy."

"Well, the guy who clobbered me was taken out of service. So I guess I came out on top."

"Out of service. Does that mean he's dead?"

"No. But I handcuffed him to the fire escape outside my window. He'll spend the night out there, and then I don't know what I'll do with him."

A waitress came by and did a double-take on my face. She was too polite to ask what kind of tree had fallen on me. I ordered a beer and another of whatever the lady was drinking. The waitress faded off.

"This hooligan in your office … what did he want?"

"To knock me out and take me away."

"To where?"

"I don't know," I fibbed, unsure at that moment how far I could trust her. "There wasn't much conversation. We were both pretty banged up."

"I'll make your pain go away tonight," my date said seductively. "You won't believe what the Incas will come up with in the next few chapters."

She was killing me — in her own way. If she noticed that my smile was on the melancholy side, she didn't let on. I gave her a weak, "Thank you."

"Did you make any progress today?"

"I don't think you could call it progress," I said.

"I bet you were watching your little football the whole time."

"Not lucky enough for that. In fact, I'll be missing some of it tonight."

"Pity. Do you usually have money riding on the scores?"

"Never."

"Then what's the point?"

"The love of the game and all that," I said.

"Is that the way you see detective work?"

"Where on Earth did that come from?"

"Only an inkling I have about you," she said.

"Well, the game I love isn't exactly the one I get to play."

"The question," she said, "is whether you ever stay on a case even after the money dries up."

"Am I being finessed into giving away a day's work?"

"You're deflecting."

I allowed myself a compressed laugh.

"You're right," I said. "And you would know all there is to know about deflection. Two nights ago, there was something you weren't telling me. Here's another chance."

The drinks came. The waitress pitied me once more, gathered up my money and walked away. My client looked at me with vigilant curiosity.

"I thought we'd been through that," she said.

"Twice. But we keep dropping it."

She straightened her back against the plush padding and said, "You're getting at something."

"Last night at The Drunk Tank, you told me you had never tasted Schnubner's famous beer. Today something occurred to me. Your employers would have wanted you to be seen drinking their product every time you had a business lunch with outsiders."

"I had already known their beer by reputation," she said with a smile. "I had certain waiters in certain restaurants joining me in a harmless conspiracy. They served me Lowenbrau in a Schnubner glass, just to keep up appearances."

"God, you're quick," I told her. "But it's too late to patch up the crack in your story. I checked with the museum this morning. They never heard of you. And the same guy has been their curator for the past four years."

"Is that so?" she said coldly.

"How about those Vikings?" I said.

"What?"

"You've heard fans talking football on Hennepin Avenue, haven't you?"

"Will you please start making sense?" Now, just for a moment, she was a little shaken. Her eyes went to the wall and swept across the room, anywhere but my face.

"Hennepin Avenue in Minneapolis," I said. "Isn't that where Tubby Tombstone has his corporate offices?"

Her look went through me like a harpoon. She breathed hard, but then the breathing and the eyes went soft. She leaned forward, calm and direct. She damn near smiled and spoke with a resigned humor in her voice.

"You do good work, my friend."

"Thanks. Maybe a little better than you were counting on when you first walked into my office."

"I'll admit it," she said. "You've been surprising me. In a lot of ways."

"Surprising as I am, I'll need a little assistance to piece this together. Help me, Rhonda."

She leaned back again, as if that would put her out of questioning range. Her mild amusement had worn off, and she looked at me under brows that were hunkered down for a fight. Though she might have been angry, she kept her head as she spoke:

"This is rather outside of your purview, isn't it?"

"Things were changing fast," I told her. "Like you, I had to improvise."

"So, Mr. Harbinger, where does that leave us?"

We were now on a last-name basis.

"I'm listening, Ms. McKinnon. Your areas are research and acquisitions, right? Exactly how do those work down at Tubby's?"

"You seem to know a great deal all by yourself."

"Not enough," I said. "I've only been running through the possibilities."

A frosted smile came across her lips and her eyes.

"Why don't you tell me what you *think* is going on?" she said.

"If that's the way you want to do it," I said, "here goes. Tubby Tombstone is a big player in the mortuary game in Minnesota and the states west of there. He's not squeamish about dead bodies and he's not squeamish about business. He wants to expand his empire by acquiring the competition, no matter how he has to go about it. He'll wave money in competitors' faces, but when that doesn't work, he's willing to use blackmail and extortion to force a sale. That's where you come in. Research. Off we go. You look closely at his target. Find a weak spot and exploit it. Find a secret and threaten to reveal it. How you find this information is *your* concern."

"What does this fantasy of yours have to do with anything?"

"Let's say Tubby looks to the east and sees Slab Kapowski, a fairly big player in his own right. If Tubby can conquer Slab's empire, he'll see a spike in his revenues. I can only guess at the figures."

"Go on," she said condescendingly.

"I'd say Tubby makes an overture, but Slab likes it the way things are. Maybe he tells Tubby to take his formaldehyde and shove it. Tubby is rankled, but undeterred. He decides to do it the hard way. He sends you out here to charm your way into Slab's life."

"What a tactful way to phrase it," Rhonda said.

"You talk your way into a cover job. You told me Slab wanted you to take a prestigious position for the sake of his image. But I'd say you had the teaching gig set up before you came to town. Tubby has you on salary and he's paying your tab at the hotel, where the registry has you under the name of Rebecca Chatterton. Tubby also gets you a car and has it registered to the real Rebecca Chatterton in Shorewood, just in case the hotel ever runs a check on your plate."

"You're sinking into quicksand."

"But you see where I'm heading with this. You find a way to meet Slab. You might even take up bowling to do it."

"How do you know I wasn't into bowling before that?"

"Don't be coy. I've seen your delivery. It isn't hard to get Slab's attention because your sex appeal is as subtle as a bonfire. You have the power to cloud men's minds — smoke from the bonfires, I guess. And your mission with Slab is to make him forget himself, get him to expose his weakness to you. You're dedicated to your job. And careful about it. You keep Slab unaware of your hotel and your Camaro. I don't know how you do that, but I'll give you credit. You start sleeping over at Slab's castle. At some point, you move in with him and start driving his GTO. You hear rumors of murder, because anyone who spends time in Slab's world is going to hear that kind of whispering."

"It's hard to avoid," she said.

"You try to mine Slab for incriminating information, but you have trouble drawing him out. You can't pin anything on him. And without a clincher, Tubby can't exert any real pressure."

I waited for a reaction.

"Don't let me interrupt you," she said with minimal tolerance.

"Not quite accurate? Well, I'm trying."

"I know you are. You're the most trying man I've ever met."

She had every right to ridicule me. I was riffing, synthesizing, building a house of cards and hoping the wind wouldn't kick up.

"Tubby is getting impatient with you," I went on. "He has a lot invested in your operation and he wants results. You decide to take a new tack, and you come to me. You tell me up front that you can't have any cops involved, but you won't say why. Obviously, that's because your business is a few turns off the straight and narrow."

"Whose isn't?" she said.

"The rest of it, we've already talked about. You dashed off some death threats and pulled the stunt with the ice pick as a way to get me feeling all gooey inside. You signed me up. You knew that if I had any brains, I'd catch on to Slab Kapowski and I'd be asking about him at Saint Opie's. You first tried to tell me you were jealous when Slab claimed to be spending time over there. That was a ruse, and you backed away from it in a hurry."

"And I told you what my real worries were. Remember?"

"That was another ruse," I said. "You didn't care about getting away from Slab. Or your financial security. You were only wondering what kind of dodgy activities he was keeping under wraps at the church. If I could find out what they were and give you the details, you'd relay the whole story to Minneapolis."

"Are you through brainstorming?" she asked.

"There's more. When it looked like I was getting close to nailing some murder evidence on Slab, you insisted on tagging along. Not because you needed to be with me but because you wanted to report what I could dig up. That was your best move as long as your boyfriend wouldn't tell you about the shady part of his life. Even when you were throwing *'The Inca Dinca'* at him."

She might have looked a little hurt, though that could have been my imagination.

"I never went near '*The Inca Dinca'* with Slab," she said. Her voice was dragging. "Anyway, I made all that up."

"Huh?"

"It was a hoax. There were some sketchy folk tales about sex in the ancient Andes. But the text was mine. I forged it in French on some old parchment and pawned it off on a collector. No harm done. He died happy."

"From chapter ten?"

"From old age."

"What about the erotic techniques?"

"I came up with those myself."

I gulped.

"Jeez," I said, breathing hard. I tried to concentrate on the case. "I suppose a summary of yesterday's legwork already went to Tubby Tombstone. That's valuable information. You probably called him this morning after I left your suite."

"What if I did?"

"A small thing, I guess, but if my investigation hadn't yielded useful results, you would have been satisfied with a deadly confrontation. I could have forgiven you for provoking that — if I lived through it. Maybe even if I found out what your real purpose was."

She shook her head. "You're not..." The protest fizzled.

"If Slab were dead or in legal jeopardy for killing me, Tubby could move in and pick up the pieces. Acquisitions. Bang, done. This was never about your plea for help. It was about financial gain. That's what was behind everything. And that's *all* there was."

FIFTY-NINE

She paused a long time, as if she were reshuffling and sorting out the playing cards in her mind. Finally, she laid down her best one.

"You're not taking my needs into account," she said.

"Maybe that's because I was the one taking the risks. All because I was sold on some crazy notion of protecting you. Let's look at the consequences. One of Slab's commandos tried to kill me and another one tried to bag me. However you break it down, Slab wouldn't be after my head unless I had gotten involved with you. I'm not sure that Slab is even dreaming of getting you back anymore. What he wants, if I know my tough guys, is to get even with me because I crossed him. You may be hidden from him. But me, he knows how to find. Hell, I can't even go to my office or my apartment anymore without a police escort."

"I'm sorry," she said as if she meant it. "If you can't go home, you could stay with me for a night or two."

"After the conversation we're having?"

"I don't hold a grudge," the lady said, still working me.

"All right. Say I hole up at your place for a couple of nights. Then what? You'll go back to Minneapolis. As long as Slab and his hired killers are still around, I'll have this mess to deal with."

"You could come work for Tubby," she said.

"As what? Vice President of Arm-Twisting?"

"I've already spoken with him about you. He could use a man of your talents. You could be on salary, a generous one. You wouldn't have to spend your time in that shabby little office or that mangy little apartment. You could have a decent place to live and a decent car to drive." She let a few beats pass by. "And I'd be there, at least for a while."

"And after that?"

"Then you'd still have the salary and …"

"Let it go, Rhonda. I can't say I know you well, but you're better than this."

"You have your nerve making judgments about me and how I make a living. At Tubby's, we don't murder anyone. And we don't think of what we do as blackmail or extortion. It's a matter of leverage."

"Just business," I said.

"That's right. It's simply business. And if mine is not an ordinary desk job, neither is yours. You, of all people, should sympathize. A regular job, even as a staff investigator for some insurance company, would kill you. You said so yourself."

"There's the matter of integrity."

"Is that what you call it? Here you are, living like some impoverished painter in some ratty little garret, suffering for your art. Only in your case, the art form requires you to get beaten up every few days. Sooner or later, you'll choose to compromise."

"There's still time for both of us to make any choice we want," I said.

Half a minute dragged out like half an hour. "You're a romantic," she said dismissively.

"I heard somewhere that love makes the world go around."

She pumped her shoulders a little. "What makes the world go around, if I remember my college physics, is the conservation of angular momentum."

It was a great shot, almost a fatal one. But she kept talking:

"And anyway, what about you? I don't see any wife and kids in your life."

"There's a void I need to fill."

"You must have had chances. There must have been someone."

"You're right. There were chances. But most women are looking for a guy with a little more stability in his life."

Suddenly, there was a half-smile on her face. "What do you want to be when you grow up?" she asked.

I laughed, although I didn't think I could.

"You've cut it to the bone," I said. "It's a rude question, but a good one. And I really don't know the answer."

"You want it both ways," the lady said. "You want to be able to do what you do, but you want stability as much as the women do. Besides that, you want magic."

"You could call it a certain rapport, a sympathetic vibration," I said. "But magic is a nice way to put it. I thought we came across a little of that over the past few days. I was also thinking maybe we could let it play out, see what happens."

She blushed and caught her breath, but then gave me the hard exterior again. And a voice that could have sliced right through steel plating.

"What do you want me to do, Jack? Settle down with you? I have to have my own space and my own way. That couldn't happen here in Pulptown. If it can't happen in Minneapolis, then there will always be some other place. As you pointed out, I can make it in Paris or Istanbul or anywhere else I decide to go. Anywhere with another ... project. All I want in the end is my freedom, financial and otherwise. No reliance on anyone. No expectations from anyone. I don't care whether it's Tubby Tombstone—"

I felt a spasm in my eyebrow.

"—God, no!" she said quickly. "It was never like *that* with Tubby. All I meant is that I won't be restricted by a corporate boss or anyone else. I won't be under the thumb of Tubby Tombstone or Slab Kapowski or even you."

"Under the thumb? Is that the way you see it?"

"That's the way it always turns out."

"Maybe so, maybe not. But when nobody expects anything from you, life is a pretty grim proposition."

She must have read the yearning on my face. "Great," she said, "I've hired the only soft-boiled detective in this country."

What she was calling freedom sounded a lot like solitary confinement. Self-imposed, except for the occasional invitation awarded to a lucky passerby. A tussle in the sack. Possibly some encores. Then a stilted parting, always on her terms. I couldn't blame her; I had plotted out my own share of one-night stands over the years. All the while, though, I had needed something deeper. That hardly mattered now, because the lady's needs were the only ones driving things. And I was just one more guy hoping to break through her walls.

I delved into her eyes, searching without a warrant. She didn't like the intrusion and looked off to the side. She took a sip from her glass and then stared at the melting ice. The untouched beer in front of me was going flatter by the second.

"You're such a sentimental sap," she told me gently.

"You never know," I said just as gently. "You may want one of those around someday."

A wave of doubt may or may not have come over her face.

"If this is where I'm supposed to cry," she said, "you'll have a long wait."

I spoke to her through an attempted smile: "I don't think a whole cannister of tear gas could make you cry."

"Then don't rescue me, Jack. I won't stay rescued."

That shut down my last try. She was no damsel in distress. And I wouldn't be slaying any dragons. I wanted to get up. I couldn't master the fundamentals of it.

Breaking the lull, she said, "The police will conduct their investigations. Even a yokel like Lieutenant Eck won't miss the mark on this one. Slab will be in jail and so indebted to his criminal defense lawyers that he'll have to sell out quickly and cheaply. Tubby will get the regional foothold he wants. And in time, a few million in profits."

"And what will happen with you?"

"I'll get kudos and a big bonus. Incidentally, if you're wondering, the real Rebecca Chatterton will wake up one day soon with a fairly new Camaro parked in her driveway. By that time, I'll be gone. Unless you're going to collar me and turn me over to the district attorney."

"You did commit fraud at the college. But you never got around to any classroom instruction. And, with all due respect to your ability, the standards at Immaculate Mind have to be pretty lax."

"Gee, thanks."

"Yours can't be the only sham resumé in their files. Half their faculty may be suspect. Hell, they might have an auto shop guy teaching quantum mechanics."

"Meaning what?"

"Meaning the administrators won't want their hiring practices picked apart in a courtroom. They won't press charges. The rest of it, your relationship with Slab, is inconclusive."

"And, I'm your client," she said, looking relieved. "That gives me some protection, doesn't it?"

"Could be, but I have no idea who my client is. Neither does anybody else. Right now, the police think you're Rene Antolini. She's an impromptu fiction, not even a ghost. Although Roxanne Delaplaine may be named as a material witness, she will have gone missing. There's a Rebecca Chatterton, all right, but she's been sitting innocently in Shorewood all this while. Even if the police look for you in Minneapolis, they're likely to learn that Rhonda McKinnon was one more alias."

She stared at me. "You're entitled to your opinions."

"Am I wrong?"

She ignored my question, sending one back with a vestige of tenderness in her voice. "What will you do now?"

"Hit the late-night mass at Saint Opie's. The parish probably holds them on Saturdays so the customers can get drunk afterward and stay drunk into the wee hours. That way, there's no stigma when they can't drag themselves to church on Sunday mornings."

She produced a small, derisive laugh.

"That's precisely why Slab always goes there on Saturday nights." The laugh didn't linger and the mood didn't lighten. "But really," she said quietly. "Stop being sarcastic. Where are you going?"

"To church, like I told you. Something is rotten there. Maybe I can find it in the catacombs, if there are any."

"You're dressed like a cat burglar. Are you planning to pick some locks?"

"That would be a sin," I said.

"Well, you're not going there to light any candles." Once more her eyes fell to the glass in her hand. She drank from it and didn't look up again. "Please be careful."

The words and the tone were kind, but they were unmistakably a sendoff. I waited a few seconds and felt foolish doing it. Somehow, I was hoping she would lower her defenses, touch my arm and beg me to stay in her life. Letting those hopes die was difficult enough. The deliberate, physical effort of standing up from the table … *that* required some heroic strength. I made it to my feet and took a good look at her. She sat there like an image in a photograph — still and silent and unreachable.

I turned and walked away from the booth. We were on the final chapter of *"The Inca Dinca."* Or maybe this was the Aztec version, the one where the guy gets his heart ripped out.

SIXTY

It seemed like a long hike through the building, down paths between rows of cars and finally out to the Mustang. Clouds in the late sky spread streaks of red and yellow over the northwestern horizon. I had an instinct to nudge Roxanne — Rebecca — Rhonda — and point up to the veiled evening light so we could share the view. No one was there but the old horse. I shook it from its sleep and guided it to the road.

I drove for miles without purpose along darkening highways and country lanes. Moving with no place to go, I spent most of the time thinking about my elusive client. The dashboard stereo was tuned to Radio Pavlov, the home of the hits as long as the hits weren't too fresh. Every song reminded me of her, although the fences, the signs and the trees had the same effect. I might have been obsessed.

I had told her I was heading over to the church, and I had meant it at the time. My vague plan was to do some skulking after everyone had gone home. But now I wasn't sure what that might accomplish. I had no real strategy and no remaining case, as if tracking down death threats had ever been a case at all.

The three disguised homicides were now partially exposed and in the hands of the Pulptown Police Department — such as it was. I had been told pretty firmly to stay out of their investigations. I ran my fingers over my bruised face. No one could argue that I deserved a few days off.

On the other side of the ledger, Slab Kapowski still had it in for me and there was no indication that he'd ever leave me alone. Also, I had his hit man handcuffed to my fire escape. I couldn't entertain my guest out there for long.

I burned gas, pulled in somewhere to refuel and kept driving nowhere.

My mind channeled back to Rance's instructions. A simpler disposal plan would have had him shooting me wherever he could find me and leaving me there. Why the complication? Why had he been told to drag me to Saint Opie's? There had to be something going on in that church besides the usual voodoo.

And what about the office that Slab had set up on their sacred grounds? Maybe I had over-interpreted a throwaway remark from one of the nuns. Maybe there wasn't any such office. But if I'd been wrong, why did Father Timothy react the way he did when I asked him about it? Why did he try to drug me and why did he call in his minions to work me over? There must have been reasons.

I couldn't go back to my apartment and listen to Rancid P. Happenstance howling through the window panes all night. Even if I spent the night in my car, parked blocks away, the questions in my head would be every bit as disturbing as Rance rattling his cuffs. There was no point in trying to sleep this off without confronting it. I pointed the Mustang in the direction of Saint Opie's and drove solemnly to midnight mass.

SIXTY-ONE

It was late by the time I drove past the house of holiness, but cars were still lining the curbs of the surrounding streets. I parked and reached into my glove compartment to grab a pen light, a roll of masking tape and a small tool pouch. I walked up a sidewalk where the length of the church paralleled a busy street. Shrubs covered an embankment rising from the sidewalk to a brick wall. There was a little-used emergency door at the upper rim of the embankment. I remembered altar boys talking years earlier about that door's part in their petty mischief. They had often left it unlocked so they could duck out before mass for a few drags on smuggled cigarettes. Maybe altar boys hadn't changed. I waited for a car to pass by and climbed through the shrubs. There were two cigarette butts, barely drawn down, in the dirt near the door. I pushed my thumb down on the ancient latch and pulled slowly on the handle.

The door opened and I eased into a dark, cramped passageway. I closed the door carefully and stepped down the hall. I could hear Father Timothy prattling through his liturgy, and I recalled enough from the mandatory attendance of my youth to know that he was nearing the end of the script. I went along the hall until I came to the familiar entrance to the vestry and Timothy's inner office. Farther down, I came to a spot where I could steal a look at the leading edge of tonight's congregation. Slab Kapowski had a front-pew seat close to my vantage point. Apparently, he had consoled himself with a new gun moll. The woman sitting next to him had a tight red dress, teased auburn hair and eyelashes like thick spider legs. She was sexy in her way, but she wasn't in Rhonda McKinnon's league. No competitor in the Central Time Zone was in Rhonda McKinnon's league. Slab looked bored and fidgety, letting his eyes roam up to the ceiling and constantly adjusting his shoulders as if he couldn't wait to get the hell out of there.

I watched as Father Timothy wrapped it up. He said, "Go in peace to love and serve the Lord," and then walked theatrically down the center aisle, strutting his vestments and nodding to either side of the gallery until he disappeared from my view. In his wake, the parishioners peeled out of their pews and followed him toward the rear doors.

The carefree voices of several altar boys came my way. Before the boys could reach the hallway, I stepped into the space behind the tall statues of John the Baptist and the woman he was dousing. The boys were committed to their chattering and didn't catch me there. They went into the vestry and started packing away the robes and tunics they had worn over their street clothes. They were winding down and doing whatever they did after a mass, preoccupied with their tasks and their conversation. I needed a place to hide until I could make a thorough search of the building. I slid down the hall without being noticed and tried the louvered door to the supply closet I had found two days earlier. It was unlocked. I stepped inside and left the door open just a crack. Between the flexible slats in the door, I could see some of the boys across the hallway. Their voices rose as they talked over each other. They gabbed about sports and summer trips until one of them titillated the others about a cache of *Playboy* magazines he had found under his dad's old yearbooks.

That's when Father Timothy swept in, concentrating on the boys and not looking my way.

"I heard everything," he said sharply. "Haven't I warned you boys about that kind of lechery?" Timothy loomed over them. "Shame on you! How are you ever going to become priests if you carry on this way?"

"I don't want to be a priest," one of the boys said. "I want to be Hugh Hefner." The others laughed, doubling up and almost falling over. They straightened and sobered when they saw the way Timothy was looking at them.

"Laugh now, laughing boys," the padre chided. "You!"

I assumed he meant the kid who had spoken up.

"Me?" the kid croaked.

"Clearly, it's time for a confession," Timothy said. "You know where my office is."

"But, Father," the boy said with dread in his voice.

"In my office," Timothy insisted. "The rest of you can go."

I pulled a quarter from my pocket, reached out for a second and sent the coin bouncing into the alcove behind John the Baptist. I closed the closet door quietly, hiding inside.

"Who's that?" Timothy said and walked out into the hallway, toward the statues and past my sightline. "What was that noise?"

Behind him, the boys were filing silently out of the vestry, sneaking past my supply closet and disappearing in the direction of the emergency exit.

Timothy came back into view, examining the coin he'd found. "What the hell?"

I heard a rush of traffic as the side door opened. Then I heard the door slamming shut. Father Timothy started toward it but stopped, kicking at something that wasn't there. He stomped through the vestry and into his office, flipping on a light. He cursed and clenched his fists in front of his chest. Apparently, all the boys had escaped. I could barely see Timothy flopping himself backward into his desk chair. He slapped both hands on the armrests and cursed again.

I stood there wondering what to do next, but suddenly Slab Kapowski took away my options. He stormed through the backstage hallway and marched himself into the vestry, then into Father Timothy's office. He stood firmly and spoke in a voice meant to peel a layer off Timothy's hide.

SIXTY-TWO

"Listen, Timmy boy, I'm tired of being put off. If things don't settle down around here, I'll throw you off your goddamn steeple faster than you can say a fucking Hail Mary."

"You've seen the list," Timothy said in a thin voice. "It's not my decision."

"I don't care whose decision it is," Slab said angrily. "I can't keep up the pace, no matter how much I'm making off the funerals. If this doesn't cool off for a month or so, I'll have the cops jumping down my throat."

"The cops have been placated," Timothy assured him.

"They can't possibly be as dumb as you say they are," Slab shot back. "At least, they can't stay that dumb forever. And besides, that private dick has been nosing around some more."

"Your man is supposed to waylay Harbinger, isn't he?"

"That's the idea," Slab said. "We'll see if Rance is up to it. Anyway, I'm on semantical for a while."

"What? You mean a sabbatical?"

Slab moved around the desk and stood over Timothy. The padre cringed and held up his hands in a defensive reflex. "No, semantical," he said. "Right. On a semantical. But you'd better reconsider things, Slab. Without the help of the church, you wouldn't be the king of the undertakers around here."

"Yeah? Well, heavy is the crown that wears out the head."

Timothy screwed up his face.

"I think you have that mixed up a little," he said helpfully.

Slab reached out savagely and clutched a fistful of Timothy's vestments.

"I'll have your goddamn *brains* mixed up in another minute, Timmy boy!"

"Don't think you can push me around," Timothy said like a man being pushed around. "Remember, I know some secrets about you."

Slab hovered over him, tightening his grip. No resistance from the priest.

"What are you saying?" Slab asked. "Do I hear the siren song of *blackmail?*"

"What?" Timothy said. "No, I think if you heard a siren song, that wouldn't be something unpleasant for you, like blackmail. A siren song would be something that you'd find … I don't know … tempting."

"Thanks for straightening me out on that, Father Timothy." Slab let go of the vestments. "That really helps."

"You're welcome. Like the siren song of fame, for instance."

Slab leaned in, slowly raised his right hand and stared at his palm as if he were reading his own fortune. Timothy looked at the hand dumbly. It sprang with a clean slap across the padre's face.

"Then how about the siren song of you shutting up?" Slab woofed at him.

"All right, all right," Timothy said, receding into his chair. He rubbed his face. "Take it easy."

"I'd be more differentiating if I was you," Slab said.

"Huh? You mean deferential?"

Slab laid another slap on him.

"You can't do that to a priest," Timothy protested.

That was a mistake. Slab switched from an open hand to a fist and let loose with a classic punch in the nose. Timothy rebounded from the back of the chair but couldn't get out of it. He brought his hands up to shield his face from another blow. When he put them down again, blood was dripping from his nostrils. There were no more punches, but Slab reached in and put a vice grip on Timothy's collar.

"You want to talk about secrets?" Slab hissed at him. "Maybe we should talk about *your* secrets, huh?" Slab shook the collar until Timothy's head bobbled. Slab let go and straightened up, towering above the priest.

"There's no need for that," Timothy said. He swallowed hard and dry, as if he had just eaten a spoonful of sand.

"Then keep your mouth shut!" Slab told him. "I'm so overworked that I had to send Mitzi home without me. I'd like to be getting drunk or laid right now. But no, I have to go over to my office and coagulate some goddamn plans!"

"In the Lord your labor is not in vain," Timothy said. "Corinthians."

"Fuck the Corinthians! And their fucking leather! Take some heat off, or I'll line your fucking coffin with it. Illuminati?"

"What?"

Slab unleashed another forehand slap. He followed up with a backhand, as if he hadn't quite made his point.

"Hey, hey, hey," the padre gibbered. "Are you asking me whether I understand? Okay, I understand."

Slab let up on him. He turned and walked out as calmly as a man going to dinner. I wanted to follow him, but I couldn't open the closet door without Timothy seeing me and blabbing about it.

Timothy wiped his face with his embroidered sleeve, grimaced in self-loathing and threw a punch at an imaginary victim. His eyes shifted all over the room. He stood up, ripped off his vestments and tossed them in a corner. He pulled a black blazer from a closet and put it on over his bloody black shirt. He sat down again, went for his desk phone and dialed.

"It's Father Timothy," he said into the phone. "I hate to have to tell you this, but there's no getting around it. Slab is an unbeliever … Yes, I know … After everything he's done for us … It was shocking … I didn't want to believe it either … No, I didn't mean it like that … I meant believing that *he* didn't believe … It all came out tonight, after mass, right here in my office … He was wavering on our cause and he let it slip … Yes, he was only in it for the money … But look, he's headed for his office and I assumed … Sorry for assuming … But I don't think it's the one at the mortuary … Right, you could catch him … I think somebody needs to teach him a lesson … No, I know it doesn't matter what I think … Of course … Certainly, that goes without saying … But I'm just agreeing with you … I don't see any other course of action … I'll be over there as soon as I can … Lars is around here somewhere … He'll lock up the church right behind me … Goodbye."

Timothy hung up. He stretched in his chair and rubbed his eyes. He got up from his desk and paced the floor, compulsively clenching his fists.

I waited for him to turn his back long enough for me to slip out of my hiding place and make for the emergency door down the hall. He wasn't cooperating, so I was stuck for a minute and had time to ponder my situation. Timothy had said on the phone that he'd leave the church for Slab's office while someone else locked up. That meant Slab's office had to be in one of the other buildings. If it was on the premises at all.

I needed to get out of my hiding place, catch Timothy's exit from the church and follow him.

I should have been worried about something else. Before I could get out of the supply closet unnoticed, Lars came by, made a little small talk with Father Timothy and then walked toward me. I stood stock still in my pocket of darkness. Lars didn't open the door, which was good. He locked it, which wasn't so good.

SIXTY-THREE

I tweaked a louver and saw Father Timothy waving to Lars before taking off down the hall.

"Coming?" Timothy asked.

"In a minute," Lars answered.

Timothy's rapid footsteps faded as a series of doorknobs jiggled and a series of door locks clicked. Lars crossed in front of me, most likely on his way out of the building. After a while, the noises died down to nothing.

My plan had been ruined, and I couldn't come up with a new one that would work. Earlier, I had lost my chance to follow Slab. Now I had lost my chance to follow Timothy.

I wanted to be reasonably sure that Lars had left before I made a move. I gave it ten minutes before I switched on my pen light. The closet door was installed to swing into the hallway, so there were no hinges on my side of it. There was no locking tab on the inside doorknob, no keyhole where I could insert a burglar's pick. Fortunately, no deadbolt. In the shelves and bays behind me, there were cleansers and sponges, rags and brushes. I had a mop and a broom, but neither one strong enough for the vandalism I needed.

I took out my gun, removed the magazine and clamped my right hand around the barrel. The pistol was now a makeshift hammer. I whacked at the doorknob. The clanging wasn't a problem because by then Lars would have been halfway home. John the Baptist was only a few feet away, but he was two thousand years old and his hearing was shot.

I broke the doorknob assembly, pulled apart the locking mechanism and pushed the closet door open. I reloaded and holstered the gun, then went down the hallway to the side exit. The old wooden door had a simple deadbolt and I had no trouble retracting it. I braced myself for the wailing of an alarm as I thumbed the inside latch and pushed against the door. The wailing didn't come. All that hit me was the humidity of the night air.

I scrambled down the embankment, then walked past the front of the church and over to the other side of the building. I stood in a small playground between the church and the east side of the school, no longer expecting anyone to come out of the church's official side door. There was no light shining through the stained-glass windows. The darkened rectory behind the church was a small living space, a cottage for a single priest. I couldn't see how Slab Kapowski could have shoehorned an office in there, even a cramped one. Behind me, the school's windows were also unlit. Its east door, in a darkened alcove, was locked. I knew there were more doors, but before I tried them, I had to check the garage. If the parish car was gone, then so was Timothy, and I'd be lost for the night.

Passing between the gym and the rectory, I found the garage. I raised myself on my toes to look through its horizontal slit of a window. A black sedan was parked in the single stall. That was a break, but where to go now?

I went back across the playground between the church and the school. I turned right onto a sidewalk that took me to the school's main entrance. The double doors were locked and the interior hallway was in shadow. I continued along the front sidewalk and rounded the corner of the building. I went down a narrow path, flanked on my right by the windows of a few blacked-out classrooms. I came to a third doorway, but there wasn't any light at that entrance either. The latch on the door wouldn't budge. I cupped my hands against a window and peered inside, letting my eyes adjust. There was no visible movement.

Stepping back, I refocused. Farther down the west wall of the school, there were no glimmers coming from any of the classroom windows. That left the basement, but there was no way to tell whether any lights were turned on down there. Spreading out from the school's wall was a second playground.

Hard to my left was the nuns' convent, a dreary stone barracks in two stories. Its windows were dark, like all the other windows in all the other buildings on the grounds. The convent's only sign of life was a lamp burning above a side entrance. In the lamp's bright radius, moths flew haphazardly and bungled against its glass panels.

I stood addled and directionless. Finding Slab's clandestine office was my best way forward, but his digs could have been anywhere within walking distance of the church. In a back room at Jiffy Cheap, for example. Or in the house of a devout neighbor with Our Lady of the

Bathtub gracing the front yard. Still, a clue I couldn't solidify — the tone of Timothy's voice or the way Pugnacia lowered her eyes under questioning — made me believe the office was much closer. I knew I had to break into one of Saint Opie's facilities, but I couldn't risk breaking into each of them.

It would have made sense for Slab to run an operation from the school's basement. There'd be plenty of space to set aside for himself. And he could be alone down there late at night. Even better, no one outside the building could monitor him in the windowless lower level.

What else did I need to remember? Had there been a neglected observation or comment?

Slab was definitely involved in a serial murder scheme, but it looked as if he wasn't in charge of it. Someone more formidable than him had been on the phone with Timothy tonight. And this was someone who could hold both Slab and Timothy accountable for what they did and what they thought. Whoever it was, the padre had been cowed under the voice of real authority. My memory went to something Timothy had said when I spoke with him two days earlier. I had chafed him with a gag about Sister Invincia, my old principal, getting kicked upstairs to take charge of the convent. He answered at the time in a peeved reflex:

I don't think you understand who does the kicking around here.

By itself, that wasn't much, but there was something else. When Flunk Vanderhovel was dying in a ravine, he said mother would kill him. I had always heard that Flunk was an orphan who never even knew his mother. Who the hell was he talking about that night? He had spoken one distinct word and then let out a long, inarticulate hiss.

Mother sssssssss.

Mother Superior?

Would she have killed him for thuggery? Would she have killed him for failing at thuggery?

I looked up again at the convent. I remembered standing in the playground as a kid, staring up at that edifice with a mixture of curiosity and apprehension. I used to wonder what it was like inside, and just as often I was glad I didn't have to find out. Most people assumed the big dormitory was a haven of prayer and virtue. I had imagined it instead as a labyrinth of toil and trouble. That may have been childhood paranoia, but there was probably some truth to it. During the intervening years, Sister Mary Invincia had become the most powerful presence in that building. What might she have been willing to conceal there? What new kinds of trouble would she have been willing to brew?

The convent was the last place I wanted to search, but it was also the last place anyone would suspect.

"I'll be damned," I said to the empty schoolyard.

A bat swooped from the roofline of the nuns' residence into the halo of the lamp, snatching a large moth in flight. I couldn't see what the bat did with its prize, but I knew it hadn't come to take hostages. There were people who would have interpreted the catch and kill as a warning from God. Me, I decided to break in anyway.

SIXTY-FOUR

The main and side doors of the convent were locked. At the far end of the building, there was a never-used back door. It had always been secured when I was in grade school, and the clumsy old padlock of years ago was still there tonight. I shined my pen light on the hardware. It was badly rusted and I might have been able to break it, but the necessary pounding would have been too loud out in the open. I bent down to a segmented window at ground level and tried to slide it open. No good.

I pulled the masking tape out of my pocket and tore strips off the roll. I cross-hatched the tape over the length and width of a single window pane. Once again, my gun made a good hammer. I broke the glass. There was a muffled *plink,* but the network of tape kept the shards hanging silently in place. Poking the gun barrel through the adhesive web, I began prying the pieces outward one at a time. The shards fell to the dirt safely and quietly. Then I used the barrel to shear the remaining fragments of glass from the rotten frame.

I reached in up to my elbow and groped. I could have found a sharp nail or a defensive snake, but I got lucky. I happened on a toggle and flipped it. Now I could slide the window to one side, creating enough room for me to crawl through.

I dropped onto a cement floor, then stood in the darkness of the interior. I shined the pen light onto cluttered shelves and stacks of cardboard boxes. I moved through the musty room to a door with no light coming from the other side. Opening it timidly, I stepped into a dark hallway. My pen light scanned rough stone walls filthy with cobwebs. I shot a barely useful beam down the corridor.

This wasn't the bottom level. At one end of the hall, I found a curving, descending stairway. I eased down the steps and came to another door at the bottom. Slivers of light seeped in at the door's edges, but there was no noise coming from behind it. I tried the knob slowly and silently, but the door was locked. I clenched the small flashlight in my teeth and took the tool pouch from my jacket pocket. I experimented until I found the pick I wanted. The lock clicked and turned. I put the tool pouch away, got a fresh grip on the pen light and felt for my gun in its shoulder holster. I pushed against the door gently.

Beyond it was a tunnel lined with more rough stone in large blocks. The tunnel extended in both directions. There was a slight draft of dank, stale air. Not far from the door, a torch rested in a sconce nailed to a patch of mortar. The torch gave off a faltering light and an acrid smell of scorched oil. The quivering rays illuminated passageways up and down the line. I turned off the pen light and dropped it into my pocket.

On my left, the hollowed-out space narrowed into a small, grated ventilation shaft. Nothing else down there. On my right, the passageway stretched out indefinitely. I moved in that direction, the torchlight fading with every step. A rat skittered past me, then disappeared into the gloom ahead. Beyond what I could see clearly, the walls reflected more glints of light, as if there were a second torch around a corner somewhere. I had no idea who or what might have been around that bend. Anxiety left me tight in the shoulders. I stepped slowly and warily toward the unsteady glow. I reached an opening in the wall on my left and angled into an offshoot of the first tunnel.

Now it was difficult to keep track of what was behind me. Uncertainty frayed my nerves and the flux of shadows played tricks on my mind. A real or imagined malevolence rolled around me like fog.

The second torch flickered up ahead.

There was yet another tunnel and I took a turn into it. I wondered whether the subterranean structure had been designed this way before the building went up. Or maybe a generation of nuns had been forced under pain of hell to dig all this out. As I walked toward yet another torch, vague forms in front of me gradually gained resolution. With a squint, I could make out a raised cabinet bolted to the righthand wall. After a few more feet, I stopped short, badly shaken. For a moment, I convinced myself I couldn't have seen what I thought I did. When I realized there was no mistake, the blood left my stomach and something like a drop of ice water trickled down my spine. The malevolence was real enough. On the top of the cabinet was a lineup of human skulls.

Breathing hard, I went in tighter. Eight of them were arrayed like a collector's exhibit. Above the lineup was a wooden plaque with the word

"Unbelievers" carved into it. Each of the skulls had been mounted on a wooden base. There was a name tag on each base, but I didn't recognize any of the names. There were several empty bases to the right of the line-up. I remembered Rebecca — Rhonda — telling me it takes weeks to get skulls ready for display. Maybe I was getting ahead of myself, but it didn't take much to imagine three of those empty bases reserved for the cranial remains of Harry Armstadt, Pete Pulaski and Norman Lumm.

The first door down from the skulls was locked, but the next one was slightly open, with no light leaking from inside a room that may or may not have been an office. I stepped up to the threshold, gun in hand, senses on edge. I pushed the door open an inch at a time until I was sure there was no one inside. With my left hand, I grabbed the pen light and turned it on. The room smelled different than the excavated hallway did, less like mildew and more like tobacco ashes. It was bleak, ascetic, devoid of anything decorative except for the icons the nuns liked to see. Broad vertical strips coated the walls. They were the color and texture of burlap. There was a gray metal desk and a matching chair lying on its side. Combination padlocks protected a gray filing cabinet.

I swept a beam of light across some papers spread over a large blotter on the desk. Beside the blotter, an ashtray held three stubbed-out cigarette butts. I got up close to the dead smokes. Printing near their filters identified them as Chesterfields, Slab Kapowski's brand. The only other items lying on the desk were a phone and a ballpoint pen. Next to the desk was a wastebasket, apparently kicked over, with torn and balled-up paper spilled on the floor. Intact, unrumpled documents were also strewn across the hardwood.

There were twin scuff marks along the floorboards. The parallel tracks extended from the desk to the door. Someone, probably Slab, must have been knocked out and dragged away with his heels leaving a trail. There was nothing to tell me how many people had been involved in the attack.

I went behind the desk. One deep drawer was open. The files in it had cryptic labels. I plucked out one of the folders. It contained funeral details and an invoice I didn't have the knowledge to question. The name of the dead customer meant nothing to me.

In another drawer I found a gin bottle, a single tumbler, a 9-millimeter pistol and a box of bullets. Others held a carton of Chesterfields, a lighter, writing pads from Slab's company and a jumble of office supplies.

Near the toppled metal chair behind me, dark spots were spattered on the floor. One of the spots was moist to the touch. I trained the pen light on my fingertip and saw blood.

The light swung across the room. Against the back wall was a pedestal capped with a small statue. Saint Francis of Assisi again — a popular choice. Woodland creatures lay at his feet. He had a moony expression on his face, but his head was dirty. I walked over and got a better look at the stain. It wasn't dirt; it was the stuff you want to keep in your veins. Francis had been doubling as a blunt instrument.

Beside the saint's pedestal, a second door was camouflaged into the wall. I wouldn't have noticed it all if it hadn't been slightly ajar. I opened it cautiously and sent a feeble stream of light down a passageway that curved and fell out of sight. I was curious about where the passageway led, but I didn't know how much time I might have to pore over the spread of papers. I turned back to them.

Almost all of the papers on the desk bore the letterhead of Last Chance Mortuary and/or the signature of Slab Kapowski. Most of them were mired in financial details and accounting jargon. I wondered whether these were pages from Slab's genuine books, not quite identical to a second set of documents an auditor would find at the company headquarters.

Slab had told Timothy that he needed to go over some records immediately. When Slab said it, he was complaining about his heavy murder schedule. The records he was talking about had to involve the killings in one way or another. Maybe he had been looking through those papers when someone came through the passageway and surprised him from behind. I searched through the sloppy pile, looking for any reference to the victims.

One of the few documents I could understand clearly was a financial analysis of what it would take to buy out Slab's competitors from here to the border of Upper Michigan. There was a neatly typed checklist with the locations and values of mortuaries and the names of their respective owners. Many of the names were drawn through in red ink. I recognized some of them from recent or older newspaper coverage. There were death notes specifying which morticians ended up in freakish falls or electrocutions or questionable hunting accidents. Next to those lined-out names and a few of the unadulterated ones, dollar figures were jotted down in red ink. The newer figure for each entry was at least tens of thousands below the typewritten value of the business. In some cases, more than a hundred grand less. The red amounts were probably the reduced prices our boy Slab had paid to frightened sellouts or the panicky heirs of deceased holdouts.

This wasn't exactly a confession, but Slab had obviously been tallying sizeable windfalls from sudden death or the threat of it.

I ruffled through the other papers on the desk and then went through a few I picked up from the floor. One of the sheets was titled *"Heretics and Apostates in Judgment Before God."* I could tell from the pica font that it came from a different typewriter. The document was a second roster of names, different from the ones on the financial breakdown. Most of them were slashed with the same red ink.

Many of the names I didn't know; some of them I did. Some matched the tags for the skulls I had just seen. Red notes next to a few of the crossed-out names said "*Caught.*" Caught and then what? Nothing good, judging from the other designations on the list. Memos beside two of the names said "*Poisoned.*" Another said "*Drowned.*" Three of the names I knew too well. Harry Armstadt's entry said *"Eaten."* Pete Pulaski's name had *"Run Through"* written next to it. The note by Norman Lumm's name said "*Chopped.*" Several of the names were not lined out and had no notes beside them. These were the targets who were still alive, I told myself. At the end of the typed list was one more name written in by hand. The ink was a shade of blue I hadn't seen on the other documents. As I deciphered the hurried penmanship, a second drop of phantom ice water slid down my back.

The name was mine.

This must have been the list Father Timothy was talking about when Slab was griping about his workload. I remembered Sister Bludgeonetta saying something about a list a few days earlier, and there had been a toxic expression on her face when she said it. Maybe this was the document she meant.

Next to the list was a chit, hand-printed in black ink. It had been crumpled and re-flattened.

M.S., I'm carrying out your nefariest bidding
but I need more time and recompensation. S.K.

The vocabulary violations were flagged in thick red lines. At the top of the chit there was a red D-minus. I shut the grade-school flashbacks out of my mind.

The documents didn't amount to a smoking gun or the holy grail, but they were as close as I was likely to find. Like Slab, I needed more time. Not to carry out anyone's nefarious bidding but to sort through the mess of papers. I wanted backup, and what I'd seen so far was more than enough to get any decent police department interested.

I set my gun and pen light on the desk, took Lieutenant Eck's card from my wallet and flipped it over to where he had supplied his home telephone number. I picked up the phone and dialed. The lieutenant came on the line after seven rings and didn't sound happy.

SIXTY-FIVE

"Yeah, what?"

"Eck, this is Harbinger."

"What the hell do you want at this hour?"

"I'm in the nuns' convent at Saint Opie's."

"The nuns' convent! What the fuck is wrong with you?"

"I found an office that Slab Kapowski has been keeping a secret."

"So what?" he said.

"You need to see some files."

"It's Saturday night, you dope." He lowered his voice. "I got a half-naked nurse in the other room."

"You're not feeling well?"

"No, no, I met her at … Harbinger!"

"There's documented evidence, Eck. Of homicide. And someone's been abducted. Could be Slab himself."

He balked. "Oh, really? You'll need to make up a better story than that."

"I'm serious. You can't afford to wait on this."

"It's not only Saturday night, but it's *late* Saturday night!"

"It's murder, Eck. That's your business, isn't it?"

"If there's a corpse at your feet, yes," he said. "Otherwise, I get time off like everybody else."

"Jesus Christ, Eck."

"Whatta ya got there, anyways?"

"Lists of names, names of dead people."

"Slab's a mortician and you're surprised he keeps track of dead people?"

"There's also a collection of skulls. You need to see this."

"So, the guy has some keepsakes laying around. Big deal. How did you get in there this late?"

"You don't want to know," I said.

"Well, a judge is gonna want to know. I'm supposed to get a search warrant on the strength of some private dick busting into a goddamn nuns' convent?"

"Besides, there's the information we gave you last night at the bar."

"Not good enough," he said. "And didn't I warn you to stay out of this?"

"I couldn't," I said. "They want to kill me, too."

"Who's *they?*"

"Slab and Timothy are involved. Maybe the nuns."

"I thought you said Slab was abducted."

"Possibly," I said.

"Who abducted him?"

"I don't know."

"Ahh, perfect. Well, whoever these people might be, I'm sure killing you is the last thing they want to do."

"You're right about that," I said. "I'm literally the last guy on their list."

"See? What did I tell you?"

"It's a *hit* list, Eck."

"It'll wait till Monday," he insisted.

"By Monday, all this evidence could be destroyed or moved off the premises."

"Hey," he said, "nobody would think to do that unless they caught you fooling around with it."

"Come on, Eck. You must have given me your home number for a reason."

"Jesus freezes, Harbinger. Okay, if anybody is standing there holding a gun on you, put him on the phone."

"Well, there's nobody here right this second."

"Then it's simple," he said. "Just get your ass out of there. Make yourself scarce tomorrow. Come down to the station on Monday morning and we'll talk about it."

He hung up.

The disconnection riled me. I punched Eck's number again. After four ring tones, his recorder kicked in. The bastard had rerouted me so he could get back to his half-naked nurse.

"Goddamn it, Eck," I said to his machine. I slammed down the phone and kept swearing.

I heard a footstep … the passageway … I should have … *BOOM* at the back of my head.

Pain flared through me, dropping me face-down on the boards. The floor performed a barrel roll or two, taking me with it. When the rolling stopped, I was nauseated, limp and defenseless. I lay there like a man thrown off a cliff.

Blurry shapes on my left stirred a few inches from my eyes. I willed myself to focus and saw a low black hem draped over a pair of black sensible shoes. Lifting my head was like lifting a piano. I saw the blood-stained statuette in the grip of a gnarled hand. The hand hung from a loose black sleeve. Above that, there was a dark mass. In the air, there was a harsh admonition.

"Thou shalt not take the name of the Lord in vain." The voice brought back memories of Sister Mary Fracturina. "You were a profane young man in the seventh grade, and you're still a profane young man."

The nun raised her weapon. I had a fleeting thought about the church powers wanting to kill me. Saint Francis of Assisi came down hard on my left temple, and then I had no thoughts at all.

SIXTY-SIX

My next awareness was of my head throbbing. A renewed bout of nausea welled up in me but I pushed it back down. Somehow, I had enough sense not to move too much or open my eyes.

My brain was frazzled but bits of information were knitting themselves together little by little. Unintelligible comments echoed from an indeterminate direction. The muffled words didn't seem to be aimed at me.

My muscles were sore and constricted. I realized I was sitting upright in a hard, armless chair. My hands were secured behind my back, and I could feel a rope chafing against my wrists. When I tried to move my hands in tandem, something tugged at them. Whoever had trussed me up had apparently looped the rope around some slats in the chair's backrest. One good thing was that I hadn't been cuffed in metal. Another plus was that there didn't seem to be any restraints on my legs or ankles.

Hell, I was one lucky guy.

My fingers could only just reach a knot between my hands. I started working it — slowly and unobtrusively twisting my wrists.

There was no telling how long I had been out. I remembered the blows to my head in Slab Kapowski's office, but I didn't know whether I had also been given a sedative to keep me under for hours. I didn't know what they had done with my gun. My shoulder holster was still strapped on, but its light weight told me the sheath was empty.

I lifted my head slightly, hoping I wouldn't attract anyone's attention. Through slits in my eyes, I scanned my surroundings. There was a table a few feet to my right. My black nylon jacket had been thrown on top of it. Peeking out from under the jacket was the grip of a gun. Maybe mine. Maybe loaded.

I widened my view. I was in a dark alcove on the edge of a large room with sweating stone walls and a high, beamed ceiling. I couldn't see any windows, which might have meant I was down another layer, deep under the convent. That was only a guess; the building could have been located anywhere. Along three of the walls, widely spaced torches burned and emitted pungent smoke. Between two torches, there was an archaic portrait of a jowly old man. The crown of his head was shaved, and he stared out from under a ring of grizzled hair. A crucifix rested on his chest and something malignant was imbedded in his eyes. I couldn't read the name plate below the drawing.

I looked for exits. There was one to my left, and as far as I could see, that was the only way out from the main floor. Past the table to my right, a display case held a human skeleton. Above that, a rotting balcony perched over a rickety flight of stairs. There was one more exit up there.

In the middle of the room there was a crude platform made of rough-hewn wood. On top of the platform, a tall man lay on his back, motionless under a gray shroud that covered his feet and most of his body. I couldn't see his face clearly. His arms were stretched back behind his head. Ropes tied to his wrists were wound tightly around a large wooden spool with a ratcheted crank.

Three figures emerged from the left side of the chamber and stepped into the light of a torch. They were Sister Bludgeonetta, Sister Pugnacia and Sister Fracturina. The holy trinity. They went over to the man on the platform. He remained still — either dead or unconscious. None of the sisters looked toward my position in the darkened alcove. They must have assumed I was still out cold.

Behind them, Father Timothy came into view. He carried a wooden bucket, and there was some weight to it. He walked up to the platform and lifted the bucket to chest level. He tilted it, splashing water onto the face of the man under the shroud.

The man coughed and snorted water out of his nostrils. He blinked hard, shook his head and raised it slightly. I could now recognize him; it was Slab Kapowski. Growling profanities at the faces around him, Slab pulled at the ropes holding him back. His legs moved under the shroud but he couldn't kick himself free of it. In spite of his new station in life, he barked as if he were still in control.

"Get me out of these goddamn ropes!" he shouted at Timothy. "Jesus, my head feels like a plane crashed into it."

"I told you not to push me around," Timothy said.

"Oh, right. You're such a tough guy and I'm such a scaredy cat. Just get me the hell out of ..." He popped his head up a little higher, looking around as best he could. "Where am I?"

"In the dungeon," Timothy said.

"In what dungeon?" Slab said angrily.

"The dungeon of … I don't know. We always just call it the dungeon."

"But I want to know *where*, you little prick!"

The priest said, "You've never been down here before? Really?"

"Look, you dumb fuck, I'll kick your ass like a goddamn pigskin all the way back to Notre Dame!"

"Better calm down," Timothy said.

"Calm down? Tell you what I'll do, I'll kick your head right through the goddamn goal posts! I'm all four horsemen of the alpaca lips! Or whatever the fuck you people call yourselves!"

"Such brave talk," came a raspy woman's voice from the darkness. "But you are in no position to intimidate."

The woman walked into the pool of light slowly, imperiously. The others gave her a subservient bow. She turned in her yoke of a habit, and when the torchlight shined on her just enough, I got a make on her. Sister Invincia was gaunt, rawboned. Her face was the same merciless mask she had worn all those times I'd been sent to the principal's office back in grade school. There were seventeen more years on her now, but she still looked as tough as a crocodile. She wore the standard uniform — the full black robes with the starched white bracket around the face — but the crucifix hanging from her neck was bigger and heavier than the ones I had seen on the other nuns.

"And so, the truth comes out," she said to Slab.

"What the hell is going on here?" he demanded.

She ignored his question. "As the truth always does."

Timothy put down the empty bucket. He hunched forward in an obsequious bow, with his neck sunken into his shoulders. His elbows hugged his ribs and his hands gripped each other at the tip of his chin. His features deformed into a perverse grin, and faint gagging noises leaked out from the back of his throat.

The other nuns gave Invincia a wide berth and let her take a position between Slab's face and a raised table. Pugnacia bent down to a box on the floor and came up with two handfuls of tools. She placed them neatly on the table and stepped back.

Bludgeonetta spoke:

"Everything is in readiness, Mother Superior."

"Very good," Invincia said.

"Ready for what?" Slab said with a glitch in his voice.

"You are a doubting Kapowski," Invincia said dispassionately.

Slab let out a desperate laugh. "Where did you hear that?" he said.

"From Father Timothy," she told him.

"But he's an invertebrate liar!"

Invincia listened but seemed unmoved. She picked through her tools.

"I'm sure you mean Timothy is an *inveterate* liar," she said casually. "That would be literally true, although your choice of words may be figuratively accurate as well. Timothy has never shown much evidence of a backbone."

Timothy opened his mouth but closed it quickly, sinking back and lying low.

"I ... guess so," Slab said meekly. "But you can't rely on what Timothy tells you. Don't you know about him?"

"I know about *you*." Invincia said. "And your guilt."

"What? Are you holding me responsible for murder? It was you who put me up to it!"

"What you call murder was the unfortunate but unavoidable corollary to the purification of souls," Invincia told him. "It is true that you have provided yeoman service to the One True Church. You have advanced the mission of cleansing and compliance, and your labors have not gone unappreciated. However, you realize the one thing I dread is interference, and you have failed to stop a lowly investigator from prying into church business. I understand that he fell into your hands at the race track. What happened when you dispatched your first incompetent to kill him there? And what happened when your second incompetent was entrusted to bring him here in chains? You appear unable to hire a decent workforce. Who is to blame for these failures?"

"Hey, you're right. Starts from the top. I'll get right on that. I'll nab the guy myself."

"Too late," she said abruptly. "We have already captured the meddlesome Mr. Harbinger, and I will deal with him later."

"Looks like it all worked out," Slab said optimistically. "You might as well let me go."

"The botched assignments of your employees are minor matters in the larger scheme of things," Invincia said. "And you have done some fine work. But your intentions have not been pure. Your recently reported skepticism is a matter of much greater significance, and you must be held responsible."

"What skepticism?" Slab said. He forced a laugh. "Are you joking?"

"I shall give you the benefit of the doubt," she said gravely.

"Thank you, sister."

"Mother Superior," she corrected him.

"Thank you, Mother Superior."

"You're welcome. And in giving you the benefit of the doubt, I assume your mismanagement and your skepticism are products of the devil."

"Well, yeah," Slab agreed. "What else?"

"Since you are possessed by Satan," she told him, "it will be necessary to perform an exorcism."

"Okay," Slab said, thinking fast on his back. "Let's regroup and get that done sometime next week. You'll need a priest, and not that goddamn Father Timothy, because we already know he's against me. Just tell me what day and time I need to show up."

"A priest is not necessary," Invincia said coldly. "By the grace of God, I am in authority here."

"Fine, all right," Slab said, wriggling on the platform. "I guess that's okay. Go on and recite your official incarnations over me and let's be done with this."

"You mean *incantations*. I've been meaning to speak with you about your vocabulary."

"All right," he said. "We can go over that another time. Just say what you have to say right now. And then we'll get the devil out of me and I'll be all fixed up. Gone are the sins of the fathers who inherit the wickedness of the young, isn't that right?"

"No, not really," Invincia said. She casually fingered through the implements on the table.

"What's … what's with all the tools," Slab said nervously.

"I'm afraid that novels and movies have distorted the public's understanding of what an exorcism involves. Certain prayers will be spoken, to be sure, but the authentic, little-known procedure actually entails a fair amount of drilling."

"Oh, you mean like drilling down. To the nitty gritty. You need to ask me some questions, is that it?"

"Well, I could. But mainly I will need to bore a hole in your head."

SIXTY-SEVEN

"*What?*" Slab shouted. He pulled hard against the ropes at his wrists. "A hole? In my head? You can't possibly mean that!"

In the background, Timothy was whisking himself into a paroxysm. He rocked and clapped his knuckles under his chin. A lower caste nun beside him was breathing hard. Another was biting her thumbs.

"Oh, okay," Slab said, calming his voice and forcing a chortle. "I see what you're doing. You're joking again."

"Am I?"

"Sure," Slab said with a flattened laugh. "You're very strict. You always liked that image. But now you're playing against type, I think they call it. Making little jokes about your tool box. That's great. Pretty funny."

"You will find I'm not a particularly hilarious person," Invincia said evenly.

"Right, I know," Slab said. "But you're dealing with a tense situation here. And so, I guess you're trying to lighten the mood. Poking fun at yourself. Nothing like a little self-defecating humor."

Invincia rested her forehead on the back of her hand.

"Lord help us," she muttered.

"Yup," Slab agreed. "Lord help us all. That's for sure."

"Perhaps the exorcism procedure may be simplified," Invincia told him. "Do you renounce Satan?"

"Boy, do I!" Slab said with a burst. "I'm so against Satan you wouldn't believe it."

"An interesting choice of words," Invincia said. "And why exactly would I not believe your renunciation of Satan?"

Slab raised his head.

"That's just a figment of speech," he said. "I renounce Satan. Satan is bad. Satan is double bad!"

"Indeed," Invincia said thoughtfully. "So, you believe that Satan's evil can be calculated as a finite figure?"

"What?"

"You said double bad. That would imply a certain numerical representation that could be doubled. Since infinity cannot be doubled, I infer that you do not believe that Satan is infinitely evil."

"Look," Slab pleaded. "I'm just a simple undertaker."

"Gangster," she said.

"Okay. Just a simple gangster. I can't be expected to keep up with all this mentalphysical stuff."

"Metaphysical!" she said sternly. "Are you doing that on purpose?"

"Just give me … just give me a minute."

"Don't try to slide out of this," Invincia pushed back.

Slab spoke, his voice getting less defiant all the time. "I wouldn't try to put one over on you, Mother Superior."

The others inhaled sharply, as if they could tell things were about to escalate. Their eyes remained riveted on the boss nun.

In the darkness, I kept twisting my wrists behind the back of my chair. I was trying to open a gap between my hands, get some slack into the rope and find a weakness in the knot.

"The biggest threat to faith is, of course, skepticism," Invincia said. "But high on the list is a lack of philosophical rigor. If you do not acknowledge Satan as infinite evil, then you do not acknowledge God as infinite goodness."

"Sure, I do," Slab whined.

"You are an unbeliever," Invincia said with an iron voice. "I can smell it on you." She turned, pivoting her body back to the others. "Sister Pugnacia, give the subject a correction."

Pugnacia rushed to the crank behind Slab's head and heaved into it. The ratchet creaked and clunked into place as Slab yelped.

"Aaahhh! My shoulders!"

Timothy's lower lip let out a string of drool. The others clenched their fists and their teeth. Watching Invincia flog a nine-year-old couldn't compare with this.

I kept working the knot.

"What do you want me to say?" Slab cried out.

"You don't believe in Satan at all," Invincia said calmly. "Admit it."

"I renounce Satan!" Slab cried out.

"I shall not rest until I get a confession out of you," Invincia said. She turned to Pugnacia and spoke a single word: "Again!"

Pugnacia cranked the traction up another notch. Slab cried out in pain.

"Do you have something to say, my son?" Invincia taunted him.

"Aaahhh … renounce …"

Invincia nodded. Another notch and more yelping.

"How can you do this to me?" Slab bawled at the ceiling.

Invincia said calmly, "Let us remember the guidance of C.S. Lewis."

"Who the hell?" Slab said.

I remembered the name coming up at the paper mill.

Invincia said, "Lewis tells us that God's benevolence allows us to pass through our suffering for the sake of a greater good. Suffering is in fact a corollary to His goodness. It is a token of His love for us. Pain is God's gift."

Slab managed a question through gritted teeth: "Couldn't God just send me a fruitcake?"

Invincia sighed and spoke in an unemotional voice. "How amusing. One more notch, I think."

The lackey ratcheted the wheel until Slab's ligaments tore. He screamed and then got a grip on his ability to speak.

"All right!" he blurted, panting and writhing. "I don't believe in Satan!"

"I knew it," Invincia said triumphantly. The other nuns applauded politely. "I have to tell you, Slab, that I'm rather disappointed in you. I've had a flower arranger on that rack and he held out much longer than you did."

"So what?" Slab whimpered.

"I'm just saying … You'd think a flower arranger …"

"No … I meant … So what if I don't believe in your crazy Satan?"

"And God? Do you believe in God?"

"What?"

"The story of God is inextricably bound to the story of Satan," Invincia said. "Anyone who has read the Bible knows that. I have always felt that disbelief in Satan can only lead to skepticism concerning God Himself."

Slab hesitated. Invincia spoke Pugnacia's name again and the assistant grabbed hold of the crank for another go. Slab gave in before she could move it.

"Okay, okay," he croaked at Invincia. "You got me." Now he was sobbing. "I don't believe in any of it."

Invincia turned to the gallery with a smug smile. "You see how easily he has fallen into my trap?"

"As so many others have been ensnared," Bludgeonetta said admiringly.

"But Jesus," Slab said. "What adult could believe in these stories? You got Satan and God working together. Bait and switch. It's all an act." Now that he was tapped out, the fancy lingo was gone. "God talks a good game, all love and kindness. But at the same time, he lets this evil Satan run around tempting people. And when the devil finally trips them up, the same loving God goes all hard-ass, turns around and damns them to hell. Christ, I've been diagnosed as a sociopath and even *I* wouldn't do that!"

"You don't understand," Invincia said.

"Goddamn right I don't understand," Slab shouted at her. "You got Noah building an ark and bringing in all the animals of the world. Two by two, right? What about bees? I actually know something about this. You have one queen bee, but you have to have a whole bunch of drones and hundreds of worker bees just to make the hive work. It's not like you can have Mr. and Mrs. Bumble Bee walking out of the ark when the rain stops and starting a nice little bee family!"

"Well, you're just nitpicking," Invincia told him. She pivoted stiffly, facing the others. "Now he's just nitpicking," she said to them.

"You got Adam and Eve," Slab said desperately. "And they had Cain and Abel and what, some daughters? So, when it came time for grandkids, who did their sons mate with? Did Adam and Eve's daughters have to make it with their own brothers to populate the world? What are we saying? That the whole human race is based on incest? Why wouldn't all the kids' brains go rotten after the third or fourth generation?"

Invincia nodded at Pugnacia. The ratchet clattered into place under Pugnacia's weight. Bones cracked. Slab let out a long scream.

"Let us not lose our focus," Invincia said.

"Maybe you're saying their brains *did* go rotten," Slab said through gasping attempts to steady himself. "Maybe all that inbreeding is the only way to explain how the human race could get dumb enough to believe this stuff!"

A tilt of Invincia's head gave another cue to Pugnacia. The ratchet clattered again with a heavier strain. More cracking, more screaming.

My nausea was coming back and I fought it hard. I took a deep, silent breath and tried to concentrate on the knot at my wrists.

"The Lord looks upon you with mercy," Invincia said. "And I do as well."

"Oh, really?" Slab said. "Well, then I'm sorry I said all that. Forget it."

"You must be freed from Satan's grip," Invincia said. "Let the exorcism begin. Sister Bludgeonetta, please hand me the large drill."

Slab's head almost jumped off the platform.

"You're not going to use that thing on me!"

"How else but opening your skull," Invincia said, "can we drain the bile of Satan from your infected brain?"

Bludgeonetta handed the drill to Invincia and picked up a rubber mallet. "Would you like me to administer an anesthetic, Mother Superior?"

"I think not," Invincia said. "In order for the ritual to be meaningful, we must proceed without tricking this man's senses. The subject needs to be conscious. For only when he is fully engaged can he confront the evil within him. And only then can he truly appreciate what we are doing on his behalf."

Slab was shrieking and Timothy was hyperventilating. Fracturina stepped closer to the platform.

"Mother Superior," Fracturina said over the noise. "If I may say so, you are wise and ethical to a fault. I can only stand in awe."

"Thank you," Invincia said. "You may reduce your nightly self-flagellations by half."

"You are so kind, Mother Superior."

"Now for the work of the Lord," Invincia said.

She laid the drill bit on Slab's temple and tightened her left hand on the back of the manual tool. She grabbed its midsection and started cranking with a strong right hand. Skin broke and blood began to spurt.

"This is gonna kill me!" Slab yelled.

"Of course, it will," Invincia said soothingly. She stopped to explain. "But it's for your own good. Your flirtation with Satan will certainly demand a price to be paid. Lord knows how many hundreds of years you will have to spend in the flames of Purgatory. But God's mercy will win out in the end. And when it does, I will be waiting for you in heaven. You can thank me then." She went back to the task, putting some muscle behind the auger.

Slab jerked his head to the side and the drill bit scuttled off its mark.

"Wait a second," Slab yelled. "Father Timothy over there is a child molester!"

Invincia whirled and faced Timothy. She was livid. "You've been at *that* again?" she railed at him. "I told you to control yourself!"

Timothy cowered where he stood. The grotesque smile had left his face, but he was still stooped over. "I flubbed up," he said as if it didn't really count.

"Flubbed up, indeed! Do you have any idea of the trouble you've caused? Now I'll have to get you reassigned to yet another parish!"

Slab went manic, shouting at Invincia.

"You mean I apply a little common sense and I get my arms pulled out of their fucking sockets? I get a hole drilled in my fucking head? Meanwhile, Timothy goes groping after altar boys and all he gets is a goddamn transfer? What kind of people are you?"

"The reputation of the Holy Church must be protected," Invincia said impassively.

Slab thrashed on the platform as if someone had lit it on fire.

"This is nuts!" he yelled. "This is completely nuts!"

Invincia stood over him, cold and unbending. She pressed the drill bit against Slab's neck to settle him down. She then placed her fingers on Slab's chin and wiggled it, measuring its degree of play.

"Sisters," she said. "We'll have to lash his head down. Better get the duct tape." The nuns converged on a cabinet and rifled through the drawers, looking for the tape. Slab cried and pleaded.

I didn't know what to do. Jumping in could end it for me in a hurry, but my options were disappearing. I could leave Slab to his fate. He was a murderer and if he died it was no loss. Besides, he had sent one man to kill me and another one to bag me and dump me here in the same dungeon.

On the other hand, I knew Slab wouldn't last long under the cranial drilling. And I knew that Invincia and her goons would strap me to the rack and start working on me as soon as they were finished with him.

I had begun to force a finger into a loose part of the knot behind me, but I wasn't there yet. I needed to stall them.

"You don't know what you're talking about," I said from the shadows.

SIXTY-EIGHT

Dead silence from Invincia … from Slab … from all of them.

Invincia glared at me and curled her lip. She turned to Slab and pointed a crooked finger at him.

"You see what I have to deal with on your account?" she sniped. "We should have been done with Harbinger long ago. But you and your hirelings appear to be incapable of carrying out the simplest task. Do you know where we caught him?"

Slab shook his head and kept silent.

"Right here in *our* convent! In *your* office!"

"And he was making a phone call," Sister Fracturina added. "To the police."

Invincia recoiled. "The police? You didn't tell me about that. You know I have to do my work in secrecy."

"It's okay," Fracturina said. "Harbinger was calling just before I knocked him unconscious. And it sounded like he couldn't persuade anyone to come here. The officers probably know what an unreliable young man he is."

"Nevertheless," Invincia said, "you should have said something. The flagellations are back on."

"Yes, Exalted One."

"We can't take any chances. Go to the armory and get pistols for yourself, Sister Mary Bludgeonetta and Sister Mary Pugnacia. Bring them back here immediately and make sure they're loaded."

Fracturina bowed and began to walk off. She paused and turned. "Shall I bring a gun for you as well, Mother Superior?"

"I am always armed," Invincia assured her.

Fracturina bowed once more and hurried away, her robes flowing in her wake.

"What about a gun for me?" Father Timothy said.

"Shut up," Invincia told him. Her voice was like a boot at his throat.

Sister Pugnacia walked over to my chair, put her face close to mine in the darkness and eyed me contemptuously. She reared back and slapped me across the kisser. I could feel my gums vibrating.

"What were you saying?" she demanded.

"Your boss doesn't know what the hell she's talking about," I told her. "She won't even be able to answer a rudimentary question."

Pugnacia's face curdled. "You need to pass our tests. We don't need to pass yours."

"Correct me if I'm wrong," I taunted her. "But aren't you people supposed to have all the answers? Ancient wisdom and all that?"

"Ancient wisdom is lost on you," Pugnacia said. She turned to Invincia. "When sister Mary Fracturina gets back with the firearms, may I have the honor of shooting him?"

"Too soon," Invincia told her. "It will be easy to fend off his inquiries. And once he sees the error of his ways, once he appreciates the reality of hell about to consume him, then he will die as his kind were always meant to die, in humiliation and terror."

Pugnacia put her hand to her chest and bowed slightly. "Yes, Mother Superior."

"First," Invincia said. "There is the matter of the exorcism. Get Mr. Kapowski's head secured."

Pugnacia laid a steely grip on Slab's head. Bludgeonetta tore strips from a roll of silver duct tape and placed them across his forehead and under his chin. Slapping the ends of the strips down onto the platform, the nuns made sure Slab couldn't slip out from whatever Mother Superior was planning for him. Invincia picked up the hand drill again and aimed the auger at Slab's temple.

"Don't move," she told Slab. "This will hurt quite a bit."

Slab screamed before she could touch him.

The door opened and Fracturina came in, buying Slab a little more time to live, buying me a little more time to work the knot. Slab went quiet as Invincia straightened up. Fracturina carried three revolvers and a heavy box to the table near the rack. The weapons weren't snub-nosed pistols. They were the old Colt .45 models, the kind gunslingers would have used when facing off on a dusty street in front of a saloon. Fracturina handed one each to Bludgeonetta and Pugnacia, then tilted the box to pour bullets into their waiting pockets. She set the box down and fished out some spare ammo for herself. All three nuns flipped out the loading gates of their guns, spun the barrels and liked what they saw. They clapped the gates back into place, then stowed the six-irons deep in the folds of their habits.

I was making some progress on the rope at my wrists. The knot was loosening slightly but not enough for me to get my fingers into the mesh. I kept twisting my hands, trying to get more slack.

Invincia rose to her full height. "Stand ready, sisters. The drilling is about to commence."

Slab wriggled and roared. "This is like the goddamn Inquisition!"

"That's the *Holy* Inquisition to you," the boss nun scolded him. Then she paused, sweeping one hand up toward the portrait of the hardened old man. "Tomás de Torquemada," she said lovingly. "His was a time of great certainty, a time when doubts were squelched before their toxins could undermine faith, a time when moral relativism was punished rapidly and decisively. Friar Torquemada is an inspiration to us all, but especially to me. During my pilgrimage to Spain years ago, I was able to acquire a pair of sacred relics. Two of the great man's teeth. An incisor and a bicuspid. They are my most prized possessions."

Slab tried to pull his head up off the platform but the duct tape had him pasted down.

"Torquemada was my role model from the day I took command as principal at Saint Opie's," Invincia said. "His strength was mine as I set about establishing order in the school. Turning youthful high jinks into submission before the Lord was a fine thing, though it may have been physically exhausting at times. As I have often said over breakfast, a ruler doesn't rap knuckles by itself."

"Amen," two of the nuns said.

Invincia went on: "Despite my efforts, and my many years of service, my holy charge at the school was interrupted by the craven appeasers at the diocese headquarters. I suffered the injustice of being replaced by a lay administrator, and I watched as school discipline was destroyed by misbehaving young barbarians."

Children, I thought to myself.

"Then, through my prayers, I learned to accept that everything happens for a reason."

That again.

"And ultimately, one day I stared at that portrait of Torquemada and I knew I had a larger mission to fulfill. And I thanked God for giving me the time and the place and the example of a great man to carry it out. Perhaps you didn't know, Mr. Kapowski, nor you, Mr. Harbinger, but this year marks the five hundredth anniversary of Friar Torquemada receiving his commission as Grand Inquisitor. It was his sacred license to do whatever was necessary to restore purity and obedience to the minds of God's subjects."

Something clicked in my memory. It was a magazine piece I'd seen more than a year before. The article said the Torquemada quincentennial was coming in 1983. It didn't mention anyone picking up where the sadistic friar had left off, but the editor couldn't be expected to account for an underground zealot in a backwater town.

"Five hundred years," Invincia said slowly and ceremoniously. "It is no coincidence that I should be alive in these times of trouble to mark the milestone. And now, through me, the spirit of Torquemada lives again in this world."

"That's a stretch," I said.

"Very funny," Slab said from the rack.

"Sorry, not what I meant," I told him. I stared into Invincia's cold eyes. "History has been a little tough on your Grand Inquisitor," I said.

She took a deep breath and let out a triumphant sigh. "The poor friar has been unfairly discredited by weak-minded historians. But that cannot possibly matter now. Only God has the right to judge, and His judgment, handed down through me, is final. Torquemada was the greatest disciplinarian of them all. And I mean to go on with his work."

Slab dropped any pretense of bravado and broke down in tears.

"She's fucking crazy," he said through the sobbing.

"Watch your language, mister. I scarcely know whether to drill your skull open or wash your mouth out with soap!"

"You know you can't justify yourself," I challenged Invincia. "This little bit of brain surgery is just an excuse for homicide."

"He's making sense," Slab said, trying to gather himself. He swallowed the crying and made himself sound almost lucid. "I don't think you can cast out any devils until you get your shit together."

"You could have said that more gracefully," Invincia told him. "But I'll concede your point for now."

She turned to me, giving me her level stare and that raspy voice.

"I knew, Mr. Harbinger, all those years ago, that there was evil within you. I remember you sitting there while I was giving the eighth graders a special lecture on the necessity of God, the necessity of there being a first cause, an eternal entity from which all existence sprang. Do you remember what you asked me then?"

"Vaguely," I said.

"You wanted to know why there couldn't always have been protons and electrons. Of all the questions you could have asked, that was your disruptive contribution to the class."

"Sounds like I forgot the neutrons, but that wasn't why you busted me."

She put down the drill and leaned forward against the platform.

"I tried to teach you a lesson that day."

"You tried to beat my brains in."

"Same thing," she said. "But you remained obstinate and irreverent. Not only on that day but afterward. You just couldn't wait to leave Saint Opie's Elementary School for the cesspool of the public education system. I knew then that if you were ever to return, Satan would be following on your heels."

"Harbinger's the guy you want," Slab pleaded with her. "Not me. I could kill him for you."

"Shut up," she told him.

I knew that putting Mother Superior on the defensive was my only chance to get more time out of her. I hit her with something out of the old days.

"Have you been throwing any more kindergarteners into garbage trucks?"

The edges of her mouth descended into a grimace. "Keep it up, buster. You are only making it worse for yourself."

"It's true you don't have your act together," I ragged her. "Even Slab can see that much."

"So, we have *two* hecklers from Satan's gallery, do we? Very well, Mr. Harbinger. If you insist on a philosophical debate, I'm happy to have one."

"Let's hold the debate at the race track," Slab said. "Bovine Downs is perfect for it, and the Fourth of July is coming up. We can sell tons of tickets."

"Sister Invincia told you to be quiet!" Bludgeonetta said firmly.

Invincia slowly took in the satisfaction of Slab's new powerlessness. Then her eyes shifted back in my direction. "Why are you fidgeting?" she asked me.

I'd been picking at the rope.

"My hands are going to sleep," I said. "The knot is too tight. How about untying me?"

Invincia threw her head back and cackled. "You'd like that, wouldn't you?" she said. "No, you go on fidgeting. After all the times you sat smirking in my office through all those years, it gives me great pleasure to watch you squirm."

The other nuns glanced at each other and nodded. Timothy moved to a stool at the back wall and sat down, hunching forward. He shriveled into some kind of secret rapture, his knees close together and his elbows digging into his thighs. His hands covered his mouth and his eyes gleamed as he rocked back and forth.

They all waited for Invincia to speak.

She waved a hand toward another dark alcove. Pugnacia and Fracturina scurried there to drag a high-backed chair out from the shadows. It was heavy, made from thick blocks of weathered wood, and the two lackeys were having a hell of a time with it. They maneuvered the throne into place between me and Slab's platform. The obedient nuns retreated to their standby positions. Invincia stepped onto a low rail and climbed aboard. She sat facing me squarely, her fingers clasping the carved griffins on the ends of the chair's long, wide arms. Torchlight flickered over her severe features. Behind her, Slab Kapowski lay writhing on the rack.

It was the principal's office — and then some.

Invincia broke the dead air. "Discipline in our time is deteriorating," she said. "I can see it happening day in and day out. Something has to be done, and someone has to do it."

"I suppose you'll have to take over the world," I said. "Is that where all this is heading?"

"If necessary," she said casually. "You challenge my authority with your cynical barbs and questions. Your very presence is a symptom of the evil that could overcome us all. Look at the world around you, Mr. Harbinger. The Latin mass is withering. Church attendance is dropping. The clergy is beleaguered. The convents are all but deserted. Lay teachers, with their dubious religious training, are filling the jobs once held by pious nuns. No wonder standards are degrading."

"Your standards were degraded a long time ago, sister."

She went on as if I had said nothing.

"Backsliding is a cancer wasting away the souls of mankind. Sin is gaining on us at every turn. Pride, greed and sloth are everywhere. Fornication and illicit cohabitation are rampant. The young scorn the mere suggestion of self-denial. In exchange for a few moments of hedonism, they blunder into never-ending damnation."

"Let's not gloss over the big one," I said. "They're even playing football in the spring."

"How about those Philadelphia Stars?" the suffering gangster said in a muffled voice.

Invincia whipped her head around, twisting her entire torso in the big chair.

"Would someone *please* shut that man up?" she said angrily.

Bludgeonetta rushed over to the rack as if to guard against any additional input from Slab.

Invincia faced me again, grinning like a wolf with its lips peeled back over its teeth. "As always, the little joke from Mr. Harbinger. But we'll see how humorous you find all this when you are in Mr. Kapowski's position." Her grin disappeared. "As I was saying, spiritual decay has been spreading its filth upon the earth. The heretics and apostates have to be silenced. Their insidious doubts and their eroding questions have to be stopped before they poison the children."

"Get off it, Invincia. To you, children never meant anything more than batting practice."

"They must be scourged for their own benefit," she said. "But they are small potatoes. I have seen my greater duty and my greater destiny. The paramount mission of our time has begun here in this town. It is imperative that dissidents learn to see the light. And if not ..."

She left the worst of it unspoken. Maybe that was a sign of weakness.

"And if not, sister? If they don't see the light your way?"

My question reverberated through the big room. Invincia paused for a long time, letting me hope for a reprieve. When she finally spoke, the answer came in a stark, impersonal voice — like a verdict from a bronze idol.

"Then may God strike them dead."

Well, that was it. There wouldn't be any weakness, any reprieve. Most likely, there wouldn't be any reasoning with her either. But I was fighting for my life with my hands tied behind me, and I had nothing to throw at her but ideas.

"Okay, Invincia. The lord taketh away. When do you think he'll get started?"

"I told you, the task has already begun. In your case, the rack will soon be open."

"I'm not talking about the rack or a drill. I'm not talking about faked accidents or piranhas in a fountain. I'm talking about an act of God. A meteorite through the head, a bolt of lightning, a killer earthquake. If your boy wants to put a toe tag on me, why doesn't he do it without your help?"

"The Almighty takes lives as he pleases."

"The hell with that, sister. You're the only one around here deciding who dies."

"God works through *me*," she said aggressively.

"Yeah, I suppose he'd have to. Because he can't strike anyone dead or get anything else done when he works all by himself."

Invincia pushed down hard on the arms of the throne and set her feet as if she were about to hurl herself at my windpipe.

"That's blasphemy!" she shouted. "And a treacherous lie!"

"No, seriously. I won a bar bet on that point just this afternoon. You should have been there."

"Your validation is a bar bet? Ha!" She stayed in her seat. My neck stayed unwrung. "It is easy to picture you in a den of iniquity. I thank the Lord God that I was never there and never will be."

My wrists were grinding, struggling against the tightness of the knot.

"Fine," I said. "Forget about the bar. But let's see if I can keep winning my bets. A few minutes ago, you were saying you'd be happy to have a philosophical debate. Up through now, you're still dodging my main question."

"Oh, I am, am I? As you shall see, Mr. Harbinger, I'm not dodging anything."

"Then tell me," I said. "Why does God exist?"

SIXTY-NINE

Sister Invincia's eyes went flat. I had hit her with a question that put her in check. After a tense few seconds, her eyes registered again. She spoke haltingly, as if she couldn't believe what she had heard. "Why does? … God exist? But … God is the necessary being."

"What made him necessary?"

"What? God is simply necessary. All creation is contingent upon Him. Nothing can come from nothing. That is a given."

"What would prevent existence from popping out of nothing?" I asked her. "If there were nothing out there, how could there have been any restraints against spontaneous existence? Where would the restraints have come from?"

"They would come from God."

"So, God would make sure nothing was there even if nothing was there in the first place? Not even him?"

"No, God would be there. God is both necessary and eternal."

"If God is necessary, then some other fundamental circumstance prior to God or outside of God must have compelled him to exist. Whatever that circumstance was, if God is dependent upon it, then he's subordinate to it."

"No," she insisted again. "God is necessary in and of Himself!"

"So, you're telling me that God's existence was undirected and unrestrained by any other condition or entity."

"Exactly," she said. "Thomas Aquinas tells us that God is the first cause."

"Okay, let's accept his assumption. That's the same as saying the first cause was itself uncaused. Isn't that right?"

"Yes. That's what I just said."

"Therefore, the God you believe in exists for no particular reason. He's existence at random. He's an accident, and his nature is accidental. He may have one set of features but he could just as easily have any others. Or his nature could be any number of changing features coming and going in chaos."

"Is there no end to your sacrilege?"

"Not until you knock down my arguments. What about them?"

"Aquinas tells us that God is perfect." Invincia said, trying to win the point with her tone of voice alone. "How could He be both chaotic and perfect?"

My fingers were digging at the knot. I had to keep her talking.

"First of all, Aquinas pulled all that stuff out of his ass."

They all gasped. "How dare you?" Invincia spat at me.

"You say God is perfect," I went on. "But that presents all kinds of logical problems."

"That's absurd! What problems could there possibly be in perfection?"

"Perfect as opposed to what?" I said. "Even if God is out there, you can't claim he's perfect just because he is what he happens to be. Perfect within what frame of reference? Perfect according to what criteria? If God has no external standards to live up to, then the concept of perfection becomes arbitrary and meaningless."

"No!" she pounded. "God is necessary and therefore omnipotent."

"Where the hell did that come from? It doesn't even follow. A chickpea could be necessary, but that doesn't make it omnipotent."

Invincia shook her head and waved her hands outward, as if pushing away the concept.

"In his omnipotence," she said, "God has the power to define perfection. Ipso facto, He must then be perfection itself!"

"But if God, by his nature alone, can't be anything less than perfect, then you're saying he isn't free to be anything other than what he is. Therefore, he must be under some set of restrictions. So much for omnipotence."

Invincia pressed her fingers tightly to her temples, as if she were trying to prevent the pressure of my logic from blowing up her head.

"It is Satan's work to confound the faithful," she said.

"You're making it damn easy for him."

"Mother of God," she prayed. She looked heavenward and shrunk into her chair. "Why does Your Grace test me so?"

"Let me see if I understand you," I said. "Necessary existence can't possibly fail to exist. Is that right?"

"Right," she said, coming slowly out of her prayer. "I suppose that's correct."

The knot was giving in a little.

"Then you have the same problem. If God is necessary, he was unable to avoid existing in the first place and right now he can't even cancel his own existence. Therefore, God is not all-powerful."

"You're twisting everything," she said.

"One of us is," I said.

"God is … God is perfect because He is all-powerful, and that is because He is necessary."

"You still haven't explained why God was not a pure accident, or why any existence at all isn't purely accidental."

"God is eternal!" she shouted. "God was *not* an accident!"

"You make a loud point, sister, but not a good one."

I reached the heart of the knot, but I didn't have much time.

"Everything must have a beginning," she said. "Except for God. God does not need a beginning … because … because God is God." She was floundering in a circular argument.

"That's empty word play," I said. "You might just as easily say that nature doesn't need a beginning because nature is nature."

"That's different!"

"No, it isn't. You and your shills define God any way you like. And then you work backward. You trot out arbitrary premises that are already loaded with the conclusions you wanted to reach in the first place. If you had any integrity, you'd start with observable data and build conclusions from that. But you won't do that because it's too much work."

"That is a vile accusation!" she said.

"But an accurate one. You haven't built your case. You're left with nothing more than rhetorical tricks. I've heard them all before, and they all have the stink of desperation on them."

I pried open a little slack and got a finger through a loop.

Invincia took one more deep, exasperated breath and then tried another tack.

"But how could human life and the human mind exist if God were not the first cause? How could everything within us and around us manifest its order and complexity unless it was designed to work that way?"

"Christ, I've already been through this with Timothy," I said.

"He's a tough nut to crack," Timothy said from his stool at the back wall.

"Oh, I'll crack him all right," Invincia answered him. "Let this impetuous fool incriminate himself, the better to exact retribution from him."

"All right," I said. "Let's look at it this way. Assume that X is the degree of complex order requiring design."

"Wait a second," Slab said, still tied down and unable to raise his head. "This is getting too complicated."

Invincia twisted in her seat and looked back toward the rack.

"I will have silence!" Her voice nearly dented the back wall. "Sister Bludgeonetta, can't you control that man?"

Bludgeonetta put a sheepish look on her face and shrugged helplessly.

"Well, give him another notch!"

"No!" Slab yelled.

Bludgeonetta wrenched the big crank. Slab screamed pitifully.

Invincia faced forward again, rolled her eyes and nodded my way.

"Go on," she told me.

"Anything of equal complexity as X, or anything of greater complexity than X, could only exist if it had been designed. Right?"

"Yes, that follows. But get on with it," she said impatiently.

"Any being capable of designing the kind of complexity we see all around us would need to have an even greater complexity than the product of his design. By the same reasoning, in order for God to design our brains, he would have needed an intelligence that exceeded human intelligence."

"Certainly," Invincia blustered. "That just stands to reason. But what's your point?"

I pulled a coil of rope down over the knuckles of my right hand.

"So, God is evidently greater than X. You've already said human intelligence is too complex to exist without a designer. If that's true, then the greater intelligence of God is even more in need of a designer than *ours* is."

She opened her mouth as if to counter, but came up empty. After an awkward pause, she reverted to the default position.

"Yours are the words of Satan!" she squawked.

"Admit it," I said. "Your own description of God has made him impossible."

"What? I admit nothing!"

"Your whole stance is an endless regression. It leads us to ask over and over again who designed the designer. It simply kicks the metaphysical can down the road."

"But you're only talking about the natural world," Invincia said. "God is supernatural."

"More empty wordplay," I said. "You hit a wall with nature and so you trot out the supernatural. When you hit a wall with that, you can trot out the super-*duper*-natural, or the *hyper*-super-duper-natural or any other half-baked idea you can dream up. All of it is a way of making God exempt from the principles you're citing when you try to prove his existence. You're saying you can't have complexity without a designer, but you're excusing a complex God from your own rule. Your maxim is always the case except where it suits you to say your maxim *isn't* the case."

"No!" she said. "Complexity is not the issue. God is simplicity itself. We know this because God cannot be broken down into components."

"You mean like the father, the son and the holy spirit?"

"Hey, zinger!" Slab called out.

Invincia pounded on the arms of her throne, twisted around and shouted:

"Sister Bludgeonetta, is there a *fucking* cattle prod in that *fucking* tool box?"

"All right, all right!" Slab said in a panic. "I'll shut up!"

"You'd better!" Invincia settled in again and redirected her anger. "That's a cheap shot," she fired back at me. "The Trinity is one, and you know it."

"Yeah? When did the one God bring Jesus on board?"

"Jesus has *always* existed as the Word!"

"Not a word or words in a limited sense, but Jesus at full throttle, right?"

"Yes, yes, yes, you scurrilous reprobate!"

"Well, in that case, the whole thing is a little sick, isn't it?"

"A little sick? Is that what you said?"

"How did Jesus get here on Earth?" I asked her.

"What? What are you driving at now?"

"Grind it out, sister. His mom was a virgin, right?"

"Well ... Jesus was ... the Holy Mother of Jesus Christ was a virgin, yes!"

"By your own account, the angel Gabriel tells Mary she'll be the mother of God by the power of the holy spirit. Sure enough, Mary magically gets pregnant. Who arranged for that to happen?"

"It was a miracle. Like all miracles, it was an act of God."

"But which parts of God? Are you telling me that only two thirds of the troika hatched that plan and carried it out? The father and the holy spirit did it all behind the son's back?"

"Well … of course not. The Word was always part of the Trinity. The Trinity is inseparable."

"So, it's one for all and all for one, like the Three Musketeers. What one does, they all do."

"Yes, that's what I told you! Whatever you're trying to say, out with it!"

"But if they're all one God, indivisible and working together, then Jesus helped to impregnate his own mother."

Invincia's jaw dropped halfway to her crucifix. The other three nuns gasped and clutched at their throats.

"What a horrid little pervert you are!" Invincia said.

"What's horrifying," I said, "is the notion that rational people could pretend to make sense of all this gobbledygook."

"Bah! That's not even …" Invincia composed herself. "You got me off the subject. I thought we were talking about simplicity. God is simplicity. He only created complexity."

"Okay, let's go with that. If simplicity can give rise to complexity, then you're admitting one of the main ideas behind evolution."

"Aah," she said with her eyes narrowing. "More of your little tricks."

"It's no trick," I said. "It's reason. You can't have it both ways."

"I'm not having it both ways," she said bitterly. "I told you that God is simplicity. Infinite and ultimate simplicity!"

My right hand came free. My left was still anchored to the chair.

"All right," I said. "Let's play with that concept for a minute. Infinite and ultimate simplicity is totally homogenous. It's featureless, without contrast or context or boundaries. Everything and everywhere would be the same. There would be no point of reference. There would be no distinction between here and there, up and down, good and bad, pure and tainted, intelligent and mindless. In fact, there's no difference between the God you're describing and an infinite expanse of nothing in particular."

"Damn you, Harbinger! You're making my head spin." She rested an elbow on her thigh and pinched the bridge of her nose. "I think I need a break."

SEVENTY

I would have liked a breather. I would have liked to stand and loosen up my legs, but that wasn't an option. It was Invincia's option and she took it. She got up and moved to the rear of her throne. Holding on to the tall backrest, she did a few deep knee bends.

I worked my fingers into the tangle at my left wrist.

Timothy stood, stretched himself and walked around a bit. Then he sat down again, frowned and picked at something sticky on the bottom of his shoe.

"Who the hell chews gum in a dungeon?" he muttered.

Pugnacia asked Invincia whether she'd like some coffee but Invincia said it would keep her up all night.

"We have Sanka," Pugnacia said. "Caffeine free."

"Not as good," Invincia said.

"I could use a beer," Slab said.

"Ours is an austere order," Invincia told him calmly. "I'm afraid we will not be offering alcoholic refreshments."

"Yeah," Slab said. "I probably should have thought that through."

As they made small talk, I looked around the cavernous room. There were shackles affixed to the damp walls, but no living or dead victims were hanging from them. In another alcove farther down to my right, there was an iron maiden, an upright and open sarcophagus with an interior studded in spikes. The big metal coffin stood ready to put the squeeze on its next tenant.

The boss nun cleared her throat and returned to her seat. She looked rested and comfortable in her element. She nodded her way through a silent roll call. The three other nuns fell into place. Timothy was still on his stool. Slab wasn't going anywhere. Neither was I.

Invincia leaned forward, once again girded for combat.

"Now then," she said, levelling her cold eyes at me. "Where were we, Mr. Harbinger?"

"You were telling me that I was making your head spin," I said.

"Oh, yes."

"Your head is spinning because I'm making you think," I told her.

"Your kind of thinking is forbidden," Invincia snarled at me.

"Obviously," I said.

A loop of rope came loose.

Invincia's face was an ugly scowl.

"The wrath of God shall soon be upon you!" she said. She shook a bony finger in my direction. "You were a silver-tongued devil as a boy, and you are still a silver-tongued devil. I've made a decision during the break, and I see no reason to indulge you any further." She rose from her throne and stepped down onto the hard, gray floor. She stood there, breathing hatred. "It is time to finish the first order of business so that we can make room for you on the rack. On this night I have wrested a confession from Slab Kapowski. And by the teeth of Torquemada, I shall extract a confession from *you,* Mr. Harbinger."

I clawed at the final snag.

"I'm an atheist and I haven't hidden it. What more would you like me to confess?"

"Errors of faith," she said. "Your willful and malicious errors of faith. Make no mistake. You'll soon recant every word of your heresy." She turned and swept back toward Slab. Suddenly, she stopped and wheeled around. Her lethal eyes took aim at me again, searing like the torches on the walls. "As for now," she went on, "sit there squirming in the dark. Await your turn for punishment. And know that you cannot escape the pain and death that are your only future on this earth."

Fracturina came forward. "Perhaps we should shut him up for a while," she said.

"Good idea," Invincia said. "There have been too many distractions already. You, or one of the others, use a gun barrel to knock him out. But be careful not to kill him. Not yet. When he awakens on the rack, he'll have sufferings to bear and heresies to renounce."

Fracturina drew her weapon. The three dark angels walked toward me.

I needed a few more seconds. I didn't have a few more seconds.

"What's the first reading at today's mass?" I asked them.

"Hmmm," Bludgeonetta said, pausing to scratch her headgear. "It was '*Genesis*,' wasn't it?"

"Depends," Fracturina said to her. "That was yesterday. It's past midnight now. Are you talking about today?"

My finger found an opening.

"That's right," Pugnacia said. "It's already Sunday. So, um, today's first reading is … let me see."

I tugged hard at the last loop.

"It isn't '*Deuteronomy*' is it?" Bludgeonetta said.

"That's it," Fracturina said.

I pulled the loop clear and flung my hands into the air.

"Look out!" Invincia yelled.

The other nuns panicked and scattered like crows.

I lunged for the table — and my gun.

SEVENTY-ONE

The sudden movement left me dizzy. Muscle contractions rippled through my arms and legs. I stumbled into the table and swept the jacket away. The gun beneath it was mine. I grabbed it with clumsy fingers and ejected the magazine. It held a full crew of nine. I shoved the magazine back into place as the first shot went off from the other side of the room. The bullet zinged into the wall behind me, chipping rocky fragments onto the floor. In the enclosed dungeon, the sound of the shot was earsplitting. I hit the deck, disoriented, with a high-pitched ringing in my ears. I forced myself to think and forced my body to gear up. Pulling on an edge of the wooden table, I kicked one of its legs to tip it over, then hunkered down behind the shield it made. More shots came in, one of them splintering the wood close to my face.

I reached around the table and fired in a defensive reaction. It was a stupid, wasted shot. I rolled to my right and saw Fracturina crouching with both hands gripping her revolver. She fired but the bullet skidded off the floor beside me. I fired back and the slug punched her in the chest. She jerked backward and fell flat, motionless.

I yelled, "Weapons down!" But the bullets kept coming. I rolled back behind the overturned table and poked my head around the left side of it.

Bludgeonetta fired at me but her aim was off. I couldn't get a clear line on her. Another two shots from her cut holes in the table top.

Still under fire, I jumped farther to my right and set myself up behind the wooden base of the skeleton display. A bullet from somewhere blew into the lower cabinet, but I got a shot off just over the top of the glass case. It missed and Bludgeonetta fired back at me. Her shot shattered a pane of glass and exploded the skeleton's bones. Pugnacia fired from a different angle. I reached around the base, and my next bullet caught her in the torso. The nun doubled over and dropped. She was finished.

Invincia took cover behind the big throne and Bludgeonetta hid behind the crossbars of the rack where Slab was still battened down. She reloaded her Colt. Timothy, unarmed, cowered under the stairs leading up to the balcony.

"Let's talk!" I shouted out to Invincia.

"There's nothing to talk about!" she shouted back. And yet, she couldn't help lecturing me. "Despite all your dismantling of philosophy, you cannot obscure the greater truth. You cannot deny the battle between good and evil. And the fact that God will one day sit in judgment of you and your abominable sins."

"I thought he'd already made up his mind about me."

"It is not yet judgment day!" she yelled.

"Doesn't matter. Your God is supposed to be omniscient. He's supposed to know in advance how things will turn out for me."

"He's well aware of your damnable sins!"

"Yeah, he would be, because he drew the flaws in my blueprints. He waits for the flaws in all of us to show up, and then he lashes out for the defects that he himself created."

Gunfire blasted the cabinet in front of me and the wall behind me.

"You're ignoring the doctrine of free will," Invincia sneered. "We can choose to be obedient or we can choose to be wicked. And if we choose wickedness, it is hardly the fault of God."

"Free will and punishment," I called out. "Another trip down the rabbit hole. You're not only torturing *people*, you're torturing logic."

Both of them fired wild bursts in my direction. I was trapped. Invincia was well hidden behind the big wooden chair. She must have started with six bullets in her gun's chambers and a pocketful of spares. Bludgeonetta was somewhat more exposed, hiding behind Slab and his platform. But shooting back at her could have meant hitting Slab. I would have no regrets if he died, but I didn't have any right to execute him.

"The paths of good and evil are laid out before us," Invincia shouted. "And we have the choice of which path to walk."

"Okay, let me see if I have this straight," I said. "One path leads to eternal euphoria. And the other path leads to eternal torment."

"Exactly," Invincia said.

"Go God's way and you're in the clover. Go another way and you're in the furnace. What kind of a phony choice is that? If we get rewards and avoid punishments just for doing what a manipulator wants us to do, then we have no more freedom than a lab rat."

"You twist and you twist and you twist!" she said. "Moral laws require rewards and punishments. And they require an unquestioned, absolute authority. Otherwise, we would be lost in a morass of moral relativism." She fired with enough anger to scatter her bullets. Bludgeonetta let off two rounds of her own and buried them in the cabinet.

"Authoritarian absolutes don't qualify as morality at all," I told her.

"And what but the approval or condemnation of God could you possibly put in their place?"

"Human empathy," I said. "Simple human compassion."

"How heart-warming," Invincia said bitterly.

"Those are the kind of emotions you wouldn't know anything about because you're stunted. You're locked into a version of morality that's nothing more than obedience."

While Bludgeonetta reloaded, Invincia fired more heat. "Only in obedience to God can any of us truly be free," she said.

"Free to do what?" I said.

"The will of God, of course."

"So, you're talking about the freedom to follow orders? That's straight out of George Orwell, lady. Substitute Big Jesus for Big Brother, work at it for six months and you'll hit the *'1984'* nightmare right on the money."

Bullets crashed in on my position.

"No!" she shouted. "There are no nightmares with Jesus!"

"Well," Slab said from between his elbows, "let's think about that for a minute."

"Just … shut up," Invincia cut him off. "Hold your fire, everyone. My point is … that God's commandments are all part of His perfect design. If God had not given us moral instruction, we would all be senseless automatons."

"You're wrong," I said. "We're not perfectly designed. We're adequately thrown together by natural selection. That's what shaped the way we think and feel — the same way it shaped the way we walk upright or work with our hands."

"To you," Invincia shouted, "we're nothing but animals. And animals have no moral rules at all."

"Morals aren't a set of rules handed down by the boss of all bosses," I yelled. "They're biologically imbedded impulses like cooperation and altruism. They're group survival strategies. They're messy and inconsistent, but like everything else in human nature, they evolved because they helped us muddle through from one generation to the next."

"Bah!" Invincia shouted. More shooting. "There is nothing uplifting in your so-called natural selection. There is nothing edifying in your stories of our descendance from apes."

"But there's something edifying about drilling a hole in a man's head to let evil spirits dribble out of his brain?"

Slab perked up from under the duct tape. "You know, the guy has an interesting slant on this."

This time Bludgeonetta didn't wait for Invincia to prompt her. She slugged Slab in the mouth. He coughed up a spurt of blood.

Invincia kept on pushing. "I make no apology for my rectitude. Or for enforcing the strict laws of morality revealed to me by God Himself."

"God's morals are like the morals of any other dictator," I said. "They're whatever he happens to decide they should be. You're stuck on the level of a child who thinks something is right or wrong only because mommy and daddy say it is. When are you going to allow people to grow up?"

Bullets blazed out of Invincia's Colt .45 and blew chunks of stone off the wall behind me.

"What about the cease-fire?" I said.

"Without God," she said, "there can be no morality at all."

"That's the trouble with religion," I told her. "It's left you unable to imagine any ethical concept that doesn't require God's reign of terror to prop it up."

Bludgeonetta reeled off a few into the cabinet. It was starting to break up. They had pretty good cover. I couldn't waste any lead shooting back at thick blocks of wood.

"The truth," I yelled at both of them, "is that you're morally vacant. If you had any decency, you would have reported your slimy Father Timothy to the civil authorities instead of watching him get transferred from one crime scene to the next."

Timothy straightened to speak.

"Now you're casting aspersions," he said.

Invincia ignored him. "I prayed mightily over that bastard," she said. "I asked God what to do and God told me to protect the Church. I had no choice but to obey Him."

"Jeez," I said. "You're no better than Abraham."

"All right, cease fire again!" Invincia said. "And just what is *that* supposed to mean?"

"Abraham was willing to sacrifice his son just because God told him to do it."

"Well," she said. "His son Isaac was probably acting up in school."

"No reason given in your Bible," I said. "No mention of Abraham even demanding an explanation. No need for him to decide whether human affection might make it wrong to kill his own child."

"That was only a test!" Invincia said. "God stayed Abraham's hand at the last moment."

"But the point of the story is that Abraham *agreed* to do it, agreed to kill a helpless kid, his own flesh and blood. He was so compliant that he was willing to do anything, no matter how depraved it might have been. And as sure as hell, we're supposed to praise him for it."

"Abraham was only following orders!" Bludgeonetta said.

"And that makes it okay? Listen to yourselves. You're taking your ethical cues from the goddamn Nuremberg defense."

Gunfire buffeted my ear drums but didn't hit me.

Invincia screamed with an acid voice: "You go too far, Mr. Harbinger!"

"You're a moral fascist," I told her. "You can't tell the difference between virtue and subservience. But people who feel affection toward each other are going to act in a humane way whether or not some spook in the sky commands it. They'll do it whether or not they're under surveillance from heaven. And people like you, people who are capable of atrocities, are always going to find a reason to inflict suffering."

"Obedience to God is no atrocity," Invincia said. "Yes, I mete out punishments. But what temporary suffering here on Earth could possibly compare to the perpetual hellfire that awaits the rebellious? I try to save people from that. And sometimes they need a little persuading."

"Is that what we're calling sadism these days?"

Another shot from each of them.

"You're taking the narrow view," Invincia said, "when what's really important is eternity. God's laws guide the way to everlasting life. Our trials here on Earth are only preparations for the hereafter."

"That's another part of your problem," I said. "You don't appreciate your time on Earth because you spend your life thinking this isn't really where you were meant to be. You believe your real life will be something else entirely, and happening in a place you can't even understand. Well, that's not the way it is. Life is here and now. And if it doesn't last forever for any one of us, we'll just have to buck up and deal with it."

More shots tore into the wall behind me. For all of Invincia's yapping about a stringent regime, target practice had been lax.

"Without eternal life in the hereafter," Invincia said, "our time in this world would be futile."

"One generation pours its life into the next," I said. "That's the only hereafter that counts. And anyone with real affection for children knows it isn't futile. But you can't get out of the way of your own mortality."

"I shall live forever in Christ!"

"You're not even living now. All this morbid hogwash about heaven and hell has made you squander every minute you've ever had. What have you been doing all this while but rehearsing for your death? Face it, Invincia, your religion is one big graveyard. No wonder you get along so well with undertakers."

"Actually," Slab said, "we're not getting along all that well."

Bludgeonetta hammered him in the mouth again. He groaned and launched a bloody tooth into the air. It rose and fell in a rainbow curve and then bounced across the floor, skittering all the way to the front of Invincia's throne. The broken tooth lay there, its roots dripping red.

"There's another incisor for your collection," I told her. "And you didn't have to go all the way to Spain to find it."

"Make your insouciant little comments while you still can, Mr. Harbinger. Because this debate will shortly come to an end."

"I take it you're conceding, then."

"There will be no concession from me," Invincia said. "You will never shake my faith."

"Faith is a belief you hold even when there's no evidence to support it."

"Silence!" Invincia raved. "You mock those who fear God."

"What you fear, sister, isn't God. What you fear is the *absence* of God. That's why you and your kind had to invent him."

"Invent God? Your arrogance is astounding!"

"It's only narcissism to say the creator of the universe is a lot like us. You tell us we were made in God's image, but it's actually the other way around. We made God in our image. And I'll tell you why."

"I will not listen to a Godless wretch!" She fired and reloaded. Bludgeonetta did the same.

I could only fire off more arguments.

"Humans invented God to have someone they can negotiate with, sister. People who can't handle uncertainty cooked up this almighty God character because they're desperate for some power over the capriciousness of life. They invented God with a human face because that makes them believe they can sit down and bargain with him."

"No one can bargain with God," Invincia shouted.

"Then what the hell is prayer? People bargain with God every day, or they pretend to. They call God all-powerful, but at the same time they think they can cajole him into giving them their due. They make material or behavioral sacrifices and then imagine that God is supposed to make sure that the volcano doesn't bury them, that their crops come in, that the plague passes them by. And the biggest and most selfish payoff they demand from God is personal immortality. There's the answer to my question, sister. That's why God exists. He's only there in our minds and he's only there for our own purposes. We don't serve God. God serves us."

"The effrontery in this room is astounding!" Invincia thundered. Her Colt erupted. Bullets bashed into the wall behind me. "Your vanity is insufferable!"

"Really? You believe that the most important being in the universe listens to your bedtime prayers, dotes on every word that comes out of your mouth, ponders every thought that drifts through your head. And you think *I'm* the one who's vain?"

Both nuns fired into the cabinet. It would be kindling in another minute.

"Your conceit," Invincia said, "is your presumption that you may pick God apart as if He were one of your philosophical theories, one of your problems in logic. But God is beyond our understanding, beyond our comprehension. He is so profound that we can never begin to fathom the depths of His being and the perfection of His plan for us."

"Oh, bullshit," I said. "Your Bible takes, I don't know — more than a thousand pages — to describe who God is and what God wants. If he's so incomprehensible, why go to all that trouble? And you, you're willing to condemn people who stray from what you call the certainty of God's commands. You're willing to put people to death merely for asking skeptical questions. And yet you're telling me that God's plan is so inscrutable that none of us could possibly be clear on what it is. To say God is beyond our understanding is to say you literally don't know what you're talking about."

"We'll just see about that," Invincia said.

I had five bullets left and a busted-up shelter in front of me. Invincia must have sensed that I couldn't risk any bad shots. She commanded Bludgeonetta to shoot and keep shooting. Under the cover of her lackey's gunfire, she dragged the throne backward. I couldn't believe Invincia's strength. She was on a rampage, overdosing on adrenalin. With the bulky frame of the high-backed chair now close to the rack, she had blocked any clear shot I might have had. She took up a position next to Slab.

"Nothing can deter me from tonight's mission," she said. "The exorcism must proceed at all cost."

For me, it was a standoff. For Slab, it was terror.

SEVENTY-TWO

"The drill," Invincia said. Bludgeonetta handed it to her, all the while keeping her gun trained on me.

"Wait just a minute!" Slab shouted at Invincia. "I've been listening to this whole conversation. I didn't understand half of it, but it was clear that you couldn't answer him. You didn't win your debate. You don't have the chops. You shouldn't be doing an exercision on *anybody*!"

"Shouldn't be doing a what?"

"I don't know what the fuck you call this crap. But it's crap!"

"Oh, screw it," Invincia said. She caught herself and paused. "No pun intended." She placed the drill bit against Slab's temple.

"What about the incarnations?" Slab screamed.

Invincia paused again, visibly annoyed. "Satan be gone," she said, flicking her wrist dismissively. "Whatever."

"That's it?" Slab yelled. "Satan be gone? That's all you can say?"

"Don't get smart with me, mister. It's late. We don't have a lot of time and there are other people who need punishing. It's not all about you."

"I'll pay you!" Slab yelled out.

"I'm not in this for money," Invincia said. "I'm in it for the glory of God."

"Who's going to carry out your murders for you after I'm dead?"

"That will be a problem," she admitted.

"You don't think that wuss Timothy has the balls to do it himself."

Timothy looked hurt. He pouted at the suffering, desolate figure of Slab Kapowski on the rack and spoke up: "You know, Slab, sometimes you can be a little mean-spirited."

"You're right about Timothy," Invincia said to Slab. "Although he did a fairly good job with the piranhas. Anyway, he will be transferred to another parish very soon, thanks to his shenanigans."

Timothy began to chirp out a weak protest. Invincia pivoted and stared at the priest hard enough to crimp his voice. Then her gaze panned away from him and she stood tall, her head bending back and her eyes beaming heavenward.

"Thou hast blessed me," she prayed. "My work, and Thine, shall go on even without Mr. Kapowski and even without Father Timothy. And there is much to be done. Other violators will have to be detained and brought to me by good, strong soldiers. I beseech Thee, oh Lord, may Thy wisdom and Thy mercy and Thy power provide all the assistance I need. Amen."

"Jesus Christ," Slab said hopelessly.

Invincia made a move to restart her cranking.

"Stop!" I yelled. Bludgeonetta fired at me again.

"I stop for no one," Invincia said, though she did stop. "By the grace of God, I shall drain the devilish bile from this man's brain. And then, Mr. Harbinger, I shall take you to task. You can't hold out there forever. I can tell you're conserving your bullets. You'll run out of them sooner or later. Or you'll be wounded. But wounded or whole, you shall eventually end up here in Mr. Kapowski's place."

"How about putting him here right now?" Slab said.

Invincia ignored him and honed in on me again.

"And I tell you this, young man. Smirk and scoff and hope for good luck all you wish, but do not cling to any fantasies that you can outsmart me or the Lord. Your recanting is inevitable, as I have said. But if you think even *that* can save you now, you're deluding yourself. You have shown your true, irredeemable nature, and you would certainly revert to it if the threat of agony were to be suspended for a single second. No, Mr. Harbinger, tonight is your final reckoning."

"Thanks for the warning," I said.

"You can thank God. I have it on His authority that no matter how many times you may snivel an admission of your guilt and remorse, no matter how many times you may plead for mercy, your insolent words have taken you far beyond the limits of forgiveness. Very soon I'll have the pleasure of hearing your pathetic attempts at atonement, and then the greater pleasure of seeing you damned for an eternity of despair."

It was only a savage face and a grating voice and some words I didn't believe in, but I had to hand it to her. All her years in the principal's office had perfected her ability to freeze a guy's guts.

Invincia snapped back into the job at hand. She aimed the drill and leaned into it. I yelled but there was no getting in her way. She muscled the drill bit home and Slab howled for his life. Red blood flew onto her black habit. She kept grinding until she broke through the skull with a sickening pop. The boss nun almost plunged in on top of her victim, but she steadied herself. Slab flopped wildly, then seized up and lay still.

A day before, he had been a kingpin in the mortuary game. Now he was only ballast for one of his coffins.

Timothy dropped to the floor. He was on all fours, and in a ghoulish trance. His hands flew up to the sides of his head. There was a bizarre smile on his contorted face. Guttural sounds rattled in his throat and saliva bubbled at his mouth.

I had never seen anyone more delighted with the way his day was turning out.

Invincia raised herself from the slaughter and caught her breath. She looked down at Slab's carcass. "You are now free of the Dark One," she pronounced. She picked up her gun and trained it on me while Bludgeonetta grabbed a knife from the tool box on the floor. The burly assistant cut Slab's body loose, sawing through the ropes at his hands and feet. She ripped away the duct tape pinning Slab's head to the platform, then pulled the body off the rack and dumped it in a corner. Invincia nodded in satisfaction. They didn't bother to wipe the blood and brain tissue off Slab's wooden deathbed. Bludgeonetta set her knife down and picked up her gun again, aiming it at my position. She stood waiting for the chief's orders.

"How about some peace talks?" I said.

"I've had all the talk from you I can stomach!" Invincia barked. Both of their guns let loose.

In the barrage of gunfire, I scrambled away from the display case and sprinted to the next recess on my right. Bullets gouged the stone wall as I ran by. I was nothing but fear and reflex. I shot but missed. I slid into the darkness and crawled behind the iron maiden. Bullets zoomed in and threw sparks as they ricocheted off the hulking sarcophagus. I stood and fired back, wounding Bludgeonetta. That was six shots from my gun.

Bludgeonetta's left arm dropped to her side and blood dripped from her sleeve. She still had her gun and a steady right hand and she used them. Between her shots echoing off the walls, I could hear a lock or a handle rattling on the other side of the main door. Then there was a pounding out there — a banging like rhythmic canon fire. I could see the door buckling under the force of a battering ram. Probably reserves from the Sisters of Divine Retribution. More hell coming and not enough ammunition to ward it off. The boss and her crony fired at me wildly. Bullets caromed off the iron maiden and the concave wall of the alcove. I risked everything, jumping out for a moment, firing at Bludgeonetta straight on. The slug slammed her backward. She got off an aimless round on the way down, but that was the end of her.

Three of us left. Two bullets in my gun. Invincia reloading. Timothy unarmed. The door breaking up. All of it raced through my mind. The boss nun fired four staccato shots, then moved slightly out from behind the platform to get a better aim. I had a moment's clear view and fired back, hitting her in the stomach, doubling her over. She wouldn't last long but neither would that door.

Mother Superior somehow kept her feet, staggering to the throne, bracing herself on its backrest, fighting to hold herself up. She made the sign of the cross with the gun barrel and loaded more ammunition.

The door burst open. Invincia sent a bullet into the breach, as if she knew there were no reserves. Eck and a squad of policemen flooded through the opening and dove onto the floor.

Eck returned erratic fire, unable to steady himself. One of the cops tried to stand up. Invincia fired again and winged him.

Father Timothy slithered out from his hiding place under the stairway and bounded up the steps to the balcony. He groped for the lone door up there and went hard at its brass lever, squalling in frustration when it wouldn't turn. He pushed and pulled madly. Nothing gave. He beat his fists on the door and begged God to let him out. God didn't answer.

Invincia struggled to an erect position, pointing her gun toward the balcony.

"Don't do it, sister!" Eck shouted.

She did it anyway. She pulled the trigger and hit Timothy in the back. He nearly went down. She let him have another one in the shoulder and he spun dramatically. He struck a rigid wall and rebounded onto the balcony's flimsy railing, breaking it and dropping twelve feet. His head crashed on the stone floor and I thought I could hear his skull cracking.

Mother Superior strained to keep standing. Holding her gun in her right hand, she pressed it high against the back of the throne. Her left hand tried to stanch the flow of blood at her belly. With a caustic smile, she said, "I always wanted to kill that son of a bitch."

She pulled down her .45 and pointed it my way but Eck didn't give her another chance. His police revolver flashed and Invincia convulsed. She defied death for a second, then fell to the floor like a plank.

One of Eck's men went over to feel for a pulse. He shook his head.

Invincia had always claimed she would go to heaven. It would have been justice for her to go to hell. But like the others, she went where no one goes and where nothing is.

When I realized the shooting was over, I tried to tamp down my pulse rate. Smoke from the torches and the guns clouded the room. A haunting desolation mingled with the smoke and settled with it over the bodies. Somewhere in the distance, against the silence, a hidden clock was ticking. It occurred to me that the faint sound was coming from my watch. I checked the time. It was a few minutes after three.

Eck walked up to me, a sergeant trailing him. "How about them Packers?" the lieutenant said.

"Right," I said. "How's your man doing?"

"He'll be fine. A little red on the shirt, but it looks like the bullet glanced off. Paramedics are coming." Eck looked puzzled. "So, Harbinger. How come Sister Invincia always wanted to kill Father Timothy?"

"Beats me. The molestation stuff didn't seem to bother her, aside from the public relations angle. Maybe it was only because he was a pain in the ass."

"At least he died doing what he loved to do," the sergeant said.

"How did you get to that?" I asked him.

He thought it over. "I don't know. I guess it just sounded nice."

SEVENTY-THREE

The two cops left me alone. Eck obviously enjoyed playing the head honcho at a murder scene, circulating among his men and ordering them through their procedures. One officer tended his wounded partner and guided him out the door. Other cops flagged bullet casings, plotted shot trajectories, drew chalk lines around the corpses and mapped out patterns of sprayed blood. Eck was grousing at nothing in particular when I walked over to him.

"Nice you could stop by," I said. "Weekend and all."

"You have your girlfriend Rene to thank for that," he said. "She kept ringing my phone off the hook until the noise forced me out of bed. She told me you two had a little tiff, but she expected you to come back. When you didn't show up, she got worried that you were gonna come down here and get yourself killed."

"Isn't that what I told you hours ago?"

"Yeah, but that was just you. When she was the one talking, it sounded more serious. Anyhow, she didn't have a clue about the convent but I knew that's where you were because of your call. She wanted to drive over here but she was pretty upset. I decided we better pick her up instead. She's on her way here in a squad car just to see you." He clapped a meaty hand on my shoulder. "I think she's falling for you, pal."

The hair on my neck stood up.

"Well," I said. "I'm glad you guys finally put in an appearance. I might have run out of ammo before Invincia did."

"We got here just in time, huh?"

"Not exactly." I pointed to the chair and then to the bloody platform. "They knocked me out and tied me to that chair. When I came to, I had to keep Sister Invincia arguing for quite a while. If I hadn't bought enough time to free my hands, her underlings would have conked me on the head again. Then they would have strapped me onto that rack. I could have been dead before you got here."

"Who's the guy dumped in the corner?"

"That's Slab Kapowski," I told him. "They already had him on the rack when I woke up. He held out for a while, but he didn't make it."

"I couldn't even recognize him under all the blood and the brains and the duct tape," the lieutenant said. "Slab on the slab, huh?" He smiled to himself, clearly proud of his way with words. "I'll be jiggered."

"Sister Invincia drilled a hole in his head. She found out he was a nonbeliever and she assumed that he was possessed by Satan."

"Possessed by Satan, huh. I bet that's how he could control all them dead fish that ate the professor."

"Well," I said, "those were just piranhas doing what piranhas always do."

"Oh, yeah, I remember now."

"The drilling was some sort of exorcism ritual."

"Really?" Eck said. "They made a movie about that. I don't remember the part about drilling a hole in anybody's head."

"Maybe the nuns had seen the director's cut," I said. "But look, I need to get my bearings because I was out of it when they brought me in here. Are we in the lowest level of the convent?"

"In more ways than one," Eck said. "We had a bitch of a time finding this place. We busted in the front door and went down a couple of staircases. Then we almost got lost in a maze except that one of my guys went down another staircase and noticed a big sign for a dungeon."

"That's good police work," I said.

"Boy, you got *that* right." He hadn't caught my tone.

"When you and your men were rooting around, did you come across a cabinet full of skulls?"

"Yeah," he said. "Scary weird."

"Two doors down from there, you'll find Slab Kapowski's secret office, the place where I called you from. There's a document in there with notes on his business rivals who were either thrown off the steeple or killed in other ways. There's also a hit list explaining how some of the other victims got their skulls appropriated."

"What was Slab's deal?"

"He wanted more money and power. He was bumping off his competitors. I think the church personnel, mainly Father Timothy, were covering for him. In return for the favor, Slab helped to kill the heretics who were fingered by the nuns. Father Timothy was covering for those murders too. He was presenting himself as an unimpeachable witness."

"They must have roped him into it," Eck said. "You know, threatened him on account of his nasty habit."

"Possibly," I said. "But from what I've seen, he liked to watch people getting hurt. Maybe the occasional ticket to torture was all the motivation he needed to join the cause. Either way, he did what he was told. Meanwhile, Slab was able to take over his rivals' territories. He also made a bundle on the heretics' funerals. But I heard him tell Timothy that he couldn't keep up the pace of murders without raising suspicion. Timothy got huffy about it and tried to put him in his place. Slab wasn't taking any guff, so he slapped the padre around. Timothy got his revenge by blowing the whistle on Slab."

"Blowing the whistle to who?"

"Sister Invincia. She was at the top of the pyramid around here. Timothy tattled to her that Slab didn't believe in God, so Invincia had her goons grab him from his office and strap him to the rack. The next thing he knew, his bones were breaking and his cranium was leaking."

"Holy shit," Eck said. "But I don't get the part about the rack. If you want to kill people, just kill 'em. But why put anybody on that thing?"

"Invincia's hero was Torquemada, who was put in charge of the Spanish Inquisition exactly five hundred years ago. Invincia figured it was time for a revival."

Eck slapped a hand across his thigh.

"The Spanish Inquisition! That's what I was wondering about back at The Drunk Tank! Remember? Damn, I sure figured *that* one out."

"You sure did," I humored him. "She thought she had a sacred mission to rid the world of heretics and doubters, and she was starting with the parish of Saint Opie's. I suppose she wanted to use the same torture equipment that her role model Torquemada used."

"She was always big on tradition," Eck said.

"True. She and her nuns did the dirty work in the dungeon. The poor bastards they dragged down here were forced to confess. The other victims required field assignments. Those were farmed out to Slab, and he put Timothy to work on a couple of killings, minimum. But Invincia called the shots for the whole gang. I'm pretty sure she was the one who made the list of infidels to kill."

Eck shook his head. "Who would have thunk it?"

"How do you like the iron maiden?" I asked him.

"The what?" Eck said.

"The upright coffin. They probably had Slab cook it up special."

"I seen them big nails on the inside," Eck marveled. "They gotta hurt, even when you're dead."

I nodded, in no mood for more controversy. "It doesn't look like they were burning anybody at the stake, though. Not down here."

"How can you tell?" Eck said.

"Not enough soot on the ceiling," I told him.

"Good point," he said, looking up. "But the rest of the place looks like some rough stuff went on in here. There's probably more skeletons laying around. I guess I've solved a few missing person cases."

"You're the real deal, lieutenant."

"Boy," Eck said, "when I look back at my school days over here … the nuns box your ears a few times and you think you know them. Now it's all the way up to homicide. Slab Kapowski and Father Timothy, murderers. They're bad enough. But Sister Invincia? Whooh, if I didn't see her execute Timothy in cold blood, I wouldn't believe it."

"I told you so," I said, and felt good about saying it. "Homicides down here, out in the industrial tracts and over at The Bishop's Retreat."

"Even in a nice, peaceful place like that," he said ruefully. "I guess we better get them little piranha buggers out of the fountain before a custodian loses a hand."

"You'll need to do some interviews with the monks," I told him. "No telling how many of them were screening for Slab and Timothy. And while you're there, keep an eye out for the Grim Reaper."

"Always," he said. He took a notebook out of his pocket and frowned.

"What's the matter?" I asked him.

"Legwork up the wazoo," he said, probably without thinking too much about the anatomical logistics of it. He jotted down a run of interview subjects, visibly disappointed over the spoiled plans he'd made for the rest of the summer. He drummed his pen on the pad and gestured to the floors above us. "There have to be a few more nuns up there, right?"

"Probably hiding under their beds," I said.

"Don't say that," he told me. "I don't like to think about nuns and beds at the same time. But hey, do you figure they're all in on it?"

"Maybe the younger ones wouldn't follow Invincia to this extreme. But who knows? They take a vow of obedience. Looks like you'll have to bring them in for questioning."

"Yeah," he said glumly. He added some items to his notebook. "There's sure gonna be a lot of papers shuffled around."

"Nobody likes that part," I said. "Not to complicate things, but you may want to check out the local chapter of the Knights of Columbus."

"Bum's crumbs, Harbinger, why don't *you* check out the Knights of Columbus?"

"Because I don't have a client anymore."

"Who *was* your client?"

"That's confidential."

"Ah, criminy," Eck said with disgust.

"Besides the Knights," I said, "there's the church deacon who went to Borneo. Guy named Dennis Canfield. He knows something about it too. The paper mill killing, at least."

"It never ends," Eck complained. "Is Borneo where Pago Pago is?"

"Pago Pago is in American Samoa," one of the cops told him.

"Maybe that's right next to Borneo," Eck said hopefully. "Heck, maybe the department will send me over there to make an arrest or something and I could get two weeks of vacation out of it."

"One more thing," I said. "Slab's alternate tough guy, name of Rance, is handcuffed to the fire escape outside my office."

"He kill anybody?"

"Don't know."

"Is he dead or alive?"

"Well, Eck, there wouldn't be any point in cuffing him out there if he was dead."

"That's logical. You keep handcuffs around?"

"Rance brought the hardware with him. He was supposed to beat me senseless, put me in the cuffs and drag me down here. Probably so that Sister Invincia could put me on that rack and add a few more inches to my spinal column."

"What did she have against you?"

"I was a disrespectful young man in grade school and I'm still a disrespectful young man."

"I can see that," he said sagely. "Oh, well. Like I mentioned, you gotta expect violence from nuns."

He snapped his fingers and one of the uniformed officers came over.

"Yes, sir."

"Take another badge and get down to Harbinger's office building."

I gave them the address.

"At the back of it," Eck said, "there's a guy named Rance. Muscle for Slab Kapowski. He's handcuffed to the fire escape. Have the fire department hoist you up there. Cut the cuffs off him and bring him down to the station."

"Hold on," I said, reaching into my pocket. "Here's the key to the cuffs."

The cop took the key and Eck went on with his instructions. "Don't tell him his boss and the rest of them are dead. If he assumes they're accusing him, maybe he'll blab what he knows. That way, we could close a few cases and put Rance away for, well, accessory to attempted murder. Or something."

"Good thinking," I told Eck.

He could see my surprise, and tapped an index finger against his noggin.

The uniform signaled a partner to go with him. When they got through the dungeon doorway, she appeared.

SEVENTY-FOUR

Rhonda McKinnon, or whatever her name might have been at that hour, stood there in perfection. Waves of blond hair fell around her sensual face. Her azure eyes were hypnotic and her lips were parted in a carnal blush of red. In a fading torch's glow, she was radiant in a sapphire dress and spiked heels that probably should have required a license. Soft light danced on gold earrings and a gold pendant. Just below the pendant, two scoops of vanilla nearly spilled out from a deep, daring neckline. Her image was about right for a nightclub in Acapulco but brazen for a convent in Pulptown. Every guy in the place had to remind himself to breathe.

"Sorry about the … inappropriate clothing," she said in a wilting voice. "When they came to pick me up it was … the handiest thing in the closet."

She stepped forward, scanned the room and then carefully surveyed the bodies littering the dungeon floor. Seasoned as she was, she looked stunned, as if the horror was more than she could take. In a way I couldn't explain, she didn't seem to be the woman I knew. If I had ever known her at all.

I walked over to her and held out a hand. I hated to lay myself open again, but I was doing it anyway. I realized what had been going on inside me hours earlier at the restaurant bar. The feelings back there had been more than frustrated desire. And they hadn't changed in spite of everything that should have run me off. I found I didn't care how many lies she had told me, why she had used me or how much danger she had put me through. Whether or not I wanted to admit it, whether or not it made any sense, I was in love with this dame.

"Let's go somewhere private and have a quiet drink and pretend this place never existed," I said.

She didn't say yes or no. She didn't take or reject my hand, and I let it fall to my side. Her hazy eyes kept panning across the bloody scene around us.

"How could this be?" she said. "What have I done?"

"You didn't do any of this," I told her. "This was set in motion long before you came to town."

She faced me directly and spoke: "When I got back to my hotel, I thought about what you said. And it made me re-evaluate my whole life. I thought about how sweet you are, and how much you had gotten to me. All I could imagine was giving myself totally to you, if only you could keep yourself alive. I'd stay with you in this tacky little town. I'd find something semi-legal to do here. I'd become your wife and bring sandwiches and bandages to your sleazy office every day at noon." Her words went coursing through me like a mainliner's fix. "But getting caught up in this bloodbath — it's taught me a lesson. There has to be something greater, something higher."

"I'll give up the private eye racket," I said.

"No, I couldn't ask you to sacrifice your way of life. This is what you were meant to do. You're all about wisecracks and concussions and a hundred dollars a day."

"Plus expenses," I said.

"Right, plus expenses. But I know now that I can't stay here. I have to dedicate myself to a radical departure from the life I've led. I have to make up for all the deceit, all the avarice, the corruption, the slinking around with men on the wrong side of the law. I've just made a decision."

"You've been traumatized," I told her. "Now is not the best time to make any big changes."

She turned and took a few steps toward the open doorway. Well short of it, she stopped, turned again and looked back at me. Her eyes darted aimlessly. I searched her face, trying to figure out whether she was doubting herself.

"Are you sure this is what you want?" I asked.

"No, not completely. And I need to be secure in my decision." Her voice was quavering. "There can't be any doubt in my mind about leaving everyone and everything behind. I can't be free of my old life if I run away from here with any emotions unresolved. There's only one way to be certain."

I couldn't inhale or even let my heart beat.

She walked slowly toward me, ravishing in the blue gown. I drank in the essence of her longingly, achingly. She looked psychologically torn.

But there was something intensely romantic, almost ethereal, in her eyes. She came in closer.

I felt — I knew — that this one kiss would have my whole future riding on it. I would have to take it all the way to the goal line or bear a devastating loss. She stopped inches away. I leaned forward, closed my eyes and reached out.

She slapped me hard across the face.

"What the …?" I tried to blink away the shock.

"Yes," the lady said. "This just feels so *right*."

"Rhonda …?"

"I've decided to become a nun."

My brain stem disconnected.

SEVENTY-FIVE

I was numb, nonresponsive, but not annihilated. Wire by wire, my mental circuitry plugged itself back in. Synapses opened their channels. Neurons began firing. I found I was able to put a simple thought into words: "Can't it wait?"

"I'm afraid not," Rhonda said. "*Fait accompli.* You're a sinful young man, Jack Harbinger. As for me, it's the cloistered life."

"What if—"

"These grounds have been tainted," she cut in. "No matter. I can enter the convent at Saint Venal's in Oshkosh. Lieutenant, can one of your officers drive me down there?"

"No problem," Eck said. "Do you need to go back to your hotel first?"

"That won't be necessary," she told him. "I'm forsaking all that I own, even the lingerie. Saint Venal's will have everything I need."

Eck pointed to one of his men. The officer pulled a set of keys from his pocket and glanced my way. With a shrug and a twist of his face, he apologized silently for something that wasn't his fault, then went out to ready a squad car.

Folding her hands with flawless piety, Rhonda turned once more and walked away from me. She passed through the exit and continued straight ahead into a long, dusky hallway. I watched until she was past the last trace of light, listened until her steady, determined footsteps faded out.

The dungeon held silent for a few moments or a few minutes — I couldn't tell which. At some point, from a far corner, mumbling finally came out of a lone cop. Other murmurings from other cops drifted randomly and then gathered into the normal volume and cadence of conversation. None of it mattered to me.

I was barely aware that Eck was standing next to me again. His voice cut through the chatter in the room and the shambles in my head. "It sure didn't take her long to get the hang of it," he said.

"Huh?"

"The nun business. Looked like she's been slapping people for years."

"Eck, does saying the wrong thing come easy to you? Or do you have to work at it?"

"Aw, hell, don't be so sensitive. By the by, what was all that talk about deceit and corruption?"

"Nothing at all," I said, summing up my world. I was as empty and forgotten as last year's bullet holes.

"Okay, Harbinger. You've had a crummy break. But you don't have time to get all weepy about it. I'll need a written statement. Now, while it's fresh."

"Come on, Lieutenant."

He glommed onto the sleeve of a passing uniform. "Shalopski, get that table back on its legs and load this guy up for some paperwork. And get one of them torches over here."

Shalopski flipped the table. He pulled statement forms and pens from a utility pack and laid them out. The lieutenant grabbed the chair I'd been tied to, dragged it to the table and laid a heavy hand on my collar to steer me into the seat.

"Anyway, Eck, it won't make sense. You realize I can't identify my client."

"Then leave your client's name out of it. Call him Mr. XYZ. We still need your full cooperation. That means the whole story. Put it all down, step by step. And don't scrimp on the details."

"Do you have any idea what time it is?" I asked.

He planted both hands on the table and leaned in with his big shoulders. He was getting testy. "Look, Harbinger, we all have to stay up all night. Me and these other guys. What makes you so special that you need a nap? And the quicker you start, the quicker you'll be done. So start."

"Start where?"

"From the beginning!" he growled.

Shalopski secured a live torch to the wall behind me.

Eck straightened. "There, you got light. You're all set. You practically have your own office down here."

After the day and night I had put in, the burden of churning out a comprehensive report seemed overwhelming. Eck might as well have ordered me to produce a thirty-volume encyclopedia. I'd been exhausted and heartsick. Now I was also angry and bitter.

He began to move away, then stopped and pivoted, probably sensing my resentment. "Another thing," he said. "It ain't my fault that all this scribbling is necessary. We need it because them nuns committed murder and mayhem right in front of you. I'm not the reason you're stuck here. If you're laying the blame, *they're* the reason you're stuck here." He went off to yell at someone else.

I slumped into the task. The stack of lined paper peered up at me, demanding to be filled. I slid a sheet of it onto a part of the table's surface that hadn't been splintered by gunfire. Then I picked up a ballpoint and got it ready to write something across page one. The pen didn't move. It just waited in my hand, expecting me to put in some effort. Hell, this was going to take forever.

Laying the blame, Eck had said. *They're the reason you're stuck here.*

The irony of where I'd landed poked me gently in the ribs. All the nuns I'd ever known at Saint Opie's were dead, but they were still making me do my goddamn homework.

ABOUT THE AUTHOR

Chuck Evanson survived Catholic elementary school in a small Wisconsin town and eventually spent more than 30 years as a private investigator in Southern California. In all that time, he never shot anybody. With this novel, he advances from a cheap imitation of Philip Marlowe to a cheap imitation of Raymond Chandler. He and his wife Dana live near San Diego.

ACKNOWLEDGEMENTS

Many thanks to my old friends and partners in comedy, Kirk Ruhnke and Lee Harrison Schmidt, whose encouragement, wise counsel and sharp eyes were invaluable.

Made in the USA
Coppell, TX
22 January 2026

68968342R00215